Children of the Lamp

BOOK FIVE

THE EYE OF THE FOREST

P. B. KERR

W9-BXY-310

SCHOLASTIC INC.

NEW YORK TORONTO LONDON AUCKLAND
SYDNEY MEXICO CITY NEW DELHI HONG KONG

ISBN: 978-0-439-93217-2

Copyright © 2009 by Philip B. Kerr.
All rights reserved. Published by Scholastic Inc.
SCHOLASTIC, APPLE PAPERBACKS, and associated logos are
trademarks and/or registered trademarks of Scholastic Inc.

12 11 10 9 8 7 6 5 4 3 2 1   10 11 12 13 14 15/0

Printed in the U.S.A.   40

First paperback printing, January 2010

This book is for Joe Gilmour

Children of the Lamp

BOOK FIVE

THE EYE OF THE FOREST

PROLOGUE

DOCTOR KOWALSKI

"All happy families are alike but an unhappy family is unhappy in its own peculiar way."

This is the first sentence of a great novel called *Anna Karenina* by the Russian writer Leo Tolstoy. Tolstoy, who wrote several great novels, had an abiding interest in children's literature and wrote a number of tales and fables for them. But even with his fertile imagination Tolstoy could hardly have explained the peculiar way in which the Gaunts of East 77th Street, New York, were unhappy.

To say the least, theirs was an unusual family with a human father, Edward, a djinn mother, Layla, and djinn twins, John and Philippa. This mixture of djinn — or less correctly, genie — and human was not, directly, what made the Gaunts unhappy, although it had something to do with it, of course. For a long time the Gaunts had been very happy and, to all outside eyes, they had even seemed like a model family with a glamorous mother, an extremely wealthy father, and two well-behaved and amiable children.

If you could have made a criticism of the Gaunts it would have been this: that they were rather richer than was, perhaps, good for them — although, in defense of their enormous wealth, it is hard to imagine that any family that includes at least one djinn as a member would not also be stinking rich.

No, what made them unhappy was this: During her flight back to New York from a recent trip to the Middle East, Mrs. Gaunt had suffered a serious accident resulting in the total destruction of her physical body. In humans — or mundanes, as the djinn persist in calling this apparently similar but entirely different species — such an occurrence would always have been fatal. But Mrs. Gaunt had cleverly managed to eject her spirit from her incinerated self and, having made her way back home to New York City in the shape of an albatross, she then set about finding herself a new body. She hardly fancied becoming a dog or a cat any more than she cared for the idea of continuing on in life as an albatross. Gooney birds, as Americans horribly call them, drink salt water and eat rotten fish heads. And having grown tired of this unappetizing diet, naturally Mrs. Gaunt was soon on the lookout for a human-shaped body.

This wasn't as easy as it might sound. Mrs. Gaunt was a member of a tribe of djinn called the Marid, which is a good tribe of djinn — one of three good tribes. Had she been a member of an evil tribe, like the Ifrit — one of three evil tribes — she would have just stolen someone else's body. But while body-borrowing is permitted to a good djinn, body-snatching is strictly forbidden by *The Baghdad Rules,* which is the code that covers all djinn conduct. At least it is forbidden unless the body is not being used.

Now it so happened that the Gaunts employed a faithful housekeeper called Mrs. Trump who, as the result of a frightful fall down a flight of stairs, ended up in the hospital and in a coma. An investigation of Mrs. Trump's situation had persuaded Mrs. Gaunt that while the housekeeper's body remained in perfect working order, the poor woman's medical condition was irreversible; and so, certain that Mrs. Trump would have approved of what she was doing, Mrs. Gaunt decided to assume total control of Mrs. Trump's body.

She could have done worse. Mrs. Trump was not a bad-looking woman. Indeed, she was a former beauty queen, although she lacked Mrs. Gaunt's obvious glamour and personality. Nevertheless, while Layla Gaunt herself could sometimes forget that she had a different body, the rest of her family seldom did. Mr. Gaunt and his two children struggled to get used to the idea that Mrs. Gaunt was now inside Mrs. Trump.

It is sometimes said that appearances can be deceptive. This was certainly very true in Mrs. Trump/Gaunt's case with the unfortunate result that Mr. Gaunt tended only to speak to her about domestic issues such as his laundry and dry cleaning and what was for dinner, while the children persisted in calling her Mrs. Trump instead of Mother or

Mom, and kept asking her to add things to the weekly grocery list.

What was worse, perhaps, was that those family friends who were unaware of Mrs. Trump's true identity or that three of the Gaunts had djinn or genie powers, found the housekeeper's apparent overfamiliarity with Mr. Gaunt a little hard to take. The way she took his hand or sometimes kissed him on the cheek. The way she never seemed to do any actual housework. The way she treated the house as if it belonged to her. The way she wore Mrs. Gaunt's furs and drove her car.

Mr. Gaunt steadfastly maintained that his wife, Layla, had gone to pursue a career as a sculptor in Australia. But keener-eyed women friends, who noticed the fact that Mrs. Trump was now wearing Mrs. Gaunt's jewelry, wondered if this might be a lie. One or two of them even speculated that Layla Gaunt had been done away with.

An increasingly unhappy situation came to a head when, one day, a police detective came to the Gaunt family house. He was a large, hairy bear of a man with a walrus mustache who was originally from the Bronx. His name was Detective Michael Wolff. He showed his detective's shield to the well-dressed woman answering the door who identified herself — to him, at any rate — as the Gaunt family housekeeper, Mrs. Trump.

"Is Mr. Gaunt at home?" asked Detective Wolff.

"No, he won't be back until this evening," said Mrs. Trump. "Might I ask what this is about?"

"I'd like to speak to him about his wife," said the detective. "She has been reported as a missing person."

"Nonsense," said Mrs. Trump. "By whom?"

"Some of her friends. Do you know where she is, Mrs. Trump?"

"She's in Australia. I spoke to her myself just the other day."

"I checked with the Australian authorities," said the detective, "and they have no record of her ever having entered the country."

"I see." Reluctantly, Mrs. Trump/Gaunt began to consider the possibility that she would have to use djinn power on the detective. "Perhaps you'd better come in."

Hardly aware of the threat that now hung over him, the detective stepped into the fine hallway and, as Mrs. Trump closed the heavy black door behind him, he glanced around his surroundings with appreciation. "Nice place," he said. "I love these big houses on the Upper East Side of New York."

"Thank you," said Mrs. Trump. Remembering who she was supposed to be she added, hurriedly, "Difficult to keep clean though."

"You don't look like no house cleaner, lady," observed the detective. "With all due respect ma'am, I never saw any house cleaner wearing jewelry like yours and a dress like that. I should know. My wife is a house cleaner."

Mrs. Gaunt usually turned humans who posed some kind of threat to her or her family into animals. But she hardly wanted to turn Detective Wolff into a wolf. A wolf on the streets of Manhattan might well be shot by another police-man in case it tried to harm anyone. And it was the detective's good fortune that she now struggled to think of a more suitable animal into which she could transform him.

"It's a matter of public record that I won the New York State Lottery a few years back," said Mrs. Trump/Gaunt.

This was true. For a long time to win the lottery had been Mrs. Trump's dearest wish and, thanks to Philippa, her wish had been granted.

"How much did you win?"

"Thirty-three million dollars."

The detective whistled. "And you kept on working as a housekeeper?"

A parrot perhaps, she thought. He whistled just like a parrot.

"I like this family," said Mrs. Trump/Gaunt. "They're like my own. I didn't want the money to change my life. You know how that story goes."

"Gee, I guess that explains a lot," said the detective. "Like why you're dressed so nicely."

Mrs. Trump/Gaunt began to relax again: Maybe she could talk her way out of this after all.

"I hope so. And thank you for the compliment, Detective Wolff."

"Only it still doesn't explain where Mrs. Gaunt is."

"As I said, Detective Wolff, I spoke to her the other day. She called here. But I have no idea where she was calling from if she wasn't calling from Australia." She paused as she came to an important decision about her own future. "However."

"Yes?"

"She did tell me that she would be coming back to New York. At the end of the month."

"She did, huh?" The detective took out his wallet and thumbed a business card that he handed to Mrs. Trump. "Would you mind asking her to give me a call when she returns home?"

"It'll be my pleasure, Detective," said Mrs. Trump/Gaunt and showed the detective out again, considerably relieved that he was leaving on two legs instead of four.

After dinner that evening, Mrs. Trump/Gaunt said that she had an important announcement to make. "I've decided to go away for a few weeks," she said.

"Where are you going, Mrs. Trump?" asked Mr. Gaunt. "Er, that is, what I meant to say was, where are you going, honey?"

"Brazil."

"What are you going there for, Mrs. Trump, I mean, Mother?" asked John.

"To undergo a procedure," she said. "A surgical procedure."

"Are you sick?" asked John.

"In a way I am, I suppose," said Mrs. Trump/Gaunt. "But not like you imagine, John, dear. I suppose you might say that I'm sick of everyone forgetting who I really am. I'm sick of people forgetting that only the outside of me is Mrs. Trump. I'm sick of people forgetting that on the inside I'm still Layla Gaunt."

"Sorry, dear," said Mr. Gaunt. Even though Mrs. Trump/ Gaunt looked nothing like the woman he had married, he could tell that she was upset. So he got up from his dining chair and came over and kissed Mrs. Trump/Gaunt on the forehead. But it was not an affectionate kiss. Mr. Gaunt found it hard to treat a woman who looked like his former housekeeper with much affection, even if she was wearing his wife's clothes. Recognizing this, he kissed her twice on the forehead for good measure. It was fortunate Mrs. Trump/ Gaunt was sitting down because, like Mrs. Gaunt before her, she was taller than Mr. Gaunt by a head. "I keep trying to remember that it's you inside Mrs. Trump's body. But some- times I forget, that's all. I'm only human, dear. Unlike you."

"Oh, it's nobody's fault but mine," she said. "I should have realized that this would be more difficult than I thought it would be. Anyway, it just got a bit more difficult, I think. You see, a detective came to the house today."

"A detective?" John's voice betrayed excitement. "Has there been a murder?"

"No, but the police think it's possible there might have been. You see, apparently someone has reported me — by which I mean me, Layla Gaunt — as a missing person."

"Oh," said Mr. Gaunt. "I was wondering when some- thing like that might happen. This kind of thing was only to be expected." He nodded. "What did you tell him, dear?"

"I told him that I — by which I mean Layla Gaunt — in person — would be back from Australia by the end of the month. Which would prove I'm still alive, of course. And forestall any embarrassing police investigation."

"How are you going to manage that?" asked Philippa. "I mean, your body. It was destroyed when you flew over that volcano in Hawaii. On your way back from Baghdad. Burned to a potato chip, you said. By the heat from a pyroclastic flow."

"And that's perfectly true, my dear. It was. I am very lucky that my spirit survived at all. No, it's just that I've decided the shape I'm in needs a bit of fine-tuning. Which is why I'm going to Brazil. You see, Brazil is recognized as the world capital of cosmetic and plastic surgery. There's a doctor there — Dr. Stanley Kowalski — who is the best plastic surgeon in the world. A number of movie stars I know have said he can work magic. And since I know Kowalski also happens to be a djinn, I'm certain that reputation is well-deserved. I intend to have him make me look exactly the way I used to look before the accident."

"How long will you be gone for, Mrs. —?" asked Mr. Gaunt.

Mrs. Trump/Gaunt smiled patiently. "Several weeks. Perhaps longer. As long as it takes, I guess."

"Can we come?" asked John. "I've never been to Brazil."

"I think not, dear," said the woman who was his mother. "Besides, I'd like you both to stay here and look after your father."

"But I don't need anyone looking after me," insisted Mr. Gaunt. "I am quite recovered, as you can see. I am myself again."

By which he meant that he was completely recovered from the Methusaleh binding that Layla Gaunt had put on her husband. This had caused him to age very rapidly. For a while Mr. Gaunt had looked like he was two hundred years old. But now he was back to his old self: a small, dapper, gray-haired man of about fifty-two, which is old enough.

"Well, at least one of us is." Mrs. Trump/Gaunt sighed. "I'm not sure who I am. Not anymore. Every time I look in the mirror I want to ask myself if there are any clean towels. Or if I could organize a visit from the window cleaner. Or if I could run down to the shops and get some coffee. You see, it's not just you who sees Mrs. Trump. It's me, too."

"Couldn't you do it with djinn power?" asked Philippa. "I mean, alter your appearance?"

"Too risky," said Mrs. Trump/Gaunt. "It's one thing to change yourself into smoke. It's quite another when you try to change the shape of your face. Believe me, terrible things have happened to djinn who've tried to make themselves better looking. For example, there was a girl I knew at school who tried to make her nose smaller. She ended up with no nose at all. And a friend of Nimrod's, whose ears stuck out like the handles on a trophy, tried to pin them back with djinn power but instead managed to make them join around the back of his head. Horrible. Which necessitated a trip to a plastic surgeon. And then there's your father. Look at him. Don't you think if I could I'd have made him taller? You can't control that kind of thing. You set out to give someone a few extra inches and they end up being the tallest man in the world."

Mr. Gaunt looked at his children and nodded. "It's true. We once discussed the idea and rejected it. Did you know that some of those guys playing pro basketball were short guys who got three wishes?"

"So what's wrong with that?" said John.

"Nothing," said Mr. Gaunt. "If playing basketball is all you want from life. I mean, when you're seven feet tall what else can you do?"

"Look, I thought you'd be pleased," said Mrs. Trump/ Gaunt. "But even if you're not, I'm going to do this. I just want to feel good about myself again. That's all."

"When are you going?" asked Mr. Gaunt.

"I already called Dr. Kowalski. He scheduled me for my first procedure the day after tomorrow. Which means I'm going to fly down to Rio tonight. By whirlwind."

They went to the rooftop of New York's Guggenheim Museum to see her off.

For centuries, a whirlwind rather than a magic carpet has been the preferred method of djinn travel. Not only is a whirlwind as fast as — if not faster than — a jet airplane, it is also a lot kinder to the environment because whirlwinds are created from nothing more than a current of warm air.

Layla Gaunt and her brother, Nimrod, had been making minor whirlwinds on the rooftop of the Guggenheim since they were children on their first visit to New York. There was something about the inverted spiral shape of Frank Lloyd Wright's famous building that made it easier to whip up a good one. There was nothing to it. You waited for a small local wind to spin on the ground and then whipped it into a funnel. And when the funnel started to lift, you just rode it up as far as a high-altitude wind and then moved off in whatever direction you chose. The trick to avoiding any surrounding structural damage was to get a quick liftoff.

On this particular occasion, however, Layla was shocked to discover that she couldn't control the wind. It wasn't that her power was in any way diminished by being inside the body of Mrs. Trump but simply that there was too much warm, turbulent air in the atmosphere.

"I don't understand," she shouted over the noise of the wind. "A little local wind shouldn't be able to turn this strong this quickly. Not here. Not in New York."

She tried to hold on to the wind but when the speed of the vortex quickly reached three hundred miles an hour, she was obliged to let it go and off it blew, west across Central Park, uprooting trees, turning over benches, and creating a National Weather Service record that was reported in all the next day's newspapers as the strongest wind to hit New York City since February 22, 1912, when the city was visited by a gale that blew at ninety-six miles an hour for five minutes. This wind, more than three times as strong, lasted for only two minutes before it disappeared up into the jet stream, fortunately for the city.

"This has never happened before," said Layla. "I don't get it. Unless . . ." She shook her head. "No. It couldn't be. Surely not so soon."

"What is it, Mother?" asked Philippa.

"Only that some djinn have speculated that global warming might eventually affect our ability to make and control our own whirlwinds." She kept on shaking her head. "But that was thought to be years off."

"There are more hurricanes around than there used to be," said Philippa. "Which might have something to do with it."

"Yes, that's right, dear. There are, aren't there?"

"How about trying it again?" suggested John.

"I don't even dare to," admitted Mrs. Trump/Gaunt. "At least not in a built-up area where the wind might damage something." She shook her head. "My goodness, I guess I'll have to take a plane, like everyone else."

And so she did, but not before telephoning her brother, Nimrod, in London, to tell him what had happened to her, only to hear that recently he, too, had experienced the same problem.

"I was about to fly over to America when the same thing happened to me," he said. "I'm spending the weekend at Frank Vodyannoy's house in New Haven, Connecticut. He's hosting a small Djinnverso tournament. But now I shall have to come by commercial jet."

"But why is it happening?" asked his sister. "It's because of global warming, isn't it?"

"Yes," answered Nimrod. "Although I think it has more to do with the destruction of the Brazilian rain forest than with things like carbon footprints."

"But what are we going to do?" said Mrs. Trump/Gaunt. "Under these circumstances, it almost seems wrong for me to take a plane to Brazil."

"Indeed so," agreed Nimrod. "At the same time, I always think one hardly feels like a djinn at all if one is obliged to travel by commercial jet. Not to mention the claustrophobia. I wonder how we are going to manage being cooped up like chickens for hours on end."

"The mundanes manage," said his sister. "Somehow."

"Only because they've gotten used to being treated like chickens."

"Before long, I fear we may all have to get used to it," said Mrs. Trump/Gaunt. "Now that's what I call an inconvenient truth."

CHAPTER 1

THE THREE DRUIDS

Considering that he was her twin brother, John Gaunt seemed to be unlike his sister, Philippa, in quite a number of ways. Most obviously he did not look like her, which is a characteristic of all dizygotic, or fraternal, twins — even human ones: She was smaller, with red hair and glasses, whereas he was tall and dark. He was a person of action rather than much thought. He liked movies instead of books. Then there was the fact that he disliked Djinnversoctoannular, which is the peculiar game of bluff enjoyed by nearly all djinn. Both John and Philippa were children of the lamp, having a djinn mother, but only Philippa liked playing this ancient pastime. John, who was not a skilled dissimulator — his sister was now classed as Incognito, the level below Expert — much preferred the honest if rather mindless kinds of games that were played on a small electronic screen. And normally he would never even have thought of accompanying Philippa to a Djinnverso party, but it so happened that he, too, had been invited to the weekend tournament at the country home of Mr. Vodyannoy, in New Haven.

Now, because John had always considered Mr. Vodyannoy to be his friend rather than Philippa's, and because he knew he was facing a boring weekend on his own in New York City, he decided to tag along. New Haven is less than two hours on the train from New York City. Besides, Mr. Vodyannoy's house, which was called Nightshakes, was, according to Uncle Nimrod, famously haunted. Not only that, but Mr. Vodyannoy had the largest collection of antique talking boards — some of them more than a hundred years old — in the world. John hoped that while his sister and his uncle and his host were busy playing Djinnverso, he himself might put the shadowy inhabitants of Nightshakes to some practical use. For it was the boy djinn's sincerest wish to enlist the spirit world in finding out for sure if his old friend Mr. Rakshasas was truly dead or not.

But first they were obliged to ask the permission of their father, for with their mother now in Brazil, it was he who was in charge of their immediate welfare.

"I can understand why Philippa wants to go," said Mr. Gaunt. "She loves playing Djinnverso. But you, John? I fail to see why you want to go. You hate the game."

"While we're in New Haven I thought I might take a look at the Peabody Museum," said John.

Philippa said nothing.

"You know, at Yale University," John added.

"I know where it is," said his father. "In case you'd forgotten, I'm a Yale man myself. I'm just a little surprised to hear you say that you want to go there."

"I don't know why you should sound so surprised," said John, feigning innocence. "They've got a pretty good collection of dinosaur skeletons at the Peabody. Matter of fact, they've got all sorts of good collections. While she's off playing games, I expect I'll spend most of my time looking at all the interesting stuff they've got there. Improving myself."

"I guess there's always room for improvement," said Mr. Gaunt. "Just don't get into any trouble, will you?"

"Me?" John laughed. "I don't see how anyone can get into trouble just walking around a silly old museum."

"What about you, Dad?" asked Philippa. "Will you be all right without us?"

"Me?" Mr. Gaunt hugged his daughter.

"Without Mom," she added.

"I'll be fine. What could possibly happen to me? But it's kind of you to ask." He tousled John's hair. "Both of you — go. Have a nice time."

For her part, Philippa welcomed John's company although she had strong doubts concerning the truth of her brother's explanation as to how he intended to occupy himself while they were weekending in New Haven. She was his twin after all, and even among mundanes, twins almost magically always seem to know things about each other without ever having to say anything. Ask any pair of twins and they will probably tell you that there exists a kind of telepathy between them that defies scientific explanation.

On their journey to New Haven by rail from New York's Grand Central Terminal, they were accompanied by Uncle Nimrod, recently arrived in New York and who was himself a keen Djinnverso player, and his English butler, Mr. Groanin. Groanin was not a good traveler, and it wasn't long before he had voiced his disapproval of American trains in general, and of the lack of proper breakfast facilities in particular.

"A snack car," he moaned. "That's all there is on this train. How's a grown man expected to get by with a flipping snack car, serving soup, salad, pizza, sandwiches, and other snacks and beverages? Whatever happened to Canadian bacon, German sausage, deep-fried bread, black pudding, eggs, mushrooms and tomatoes, toast and marmalade, and lashings of hot sweet tea? I wish, I say, I wish there was a proper dining car on this train."

"You had breakfast at the hotel, before we left this morning," said Nimrod.

"That was in the hotel," said Groanin. "Trains always make me hungry."

John, who was himself starting to feel quite hungry as a result of Groanin's description of breakfast, decided it would be amusing if he were to grant the butler's wish and, a few minutes later, they were all sitting down to eat in an elegant dining car that would not have disgraced the old Orient Express.

"You're going to have to stop doing that," Nimrod told his nephew.

"It was just this one time," said John.

"Even so," his uncle said sternly. "You know it risks drawing attention to us. To say nothing of the unseen, unpredictable consequences that can result from granting someone's wish. Remember what Mr. Rakshasas used to say? Having a wish is like lighting a fire. It's reasonable to assume that the smoke might make someone cough."

"Speaking for myself," said Mr. Groanin, "I'm glad the boy did grant my wish, sir. There's no journey that's not improved by a good English breakfast. Especially one that comes with a nice white tablecloth and some proper silverware."

"Well, I can't argue with that," said Nimrod, and smiled indulgently at his nephew.

"I can't see why we're going by train at all," objected John. "Instead of by whirlwind."

"Perhaps you've forgotten what happened to your mother," said Nimrod. "As it happens I've taken a sounding among other djinn of my acquaintance and discovered that whirlwind travel has become problematic for us all, good and bad. Until someone, somewhere, works out what to do about this situation we shall simply have to travel like mundanes. Where air travel is concerned, that is unfortunate. But where, as in this case, there is a perfectly good train, I can see no real objection."

"I don't know about perfectly good," said Groanin.

"Need I also remind you, John," continued Nimrod, ignoring his butler, "of the effect that the profligate use of djinn power has on your life force? How many times have I told you? Every time we use djinn power it dims the fire that burns within each and every one of us. Do try to remember what happened to poor Dybbuk."

"I remember," said John, but by now, and like the good uncle he was, Nimrod was intent on reminding him, anyway.

"He exercised his power in such a reckless way that he quite used it up. Completely. Forever, I shouldn't wonder."

"*I* wonder where he is now," mused Philippa.

"It was his choice to put himself beyond our world," Nimrod said quietly. "Dybbuk's gone somewhere beyond our sympathy. Into the cold. Quite literally, I'm afraid."

"Does anyone ever come in from the cold?" asked Philippa.

"I'm afraid not," said Nimrod. "Not in my experience."

"Where will he go?" asked Philippa.

"Egypt probably," said Nimrod. "That's where I'd go if I'd gone cold."

"Poor Dybbuk," repeated John, and then ordered his hot breakfast.

Edward Gaunt left his house, as he always did, at exactly 7:30, and glanced right to see his gray Maybach limousine waiting for him. Hardly lifting his eyes from his newspaper, he came down the steps and ducked into the back of the car. He poured some water into a silver goblet and settled back in his leather seat to look at the market prices, which was what he always did. Even creatures of habit looked irregular in their habits compared with Edward Gaunt. They were several blocks down Park Avenue before Mr. Gaunt realized that he was not being driven by his usual driver, but by another man.

"Where's Mr. Senna?" he asked.

The man was tall and bald and wore a uniform identical to Mr. Senna's.

"He's ill, sir," said the man. "My name is Haddo. Oliver Haddo. I'm an old friend of Mr. Senna's. A chauffeur like him. He asked me if I could fill in for him."

"I've never known Senna to miss a day's work in his life," said Mr. Gaunt. "What's the matter with him? And why didn't he telephone and let me know personally?"

"I believe he wanted to, sir," said Haddo. "But due to the nature of his virus, he found himself unable to do so."

"You're English, aren't you, Haddo?" said Mr. Gaunt.

"That's right, sir."

"My wife was born in England," said Mr. Gaunt. "Although you wouldn't know it now. Which part of England are you from?"

"From Strangways, sir. In Wiltshire."

"Don't know it."

"It's about a quarter mile up the road from Stonehenge, sir."

"You mean the ancient stone circle of the druids?"

"Yes, sir."

"That's a strange place to come from," said Mr. Gaunt. "And what's that strange smell?"

"In many ways Strangways is rather a strange place, sir," admitted Haddo. "Oh, and the strange smell is probably me, sir. You see, when you brush up against evil, sometimes a little of it rubs off."

"What does that mean?"

"As well as being a chauffeur, I'm also a druid, sir. Only not a white druid. They celebrate good. I'm a black druid." He chuckled unpleasantly. "We support the other team."

"I think I'd like to get out," said Mr. Gaunt. "Stop the car."

"As you wish, sir," said Haddo. "I'll pull up at the next corner if you like."

"Yes, please do."

Amid much honking from the many taxis and cars behind, the Maybach drew almost silently to a halt on the corner of Park and 57th, but before Mr. Gaunt could get out, the heavy doors opened and two even stranger men got into the back of the car beside him. The odd smell in the car seemed to grow even stronger.

"Thank you, Mr. Haddo," said one of the two men, who was also English.

The car pulled away again and, sensing some danger now, Mr. Gaunt made an attempt to get out of the car only to find he could not move.

"Don't worry," said one of the two men. "The odor on Mr. Haddo's body is a hypnotic unguent to render you harmless to us and to yourself."

"What's happening?" said Mr. Gaunt. "Who are you people?"

"We're your kidnappers," said the man. "And you're being kidnapped."

"I suppose you want money," said Mr. Gaunt.

"Money?" The man laughed. "No, no. Nothing so mundane."

CHAPTER 2

THE TALKING BOARD

Founded in 1638 by five hundred Puritans who promptly murdered the tribe of Quinnipiac Native Americans who were already living there, New Haven is on the northern shore of Long Island Sound and best known as the home of Yale University. Philippa knew that seven U.S. presidents and vice presidents had gone to Yale (not to mention one Turkish prime minister, and her own father) and, one day, she intended to go there herself. Other than Mr. Gaunt, the only Yale alumnus known to John was Charles Montgomery Burns, the owner of the Springfield Nuclear Power Plant in the hit cartoon television series, *The Simpsons,* which was his favorite show on TV. For John, the idea that Mr. Burns had gone to Yale told him all he thought he needed to know about the place.

Mr. Vodyannoy, who also owned an apartment in the creepy Dakota building on New York's Central Park, welcomed the twins, Uncle Nimrod, and Mr. Groanin to a giant-sized house on the seashore that looked more like a medieval castle with proper turrets and arrow windows. John was impressed. Mr. Vodyannoy's house was even creepier than the Dakota.

"This is one heck of a house, Mr. Vodyannoy," he said. "Have you lived here long?"

"I assume you know that heck means hell," commented Mr. Vodyannoy. "This is truer of Nightshakes than perhaps you know. When I bought it, around seventy years ago, the house came with a curse, which, among several other things, required me never to stop building, and curses are something one takes very seriously in this part of the world. The house had just thirteen rooms when I acquired it. Since then I have added another seventy rooms, mostly to the east wing which I advise you never ever to enter."

"Is that the haunted part?" John asked.

"Worse than haunted," said Mr. Vodyannoy. "The east wing is the ill-favored, unfortunate part of the house. And it has amused me to reflect this in the way all of the building work has been undertaken. For example, there are thirteen cupolas and thirteen passages. All of the windows have thirteen panes, all of the floors have thirteen boards, and all of the staircases have thirteen steps. In the east wing of Nightshakes, there are corridors that lead nowhere and doors that open into the open air, and the house is now too huge to navigate without getting lost. So, I advise you to remain in the west wing at all times. Or face the consequences, which might be terrible. Even for a djinn. Should you be unfortunate enough to find yourself lost there, I advise you to scream as loud as you can and for as long as you can and then, perhaps, some intrepid soul will dare to come and find you. Unless it is after dark, of course, in which case you will have to take your chances until morning."

Mr. Groanin shivered and said, "Catch me creeping around this place after dark and you can send me to the local loony bin."

"That is certainly a possibility," said Mr. Vodyannoy. "You see, before I bought the place, it *was* the local loony bin."

Given his somewhat eccentric appearance, anyone would have been wise to take Frank Vodyannoy's warning seriously: He was tall — taller than Nimrod — with a red beard and an eagle's beak of a nose, and on his finger he wore a large ring with a moonstone that was the size and color of an alligator's eyeball. Mr. Vodyannoy had lived in New York for seventy-five years but occasionally some traces of his real Russian origins appeared in his conversation. "But enough of this talk. The Djinnverso tournament will begin this afternoon in the library, at three. Until then, if there's anything you need, ring for my butler, Bo, who will show you to your rooms. Bo?"

A large, misshapen man came forward and, taking hold of all the luggage at once — which amounted to more than a dozen bags — lifted it like so much shopping. Leaving Mr. Vodyannoy to greet Zadie Eloko, a new guest, Bo led them to their respective rooms in silence, which was Philippa's opportunity to quiz her uncle about her host's comments regarding the east wing.

"After our last adventure," she said, "it was my impression that the spirit world had been more or less cleared out. That there are no more ghosts. That Iblis had destroyed nearly all of them."

"That is true," said Nimrod. "Of course, new ghosts are being created all the time. People die and sometimes they become ghosts. But it is certain that things are not what they were. It will take many centuries for there to be as many ghosts as once there were. However, you must allow a man with a house like Nightshakes a little poetic license. Besides, there are more things in heaven and earth besides ghosts than perhaps you can yet imagine, Philippa. At least I hope so."

"Now there's a comforting thought," mumbled Groanin. He went into the room that Bo had indicated, closed the door behind him and looked around, nodding appreciatively as his eyes took in the enormous bed, the wide-screen TV, and the many marble acres of the bathroom. He had just dropped his bag and spread himself out on the bed when there was a knock at the door. It was John.

Groanin smiled as best he was able. "What do you want, young man?" he asked the boy. "I say, what do you want?"

"I assume you have no real interest in the Djinnverso tournament," said John.

"You assume correctly. I dislike all games except soccer and darts."

"In which case I was wondering if you might like to accompany me to the Peabody Museum."

Mr. Groanin thought about John's invitation for a moment. In truth the idea was not an attractive one to him. Groanin had disliked museums ever since the time he had been attacked by a tiger while working in the library of the British Museum. But he was fond of John and decided to go with him if only to keep him from getting into mischief, because boys will be boys even when they are also djinn.

The Peabody is a large redbrick building that looks more like a church than a museum. But there can be few if any churches that are possessed of the type of outside statuary that blesses the Peabody. For, mounted on a granite plinth in front is a life-sized and reasonably lifelike bronze of a *Torosaurus*, which is a species of dinosaur that most resembles a *Triceratops*.

Mr. Groanin was not impressed.

"Now, why would anyone want to make a statue of an ugly-looking beast like that?" he grumbled. "I've never understood the fascination people have with these daft creatures. Big, nasty things with sharp teeth and clumsy feet." He shuddered. "Horrible."

John did not agree. "I think it's amazing," he said. "Just imagine what would happen if it came alive. The damage it could cause. Awesome."

"If I was lucky enough to have a wish from a djinn right now," Groanin said pointedly, "it would be that this big horrible monstrosity could stay exactly where it is, forever. Is that clear?"

"Yes," said John. "I was just imagining, that's all."

"Well, don't. When you imagine something, most normal folk feel obliged to reach for a tin hat."

They went inside and spent a meandering couple of hours looking at collections of historical scientific instruments, meteorites, Egyptian antiquities, and various items of South American gold and pottery. John would have been bored except for the curious sensation they were being watched. A couple of times he even turned around suddenly, hoping to catch sight of someone spying on him, but spotted nothing out of the ordinary and his behavior only earned him some strange looks from Groanin.

"What's wrong with you, lad? You're as jumpy as a sack full of cats."

"Nothing," said John. He glanced out of the window, where a wind was strengthening. "I expect it was just the wind." He glanced at his watch. "Come on, let's go back to the house. This place is boring."

"Never a truer word spoken," said Groanin. "I've seen the contents of handkerchiefs that were more interesting than this."

At Nightshakes, the Djinnverso tournament was in full swing and nobody paid any attention to John, which, for once, suited him very well, and after dinner, he sought out Bo, Mr. Vodyannoy's weird butler, to ask him a question. He found Bo in the butler's pantry in the basement reading a magazine about boxing, which was a sport in which Bo, who was the size of a mountain gorilla and almost as hairy, had once excelled.

"Excuse me, Bo," John said nervously. "But I was wondering if you could direct me to Mr. Vodyannoy's collection of talking boards. I'd like to take a look at them, see. On account of how they're supposed to be valuable antiques 'n' all."

Bo growled quietly, stood up, fetched his improbable jacket, and from a pocket, produced a map of the house that he then spread on the pantry table. He spoke in a voice that was a strong combination of coffee, many sleepless nights, cigarettes, an old punch in the throat, and Hungary.

"We're here," he said, pointing a forefinger as thick as a tree sapling to a small square on the map. "You go along this corridor and up these stairs to the hall of mirrors. Exiting the hall by the east door, you head quietly through the portrait gallery and then the music room, to the summer drawing room. Exit the summer drawing room by the tall door and walk through the conservatory to the spiral staircase. At the top of the spiral staircase, with fortune you will find yourself in an observatory, easily recognizable by the presence of a large reflector telescope. Counting your blessings as you leave the observatory by the green malachite corridor, you will then pass through a trophy room to the hall of shadows. There, in thirteen large drawers labeled BEWARE, you will find what you are looking for, sir." Bo folded the map and handed it to John. "Here. Take it. In case you get lost."

"Thanks," said John. "Incidentally, why are those thirteen drawers labeled BEWARE? Is it because the talking boards are so valuable?"

"It's not that they're so valuable, sir," Bo said stiffly. "Just that they are quite hazardous and should on no account be handled by anyone who has no knowledge of how they work. Let alone a boy of about twelve or thirteen years old. Of course, you, sir, being a djinn, will doubtless know exactly what you're doing."

"Yes," said John, who, despite the faith Bo placed in him, had almost no idea of what a talking board could do. "You're right. I do know what I'm doing. Of course." He pocketed the map and moved toward the door. "Thanks for all your help."

"Not that way, sir," said Bo, pointing in the opposite direction to the one John was moving in. "This way. By the way, sir, the hall of drawers is on the very edge of the west wing. This means that it is on the very border of the east wing, which is not a place to go after dark. Not even for a djinn such as yourself. Eight months ago, my own sister, Grace, went missing in the east wing."

"How long was she missing for?" John asked brightly.

"I regret to say she is still missing," said Bo. "Occasionally we hear her weeping in some faraway corner of the house, but although we have often looked, we have never been able to find her. We leave food out for the poor creature, of course. And the food disappears. So we presume that she is still alive."

"But surely Mr. Vodyannoy could find her, with djinn power."

"Didn't Mr. Vodyannoy explain about that?" said Bo.

"Explain what?"

"There is a djinn binding on this house that stops djinn power being used in it. That is the Nightshakes curse, sir. Before it was a loony bin, sir, the house was previously owned by a member of the Ifrit tribe. A very nasty lot. In fact, sir, if you will pardon my language, they are an absolute shower."

"Yes, I've met them."

"You will be careful, won't you, sir?" said Bo in a voice as deep and rough as an alligator's. "We should hate to lose two persons. Once has been unfortunate. Twice would look like actionable negligence on my part."

"Yes. I'll be all right."

For an instant, the wind and rain rubbed against the windowpane like a hungry dog and, momentarily, a flash of lightning illuminated the butler's pantry like someone playing with an electric switch.

"A storm is getting up," observed Bo.

"I'd say it has gotten up, had breakfast, and is already at work," replied John.

Bo did not smile at John's joke.

"I mention it, sir," he said, "because the power in that part of the house is always uncertain. Especially during an electrical storm. I would advise you to take this flashlight."

Bo handed John a flashlight and then sat down to finish reading his magazine. Somewhat unnerved by the butler's remarks but not quite deterred, for he was a stubborn, often courageous boy, John set out for the hall of shadows.

It was another half hour before John reached the hall of shadows, by which time he was talking to himself almost constantly to keep from being frightened. The portrait gallery had been full of pictures of Mr. Vodyannoy's ancestors, several of whom seemed to belong in a carnival freak show. Especially the great aunt with the red beard. The summer drawing room had been as cold as a crypt, which was hardly surprising since the several stone gargoyles there had been taken from the Vodyannoy family burial vault in Vienna. Exiting the so-called summer drawing room by a door as tall as a basketball hoop, John had passed through a cobwebby conservatory and climbed up a wobbly spiral staircase, at the top of which there had been an observatory where a human skeleton sat in a red leather armchair apparently staring through the telescope at the moon. Then, leaving the observatory by the green malachite corridor, he had entered a trophy room. These were not silver trophies but some very lifelike animals which had been shot and expertly stuffed and arranged around the room like so many pieces of fierce-looking furniture: a Kodiak bear, a lion, a tiger, a jackal, a hyena, a wolf, a jaguar, a rhinoceros, and an elephant with a homicidal glint in its amber eye.

"Forget the Peabody, dude," he said to himself. "You should have looked around this museum. Place gives me the creeps."

But he remained firm of purpose, determined to use one of the talking boards to make contact with some sort of spirit and discover the fate of poor Mr. Rakshasas. A month or two before, Mr. Rakshasas's spirit had disappeared from the Metropolitan Museum in New York, apparently absorbed by a ghostly Chinese terra-cotta warrior. His body, which had been left for safekeeping at the Gaunt family home on East 77th Street, had subsequently vanished. John missed the old djinn, and his peculiar, wise Irish sayings, dreadfully.

The hall of shadows was well-named. The ceiling chandelier seemed not to be working but a log was burning in the huge grate and this made everything seem uncomfortably vivid and penumbral, as if the room itself might be moving. John turned on the flashlight, let out an unsteady breath, and gritted his teeth for a moment.

"Nothing to be scared of," he said. "Just the fire, that's all."

In the center of the room stood a tall hexagonal cabinet made of Chinese red lacquer. In the firelight, it looked quite infernal. It had exactly thirteen drawers. On each drawer was painted one word in gold lettering: CAVE. For a moment John wondered if he might have the wrong drawers until he remembered that *cave* was the Latin word for "beware." But it was another Latin phrase that immediately presented itself to John's nervous mind.

"*Carpe diem*," he said. "*Carpe diem*. Seize the drawer handle." He seized one of the drawer handles and pulled.

"Looking for something?"

John let out a yelp of fear and, spinning around, saw a woman sitting in a high-sided chair who looked like the witch of the place. She had long unkempt hair, dirty clothes, and a strange smile on a grubby face that was all yellow skin and bone. Instinctively, he guessed this strange creature must be Bo's lost sister.

"You must be Grace," he said, swallowing his fear.

"I don't think I know you, boy," she said.

"Your brother, Bo, told me about you," said John.

"What did he say?" Grace asked sharply.

"Nothing. Only that you had gone missing in the east wing."

"That's easy enough in this house, right enough."

"You're in the west wing now," said John. "I can show you the way back if you like. When I've done what I came here to do."

"I suppose you want to play cards. Do you want to play cards?"

"Cards? No, not particularly."

"What are you doing in those drawers? There are no cards in those drawers, if that's what you're after. And no food, either. I've already looked."

"I was looking for one of Mr. Vodyannoy's talking boards," answered John, and removed one of the boards from the open drawer. It was rather a fine wooden board, with a picture of what looked like several Native Americans and a man with a beard, who was wearing armor.

"Those boards," said Grace, "they're dangerous. You shouldn't mess around with them."

But John wasn't listening. He took the board and a little balsa-wood heart, which acted as a kind of pointer, over to the fire, laid it on the rug, and sat down in front of it. Printed on the board was an alphabet, ten numbers from one to zero, and the words *sí*, *no*, *hola*, and *adiós*. Curious to see what might happen, Grace came over and sat opposite John. She was close enough for him to smell her, and it was not a good smell, but John was too polite to tell Grace she stank and to move away. Besides, he was still a little scared of her as she obviously was quite mad. He took a deep breath, placed his hands on either side of the board, and stared at it intently.

"My name is John Gaunt," he said loudly. "I'm trying to get in touch with a friend of mine, named Mr. Rakshasas, to find out if he has passed over to the other side. If Mr. Rakshasas is there, or if there's someone here with us who might know Mr. Rakshasas and where he is, then please make yourself known to us."

Nothing happened except that Grace shook her head. "Listen to me, boy," she whispered. "This is not something a child should ever do."

"Quiet," hissed John. "Please. I'm trying to make contact with the other side."

"The other side of what?" sniggered Grace.

"I dunno, exactly," admitted John. "But a medium made contact with me once. And that's the kind of thing she said."

"A medium made contact with you?" Grace frowned. "Are you dead? You don't look at all dead."

"Look, don't ask me to explain it now," said John, and moved his hands onto the board, which seemed to work because almost immediately the little wooden heart moved.

"You moved that yourself," said Grace.

"No, I didn't."

"Yes, you did."

John decided to ignore her and concentrate on the talking board. "Is anyone there?" he asked, and looked around nervously as he heard something tap on the windowpane. But it was just the branch of a tree outside. The wind moaned in the fireplace, stirring the flames, and a small wisp of wood smoke drifted across the board. Then the heart moved again, this time more noticeably than before, pointing to one letter, then another, and then another. John spelled out the letters.

"P-A-I-T-I-T-I."

Then the heart stopped.

"Paititi? Is that a name? A word? I don't understand."

Now the heart began to move rapidly, and John found himself struggling not just to spell out the words, but to understand them, too.

"You're going too fast," he said. "Slow down. And, please, what language is this? I don't recognize it." Finally, he shouted, "Look, whoever you are, what language is this?"

The heart stopped for a moment and then slowly moved again.

"M-A-N-C-O-C-A-P-A-C. Mancocapac? I'm afraid I don't speak Mancocapac. I mean, I wish I did. But I don't."

Now, in all normal circumstances John's wish that he spoke Mancocapac would have done the trick because he was a djinn, after all. Once before, in Berlin, John wished he could understand German, and immediately found that he could. But the ancient Ifrit binding on Nightshakes meant that John's wish went unfulfilled, and unfortunately, he was left none the wiser as to what his invisible interlocutor wanted to communicate.

The heart began to vibrate on the board.

"I think you've upset him," said Grace.

The next second, the little heart flew into the fireplace as if flicked there by some unseen, powerful forefinger. Even as John quickly retrieved the antique heart from the fire, something picked up the talking board and hurled it across the room, hitting one of the thirteen panes in the window and breaking it. The log fire seemed to stretch out to this new current of oxygen. A huge gust of smoke, which billowed down the chimney and into the room, seemed to clothe an invisible figure, and, for the briefest moment, John saw what looked like a man with the longest earlobes he had ever seen. The man had a fringe of hair that almost covered his eyes and was wearing a cloak of feathers so that he looked like an enormous peacock. Then the man disappeared from sight, although not from the room, it seemed, for something hauled every one of the thirteen drawers out of the hexagonal red lacquer cabinet, emptying all of Mr. Vodyannoy's talking boards onto the floor. A moment later, the window burst open and the spirit — for John was sure that was what it was — disappeared into the stormy night.

"He's gone," said Grace. "Good riddance, too, if you ask me. Smashing up the place like that. Diabolical liberty."

John pressed a finger to his mouth because something remained behind. Something hidden in the shadows of the hall of shadows. Something that had not been there before.

It sounded like a rumble of thunder. Or perhaps a very large man snoring after a heavy lunch. A very large man with powerful jaws and sharp teeth. A very large man who was rather more feline than human. John felt the hair rise on his head, as it suddenly dawned on him that this sounded less like a large man and more like a very big cat. The kind with spots on it. Like the one he'd seen in the trophy room. The growling came closer and he saw a definitely catlike shape edging forward from the corner of the room.

"What is it?" gulped Grace. "A sheep?"

"It definitely isn't a sheep, you crazy witch," whispered John.

"Then what is it?"

John didn't answer. But already he recognized the kind of big cat he was dealing with. It was a South American jaguar, or *otorongo*. A big one, heavily muscled, about six feet long and probably weighing as much as two hundred pounds.

"Are you sure that's not a sheep?" asked Grace.

It is said that adrenaline will enable a man being chased by a bull to leap a gate at one bound or a child to lift a very heavy object off its stricken parent. It was the same with John, except that he was a djinn and, as anyone knows, the djinn are made of fire. The boy did not think. He just did what survival urgently obliged him to do. He reached into the blazing fire, lifted a burning log and, in the same moment that the *otorongo* raced toward him, thrust it into the cat's open jaws. The *otorongo*'s roar turned into a high-pitched scream, and the big cat shrank back from the fire in John's hand. It turned all the way around, took another look at John with luminous eyes, as if judging the wisdom of mounting a second attack against someone armed with fire and, seeming to think better of it, gathered itself like the string on a crossbow and then shot out of the window.

John let out a breath and tossed the log back into the fire. "Man, that was close," he said.

"Funny-looking sheep," said Grace.

"Wasn't it?" said John. He could see little point in arguing with her.

Grace grabbed John's hand and looked at it with astonishment. "Your hand," she said. "There's not a mark on it. No burn. Nothing. Not even a smudge."

John looked at his hand and was a little surprised to discover that she was right: His hand was quite unscathed.

"You're not human," she said almost triumphantly.

John smiled and for once hardly cared that a human should know the truth about who and what he was. "No," he said. "I'm not."

A little fearfully, Grace dropped his hand. "Hey," she said, "don't tell me you really are dead."

"No," said John, "I'm not dead. I'm a djinn."

"Is that like a sheep?"

"Yes. It's just like a sheep. Look here, why are you so interested in sheep?"

"'Cause I'm a sheep myself. Not only that, but I'm a sheep that's lost. If I find some of the other sheep that are lost, then I figure my brother, Bo, might come and find me. You know. Like in the nursery rhyme."

John, who thought this was just about the saddest story he had ever heard, persuaded Grace to come back with him to the butler's pantry where Bo was very pleased to be reunited with his sister.

"I'm afraid there's a bit of a mess in the hall of shadows, Bo," said John. "Like, the talking boards are all over the floor. But I kind of figured it was better to bring Grace back here ASAP rather than spend time cleaning up."

"Please, sir, leave it to me." Bo hugged Grace, who now started to cry almost as if she finally realized what had happened to her. "I am very grateful to you, sir, and am forever in your debt. If there is anything I can do for you." And so saying, he kissed John's hand gratefully.

"There is *something* you could do," said John, taking back his hand, for he disliked being kissed on the hand by anyone, least of all a grown-up man. "I'd appreciate it if you didn't mention this to anyone. My uncle Nimrod might get a bit uptight about it if he found out what I'd been up to. He's English, you see."

"Yes, sir. I understand perfectly. No further explanation is required. I used to work for a junior member of the British royal family, and they don't get any more uptight than that, let me tell you. Those people are so stiff they could whip eggs into a meringue with one look."

"Yes. That describes it very well, I think."

Bo took John's hand into his own, and John decided to go to bed before the Hungarian butler could kiss it again. He felt the evening had not been a complete waste of time. He had failed to gain any information about Mr. Rakshasas but at least he had rescued Grace.

As John went up the stairs, he saw Philippa and his uncle were still playing Djinnverso in the library. It looked like they were going to go on all night. Now that really was a waste of time, thought John. As complete a waste of time as you could have found on any college football field.

CHAPTER 3

MANCO CAPAC

The next morning, John came down to the breakfast room to find Uncle Nimrod and Mr. Vodyannoy wearing the same clothes as the day before and expressions that were brimful of accusation.

"It seems that there was an incident last night," said Nimrod delicately.

John made a fist and cursed Bo for opening his mouth. No. That was unfair. Bo wasn't the type to squeal on a guy. Not even when his master was a powerful djinn. His crazy sister, Grace, must have mentioned something. John bit his lip and hoped he could bluff it out.

"Oh, really? What kind of incident?"

"It seems there was a break-in at the Peabody Museum," explained Nimrod.

John breathed a sigh of relief and tried to conceal a smile as he helped himself to a large steak.

"A violent break-in of a most peculiar nature," continued Nimrod. "The front door of the museum was battered down by a large object, and a number of valuable artifacts were thrown about the place."

"I don't see what that has to do with me," said John.

"You were at the Peabody for two hours yesterday afternoon, were you not?" asked Nimrod.

"Sure," said John. "And it was dullsville. I certainly didn't steal anything from the place, if that's what you were suggesting."

"Let me finish telling you exactly what happened," said Nimrod. "And then you will understand why I am speaking to you about it at all, John. You saw the *Torosaurus* outside the front?"

"Yes. It was cool."

"This *Torosaurus*?" Nimrod handed John a photograph of the bronze dinosaur on the granite plinth in front of the Peabody.

"Yes."

"It might interest you to know that this is what the *Torosaurus* looks like now." He handed John a second picture.

John shrugged. "I don't see . . ."

"It's the wrong way around on the plinth," said Nimrod. "It now faces the museum, instead of facing away from the museum."

John felt his jaw drop.

"You see the problem, John. Like a real *Torosaurus*, the bronze statue weighs several tons. So this goes beyond any normal student prank. In other words, it is impossible to imagine how anyone could do this who was not in possession of a very large crane, which seems unlikely. So the implication is clear. Someone must have used djinn power to have that *Torosaurus* climb off its plinth and batter the door down with its horn. Why, I'm not sure. Anyone who could achieve such a feat had no need to draw attention to their crime."

Mr. Vodyannoy shrugged apologetically. "The police are baffled, of course. But they have found pieces of the Peabody's front door on the bronze statue's horn."

"Mr. Groanin tells me you were most impressed with the statue," said Nimrod. "That you actually mentioned what might happen if ever it came alive."

"Yes, I did," said John. "But look, I had nothing to do with the break-in. Honest."

He was about to say more and then checked himself. Was it possible that this strange occurrence had something to do with the incident involving the talking board in the hall of shadows? Could the ghostly man with the feathered cloak he'd summoned from the other side have brought the bronze statue to life and broken into the Peabody Museum?

"Yes?" Nimrod said. "I think you were about to say something?" He waited for a moment. "Odd, don't you think, that something as bizarre as this should happen on the very same night that Bo's sister, Grace, is rescued from the east wing of Nightshakes after being missing for eight months? Or is that merely a happy coincidence?"

"I didn't do anything to that *Torosaurus*," said John. "And I certainly didn't steal any silly old artifacts."

"Perhaps. However I'll hazard a guess that you can offer a better explanation for what happened than the one we have at the moment, which is to say, no explanation at all."

John sighed. He could see no way around a full and frank confession now. Nimrod was onto him. Of course, John was hardly surprised about this, given the amount of fish his uncle ate. The guy had a brain as big as a basketball. He was busted. So John told his uncle and Mr. Vodyannoy what had happened with the talking board on the outermost limits of the west wing.

"Light my lamp, are you mad, boy?" exclaimed Nimrod.

"Those boards should never be used," added Mr. Vodyannoy. "They're extremely dangerous. That's why they're kept hidden away."

"I'm sorry," John apologized. "I meant no harm, really. I only wanted to try to make contact with Mr. Rakshasas."

Nimrod nodded. "I miss him, too, you know." He put his hand on John's shoulder.

"Do you really think it's possible that my using the board is what caused the incident at the Peabody?"

"I'm afraid that's the conclusion we must form," said Nimrod. "Whoever it was you summoned would have been very upset."

"Yes, but why?" asked John.

"Because he must have failed to do the one thing he had

46

been summoned by you to do, which is to communicate," said Mr. Vodyannoy. "He was probably furious that you couldn't speak his language. Can you remember what it was? Or any of the words he used?"

"No," confessed John.

"Then we'll have to work it out from the board you used. You see, each one will summon a different entity, from a different part of the world, depending on the origin of the board. Do you think you could remember what the board looked like?"

"If I saw it again, I'm sure I'd recognize it," said John.

They went back to the hall of shadows. In daylight, it looked quite different from what he remembered. *Hardly creepy at all,* John thought. Bo had tidied all of the boards away into the thirteen drawers of the red lacquer cabinet and was already repairing the broken windowpane. He was even whistling. Mr. Vodyannoy opened the drawers and started to show John the various boards in his collection, and it wasn't long before John recognized the one he'd used the night before.

"That's it," he said. "That's the one. I recognize the Native American pictured on it. And the man in the armor."

"Actually," said Mr. Vodyannoy, "the Native American, as you call him, is an Inca. And the fellow with the armor is supposed to be Pizarro. This is the conquistador design. And it was made in South America about a hundred and fifty years ago. This makes it much more likely that the spirit you summoned, if spirit it was and not a demon or an elemental, came from that part of the world. It would certainly explain the *otorongo*."

"I do remember the man had very large earlobes," said John. "And a cape of feathers."

"Then you actually saw him," said Nimrod.

"Just for a second. A gust of wind from the chimney blew out some smoke that seemed to give his body a kind of form."

"If only you could remember his name," said Nimrod.

"We'll go to the Peabody," said Mr. Vodyannoy. "Perhaps one of the museum's many South American exhibits will help to jog the boy's memory."

There was a police line in front of the broken door of the Peabody, and nobody was being admitted except museum officials and crime scene unit investigators from the New Haven police department. But none of this presented an obstacle to the three djinn. Away from the curse of Nightshakes, they simply left their bodies in Mr. Vodyannoy's car and walked invisibly past the policeman on duty in front of the wooden smithereens that had once been the front door. But not before pausing to listen to some of the various local explanations of the same story that were being told to the several reporters, photographers, and television crews who now surrounded the *Torosaurus*. Some people suggested that students were somehow responsible for the new position of the bronze statue. Others pointed to the skies and insisted that aliens must have done it. An eccentric geologist claimed he had measured a small earthquake in the immediate vicinity of the university museum, which might, he claimed, have turned the statue around on its plinth. A few religious eccentrics were suggesting a divine explanation, while a group of conspiracy theorists were mooting the possibility that the *Torosaurus* had never been made of bronze at all, but had been a real *Torosaurus* in some kind of suspended animation.

John laughed out loud at some of these wildly different ideas and commented on their stupidity to Nimrod, forgetting for a moment that he was invisible and that someone might hear him. Someone did. One of the policemen. And he quickly told a television reporter that, in his opinion, the museum was haunted.

Inside the museum, the three invisible djinn — who were holding hands so as to avoid getting separated from each other — went into the rooms exhibiting South American artifacts and learned for the first time that these were the rooms that had been vandalized. Several glass cases had been smashed and their mostly golden contents now lay strewn on the floor, where a police photographer was busy recording the scene of the crime.

"Well, that makes sense, I suppose," whispered Nimrod.

"What does?" asked John.

"That our anonymous South American friend in the cape of feathers should have come here. To the Hiram Bingham treasures."

Mr. Vodyannoy told John that many of the artifacts in the Peabody had been brought to Yale from Machu Picchu, a lost city of the Incas discovered in the Peruvian Andes by Hiram Bingham — who was perhaps the model for Indiana Jones — in 1911. "The Peruvian government has long petitioned Yale for their return. Perhaps our invisible friend has lent his weight to the Peruvian cause."

"That is one possibility," admitted Nimrod.

For a few moments, they eavesdropped as a police detective spoke to a bespectacled man wearing a gray suit and a yellow bow tie.

"Can you tell us what's missing, Professor?" asked the detective.

"Three rather large coins or medals," said the professor. "Made of solid gold and Incan in origin. And some *khipu*. Incan message cords."

"Anything else?"

"Yes. One of our Incan mummies is missing."

"You mean like an Egyptian mummy?" asked the detective. "Wrapped in bandages 'n' stuff?"

"It wasn't just the ancient Egyptians who mummified their dead aristocrats, Lieutenant," said the professor. "A number of pre-Columbian South American civilizations did so, too. Only they didn't wrap them in bandages. And they didn't seal them inside pyramids. At least, the Inca didn't, anyway. They carried their dead kings around with them and got them out for ceremonial occasions. For all intents and purposes, they treated them like they were living people."

"So what did this mummy look like?"

"Actually, rather ghastly. Like someone who had been dead for a very long time. They were embalmed, of course, but the effect is still somewhat horrific."

"And who was this mummy, exactly?" asked the police lieutenant.

"I have no idea. Hiram Bingham was more of an explorer than an archaeologist and infuriatingly careless about properly identifying the Incan artifacts he brought here from Machu Picchu, the lost city of the Incas. It could have been anyone, really. That is, any member of the Incan royal family."

"Interesting," murmured John.

"What's that you said?" asked the professor.

"I didn't say anything, Professor." The detective shook his head. "Why do you think anyone would want to steal a mummy?"

"I was kind of wondering that myself," whispered John, and felt Nimrod pull him quickly away as the detective and the professor stared suspiciously at each other.

"You must learn to be silent when you are invisible, John," hissed Nimrod.

"I'm sorry, but I really couldn't help it. With all that gold on the floor, a mummy seems like such a weird thing to steal, that's all."

"I very much doubt that it has been stolen," said Mr. Vodyannoy. "After all, you can hardly steal something that belongs to you in the first place."

"You think the mummy belonged to the guy in the feather cape?" asked John. "That it was his own mummified body?"

"I can't think of a better explanation," said Mr. Vodyannoy. "Can you?"

"Which makes it all the more imperative that we try to identify him," said Nimrod.

"I don't see how," argued Mr. Vodyannoy. "You heard that professor. They have no idea who it was."

"Let me think for a minute," said Nimrod.

The three invisible djinn stopped in front of a wall-sized photograph of Machu Picchu. John recognized it from a history lesson at school: a lost Incan city on top of an eight-thousand-foot-high plateau in the middle of the Peruvian jungle.

"It can't be easy to lose a whole city," said John. "I mean, it's not like a set of keys, is it? Or ten dollars. A city's not exactly something you leave lying around. I mean, I bet there were lots of local Peruvian people who knew it was there all along. I bet it was never really lost in the first place. I bet this Hiram Bingham decided to say it was lost just to make himself famous."

"Bravo," said Nimrod. "I think there's a lot of truth in what you say. There is, of course, a proper lost city of the Incas. But Machu Picchu isn't it. Never was. That was just Hiram Bingham's wishful thinking."

"So what's this other lost city, then?" asked John.

"Paititi," said Nimrod.

John's heart skipped a beat. "What did you say it was called?" he asked.

"Paititi," repeated Nimrod.

For a moment, John's mind's eye pictured the heart on the talking board spelling out the word. "Is that P-A-I-T-I-T-I?" he asked.

"Yes," said Nimrod. "Why? And do try to speak more quietly. I just saw a policeman cross himself."

"Paititi was the first word that got spelled out on the talking board," said John.

"Are you sure?"

"Yes." After wringing his brain like a sponge for a moment, John added, "I'm sure. There was one other word I was able to distinguish. The language being written. I think it was Mancocapac."

"Manco Capac?" Nimrod asked.

"Keep your voice down," said John.

"Did you say Manco Capac?"

"Yes."

"Manco Capac isn't a language," said Mr. Vodyannoy. "Manco Capac is a name. Manco Capac was the founder of the Incan Dynasty in Peru. This is why he is sometimes known as Manco the Great. That was who you summoned in the hall of shadows, John. That was who you saw. It was Manco Capac himself."

Mr. Vodyannoy gasped.

"Oh, my goodness," said Mr. Vodyannoy. "Nimrod, do you remember that photograph in the newspapers a few days ago? From the South American jungle. The Eye of the Forest?"

"I've hardly thought about anything else since I saw it," confessed Nimrod. "Are you thinking what I'm thinking?"

"The prophecy," said Mr. Vodyannoy. "Of course. What else could it be?"

"What prophecy?" asked John.

"Do you suppose we could try to summon Manco Capac again?" Nimrod asked Mr. Vodyannoy. "With the talking board?"

"Not now he has his own mummy back," said Mr. Vodyannoy. "He'll use that for any future manifestations rather than a talking board."

"Then we've missed it," Nimrod said. "We've missed our best chance to avert a disaster. We missed it."

"Strange, don't you think?" said Mr. Vodyannoy. "That it should have been the boy who summoned him. Given that he's a twin. I suppose it means that John and Philippa are the twins, after all. The ones who were foretold."

"I hardly want to think about it," said Nimrod. "But I was afraid of that, of course. Always have been, really. I suppose I'd better inform Faustina."

"Would someone mind telling me what this is all about?" John said as loudly as he could without scaring another policeman.

"I think it would be better if your sister was present when I explained how things are," said Nimrod. "Since this affects her just as much as it affects you. But Manco Capac wasn't just the first Incan king, he was also a djinn. A very great djinn."

"And the prophecy?" asked John.

"The prophecy?" Nimrod sighed a great sigh. "The prophecy is called the *Pachacuti*," he said quietly. "Something feared by all the tribes of djinn, good and evil. It's an Incan word. It means the 'great earth shaking.' It's a prophecy about the end of the world."

CHAPTER 4

PACHACUTI

Between Djinnverso games at Nightshakes, Philippa went to her room and wrote in her diary, which was a favorite habit since the time she had spent at Iravotum, the official residence of the Blue Djinn of Babylon. One of her opponents at Nightshakes was Zadie Eloko. This is what Philippa wrote about Zadie Eloko:

> Zadie Eloko is about the same age as me, I think. She's a member of the Jann tribe — like Mr. Vodyannoy — with a Bahamian father who's a politician and an American mother who used to be a famous actress. Her older brother is a famous comedian. She is rather precocious and tells me that she wants to become a conceptual artist. Some people suck a lollipop, but Zadie sucks a toothbrush and always seems to be cleaning her teeth. She says she's in love, but she won't say with whom. Her focus word is KAKORRHAPHIOPHOBIA, which she tells me means having an abnormal fear of failure — something she herself seems to suffer from. But in spite of that, I've already

defeated her! More than once! She seldom uses djinn power because she says it's lazy and says she much prefers "doing it for herself." I kind of like her but she has the room above Mr. Groanin here at Nightshakes and drives the poor man crazy because when she isn't playing Djinnverso, she is practicing her tap dancing on the wooden floor on account of how she's in some kind of beastly show at her school. Groanin says he'd like to strangle her.

Zadie seems to think I've led a much more interesting life. I told her that it's not always good to have an interesting life because that's just another way of saying that lots of things have happened in it, and not all of them good. Like the time I spent in Iravotum with Ayesha. And our trip to Kathmandu when that smelly guru wanted to steal our blood. To say nothing of that horrible terra-cotta warrior who absorbed poor Mr. Rakshasas. Anyway, to cheer her up after our last match — she hates losing — she made me make her a foolish promise that the next time I go anywhere interesting with John and Nimrod she can come with us. It was a djinn promise, which is binding, of course. John will be upset with me, I think. But I won't tell him about it for a while. Not until our next adventure, anyway.

Hearing a car outside the house, Philippa put aside her diary and got up from the writing desk. Looking outside her bedroom window she saw an enormous Rolls-Royce pulling up at the front door. Out of the driver's side of the car stepped a little man she recognized. He was wearing a neat dark suit, a bow tie, and a pair of yellow driving gloves. It was Jonah Damascus, the Blue Djinn's chauffeur, bodyguard, and handyman from her unofficial residence in Berlin.

Jonah went around to the rear passenger door, opened it, and out stepped Faustina herself.

"What's she doing here?" Philippa murmured, and went downstairs to find out.

Faustina had become more glamorous since becoming the Blue Djinn. The necklace and earrings she wore were made of sapphires as big as bottle caps. And her clothes were all djinn-made copies of expensive Italian designers, only better. She shrugged a *Smilodon* fur coat into Bo's hands, placed a folded newspaper on the sideboard, and greeted Philippa coolly. "Is your uncle about?" she asked. "Or Mr. Vodyannoy?"

"They went to the Peabody Museum," said Philippa. "With John. But I don't think they'll be very long."

Zadie showed up in the entrance hall with some of the other guests, among them Patricia Nixie from Germany and Yuki Onna from Japan, both of whom bowed on seeing the great Blue Djinn of Babylon. But after all they had been through together, Philippa couldn't bring herself to bow to Faustina.

"Did you come for the tournament?" asked Philippa.

"No, of course not," said Faustina. "I've got much more important things to do these days than watch or play Djinnverso."

"Like what, for instance?"

"Like coming here on official djinn business."

"Is there any news of your brother, Dybbuk?" asked Zadie.

"No," said Faustina. "He was last heard of in England. Since then he's disappeared completely."

"That seems to be an occupational hazard in your family," said Philippa. When Faustina scowled at her, she realized she might have given some offense and added quickly, "What I mean is, I expect he'll turn up safe and sound, just like you did, after you disappeared for a while."

Faustina nodded, acknowledging the debt she knew she owed John, Philippa, Nimrod, and Mr. Groanin. But for them, she might still have been little better than a corpse in an Italian crypt.

Bo showed Faustina into the library and fetched her some tea. But she didn't have long to wait before Nimrod, John, and Mr. Vodyannoy returned from the Peabody Museum.

"Faustina," said Nimrod. "Light my lamp, how very fortunate that you're here. We were just going to call you with some extremely grave news."

"If it's about the *Pachacuti* Prophecy," said Faustina, "then I may have anticipated you, Nimrod. Mr. Vodyannoy, is there somewhere private the three of us can talk?"

"Of course," said Mr. Vodyannoy, and led Faustina and Nimrod out of the huge library and into his office, closing the door behind him.

"She's changed," observed Philippa.

John bit his lip and nodded. There was a time when he had been extremely keen on Faustina. "She didn't even say hello," he murmured.

"So, what's it all about?" Philippa asked her brother. "Nimrod looks worried."

"I'm not entirely sure," admitted John. "But it's almost certainly a matter of life and death. Given what Nimrod was saying, I think it might even be more important than that."

"Is this another adventure, do you think?" Philippa asked.

"It's beginning to look that way," admitted John.

Philippa glanced at Zadie, whose eyes had widened at the very mention of the word "adventure." *No time like the present,* she thought. Especially since John already seemed to be in a mood about Faustina.

"John, you remember Zadie, don't you?"

John looked at Zadie and nodded glumly.

"Okay, don't get mad," said Philippa, "only, I kind of promised Zadie that the next time we had an adventure, we'd take her along."

"You did *what*?" John looked horrified.

"I invited her along on our next adventure."

"Why would you do that?"

"Because she asked me."

John looked at Zadie accusingly. "What's the matter?" he said. "As if being a djinn is not a big enough adventure already. Why don't you just go and grant some poor mundane three wishes? That usually provides enough excitement for most of us."

Philippa frowned. "John. Don't be so rude."

Zadie removed the toothbrush from her mouth and smiled a big smile that made John feel like a heel. "That's okay," she said.

"I'm sorry," John told Zadie. He pointed at Mr. Vodyannoy's office door. "I just don't like being discussed by the three of them, that's all." And he proceeded to tell Philippa and Zadie everything that had happened in the hall of shadows, as well as all that he had heard in the Peabody Museum. "Mr. Vodyannoy mentioned a picture they'd both seen in a newspaper a few days ago that's got them both worried about some kind of prophecy. A prophecy that involves us, Philippa. I'm certain of it."

"This is the newspaper that Faustina arrived with," Zadie said helpfully. "And it appears to be several days old. I wonder if it could be this newspaper."

John and Philippa stood over Zadie's shoulders as she turned the pages.

"There," said John, pointing to a picture. "That's the one."

The three young djinn took a minute to look at the black-and-white picture. Several bearded explorers were grouped around a strange stone doorway in the South American jungle. The doorway was shaped like an eye and overgrown with vines and creepers. But the strangest-looking thing about the doorway, which was complete with a heavy wooden door, was that it seemed to lead absolutely nowhere except to more thick jungle.

Zadie read the picture caption. "'The Eye of the Forest,'" she said. "'The door was discovered in Peru, in the remotest depths of the upper Amazonian rain forest by a team of English explorers and archaeologists. There are no other buildings about, not even the foundations of buildings now ruined. There is just this unusual eye-shaped door that the local Indians call the 'Eye of the Forest.' Believed to be of Incan construction, the door possibly marks a site that was considered holy, although no one knows why.'"

Zadie let John take the newspaper so that he might look at the picture more closely. "Weird, huh?" she said.

"What could that have to do with us?" Philippa asked John.

"I have no idea," said John as the door to Mr. Vodyannoy's office opened again. "But I have a feeling we're about to find out."

Mr. Vodyannoy stroked his beard, which was redder than a foxtail, the result of applying a henna-based dye to a beard that was, in reality, white. "Horror show," said Mr. Vodyannoy.

At least this is what John, Philippa, and Zadie thought he said. In fact, as he often did, Mr. Vodyannoy was using a Russian word to begin an English sentence, a word that only sounds like "horror show."

"There were eight Egyptian djinn," he said. "Four brothers and four sisters who decided to leave ancient Egypt and find another country in which to live. They traveled by a system of underground caves that were known only to the djinn and that once connected a djinn-made world with the human one. Eventually, their journey led them to what we now call Peru. The youngest but strongest of these eight djinn was called Manco, and secretly he had decided to make himself a great king and a god among the ancient Incas. Of course, he knew his brothers would never agree to that and so one day, when they least expected it, he turned them and his oldest sister into solid-gold statues. Then Manco married his other sisters and, claiming to be descended from the sun god, he set himself up as lord of the valley. Using djinn power, he easily conquered other tribes and became known as Manco Capac, for *Capac* means 'warlord.'

"Of course, as in ancient Egypt, sun worship was common among the djinn at that time. But it was not generally understood by the djinn back then how heat gives us power. Nor was it understood how at higher altitudes the cooler temperatures there could cause a djinn to lose his power. This was what happened to Manco. And since he had come to use his power almost exclusively for the creation of gold to enrich himself and his kingdom, his sudden inability to do this anymore was how Manco believed that his djinn power had deserted him.

"Now Manco thought that his power had gone not because Cuzco, his capital city, was located at a height of some 11,500 feet and too cold for djinn power, but because the sun god — who the Inca called Inti — was angry with him. So Manco, seeking spiritual advice, summoned several Incan priests to the holy city of Paititi, whose location was a closely guarded secret, although it is said that their route to the holy city lay through a magical door known as the Eye of the Forest, hidden somewhere in the jungle, and which Manco had especially constructed for this purpose. When at last the priests arrived in Paititi, Manco asked these priests to help him devise a special ritual to honor the sun god, Inti, which would restore Manco's power."

"And did it?" asked John. "Did the ritual bring Manco's power back?"

"All of this happened a very long time ago," said Mr. Vodyannoy. "We cannot be sure of very much with so little archaeological evidence. So much of that was destroyed afterward by the Spaniards. But it is said that the ritual *was* successful, that Manco's djinn powers were indeed restored, and that the number of gold objects in the kingdom was increased tenfold, so that the Incas grew rich again. Even so, a short while later Manco became sick and was near to death. But before he died, he summoned his priests to Paititi once again. There he promised them that if ever they should have need of him, he would return one day to destroy the enemies of the Incas in a great destruction called the *Pachacuti*. All their priestly descendants would have to do would be to lead the enemies of the Incas through the Eye of the Forest, and Manco Capac's spirit would do the rest.

"Hundreds of years passed, and for thousands of square miles, the Incas ruled without opposition. So powerful were they that no one could even conceive of them having any enemies at all, and their only enemies were themselves. The location of the Eye of the Forest was almost forgotten. And Manco's promise was known to only one or two select priests who kept the story secret for fear that one Incan ruler might try to use the power of the Eye against another.

"But then one day in 1532, all that changed forever. The Spanish conquistadors, commanded by Francisco Pizarro, arrived in Cuzco and proceeded to brutally rob the Incas of everything they had, after which they enslaved or murdered them. Their hunger for gold seemed insatiable. For as much as the Incas gave them, the Spaniards still wanted more. The Incas fled the Spaniards, retreating into the high Andes. But the Spaniards pursued them relentlessly, murdering many and always hungry for yet more gold. Then, a priest named Ti Cosi, remembering Manco Capac's words, sought to find the Eye again in order to lure the Spaniards into the jungle and through the Eye of the Forest so that they might be destroyed in the *Pachacuti*, as Manco had promised.

"Well, of course, it never happened. The Spaniards were not destroyed and their descendants govern Peru to this day. Because before he could lead the Spaniards to the door, Ti Cosi was captured. Worse still, he caught smallpox, which was one of many diseases the Spaniards had brought with them, and to which none of the Incas had any resistance. On his deathbed, hoping still to draw the Spaniards into the trap Manco Capac had created for the mortal enemies of the Inca, Ti Cosi told a Spanish priest named Father Diego that El Dorado, the city of gold, which the Spaniards were convinced existed hidden in the jungle, was really Paititi, and how it could only be reached through the Eye of the Forest. Ti Cosi also told Father Diego that in Paititi lay the secret of turning base metals into gold and that this was why the Incas had so much gold in the first place. That the secret of making gold was contained in a ritual called the *kutumunkichu*, which some believe was the name of the very ritual carried out earlier by Manco himself. The same ritual by which he had restored his own djinn power. And what seems more than likely is that if Ti Cosi meant the Spaniards to have the secret of turning base metal into gold, then he also believed that it would bring about their total destruction. Although to this day no one really knows how. Anyway, it is said that Ti Cosi drew a map for Father Diego. But that the map was lost. And neither Paititi, nor the chronicle describing the *kutumunkichu* ritual dictated to the Spanish priest, has ever been found."

"That's such a cool story," said John.

Mr. Vodyannoy winced. The word "cool" was anathema to a djinn like him for whom heat is everything. He scratched his beard and hesitated just long enough for Faustina to take up the story.

"Several weeks ago," said Faustina, "some valuable artifacts, including a rare golden staff of Incan origin and several *khipu*, were stolen from the Ethnological Museum in Berlin."

"What's a *khipu*?" asked Philippa.

"*Khipus* were an Incan method of recording, a sort of abacus made of ropes," said Mr. Vodyannoy. "But rather like the ancient Egyptian hieroglyphics two centuries ago, no one really knows what they mean. You could say that until some-one discovers the equivalent of the Rosetta stone, they're likely to remain one of the ancient world's last great mysteries."

"The museum in Berlin has almost three hundred of them," said Faustina. "It's the largest collection in the world, so I didn't think too much about it when the theft was first brought to my attention."

Faustina nodded at the newspaper in John's hand.

"However, when I saw the picture of the Eye of the Forest in that newspaper, I realized these two events might be con-nected. And straightaway, I decided to come here and speak to Nimrod and Mr. Vodyannoy, who is an expert in Incan matters."

"Not such an expert," Mr. Vodyannoy said modestly. "If I was more of an expert I might know the meaning of the *khipu*."

"It was my hope to arrive here and use one of Mr. Vodyannoy's special talking boards to try to speak to Manco Capac's spirit myself," said Faustina. "To ask for some clari-fication regarding the *Pachacuti*. He was a powerful djinn, after all, and it is always prudent to take djinn promises regarding such things seriously. But it seems I'm too late. It seems that someone has already taken this opportunity for their own selfish purposes and squandered it."

Faustina looked pointedly at John, who felt himself color with embarrassment.

"Sorry," said John. "But I really had no idea."

Faustina brushed aside his apology with a wave of her hand as if it was of little or no consequence.

"Until now the secret of where the Eye of the Forest was to be found has been vouchsafed only to the Blue Djinn of Babylon in an ancient copy of Father Diego's map," she said.

"So you've got the map," said John. "Well, that's something."

"Yes, I have a map," said Faustina, "but sadly not the chronicle describing Manco's *kutumunkichu* ritual. Nor anything about the *Pachacuti* — the promised destruction. I might have assumed that whoever found the Eye of the Forest had stumbled onto it by accident. But the theft of these Incan artifacts would suggest that someone has devised another means of finding the Eye. Clearly its location is a secret no longer. Perhaps someone has managed to decode a message contained in one of those *khipu* to mount an expedition to find the Eye of the Forest. Someone with a knowledge of the esoteric. But who that someone is, or what their motive might be, I have no idea." She looked squarely at Nimrod. "I had hoped that Manco Capac, you, Nimrod, or you, Mr. Vodyannoy, might have been able to shed some light on the matter."

Nimrod took the newspaper from John, looked closely at the picture of the South American explorers, read the caption naming them, and then shook his head. "I can't say that any of these people are familiar to me." He handed the paper to Mr. Vodyannoy. "Frank?"

Mr. Vodyannoy glanced at the picture and shook his head. "I'm afraid not."

"No, I thought as much."

Faustina let out a heavy sigh and, taking Nimrod and Frank Vodyannoy by the hand, she said, "Gentlemen, as you know, I have only been the Blue Djinn of Babylon for a very short while. And I hesitate if it seems like I'm stating the obvious to more mature and experienced djinn such as yourselves, but it seems to me as though someone must travel to South America as soon as possible with the aim of preventing the *Pachacuti* promised by Manco Capac."

"I agree," said Mr. Vodyannoy.

"Without question," said Nimrod.

"I can't tell you how relieved that makes me feel," said Faustina, whose extensive studies of *The Baghdad Rules* had enabled her to resist the cold voice of Logic, and unlike previous Blue Djinn, to retain her feelings. "Knowing that I can rely on the both of you. Frankly, I have been at my wit's end about what to do."

"Do you really think that Manco Capac could still destroy the world?" Philippa's voice was full of doubt.

"It may just be a legend," said Nimrod. "Then again, Manco was a very powerful djinn and I'm not sure we can afford to take the risk. You see, Philippa, it's always difficult making prophecies. Especially the kind of prophecies that involve trying to foretell the future. For this reason, djinn very rarely make prophecies. But when they do, it's usually best to pay attention to them."

"I shall make you a copy of the map I have that describes how to find the Eye of the Forest," Faustina told Nimrod. "If necessary, you must if possible create a binding that renders the Eye secure. But, at all costs, you must if possible try to stop these foolish explorers from even entering the Eye."

"And if they have already done so?" asked Mr. Vodyannoy.

"Then you must follow them and, at the very least, if it does lead to the lost city of Paititi, you must try to stop them from reaching it and from executing the *kutumunkichu* ritual. Is that clear?"

"Quite clear," said Nimrod, and bowed gravely to the Blue Djinn of Babylon, blessed be her name.

"There is one more service you can perform while you are up the Amazon," said Faustina. "A useful ecological service."

"Name it," said Nimrod.

"It will not have escaped your attention that, at present, none of us are able to create the whirlwinds by which we djinn normally travel. I have done some research in the library at Iravotum and it seems there is a giant tree in the upper Amazon called the lupuna. This tree contains certain ancient properties that affect the atmosphere. Unfortunately, deforestation in the Amazon jungle has meant that loggers and lumberjacks have started chopping down lupuna trees, with the result that we can no longer control the whirlwinds we create. So, I would like both of you to plant some new lupuna trees. And to find a way of protecting them against the loggers."

"Consider it done," said Mr. Vodyannoy.

"We'll leave immediately," said Nimrod.

"Wait a minute," said John. "I feel like I'm the one who set all of this into motion by summoning Manco Capac with the talking board. So I'm going with you."

"Me, too," said Philippa. "Because I go where he goes."

"I'm not sure it's a good idea," said Mr. Vodyannoy.

Nimrod sighed. "But I suppose you'd find a way to come, anyway, even if I tried to prevent it."

"You bet we would," said John.

"Faustina?" said Nimrod. "It's up to you to decide."

"No sacrifice is too great where the future of the world is concerned," she said. "If John or Philippa feel inclined to risk their lives to prevent the great destruction, then so be it."

"What about your mother?" said Nimrod. "We'll have tell her you're going to South America."

"As it happens, right now she's in South America herself," said Philippa.

"She's in Brazil, having plastic surgery," said John.

"Yes, of course," said Nimrod. "I'd forgotten. Your father then. We'll have to tell him something."

"We'll leave a note for him," said Philippa. "We'll tell him that we've gone to Brazil to visit Mother."

"Half the time he doesn't know where we are, anyway," said John.

"All right." Nimrod sounded reluctant. "If you're sure."

"There's one more thing," said Philippa. "If I go, then Zadie has to come, too. I made her a binding promise that I would bring her along."

John stayed silent.

"Very well," said Nimrod. "I suppose it might be useful to have another djinn in our party."

Zadie whooped with delight.

"What about you, Faustina?" asked John. "Are you coming?"

"I'm afraid I can't," said Faustina. "While the *Pachacuti* affects both good and evil tribes of djinn, my position still requires that I don't get involved other than to order you to try to prevent it."

"She's right," said Nimrod. "It's important that Faustina remains at a distance. There are some evil djinn who might think that the destruction of the world — even a destruction that would include them — is something to be welcomed."

"This is going to be fun," declared Zadie.

"It won't be any picnic, you know," declared Mr. Vodyannoy. "We'll be going to one of the most inhospitable places on earth. It's not called the rain forest for nothing. It rains in the Amazon. A lot. As a result it can be cold and wet, and you know what that means. The use of djinn power may be uncertain. For you younger djinn, at any rate. Giant anacondas, bull sharks, vampire bats, electric eels, bird-eating spiders, and let's not forget *el Tunchi*."

"*El Tunchi?*" asked Zadie. "What's a *tunchi*?"

"Let's hope you never find out," said Mr. Vodyannoy.

Nimrod smiled. "Groanin won't like this trip. He won't like it at all. Groanin simply hates snakes."

This prompted Mr. Vodyannoy to continue with his catalog of South American hazards. "Horror show," he said. "Not just snakes. Poisonous tree-frogs, killer bees, monster alligators, piranha fish, big fierce jaguars — the one in the trophy room is considered small — and headhunters."

"Headhunters?" exclaimed Philippa. "In this day and age? I don't believe it."

CHAPTER 5

BRING ME THE HEAD OF FRANCISCO PIЗARRO

They flew by passenger jet to Lima, the capital of Peru, which is a very nice city and full of extremely friendly people. Unfortunately, these were not always to Mr. Groanin's taste.

"I wish people would stop smiling at me," he complained upon arrival at their hotel, the five-star Primer Paraíso Excelente con las Campañas Encendido, in Lima city center. "It makes me nervous. Like they all know something I don't. I can't abide people who look happy all the time. I say, I can't abide people who are always happy. Give me men about me who scowl and are miserable. You know where you are with a man who looks gloomy. Give me a man from Manchester every time, not these smiling rogues."

"Speaking for myself," said Philippa, "I like people to look happy. It makes me feel all warm inside." She went out onto the balcony of her suite, which had a superb view of the main square and the cathedral across the street.

"I'm not in the least bit warm," said John. "Being so close to the equator, I thought it would be hot here in Peru. But it's actually kind of chilly. The minute I got off the plane I felt my power diminish a little."

"Horror show," said Mr. Vodyannoy. "Most people make that mistake about Lima. It's really not that warm here. And all because of the cold Humboldt Current that runs along the Peruvian coast."

Groanin consulted the thermometer on the wall. "Sixty degrees Fahrenheit," he said. "I'll grant you, this is a few degrees off being perfect. But I prefer it like this to being too hot or too cold. If you ask me, hot weather is the great enemy of civilization. No culture that's worth a spit can survive where it ever goes much above seventy. That's what makes England the most civilized place in the world. Because the weather is always fair to middling."

"Same old Groanin," said John.

Zadie did a little tap dance across the floor with excitement. Chilly or not, she seemed delighted to be on an adventure in Peru with John and Philippa and Nimrod and Groanin and Mr. Vodyannoy.

"So what's our next move?" she asked Mr. Vodyannoy.

Mr. Vodyannoy pointed at the Lima Cathedral, which, especially at night when it is lit up and glows like burnished gold, looks more like a presidential palace than an important church. "We go in there," he said, looking at his pocket watch. "We have an appointment with Francisco Pizarro. In thirty minutes."

"Francisco Pizarro?" exclaimed Philippa. "But he's dead, isn't he?"

"I sincerely hope so," said Mr. Vodyannoy.

As they walked across the main plaza with its ornamental fountain and palm trees, Mr. Vodyannoy took a deep breath.

"Horror show," he said. "It's good to be back in Peru."

"What does that mean?" asked John. "Horror show? You say it kind of a lot, Mr. V."

"Not 'horror show,'" said Mr. Vodyannoy. "*Khorosho*. It's Russian. It means 'well,' or 'okay,' or 'right then.' It's a habit and I'm afraid I don't always know when I've said it."

"*Khorosho*," said John.

"Pizarro," Philippa interrupted. "He was Spain's most notorious conquistador, right?"

Mr. Vodyannoy nodded.

"That's right. Francisco Pizarro arrived here in Peru in 1531 with just one hundred and sixty-eight Spaniards. At first, they and the Incas kept their distance. Then, in 1532, Pizarro led his men up into the Andes to meet the Incan king, Atahualpa, who was camped with an army of almost one hundred thousand men following a great military victory over his brother and rival, Huascar. Curiosity about these strange foreigners and their horses, which the Incas had never seen before, got the better of Atahualpa and he came to take a closer look at them, at which point Pizarro and his men took the king prisoner and killed some five thousand of his retainers. They were, of course, interested only in gold and promised to release the king if he paid them a ransom. So the king promised to fill the room in which he was held prisoner with treasure, and was as good as his word. Sadly, the Spaniards were not. And as soon as the room had been filled with gold they executed poor Atahualpa. So began the conquest of Peru and the near extermination of the Inca people by the Spaniards."

"He sounds really horrible," said Philippa.

"Oh, he was," said Mr. Vodyannoy. "Although by the standards of the day, he wasn't much more horrible than anyone else. Atahualpa himself was no saint. Having founded this city, which used to be called the City of Kings, and ordered the construction of the cathedral where we're going now, Pizarro ended up fighting with some of his own men and was murdered by his fellow Spaniards in 1541."

"Serves him right," said John.

"Hear, hear," said Groanin. "Now you know what we were up against. Spanish Armada? 1588? They tried to invade England. But we saw them off. No thanks to you Yanks. Just like in 1939. Where were you then, eh?"

"The United States didn't exist in 1588," said Philippa. "The USA didn't exist until 1776. So we couldn't have helped even if we'd wanted to."

"That's a feeble excuse," muttered Groanin.

"Anyway, Pizarro was buried in the cathedral," said Mr. Vodyannoy. "And today his tomb is one of the main tourist attractions. However, that's not where his remains really lie. His true remains are kept hidden elsewhere in the cathedral. Which is why we're going there now."

They walked into the cathedral and went up to the archbishop's office, where they were met by a priest with bright blue eyes and a black mustache shaped like a tooth-brush. Philippa thought he looked a bit like Charlie Chaplin. Groanin thought he looked like someone else. Mr. Vodyannoy introduced the priest as Father Polzl. Father Polzl shook everyone's hands warmly and welcomed them to Peru.

"Mr. Vodyannoy and I are old friends," Father Polzl told the children. "After the last earthquake he helped to repair a number of cracks in the walls of the cathedral." He smiled warmly at Mr. Vodyannoy. "It gives me such enormous plea-sure to be able to do you a good turn, Frank."

"It's really just a precaution, Father," said Mr. Vodyannoy. "But as you know, where we're going this sort of thing some-times comes in handy. If we run into any trouble, it might make a useful offering. In which case, I'll certainly replace it with an exact copy."

"Say no more, my friend, say no more. Mum's the word, eh? Please. Come this way. He would be no loss to anyone, I think."

Father Polzl led his six guests into a small private chapel where a polished wooden box about the size of a soccer ball stood on a little oak table. He went over to the table, crossed himself devoutly, and opened the box. Inside lay a yellowing human skull.

Zadie gasped. John whistled. The Father smiled.

"Whistle away, young man, whistle away," the Father said indulgently. "And well you might. For this is the head of none other than the first governor general of Peru, Don Francisco Pizarro Demarkes himself, which was discovered hidden away in the crypt underneath the main altar as recently as 1977."

"Ugh," said Philippa, turning away.

"Wow," said John, staring into the box. "Did someone cut it off?"

"That's generally the best way to remove a head," observed Groanin. "Where's the rest of him when he's at home?"

"In a separate box," said the Father. "Also in the cathedral."

"Ask a stupid question," muttered the English butler.

"Why do you keep them separately?" asked Zadie.

"Because that's how they were found," explained Father Polzl. "There's an inscription on top confirming it's Pizarro's head, as you can see for yourselves. But we also had it verified by a forensic scientist. Just to make absolutely sure."

"Well, you wouldn't want to make a mistake about that kind of thing, would you?" muttered Groanin.

Nimrod seemed to be more interested in the box than in the skull. "That's curious," he murmured. "It appears to be made of wood from a lupuna tree."

"Look, there's a sort of hole in it," said John, who was only interested in the skull. "What's that from, Father Polzl? A bullet? A sword?"

"It is said that Pizarro, his sword stuck fast inside the poor man he was in the process of stabbing, was struck on the head with a water bucket, which knocked him to the floor."

"I've heard of water on the brain," said Groanin. "But I never knew it was fatal."

The Father crossed himself again. "While lying there, he was stabbed by up to twenty of his former followers. All of them Christians and Spaniards I regret to say, although, of course, he was hated in equal measure by the poor Incas he had robbed and persecuted with such wanton cruelty. Perhaps them most of all."

"What did they fight about?" asked John. "The Spaniards, I mean."

"The same thing men always fight about. Power. Money. Revenge. Pizarro died as he had lived in this much-abused country. By the sword."

The Father closed the box and handed it carefully to Mr. Vodyannoy who, finding the object heavier than he had expected, proceeded to give the ancient-looking box to the stronger Mr. Groanin.

"Just what I always wanted," muttered Groanin. "You shouldn't have, really." And then: "Is there a gift card?"

"But I don't understand," said Philippa. "Why on earth do we need to bring along Pizarro's skull?"

"Haven't you heard, Miss Philippa?" said Groanin. "Two 'eads are better than one. Even an 'ead with an 'ole in it. I say, even an 'ead with an 'ole in it."

"Do shut up, Groanin," said Nimrod.

"Yes, sir."

"You'd better take it and get back to the hotel."

"Yes, sir." And still carrying the lead-lined box containing the conquistador's skull, he shimmered out of the little chapel.

"My butler," Nimrod said to Father Polzl, as if that was explanation enough.

Father Polzl smiled. "He's quite a card, isn't he?"

"Yes, but not always the winning kind," said Nimrod.

They stayed talking to the Father for another fifteen minutes until it was time for him to go and conduct mass. The cathedral was already filling up with people for whom Pizarro was just an unpleasant name in history. And having thanked the Father for his help, the five djinn went outside and onto a plaza made chillier by the spray from a fountain that seemed to have its own police guard.

"So what's the head for, Mr. V?" asked John, bursting with curiosity. "A gift for the headhunters, perhaps?"

"There are no headhunters in South America," insisted Philippa. "Possibly, there never were. Most likely, it was just a story invented by explorers who wanted to make a bigger deal out of coming here."

Mr. Vodyannoy said nothing to Philippa, preferring to

answer John's question than to argue with his sister. "If ever we come across Manco Capac," he said, "or any of his descendants — most of the Indian tribes in the upper Amazon are probably related to the Incas — it might be very useful to be able to hand over the head of the Incas' greatest enemy."

"But Manco himself died long before Pizarro came to Peru," said Philippa. "In which case Pizarro's name will probably mean nothing to him."

"Must you be so literal, Philippa?" exclaimed Nimrod. "Try to remember that you are a djinn, not an attorney in a court of law. Given Manco Capac has almost certainly returned from the dead, I think we can agree that he might be capable of almost anything, don't you?"

"Good point," said Philippa. "Sorry. Since that time I spent in Iravotum, I still get bogged down with logic sometimes."

"Yes. Yes, of course," said Nimrod. "I'd quite forgotten about that."

"I wish I could," said Philippa.

Mr. Groanin walked slowly back to the hotel with the box containing Pizarro's skull under his arm.

"The things you get asked to do when you're a butler for a djinn," he muttered to himself. "I feel like flipping Hamlet walking around with old Yorick here."

Seeing a café, he decided to stop for a quick drink, thinking it would be nice if someone waited on *him* for a change. Groanin sat down at an outside table and, seeing a waiter, he was about to order a cup of tea until concern about the local water quality prompted him to change his mind and order a lemonade instead. And while he waited for the waiter to return, he started to think about how lemonade is made: from adding lemon to water and heating the result. But suppose, thought Groanin, the water came straight out of the Amazon, for instance? And did they actually boil it? Was the lemonade in Peru safe to drink? These were the questions that occupied poor Groanin's mind in the time it took for the waiter to return with his lemonade. By which time he'd thought better of drinking it.

"Blast this country," he muttered, and stood up. "I should have ordered a beer. They boil that." He was about to leave when he noticed, at the next table, a very attractive woman weeping copious amounts of tears. "What's the matter with you?" he asked. "I say, miss, what's the matter with you?"

The woman pointed to the other side of the main plaza. To Groanin's surprise, she spoke good English. "Do you see that man in the red jacket, *señor*?" she said. "He just ran away with my handbag."

"You're joking," said Groanin. "You mean he stole it? In broad daylight?"

The woman blew her nose and then nodded. "It had my whole life in it. My purse. My keys. My phone. Everything. I really don't know what I'm going to do."

Groanin stared into the distance. "The fellow in the red shirt, you say?" The woman nodded. "Wearing the blue trousers?" The woman nodded again. Groanin placed the antique box containing Pizarro's skull on the table in front of her. "Stay there," he said. "I said, stay there. I'll sort this out. I'm English." And with that, Groanin walked swiftly across the plaza in the direction of the man in the red shirt. He was a sucker for a pretty face.

When he was halfway across the square, Groanin turned and looked back. The woman was standing up, watching him, as if hoping he was going to recover her handbag. Groanin waved and walked on. But now that he was nearer, he saw that the man in the red jacket was actually a man in a ceremonial military uniform. Under his arm he had a tall red hat with a plume on it and the only bag he was carrying was the cartridge bag on his Sam Browne military belt. The man was a policeman. Groanin gulped as he realized he'd been had and ran back to the café, but the woman was gone. And, what was worse, the box containing the skull was gone, too.

It was then that he saw Nimrod and the others.

"I've lost it," Groanin said flatly. "That box, with Frank thingummy's skull in it. I say, I've lost the flipping thing."

"You've lost the head of Don Francisco Pizarro?" Nimrod sighed loudly.

"That's what I said, isn't it?" said Groanin unhappily. "Some Peruvian bird tricked me into thinking her handbag had been pinched and then nicked it."

"That was pretty stupid of you," said Zadie.

Groanin shot her a poisonous look.

"Give me your hands, Groanin," Nimrod said gravely.

"It were an accident," said Groanin. "I say, I'm sorry, sir. Look here, you're not going to do anything unpleasant to me, are you?"

Nimrod took hold of Groanin's hands. "Not to you, Groanin," said Nimrod, and closed his eyes.

"What are you doing?" demanded Groanin. "She can't have gone far. We've got to find her."

"That is precisely what I am trying to do," said Nimrod. "If you will shut up and let me get on with it." Nimrod lifted Groanin's hands to his nose, inhaled deeply several times and muttered his focus word: "QWERTYUIOP!"

"What's he doing?" whispered Philippa.

"Don't tell me you don't know about *odorari*," scoffed Zadie.

"*Odorari*," said Mr. Vodyannoy. "It's a mystical technique practiced by only the most powerful djinn. You see, traces of the box's atoms are still on Groanin's hands. Another few minutes and it would probably have been too late. You just watch. Nimrod will get the scent in a moment or two."

Nimrod took another deep breath from the sweating palms of his butler. He could smell some cheese, bread, throat lozenges, a trace of lemonade, and some soap. Then, finally he had it. Just a few particles of lead from the box lining but more than enough for his immediate purpose. Nimrod lifted his distinguished, fastidious nose high into the air and drew in a mixture of coffee, beer, cigarette smoke, fried food, human sweat, soap, silicon, water from the fountain, wood smoke, carbon monoxide, lead from gasoline, and finally the same carbon he had detected on Groanin's large hands. Then he opened his eyes and smiled.

"I believe I have them," he said quietly. "Wait here."

The woman from the café carried the box containing the skull around the corner to where her friend and accomplice was waiting in his car. She hadn't had time to look inside the old box, but she thought maybe it was an antique and probably very valuable on its own. She opened the front passenger door and sat down with the box on her lap. Neither of them noticed the invisible figure that crept into the backseat behind her.

"What is it?" asked the man, and nodded at the box.

"I don't know, but there's a name on the lid. Don Francisco Pizarro Demarkes."

"Never heard of him. But he sounds rich."

"It looks kind of creepy. But valuable, don't you think?"

The man grinned wolfishly.

"Perhaps there's something even more valuable inside," he said.

"There is only one way to find out," said the woman, and lifted the lid.

Nimrod was not a cruel man but he had little sympathy for thieves and felt that giving this pair a good fright — especially the kind of fright that might cause them to stop stealing — would, in the long run, be in both their moral interests. For a moment, he considered changing his appearance to something much more frightening and then rejected the idea, for he had no wish to give the two thieves heart attacks. So he confined himself to looking like Pizarro, as imagined by the English painter John Everett Millais, in a picture Nimrod had once seen in London's National Gallery, which is to say he wore a beard, a red doublet, a golden breastplate, a ruff around his neck, a soft hat with a feather in it, and carried a sword in his hand. This sudden appearance in the backseat of the car was accompanied by a bang as loud as an exploding paper bag.

The two thieves screamed and reached simultaneously for the door handles, only to find that these came off in their hands, and the doors stayed locked. In her haste to be out of the car, the woman managed to empty Pizarro's skull from the lead-lined box and onto her lap, which only caused her to scream even louder. And then she tried to climb up onto the dashboard of the car, at which point the skull bounced onto the floor.

"Who dares to purloin and then fumble my head like a pomegranate?" demanded Nimrod in a loud, imperious, and quite frighteningly Spanish voice. Leaning forward in his seat Nimrod allowed a very garlicky smell to escape from his mouth and nostrils, fouling the confined atmosphere of the car, before he added, "You dogs. You curs. You mongrels. You felons. You, who stole that precious box and the head of Don Francisco Pizarro Demarkes, must prepare thyselves to suffer the most terrible of punishments."

"Please," whimpered the man, twisting around in his seat, his hands clasped as if in prayer. "I beg you, Don Francisco, please don't kill us."

Nimrod sneered in his face sulfurously and rattled his sword in its scabbard. "You dare to entreat me, thief?" He was almost enjoying himself, as an actor might enjoy hamming it up as the villainous genie in some crummy Christmas pantomime. "Ask of me only by what mode of death thou wilt die and by what manner of slaughter shall I slay thee and thy worthless accomplice. Thou Mother of Amir, thou hyena, thou leper. Speak only that thou wilt swear on the life of thy mother and thy mother's mother that thou wilt never steal again, and then, perhaps, will I spare your worthless lives. Otherwise, hold thy tongue, for thy last lying breath is in thy thieving nostrils and in thy dishonest mouth."

"Yes, yes, yes," said the man. "I swear it. By my mother and my mother's mother. I'll never steal again. We both do, don't we?"

"Yes," squeaked the woman lying across the dashboard. "I swear it."

"I believe thee not," growled Nimrod, and made the car vibrate with his wrath until the radiator began to overheat. "For thou dost say nothing of returning my skull to the poor fool thou stole it from who must himself die a terrible death. And I hear thou sayest nothing about making amends to all the other fools whom thou hast tricked and robbed.

But perhaps because thou hast both softened my heart a little I will give thee a choice of terrible deaths. Now then, shall I shut thee both in a leaky jar and then cast it into the dirtiest sea on the planet? Or feed thee both slowly to a boa constrictor with very bad breath?"

"No, no, no," said the woman, "we will take the skull straight back to him. I promise. And I will give all the money I have ever stolen to the church. I swear it."

"Me, too," squeaked the man.

Nimrod nodded. "Very well," he said. "I do believe it. But if either of you ever again so much as steals a bit of stationery, avoids paying a bus fare, or causes a book to become overdue at the library, I will come back and replace your heads with elephant dung and make scarabs of your ears. Do I make myself perfectly clear?"

"Yes, yes, yes."

"Now go. Return the box and the skull to the cream-faced loon in the square." Nimrod caused the doors of the car to fly open and the two scrambled out, pausing only to collect the box and return Pizarro's skull to its lead-lined interior.

Chuckling a little, for he had rather enjoyed himself, Nimrod got out of the car and watched them run away. Thinking he might just remind them of the need to turn over a new leaf he turned to the car, muttered his focus word, and made a few alterations to the basic design — blacking out the rear windows and adding bars to them so that it looked more like a prison van. For good measure, he even laid out two orange jumpsuits and two sets of shackles on the seats.

"Who says you can't reform criminals?" he said.

"Does she have to do that?" said Groanin as Zadie tap-danced her way around the café table where he, John, Philippa, and Mr. Vodyannoy were awaiting Nimrod's return. "I don't mind telling you I'm hoping there's a mantrap or an open drain cover somewhere around this square."

"That's a little cruel," observed Philippa.

"I don't think so," said John.

"She's driving me mad. All that dancing. Who does she think she is? Gene Kelly? Ginger flipping Rogers? Is she hyperactive or something? I say, is that daft girl hyperactive?"

"I believe she might be, yes," said Mr. Vodyannoy. "It's what we djinn call a fugue state. Like when someone chases a sort of baroque tune around a church organ. Quite a few djinn suffer from it when they're young."

"There you are," said Philippa. "She can't help it. That means we have to be sympathetic."

"Speak for yourself," said John.

In truth, however, Philippa was already regretting having asked Zadie along on their South American adventure. It wasn't the tap dancing she minded or even the toothbrush that was always in Zadie's mouth so much as the other girl's sharp and often critical tongue. That really bugged her.

Zadie was still tap-dancing when the woman who had taken the box presented it and then herself at the table on the plaza with a cringing, fearful bow.

"I'm very sorry," she said. "I apologize. I'll never ever do it again. Please forgive me, *señor*."

"Aye, well, that's easy to say," said Groanin. "You should be ashamed of yourself, young woman. I've a good mind to go and fetch the police and have you locked up. I say, I've a good mind to fetch a copper, do you hear? I've no time for thieves. Really I don't. Especially not when they steal other people's property."

The woman smiled abjectly and, wringing her hands piteously, bowed again. "Please, forgive me," she repeated with tears in her eyes.

"Never," Groanin said firmly.

"Groanin," Philippa said sternly. "I seem to remember that you were once a thief. In fact, that's how you met Nimrod, isn't it? Because you stole a decanter that he happened to be inside."

The English butler harrumphed loudly and looked at Philippa stiffly. "Yes, well, that's as may be. Thanks for reminding me of that, miss. Now you come to mention it, I suppose I had rather forgotten my former life."

"It is human to err and divine to forgive," said Zadie.

Groanin bit his lip. It was one thing being lectured by Philippa, whom he loved dearly, but it was quite another being lectured by the intensely irritating Zadie. "And to think I ever complained about that lad Dybbuk," he murmured.

"Hmm?" said Zadie, who wasn't listening, anyway.

"I say that's fine and dandy for them as seem to be almost divine," said Groanin. "But for us mundane mortals, things are a bit different." Groanin waved at the woman irritably. "Go on, be off, you baggage, before I change my mind and have you in the stocks or whatever it is they do to thieves in this pigging country."

The woman turned and fled.

"There," said Groanin triumphantly. "That told her, I think."

CHAPTER 6

SICKY'S SHRUNKEN HEAD AND SOME OTHER REVOLTING AFTER-DINNER STORIES

They chartered a plane and flew to Cuzco, the old Incan capital, high in the Andes. The plane was a Cessna Caravan, which it needed to be, given all the equipment they had brought from New York. While the plane was being refueled in Cuzco, they took a helicopter ride up to the citadel of Machu Picchu, the so-called "lost city" found by Hiram Bingham in 1911.

Machu Picchu almost seems to be up in the clouds, and the twins thought it one of the most spectacular things they had ever seen. Almost as good as the pyramids, although it was more recent in origin.

"Hard to believe the Incas moved all these huge rocks up here without djinn power to build this place," observed John.

"Well, they did," said Nimrod. "This place was built in 1450, long after the djinn king of the Incas, Manco Capac, had died."

"There's not much humans can't do when we put our minds to it," Groanin said breathlessly, because at nearly eight thousand feet above sea level, the air in Machu Picchu is quite thin. "Except perhaps treat a place like this with a bit of pigging respect. I must say, it doesn't look very lost. Look at this place. I say, look at this place. It's like Heaton Park in Manchester on a bank holiday. There are folk chatting on their cell phones or having picnics, hippies selling postcards, religious nutcases having prayer meetings — flipping heck, there's even a group of Yanks over there making an advertisement for suntan lotion."

It was true, the ancient citadel was crawling with tourists of all nationalities, and John came away from Machu Picchu with the thought that it might have been best if Hiram Bingham had kept his discovery of the site a secret. Philippa found herself thinking it was rather hard to believe that another site like it — in Machu Picchu, there are one hundred and forty different constructions covering five square miles — such as Paititi, really could await discovery.

At least she did until they got back on their Cessna and

flew east and over the other side of the Andes to a little town named Manu, in the heart of the Peruvian Amazon.

The Amazon rain forest is the largest tropical rain forest on Earth and covers almost three million square miles. The Peruvian Amazon is only a small part of that huge total, but it is the wildest, least accessible, and hence, the most unexplored rain forest in the world. As the plane dipped low over the near-unending canopy of trees, Philippa decided that it was almost as if she was looking down at a thick layer of green cumulus clouds.

"Wow," she said to John. "It just goes on forever, doesn't it? I mean, when you see how thick that canopy of trees is, it's a lot easier to buy the idea that there really might be some kind of lost city down there, isn't it?"

"You bet." John smiled and nodded back at his twin sister. "Isn't this cool?"

Groanin, however, was doing his best to ignore the view.

"I hope that pilot knows where he's going," said Groanin. "I should hate to run out of gas and have to start looking for a good landing spot down there."

John clapped the butler on the shoulder. "Good old Groanin," he said. "Always looking on the bright side."

"Someone has to," said Groanin. "That way nobody's surprised when things go wrong."

John laughed.

"I'm glad you find it so amusing, John," said Zadie. "Because I don't. I'm not a good air passenger at the best of times."

"Somehow I suspected as much," said John.

"Look on the bright side," Groanin told him. "At least she's stopped tap dancing."

"Did you know that there are a thousand different species of birds down there?" said Philippa. "To say nothing of sixty different species of bats, including five different kinds of vampire."

"Do please say nothing about the bats," said Groanin. "Especially the vampire bats. I hate bats. Nasty things. Like rats with wings."

"Unless you're careless enough to leave a foot sticking outside your tent at night," said Mr. Vodyannoy, "there's very little chance of you being bitten by one."

"There's very little chance of me leaving so much as a single hair outside my tent at night," declared Groanin. "Some of us have got more sense than to go gallivanting about in the jungle with all them headhunters about."

"I can't see anyone wanting your head, Mr. Groanin," said Zadie. "For a start, there's not much hair on it. And not much in it, either."

Groanin swore at her under his breath and began to eat a jar of Baby Balance Scrummy Tuna Penne, which, unless he was very hungry, was the only kind of food he intended to eat while they were in the Amazon. He hoped that at least there would be something nice to drink. He'd heard the local beer, *chichai*, was delicious. And Groanin was fond of beer.

"Look here," said Philippa, "can we dispense with this ridiculous myth once and for all? There are no headhunters in the Amazon rain forest. Possibly there were headhunters, about a hundred years ago, but not anymore. Isn't that right, Uncle Nimrod?"

"You might very well be right about that, Philippa," said Nimrod. "Then again, this is the Amazon we're talking about, not Yellowstone National Park. This is the last great primeval forest on Earth and there are three million acres of it, most of it untouched by humans or, for that matter, djinn. So we really have no idea what might be down there and what might not. But at the very least I should say that all of us are in for some surprises when we step on the ground."

They were met by their South American guide and expedition manager, Sicky, and his cook and boatman, Muddy. These two were old friends of Mr. Vodyannoy's, having accompanied him on previous trips up into the jungle.

Sicky was extremely tall for an Indian, with huge hands and enormous feet, and his arms, neck, and chest were covered with a variety of strange tattoos that he was more than happy to show John. All except the tattoo on his stomach. Sicky told John that he kept this particular tattoo hidden because, just like a Gorgon, it had the power to turn all living creatures to stone.

"Gee," said John. "I'd like to know where that tattoo parlor is."

"Many years ago, Mr. Vodyannoy gave me three wishes," Sicky explained. "And that tattoo was one of the things I wished for, so that I could always defeat my enemies even when I wasn't armed."

"Wow," said John. "Do you have many enemies?"

Sicky smiled. "Not anymore."

Otherwise, Sicky was kind, with a good sense of humor, very reliable, and scrupulously honest. It seemed he was also quite an accomplished sculptor. Or so the children thought. But chiefly Sicky was remarkable for the size of his head, which was no larger than a grapefruit or, for that matter, his own fist. John and Philippa tried to pretend Sicky's was a perfectly normal-looking head, but this was difficult when Sicky was talking since his English wasn't great, and they had to look closely at his lips to be sure of what he was saying. These lips were almost as strange as his head. The twins had seen body piercings before. There were plenty of weird people walking around New York with strange pieces of metal in their noses, ears, lips, and belly buttons. But Sicky was the first person they had ever seen with lengths of colored cotton cord sewn into his lips, like several Fu Manchu mustaches. And, for several hours at least, how he had come by these remained something of a compelling mystery.

The origin of his nickname was easier to understand, however. Every time someone asked Sicky a question like, "How are you today?" Sicky would always answer, "Not so good. I'm a little sick today." Of course, the twins were much too polite to ask Sicky about his small head and unusually decorated lips. Zadie lacked their diplomacy and good manners, however, and it eventually was she who blurted out the question that was on all of their minds.

This is how it happened: They were having dinner at Sicky's wooden lodge in the village named Manu, on the edge of a palm-rimmed, sparkling oxbow lake where they were to spend their first night in the Peruvian Amazon. A delicious goat stew had been prepared by Sicky's cook, Muddy, who was an excellent chef and a fine guitarist to boot. Zadie had drunk several glasses of something she had enjoyed so much that she had asked Sicky what it was and how it was made.

"It's *chichai*, a sort of local beer invented by the Incas," said Sicky.

"There's nothing like a glass of decent beer," said Groanin, and toasted Sicky happily.

"Adults like Mr. Groanin have alcoholic *chichai*," Sicky told Zadie. "Which is called *chichai*. But Mr. Vodyannoy said to give you the zero-alcohol version, which is called *holy chichai*, so that is what you are drinking. It has all the taste of *chichai*, but without any of the alcohol. And zero calories, too. Of course, if you weren't American kids, I'd have given you regular *chichai*. But Mr. Vodyannoy said —"

"Yes, I understand all that, of course," said Zadie, interrupting him. "But what's it made from? What's in it?"

"Corn," said Sicky. "Same as any other beer. And saliva. Human saliva."

Zadie swallowed uncomfortably. "Excuse me, did you say human saliva?"

"Yes," said Sicky. "Spit." He picked up his empty glass and, gathering the cords in his lips to one side, dribbled copiously into it as if it might remove any doubts that still remained after his explanation. "Like this. Yes?"

"You're joking," she said.

"I'm afraid he's not," said Mr. Vodyannoy, lighting his pipe.

"I'm not joking," said Sicky. "It's a very old Inca recipe. Very old. Good, huh?"

Philippa smiled politely. "And do you buy the *chichai* in bottles?" she asked. "From a supermarket?"

"No, Muddy makes it himself," said Sicky.

"So, let me get this straight." John's inquiry was sadistic and meant entirely for the effect it might have on Zadie and Groanin. "This *chichai* is homemade. Muddy makes it with his own spit, right, Muddy?"

Muddy stopped playing his guitar and, standing up, took a bow as if proud to acknowledge the true origin of the spit in the *chichai*. He wasn't much taller than about five feet and, standing up, was no bigger than Sicky sitting down. But he had a big heart.

"My own spit, yes," said Muddy, and spat into the bushes as if he was keen to add some further evidence to what he had alleged. "I like to spit. I can spit pretty good, too. I can spit maybe thirty feet and hit what I aim at."

"There's not a man in the whole of South America who spits better or more than Muddy," said Sicky.

Groanin got up and left the table quietly.

"Oh, dear," said Nimrod. "Poor Groanin. Perhaps I should have told him before he got the taste for it. He's had several large glasses of the stuff."

"Delicious," said Mr. Vodyannoy, and drained his glass.

"Can we talk about something else?" said Zadie. She was clutching her stomach in horror and feeling too nauseous to follow the butler into the bushes, where he was already throwing up loudly.

But John wasn't about to let this subject go. Not yet. "About how much of your own spit do you need, Sicky?" he asked. "To make, say, a gallon of this stuff."

Sicky nodded and dribbled several mouthfuls of saliva into his empty glass. "About this much," he said, holding up several inches of thick yellow saliva. "For the *chichai*. More for the *holy chichai*."

"Please, if you don't mind, John," said Zadie. "I really think we've heard enough." And thinking John and Muddy would only be diverted from the disgusting subject of *chichai* if she provided another topic of conversation, she smiled brightly and said, "So, Sicky. How come your head's so small? And how did you come by all these weird pieces of string in your lips? Did you sew them in yourself?"

Philippa gasped that anyone could ask such a direct question to such an obviously afflicted person. But Sicky didn't mind. He was used to it.

"I am a Prozuanaci Indian," said Sicky. "The Prozuanaci are old enemies of the Xuanaci Indians. The Xuanaci are plenty more savage, plenty more uncivilized than we are. The country they inhabit is plenty inhospitable, too, with no tracks through very dense jungle, and they are seldom seen by anyone. Which is just as well. Anyway, plenty long time ago, when I wasn't much older or bigger than the boy, I was captured by Xuanaci Indians. Except for my young age, they would have cut off my head as a war trophy. What they call a *tzantza*. Instead, to humiliate me and always make me be reminded of how they had captured me, they decided to shrink my head while it was still on my shoulders. Something that we Peruvians call *pernocabeza*."

"But surely that's impossible," said Philippa.

"Not for the Xuanaci. The Xuanaci know plenty things about taking and shrinking human heads as trophies. First of all, they tied me up tight and sucked the fat out of my face with little straws. Then they shaved my head and painted it with special oil from a rare plant that grows only in the Amazon, and which is known only to the Xuanaci. Then they made me lie with my head in a bucket of other secret herbs and hot sand for many weeks, drying it out before painting it again with the special oil, and drying it once more. And always they kept sucking the fat from my face."

"Kind of like liposuction," said John. "I get it."

"This happened plenty of times," said Sicky. "And all the time my body was growing, my head was shrinking. Of course, I would have cried out for help. Because my own people were looking for me. And to prevent this, the Xuanaci sewed my lips together with these cords that you see I still wear."

"What happened next?" asked John, who was fascinated by Sicky's story. "Did they let you go?"

"When my head was plenty small they held a special *pernocabeza* — a feast at which I was the guest of honor. They gave me a drink that contained all of the fat drained from my own head."

"And did you drink it?"

"Of course. If I had refused, they would have killed me for sure. This fat made my body much bigger than it would have been, and which made my head seem much smaller, too."

"Makes sense, I guess," observed John. "What happened then?"

Sicky shrugged. "They gave me a mirror that they had once traded for a shrunken head and let me look at myself. Which they thought was plenty funny."

"And how *did* you feel?" asked Philippa who, in spite of herself, was equally fascinated.

"Sick," said Sicky. "Very sick. Sick to my stomach. How would you feel?"

"Sick," agreed Philippa.

"Then they let me go. I went back to my village and everyone was plenty pleased to see me, but also very sad because of what the Xuanaci had done to me and my head."

"And did you ever get revenge on them?" asked John, who, being a boy, was inclined to think that way.

"Oh, yes. But many years later." Sicky looked at Mr. Vodyannoy and smiled.

"I was on vacation down here," said Mr. Vodyannoy, "and Sicky saved my life. Stopped me from being bitten by a *Scolopendra gigantea*, a Peruvian giant centipede. These are highly venomous and quite deadly. Even more so to djinn than to mundanes."

"I guess that's only fair, given that we're immune to snake venom," said John.

"How giant are they?" Philippa asked.

"They can easily reach fifteen inches in length," said Mr. Vodyannoy. "Anyway, I gave Sicky three wishes. And after wasting the first one —"

Sicky grinned sheepishly as he remembered it. "I wished that I knew if he was telling the truth or not. And then, of course, I did."

"So, forgive me," Zadie said carefully, "and no offense, Sicky, but why didn't you wish for a normal-sized head?"

"Because I didn't want one," Sicky said simply. "I was used to my head the size it was. So was everyone else. It didn't seem that important."

"I get it," said John. "Your second wish was to have revenge on the Xuanaci."

"Oh, no," said Sicky. "My second wish was to have my own business. Here in the jungle. To support my family. Which is how I have this tour and expedition company. My third wish was to have the tattoo I told you about. The one that turns things to stone."

"And I thought you were a sculptor," said Philippa.

"Those very lifelike statues of animals I've seen around the place. Those were once real animals, weren't they?"

"Yes," said Sicky. "I make some money by selling them to tourists."

"And the Xuanaci?" said John.

Sicky grinned sheepishly again. "You are right, boy. One day, using this tattoo, I went deep into the jungle, looking for some Xuanaci and turned some of them to stone, too."

"Wow," said John. "How did you feel about that?"

"Sick," said Sicky. "Very sick. Sick to my stomach. It gave me no pleasure to do that. Anyway. Perhaps you will see the statues for yourselves since we will have to go upriver, deep into Xuanaci country, to get to where you want to go."

Groanin returned to the table.

"Do they still hunt heads?" John asked with one eye on Groanin.

Sicky shrugged. "Difficult question. I have not seen any Xuanaci for a very long time. So, maybe yes. Maybe no." He smiled at Groanin and added quietly, "Keep very still please, Mr. Groanin."

"What's that you say, Sicky, old chap?"

"Keep quite still, please. There is something on your back."

Groanin gulped and turned very pale. "Something? What sort of something? You mean a creepy crawly something?"

Sicky's hand disappeared behind Groanin for a moment and when it returned it was holding a giant centipede. It had about twenty-eight red leathery segments and a couple of dozen pairs of yellow claws that were bigger than the teeth of a large comb. The centipede looked like something from another planet, and an inhospitable planet at that.

"Holy centipedes," exclaimed John, rising from the table. "A *Scolopendra gigantea*."

"Precisely," said Nimrod.

"Biggest I've ever seen," said Sicky, and held it up to the light so that everyone could get a better look at it. Even in Sicky's hand the giant centipede looked as big as a snake. "This one must be twenty inches long. Plenty poisonous, too."

"You look a bit pale, Groanin," said Nimrod. "How do you feel?"

"Sick," said Groanin. "Very sick. Sick to my stomach. How do you think I feel?"

And then he fainted.

Sicky did not, however, kill the giant centipede or even throw it away. Later that same evening the three children discovered he was keeping the centipede in a large box and feeding it with mice and cockroaches.

"Ugh," said Zadie. "Why are you keeping that disgusting thing, Sicky?"

"I'm going to feed him up until he's plenty bigger," said Sicky. "Then I'm going to show him the magic tattoo on my belly and turn him to stone. He'll fetch a good price as a piece of sculpture, from tourists. Same as the others."

He pointed at some of the beautifully detailed stone animals that were on the veranda outside his living quarters. There was a bird-eating spider, an anteater, a sloth, an opossum, a howler monkey, a short-eared dog, a tapir, a porcupine, and a puma. It looked like quite a cottage industry Sicky had going at his simple wooden home at Manu.

"Is that how you make all your sculptures?" asked John. "You just show them your belly?"

Sicky nodded. "I used to have a stone Xuanaci Indian," said Sicky. "But a famous British artist bought him and sold him to a modern art museum in London for plenty money."

"How did that make you feel?" asked John.

"Sick," said Sicky.

"I can see why someone might want a stone puma," said Philippa. "Even a porcupine. But what kind of weirdo would want a stone centipede?"

"Oh, I don't know," said John. "I wouldn't mind one. Tell you what, Sicky. I'll buy it."

"I guess you just answered my question," said Philippa.

"That is, when you've completed the, er, the actual transformation into stone," John added quickly. "It might look good on my mantelpiece at home."

So John was a little disappointed when, a little later on, just before bedtime, Sicky informed him that the giant centipede had escaped from the box.

"I think he was a very clever centipede," said Sicky, scratching his grapefruit-sized head with puzzlement. "I think maybe he pretended to be a lot smaller than he was. Stretched out, he must have been longer than I suspected. Anyway, he's gone now. We won't see him again."

"I certainly hope so," said Zadie.

But while she instinctively disliked centipedes, it seemed that Zadie felt rather differently about bats, for the twins were surprised to discover that she was keeping one on her arm as a pet. "I found it hanging on the wall in my room," she explained, and invited the twins to stroke it. "It's quite tame, really."

Mr. Vodyannoy inspected the creature. "It's a *Sturnira erythromos*," he declared authoritatively. "A yellow-shouldered bat. Quite harmless."

"Its fur is very soft," said Philippa, rubbing the bat's head with her finger.

"The Incan Emperor Atahualpa had a robe softer than silk that was made from the very finest bat skins," said Mr. Vodyannoy. "So, one of Pizarro's brothers, Pedro, informs us in his account of the conquest of the Incas."

"I'm calling it Zotz," said Zadie. "After Camazotz, the death bat god of the Maya Indians."

Muddy's dog, Hector, growled at the bat when Zadie attempted to introduce them, which earned him a pat on the head from Groanin.

"I couldn't agree more, Hector, old chap," muttered the butler. "There's something plenty wrong with that girl."

CHAPTER 7

HERE BE MONSTERS

Very early the next morning, with a thick mist rising above the water to meet an even thicker mist coming down from the trees, the party set off along a narrow tributary of the Amazon river, aboard two long dugout canoes powered by small outboard motors. Sicky, Nimrod, John, and Groanin traveled in the first canoe, and Frank Vodyannoy, Muddy, Muddy's dog, Hector, Zadie, and Philippa traveled in the second. Steering the first canoe, Sicky led the way and, early on, he pointed out a giant river otter, a red brocket deer, and, among the tall trees, a sheer cliff face that seemed to be swarming with noisy macaws. They were following the route described on the map that Faustina had given to Mr. Vodyannoy, which, they assumed, was the same route to the Eye of the Forest chosen by the earlier expedition — the one that had appeared in the newspaper. Sicky had asked all of the other jungle guides in the Manu National Park for information concerning the other expedition, but this seemed to be shrouded in mystery or secrecy and nobody had anything to report other than the fact that its members were mostly English and German archaeologists. With one notable exception: It seemed one of the team was a boy of about fourteen years old.

"Did anyone describe this boy?" John asked Sicky as the dugout canoe chugged steadily through the limpid green water.

"Just a boy. That was all they said. English. Maybe American. Just a boy. Bit like you, maybe." He grinned. "Maybe not so friendly."

"You would think a boy of fourteen would be in school," said John. "Getting an education."

"I might say the same to you," observed Nimrod.

John shrugged. "Travel broadens the mind. Isn't that what they say?"

"Yes, but first you have to have a mind," said Nimrod. "And there's only one way to get that. Reading. School. College. University. Not gallivanting around the jungle."

"If you ask me, all travel's wasted time," grumbled Groanin. "I mean, what's the point of coming halfway around the world to look at a bunch of pigging otters and parrots. Worth seeing, perhaps. Just about. Maybe. But hardly worth *going* to see. There's a subtle difference. I say, there's a subtle difference. And none of this beats the beach at Lytham St. Annes in summer."

"There speaks the true born Englishman," said Nimrod.

Around five o'clock, after a full day on the river, they

stopped on the shore at a picnic spot, where they ate an excellent dinner prepared as usual by Muddy. But after the unfortunate business with the *chichai*, Groanin could not be tempted to eat anything other than a few of the sterile jars of baby food he had brought with him from England.

When the meal was over, Sicky and Muddy built up the fire and then settled down in hammocks, which was their usual custom in the jungle and, wrapping himself in several yards of mosquito net, Groanin did the same. Hector lay down beside the fire and went to sleep. Nimrod and Mr. Vodyannoy played a game of *perudo*, a South American game that is not unlike Djinnverso, while the three children sat around the campfire and talked excitedly about their first day on the great Amazon river.

"Do you think there are any piranhas in that water?" John wondered aloud.

"Why don't you leave your hand trailing in the water tomorrow and find out?" suggested Zadie.

"Very funny."

"Where's Zotz?" Philippa asked Zadie.

Zadie glanced at her upper arm which, until recently, was the bat's preferred resting place, but this was now empty.

"Oh," Zadie said sadly. "He must have flown off somewhere. I hope he comes back."

"It is dark," said Philippa. "I mean, bats are nocturnal, right? So I expect he's gone off to get some fruit or something."

"I gave him some orange," said Zadie, and looked around anxiously. "I'm not stupid."

"I'm sure he'll come back," said Philippa. "You'll see."

Suddenly, Sicky sat up in his hammock and reached for his rifle. Nimrod tossed his cigar away and stood, looking expectantly at Sicky. The guide's head may have been unusually small but there was nothing wrong with his hearing or indeed his sense of smell. He lifted his tiny nose in the air and inhaled. Hector did the same and growled quietly.

"I smell dead mouse," said Sicky.

"Zotz, perhaps?" said John. "Zadie's bat?"

Sicky shook his head. "Bigger," he said. "Something is hunting us. Something that eats a mouse." Quietly, he worked the breech on his rifle.

Everyone looked around and moved instinctively closer to the fire. That is, everyone who was awake. Groanin was already snoring like a small outboard engine.

"I thought maybe I heard something about ten minutes ago," said Sicky, swinging his legs out of the hammock and placing them firmly on the ground. "And now I'm sure of it."

Something shifted in the undergrowth. Something large. Hector tucked his tail between his legs and whimpered. Zadie went to stand closer to the fire. It seemed like the safest place to stand. John and Philippa moved alongside her. Placing his hands on his head, John tried to flatten the hairs that were already standing on end. To his surprise, he realized that both Nimrod and Frank Vodyannoy were also pointing guns at the undergrowth behind Groanin's hammock.

"Whatever that thing is," said Nimrod, "it appears to have poor Groanin on the menu."

Sicky raised his gun to his shoulder. And there was a long silence. A minute later, the thing attacked, swooping down on the butler's hammock with a slithering, scrambling sound that was like a dozen pairs of claws on a kitchen table, and a dreadful hiss that was part cockroach and part snake.

At first, they thought it was a very large boa constrictor or anaconda, but no snake ever moved so quickly, or had *legs*. *Twenty-eight pairs of orange legs*. And no snake had *antennae*.

For half a moment, Philippa imagined they were being attacked by some kind of creature from outer space, and screamed involuntarily.

The next second, there was a deafening roar as Sicky, Nimrod, and Mr. Vodyannoy fired almost simultaneously and the leathery, brown, segmented creature, still partly hidden by thick jungle foliage, howled like a careening bird of prey and twisted around in a vain attempt to make its escape. The three armed men fired again and the enormous centipede — this one was as big as a horse — collapsed dead beside Groanin's hammock, oozing a hideous yellow muck from the six holes that now perforated its saddle-like back.

Groanin sat up in his hammock and yawned. "What's all the racket about?" he demanded. "Can't you see there are folk trying to get some sleep?"

Sicky laughed with relief and kicked the thing where it lay on the ground. Hector began to chew the creature furiously.

"Pity him dead," said Sicky. "Biggest centipede I've ever seen. Make plenty of money in a zoo. Looks like the big brother of the giant Peruvian centipede we find back at lodge."

"Centipede? What centipede?" Groanin was looking at the front and then the back of his shirt.

Mr. Vodyannoy knelt beside the huge centipede and began to examine it more closely. Each one of the orange legs was as big as his forearm. "The very big brother," he murmured. "Rather too big, wouldn't you say, Nimrod?"

"Yes," agreed Nimrod. "Unnaturally so."

Groanin looked over the edge of his hammock at the huge creature lying dead beneath him and swallowed biliously. "You don't think it intended —?"

"To eat you?" Nimrod put down his rifle. "It's a distinct possibility."

Groanin fainted, again.

Sicky and Muddy took turns to sit up and keep watch. And Nimrod used djinn power to create a propugnator, which is a sort of protective wish that acts like a perimeter fence, surrounding their camp to prevent any further attacks. But that night, nobody slept particularly well. The thought that there might be similarly large and hideous monsters lurking in the rain forest was on everyone's mind, and they all looked forward to resuming their journey up the Amazon. The river was in the open, after all, and it seemed a lot harder for something to creep up behind you when you were traveling in a boat. At least it did until the next morning, when several miles farther up the Amazon, Zadie reminded them all that on the river it was also easier for some silent monster to swim unseen underneath the boat.

"Anything could be under this dugout canoe and you wouldn't know a thing about it," she said, shifting a toothbrush from one side of her mouth to the other, like Mr. Vodyannoy's pipe. "Piranhas, anacondas." Even as she spoke, an alligator on the riverbank slipped into the water and moved into the depths like a wooden torpedo. "To say nothing of all the river crocs and alligators."

"If you can't say anything helpful," said Groanin, eyeing the water suspiciously from the other boat, "best not say anything at all. That's what my old mum used to say."

"I was only saying," said Zadie.

"Well, don't," said John. "Don't say a word."

"If you like, I could sing a song," she offered brightly. "To keep everyone's spirits up."

"I can't see how you singing could possibly achieve that result," Groanin said sourly. "In fact, speaking for myself, it would have entirely the opposite effect. But if you want to tap-dance on the water, don't let me stop you."

John laughed cruelly. And Zadie pulled a face at them.

A little later on Zotz the bat came back and settled on Zadie's arm, which cheered her up a lot. And after that, it seemed that the bat was always coming and going. Somehow, like a racing pigeon, he always seemed to know exactly where to find them in the forest or on the river.

It was about midday when they encountered the next obstacle to their progress. Sicky's head may have been unusually small, but there was nothing wrong with his eyesight. He cut the dugout's fifty-five horsepower engine and sat silently staring in front of him.

"What is it, Sicky?" asked Nimrod.

"Something is in front of us, boss."

Sicky pointed up the river. In the distance, a black cloud hung over the water ahead of them. The cloud shifted shape but it did not move away, and it was immediately obvious to everyone that so long as they remained on the river, they could not go around it. Nimrod fished out his binoculars and took a closer look.

"That's odd," he said. "It appears to be an unusually large cloud of mosquitoes."

"What's odd about that?" said Groanin. "We're on the Amazon. The whole country's crawling with this and that."

"Yes, but mosquitoes mostly feed at night. It's very peculiar to see them venture out into the heat of the day in such large numbers. I'm afraid they could be extremely hazardous to the human members of our party. Normally, insects don't bother djinn very much. But, given their sheer number, it's safe to assume that these mosquitoes might be different."

"Protective bee suits?" suggested Mr. Vodyannoy.

"It seems like the obvious solution," said Nimrod, and was about to utter his focus word when Mr. Vodyannoy raised his hand.

"Here," he said. "Let me do it." He thought for a moment, stroked his red beard, and then murmured, "ZAGIPNOTIZ-IROVAVSHEMUSYA," which is a Russian focus word meaning "to him who has hypnotized himself."

Seconds later, they were all wearing bee suits — including Hector the dog — and heading through a swarm of mosquitoes that hummed furiously like a million little currents of electricity.

"I hope these suits work," said John, who was already sweating profusely inside his protective outfit.

But seeing the river travelers seemed to drive the mosquitoes into a frenzy, and it wasn't long before one had managed to bite someone because it is a little-known fact that forty percent of mosquitoes are able to bite through clothes, even protective bee suits.

"Yaroo!" yelled Groanin. "One of the little blighters got me."

"And me," shouted John.

Hector barked loudly as if he, too, had been bitten through the suit.

Nimrod clapped his hands in the air, crushing one of the insects. Opening his gloved hands he saw that the mosquito he had killed was three or four inches in size, with a proboscis at least as long as and sharper than a hypodermic needle.

"It's no wonder," he said, wincing as a mosquito managed to penetrate the suit on his behind. "These mosquitoes are unusually large."

Mr. Vodyannoy conjured a large aerosol of insecticide out of nothing and began to spray the air around him. John tried to follow his example, but got stuck trying to imagine the synthetic chemical compound of the spray and managed only to create a room deodorant, which did little to deter the airborne plague that now afflicted him.

Philippa had better luck, and uttering her own focus word — which was FABULONGOSHOOMARVELISHLY-WONDERPIPICAL — she successfully created several large dragonflies, which eat mosquitoes. But there weren't nearly enough of these to put a real dent in the sheer number of insects now swarming around the two boats.

"Yaroo!" yelled Groanin again. "Do something, you great fathead, sir. Before we all get eaten alive."

"More speed," Nimrod shouted at Sicky, who shook his diminutive head hopelessly.

"We already going at full speed, boss," said Sicky, waving the insects away from the visor on his shrunken hood. "No more power in engine."

"I'll soon fix that," said Nimrod and, uttering his focus word — QWERTYUIOP — he doubled the horsepower of the outboard engines for both of the boats.

And with that, finally, they made their escape.

Another fifteen minutes' travel took them to the end of the river, where Sicky snatched off his hood and let out a euphoric breath. "That was close," he said. "I thought we get killed for sure."

"Did you get bitten, Sicky?" John asked him.

"Bitten plenty," said Sicky, pulling the front of his suit down and showing John several livid-looking bites on his shoulders.

"You feel all right?" said John.

"I feel sick," said Sicky. "But I is okay." Gradually, he slowed the engine and the two boats coasted toward the riverbank.

"I'm itching all over," complained Groanin. "I feel like a Scotsman's picnic blanket." He inspected one of the insects he'd killed with a rolled-up newspaper. "Look at the size of these," he exclaimed. "They're monster mozzies."

"Monster mozzies is about the size of them," agreed Philippa.

"In comparison with normal mosquitoes," said Zadie, "I should say they're every bit as large as that centipede last night was in comparison with a normal giant centipede."

"Yes," said Nimrod thoughtfully. "Yes, you have a point there."

"I think we should go back," added Groanin.

"What?" said Philippa, appalled at the very idea.

"I mean, if this is a sample of what we can expect," continued the butler, "we should return home. Immediately. Or, at the very least, right now."

"We can't go back," said John. "You heard what Faustina said back in New Haven. We have to stop these explorers from reaching the lost Incan city of Paititi. As soon as possible. With the aim of preventing the *Pachacuti*. The great disaster foretold by Manco Capac. We simply have to go on."

"Well said, John," said Nimrod. "What do you say, Philippa?"

Philippa shrugged. "John's right. We have to continue. No one said this was going to be a walk in the park."

"Frank?"

Mr. Vodyannoy nodded. "I'm for going on, Nimrod," he said. "Always."

"You're all crazy," insisted Groanin. "Look at the size of that mozzie. It's a monster."

"That's something we agree on, anyway," said Nimrod. "But the fact is, it's big because someone made it that big. Deliberately. Something or someone appears to be trying to slow down this expedition."

"Well, we are slowed down," said Zadie. "I need a break. For the sake of Mr. Groanin."

"Someone?" said John.

"After that picture of the Eye of the Forest," said Nimrod, "whoever is leading the other expedition must have known that they would be followed. Which means there may very well be other similar surprises that lie ahead of us in the forest. Groanin? You could go back to the lodge with Zadie, if you want. I'm afraid we'll be on foot from here on in."

"I said I needed a break," said Zadie. "I didn't say I wanted to go back."

"How can you look at the size of that bug and want to go on?" Groanin asked. "To say nothing of that thing last night. It could have killed any one of us. And me in particular."

"You're forgetting something, aren't you?" said John. "We have djinn power to protect us."

"I wasn't forgetting it," said Groanin. "And I still wouldn't mind going back."

"Nothing's going to happen to any of us," insisted Nimrod. "We're armed with djinn power and rifles."

"You promise?" said Groanin.

"Yes, yes, yes," said Nimrod.

Groanin nodded. "Very well, sir. Please forgive my earlier cowardice. I'm a little unnerved at this latest turn of events, that's all."

"Don't mention it, old fellow."

Groanin looked at Zadie and nodded back at her nervously. "Er, thanks, miss," he said. "For what you said back there."

Zadie pulled a face. "It's no big deal," she said. "All I said was that maybe we needed to slow down and take a break." Hearing a fluttering sound she looked up and smiled as her pet bat settled on her sleeve. It was Zotz. "Don't you worry about me. I'll be all right."

"Well, that's a relief, I'm sure," said Groanin.

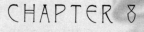

CHAPTER 8

CAT PEOPLE

It was getting dark and, after they had pitched camp and while they were still able to see it, they all inspected the beginnings of the trail indicated on the map given to Mr. Vodyannoy by Faustina.

"May I see the map?" asked Zadie.

"Of course," said Mr. Vodyannoy, handing it to her.

"Do you think this is the way the other party could have come?" asked John.

"There's no sign that anyone has been along here with a machete," said Sicky.

"It must be the way they came," said Zadie, and advancing several yards into the undergrowth, stooped to pick something up before turning to show everyone the contents of her hand. "Look."

She was holding an English candy wrapper and a cigarette butt that she handed to Nimrod, who then inspected these two objects with a forensic closeness that would not have disgraced Sherlock Holmes.

"You see this gold *E* and *S* on the paper?" said Nimrod. "That stands for Empha Seema. An English brand of cigarettes. And this candy wrapper is from a Callard's English toffee."

"So I guess we're on their trail, after all," said Philippa. "It's typical of Europeans that they should leave their garbage lying on the forest floor. Eh, Sicky?"

But Sicky was no longer listening. He pointed silently into the distance and eventually Nimrod managed to distinguish what the guide was looking at. Lying in the boughs of a tree were a couple of jaguars.

"You don't think they're meaning to ambush us?" asked Nimrod. "I mean, they're very close to the trail."

"I don't think so, boss," said Sicky. "For one thing, they would never have allowed us to see them if they was planning anything like an ambush. 'Sides, these big cats are half asleep. Probably they're just having a *siesta* until it gets dark. Then they'll go a-hunting." He sighed wistfully and rubbed his tiny head. "Be nice to see what else lies along this trail, boss. Before we're on it, don't you think? Just like them two cats."

"Yes, wouldn't it just?" said Nimrod.

Sicky looked up at the sky. "Too late now, of course. Soon be too dark to see very much at all. Unless you've got cat's eyes."

"You've given me an idea, Sicky," said Nimrod.

Upon their return to camp, Nimrod told everyone what his idea was.

"I think it's reasonable to assume that the other expedition might have planned some other surprises in store for us farther along the jungle trail," he said. "Therefore, what I think we should do is to separate for a while. John and I will scout ahead and check that things are safe. If they're not, we'll come back and warn you. What do you say, John? Are you up for this?"

"I'm game for anything," said John.

"That's the spirit."

"What if it's not safe?" objected Zadie. "Won't you just be putting yourselves at risk instead of everyone?"

"I'm glad you mentioned that, Zadie," said Nimrod. "We could go invisibly, of course. But it's very easy to get lost when you're traveling with someone you can't see. So what I propose is this: You recall those two young male jaguars we spotted sleeping in a tree? Well, John and I will borrow their bodies for a while and scout the trail ahead. Nothing moves more silently in the jungle than the jaguar."

"Except perhaps the snake," said Zadie. As if evidence of this was required, she pointed to a Peruvian coral snake that was slithering almost invisibly across some dead leaves on the rain forest floor.

"True," admitted Nimrod. "But I've never much liked being a snake."

"And soldier ants," said Zadie. "And spiders. And bats. They all move more silently than the jaguar."

Nimrod smiled patiently. "I've never much liked being those creatures, either." Seeing that she was about to add some more animals to an extending list, Nimrod raised his hand to silence her. "Anyway, as two jaguars we'll very likely see if there are any surprises that lie in store for us in plenty of time. So that then we might deal with them."

"I don't think I like the idea of us splitting up," said Philippa.

"Me, neither," admitted Zadie.

"You'll be fine with Mr. Vodyannoy and Groanin and Sicky," said Nimrod. "And it's just for a few hours. Until tomorrow morning at the latest."

"No harm will come to you while I'm here," insisted Mr. Vodyannoy. "Trust me."

John and Nimrod walked up the trail to the giant red cedar where the older djinn had seen the two jaguars.

"There they are," said Nimrod. "*Panthera onca*. They're beautiful animals, don't you think?"

"Very," agreed John. "This is going to be cool."

"I'm rather looking forward to it, myself," admitted Nimrod. "In my experience, there's nothing that's as much fun as being a cat. And among cats, the jaguar, or *otorongo*, is one of the most exciting. I'll take the bigger one, on the left." He paused. "You've done this before, haven't you? Animal possession? I mean, I seem to remember your mother telling me you've had experience of being a bird."

"I was a peregrine falcon once," said John. "In Central Park."

"After you've been a peregrine falcon, frankly, being a jaguar is a piece of cake," said Nimrod.

John looked around them. "Where are we going to leave our own bodies?" he asked a little anxiously. "Just about anywhere around here, and we're likely to come back and find something eating them."

"Good point," said Nimrod. "I don't suppose you thought to bring your lamp."

"Er, no," said John. "Should I have?"

"It's a good habit to get into. That way you're never stuck for somewhere to lurk while you take your spirit off somewhere else. Don't worry. You can share my travel lamp."

From his coat pocket, Nimrod produced a small silver bottle and placed it in the trunk of a tree. "Right," he said. "We should be safe enough in there."

"I'm afraid I haven't done this before," said John. "I can transubstantiate all right. But I don't know how to separate my transubstantiated self from my spirit."

"It's called decanting," said Nimrod. "And it's relatively straightforward as long as you make sure to leave the stopper out of the bottle, or the lid off the lamp. My travel lamp has no stopper so there's nothing to worry about."

John uttered his focus word and was gradually enveloped by an almost animated white smoke. As he returned to his natural element, which was fire, he took a deep and euphoric breath of the many millions of carbon atoms that were his combusted self and, with a tremendous sense of well-being and deep relaxation, he gave himself up to his own true form. Each time he transubstantiated, John felt as if he had achieved some deeper understanding of who and what he was, like a kind of holy man finding nirvana. It was akin to coming home after having been away for a long time.

Inside the bottle, a feeling of anxiety overcame John momentarily, as it always did when the moment came to become pure djinn. He gathered his atoms urgently, like someone catching dollar bills caught by a gust of wind, and put himself back together, as he always did, fearing that he would forget some small but important part of himself. But somehow he always managed it successfully. Nimrod had already reassembled and was inspecting the inside of the travel bottle which, as was normal, was many times larger on the inside than on the outside. John still didn't know how that worked.

The interior of Nimrod's bottle was furnished like the lounge of an elegant hotel, with many fine paintings, several large leather sofas and chairs, and a blazing log fire. Nimrod sat down, removed his shoes, and invited John to do the same.

"Just think of decanting as a normal out-of-body experience," he told John. "A few deep breaths and then out through the top of the bottle. All right?"

John nodded.

"One more thing. I nearly forgot. A decanting is much more effective if you leave the body not on an inhalation but on the exhalation."

"What's an exhalation?"

"I'm sorry. I forgot you're an American. English words of more than three syllables are a foreign language to you."

"That's a bit harsh."

"But true." Nimrod smiled sweetly. "You leave the body as you breathe out. That way, when later on you reenter, you can do it as if breathing in again. This is where the Indian yogis got all of their ideas about breathing. From us."

John let out a deep breath and let himself lift up through the neck of the bottle. This felt very different from a transubstantiation. Whereas that was about smoke, this was all about air and free spirit. This felt like an incredible lightness of being.

The two jaguars lazed in the high branches of the tree, paws hanging down on either side of the bough, and their eyes closed, although neither was asleep. Jaguars don't like to miss anything. And seldom do. They were brothers and quite young and not yet the solitary hunters that most jaguars become. Several hours before, they had just enjoyed a light lunch of river turtle and were looking forward to hunting down a more substantial supper such as a capybara, a peccary, or perhaps a monkey. Their mother was already a distant memory.

John slipped into the smaller of the two big cats and immediately set about licking his paws, on which there was still a trace of turtle meat. Meanwhile, Nimrod stood up and after vocalizing a few mews and grunts, he opened his lungs and let out a powerful roar. John almost jumped out of his beautiful rosette-covered coat and temporarily lost his footing. For a second he clung onto the bough of the tree with his huge sharp claws before his own body weight got the better of him and it seemed easier to drop down on the ground. He looked up at Nimrod and waited, flicking his long tail impatiently. Nimrod roared again, as if demonstrating his superior size and strength.

"What's that for?" John's question was telepathic, for the simple reason that, in common with most other animals, jaguars can't talk. "You scared the heck out of me."

"Just opening my chest," explained Nimrod. "This fellow's been lying across a tree for three hours and he's a bit stiff."

As soon as Nimrod jumped down from the tree, John bounded along the forest trail.

"Not so fast, John. Remember, the whole point of this exercise is to spy out the land ahead of us. To move stealthily. To exploit the natural characteristics of this wonderful member of the Felidae family. And we should stay to the edge of the beaten track rather than be on it. I mean, there's no point in being a jaguar at all if we just march along the trail like a couple of stupid tourists." And so saying, he stepped into the dense undergrowth and almost immediately vanished from view. The dark brown rosettes on his tawny yellow coat were perfect jungle camouflage.

John growled and then followed the other jaguar. For good measure he growled again. He liked growling. In fact, he liked everything about being a jaguar and couldn't imagine why he'd never before tried out being a big cat. And he was a very big cat. About five feet long and thirty inches tall at his shoulders, John weighed nearly two hundred pounds. Nimrod was an inch or two longer and several pounds heavier.

For a whole hour, they made easy progress through the jungle. Their short and stocky build made them adept at climbing, crawling, and swimming — for, as with the tiger, the jaguar is a cat that enjoys and excels at swimming. But while they were crossing a tributary of the Amazon, John caught sight of a turtle and, suddenly feeling hungry, grabbed it in his powerful jaws.

"What are you doing?" Nimrod's telepathic voice was impatient.

"I'm hungry."

"This is no time to stop for a snack." Nimrod licked his lips. "Even if it is a delicious-looking turtle. Besides, if this jaguar's memory serves me right, we had turtle for lunch."

"I don't think we have time to hunt anything larger." John kept hold of the feebly struggling turtle in his jaws. "Do we? Hunting a deer or a tapir could take hours. And now that I've got this — well, it's a bird in the hand, isn't it? In a manner of speaking."

"You're right," agreed Nimrod. "I suppose I am feeling a bit peckish myself, and he is a beauty, isn't he? I don't suppose it'll do any harm if we eat something."

"Unless you're the turtle." There was a harsh laugh and something of the jaguar's cruelty in John's thoughts because, after all, it is impossible to be a jaguar without becoming just a bit like a jaguar. The next second, John bit down hard into the turtle and, since the jaguar has the strongest bite of all felids — stronger than a lion or a tiger — his powerful jaws pierced the turtle's protective shell easily and killed it instantly.

Nimrod took hold of the back half of the turtle, and the two jaguars tore the poor creature apart and ate it quickly.

"I had a pet turtle once," admitted John, licking his chops. "When I was a kid. But I never liked it much. It was always biting me."

"I think you just had the last bite," suggested Nimrod, crunching his way through the last bits of shell and turtle meat. Later on he would throw up what he couldn't digest. "Now then. Can we get on? While it's still dark and we can enjoy the advantage of being able to see in the dark. I can't remember when I enjoyed such perfect eyesight. I really must make myself a better set of glasses when I'm in a human shape again."

They were just about to move on when a rhythmic noise filled the damp forest air.

"What's that?" wondered John.

"It sounds like jungle drums."

"Do you think it's those headhunters Sicky was talking about?"

"There are two tribes of Indians in this part of the forest, John. The Xuanaci and the Prozuanaci. Only the Xuanaci seem inclined to be warlike."

"Maybe we should go back," suggested John. "See that everyone is all right."

"Mr. Vodyannoy is more than equal to the task of protecting everyone," answered Nimrod.

"If you say so."

They resumed their reconnaissance, walking alongside the trail Nimrod had memorized from his last perusal of the map. After an hour of walking, during which the drums continued to beat, John halted and passed a thought through the air to Nimrod. "It all seems safe enough. Don't you think we should go back now?"

"We'll just see what's over the next hilltop," argued his uncle, slinking forward underneath a fallen tree trunk and through a thick bush without as much as moving a solitary leaf. A second or two later he stopped dead in his own tracks as if something had frozen him to the spot.

"What is it?" wondered John.

Nimrod did not answer and, after almost a minute, he settled down on his stomach watching something that lay somewhere ahead of them. John crept alongside him and tried to make out what this was.

It began to rain. And still Nimrod did not answer.

John flicked the rain off his ears and, narrowing his eyes against the relentless stream of water, stared into the darkness. Nimrod was looking at the twisted trunk and boughs of a small tree that was twenty or thirty feet ahead of them and about which there seemed nothing at all remarkable. Try as he might, John could see nothing in the tree but, trusting his uncle's experience, he waited, and it was fortunate that patience comes easier to jaguars than to boy djinn, for eventually this patience was repaid.

Almost imperceptibly the tree was moving. Not moving in any direction. It was as if the tree was breathing very gently. Then something flickered on the tip of one of the branches, like a bird or an insect, and suddenly John felt a chill of fear as he realized that the tree was not a tree at all. He let the thought drift out of his mind to the creature lying beside him.

"It's a giant anaconda."

"To be rather more accurate," Nimrod replied silently, "it is a *giant* giant anaconda. Normally, these snakes grow to twenty or thirty feet in length. But this one appears to be at least twice that size. Perhaps even bigger. It's hard to tell in the dark. But given its size and position immediately next to the trail, there can be no doubt that it has been placed here to ambush us."

"How are they doing this?" asked John.

"I don't know," admitted Nimrod. "But however they're doing it, we have to get rid of that snake."

"We're going to need a very large gun."

"There's no guarantee it will be in the same place tomorrow," said Nimrod. "And, despite its enormous size, in our human shapes we might never even see it. Not until it was too late. No, John, we must attack it together. We must try to kill it right now."

"But it's huge," argued John. "The trunk must be three or four feet thick. You could bite it all day and probably not get anywhere."

"We have one or two advantages in mounting an attack. For one thing, the rain will help to conceal our movement. Also, we have already identified the snake's head. That is the best place for us to concentrate our attack. You will employ the deep-throat bite and suffocation that is usually practiced by jaguars. I will bite its skull, between the ears, piercing the snake's brain in exactly the same way you cracked that turtle's shell. With any luck, the snake will not be expecting anything like this to happen. Especially since it will be looking only at the trail and we'll be attacking from the jungle, behind the snake's blind spot. That's another advantage. But we must also be very careful. If the snake manages to get ahold of us in its coils, we will be crushed like a jam sandwich. If that happens, you must lift your spirit out of the jaguar without hesitation. Then find some other creature and make your way back to the place where I left the bottle containing our transubstantiated bodies. Clear?"

"Clear," declared John.

They began to inch their way forward through the jungle. Whenever Nimrod disturbed a leaf, he stopped to wait for it to stop moving again. Half an hour brought them only ten or twelve feet closer to the giant anaconda. This seemed to galvanize the jaguar possessed by Nimrod. His sinews stiffened and his muscles tensed up and his huge claws extended from his big powerful paws. John copied his example. *The snake's throat,* he told himself. *Bite and suffocate. Bite and suffocate.*

When it came, the charge was silent. A jaguar's roar might have helped to terrify and subdue a smaller animal, but it would only have alerted and therefore helped the huge snake. Both jaguars hurled themselves simultaneously through the dripping wet jungle foliage toward the snake's shovel-sized head like the arrows from two crossbows.

The attack had begun.

CHAPTER 9

A LITTLE TOUCH OF FROGGY IN THE NIGHT

The little party of three djinn and three humans camped by the river had, except for Groanin, just finished eating Muddy's excellent dinner when the drums started to beat, rolling rhythmically through the jaguar-haunted night air like a distant locomotive.

Muddy's eyes widened and he looked afraid. Sicky threw his chicken leg aside and stood up, inclining his head toward the treetops. The guide's head may have been unusually small but there was nothing wrong with his sense of direction and, after a moment or two, he pointed westward and picked up his rifle. "Five miles that way. Maybe farther."

"Talking drums?" Philippa asked him.

"Not talk," said Sicky. "But drums send a message still the same."

"Oh, what's that?" asked Zadie.

"Let people know they are there. And to be plenty afraid."

"Prozuanaci Indian drums?" Groanin's voice was hopeful.

Sicky shook his small head. "Prozuanaci Indians don't drum no more. Prozuanaci Indians prefer to use the telephone. Prozuanaci is private people. Don't like everyone to know their business. Them is Xuanaci Indian drums. Xuanaci don't care who knows what they're talking about. Xuanaci Indians is bad people. Xuanaci drum to make people feel plenty scared. Make people feel nervous." Sicky took hold of his small jaw and drew a hand across his even smaller throat. "Make tourist people worry about losing heads."

Groanin swallowed noisily. "Well, they got that right," he said. "I do worry. I've grown kind of attached to this head of mine. And it's grown rather attached to me. I should hate to see it on some local witch doctor's bookshelf."

Sicky shook his head. "Xuanaci probably not interested in cutting your head off, Mr. Groanin," he said, and gently patted Groanin's bald pate. "You got no hair. Bald head no good for Xuanaci. They prefer plenty of hair to hang shrunken head on trophy pole. Slap head like fat baby no good."

"Well, that's a relief, I'm sure," Groanin said stiffly. "Slap head, indeed."

"Really, there's nothing to worry about," insisted Mr. Vodyannoy. "I am a djinn, after all."

"Then do something to make us all feel safe," insisted Groanin. "I say, do something."

"Such as?"

"How about a stockade?" suggested Groanin. "Better still, a castle. With a drawbridge and a portcullis. And a hundred archers to defend us."

"You're overreacting, Groanin," said Philippa.

"Am I, miss?" Groanin smiled thinly at her. "That's easy to say when you're a djinn and you can disappear inside a little bottle when the going gets tough. But things are different for the likes of Muddy and me. Every time I look at Sicky here, I get a funny feeling on the back of me neck."

"If it makes you feel better, I'll use djinn power to create another propugnator," said Mr. Vodyannoy. "A protective perimeter wish. Like the one Nimrod made the other night. To deter anyone or anything that gets too close to our camp."

"Please do that," said Groanin.

"Horror show," said Mr. Vodyannoy and, with his finger, drew a circle in the air, while at the same time he uttered his focus word: "ZAGIPNOTIZIROVAVSHEMUSYA."

"Is that it?" inquired Groanin.

"Yes," said Mr. Vodyannoy. "You'll be quite safe now. More or less."

"More or less?" Groanin frowned.

"Yes," said Philippa. "What do you mean?"

"Don't you know, child?" exclaimed Mr. Vodyannoy. "You can't use djinn power inside a propugnator."

"Oh. No, I didn't."

"Yeah," said Zadie. "Didn't you know that?"

Philippa bit her lip and tried to contain her irritation.

"I don't know what they teach young djinn nowadays," said Mr. Vodyannoy. "Why, in my day, we were told all this kind of thing before we even had our wisdom teeth."

"What does it matter?" Groanin said impatiently. "I mean, once we're inside this, er, propugnator thingy, then it won't matter what happens, so long as we're safe, eh?"

"That's right," said Mr. Vodyannoy. "As safe as houses."

Safe, but not, it seemed, as dry. Because when Muddy and Sicky went to erect the tents, they found that Muddy's dog, Hector, had been chewing them and that these were now full of holes, which prompted Muddy to throw stones and sticks at the poor brute until Philippa restrained him.

"Leave him alone," she said. "He didn't know what he was doing."

"Miss Philippa is right," Sicky told Muddy. "Hector's plenty nervous because of the drums, probably."

"Me, too, I guess," agreed Muddy. "I wouldn't normally hit old Hector. But them tents is ruined."

"Don't worry," said Philippa. "It's no big deal. We'll use djinn power to repair them in the morning."

"Let's just hope it doesn't rain tonight," said Groanin.

The Amazon gets nine feet of rain every year, about twice as much as eastern parts of the United States, and that night, it started to rain and rain heavily. Not for nothing is the rain forest called the rain forest. The damaged tents afforded little or no protection against the deluge. Philippa and Zadie awoke to find themselves soaked to the skin. They were cold, too, very cold. Zadie had already donned a scarf and some gloves. The fire had gone out, and Sicky and Muddy were having no luck in relighting it. Groanin was sitting in a pool of water holding a folded newspaper over his head like a hat but it wasn't doing much good; he might as well have been standing in the fountain back in Lima's main square.

"Marvelous, isn't it?" he complained. "The one night our tents get chewed up by that daft dog and it rains. Like Manchester on a bank holiday, so it is. I couldn't be more wet if I had a rubber duck and a loofah in my hands."

"Listen," said Zadie.

Groanin cocked a wet ear at the rain. "Don't tell me, it's raining," he said bitterly.

"The drums," said Zadie. "They've stopped."

"If they've got any sense, them Indians have gone indoors to keep dry," said Groanin.

"She's right," said Philippa.

Groanin shrugged.

"Don't you get it?" asked Philippa. "If the drums have stopped, then maybe we don't need the propugnator. We could use djinn power to repair the tents and get warm and dry again."

"You're right," said Groanin. "You'd better go and tell Mr. Vodyannoy. Wherever he is. I can't imagine he's sleeping in this downpour."

They went to Mr. Vodyannoy's tent, which was as badly chewed up as anyone's and found him fast asleep on his camp bed. Groanin cleared his throat loudly.

"I say. Mr. Vodyannoy." Groanin took hold of the djinn's shoulder and shook him gently. Groanin tutted loudly. "How does he manage to sleep in all this water?" he grumbled. "That's what I should like to know. I say, wake up, sir. We need to fix these tents and pronto. On account of the fact that we're all soaked to the skin."

But Mr. Vodyannoy apparently remained fast asleep.

"There's summat up here," said Groanin. "It ain't natural for anyone to sleep in all this rain."

"Maybe he's dead," said Sicky. "I don't feel so good myself. All this rain is making Sicky's head shrink."

"Rubbish," said Groanin. "Look." He pointed at Mr. Vodyannoy's blanket. "His hands are moving."

"Them no his hands," said Muddy.

"Course they are," said Groanin, and hauled the sodden blanket off Mr. Vodyannoy's chest to reveal, sitting on the djinn's bare chest, a small, bright yellow frog.

Sicky let out a scream, which made Philippa scream in her turn, and Hector bark in his, so that Groanin nearly had a heart attack.

"Don't do that," Groanin said irritably. He pointed at the small creature sitting on Mr. Vodyannoy's bare chest. "It's only a flipping frog. Anyone would think it was a pigging snake. Not that it would matter. Djinn are immune to snake venom. So I've been led to believe, anyway." The English butler bent down to pick up the frog and yelled as Sicky smacked his hand away.

"What's the matter, you daft halfpence-worth?"

"No touch that frog," yelled Sicky. "That is golden poison dart frog."

"You what?" said Groanin, clutching his fingers to his chest.

"Just about the deadliest creature in the world, that's what," said Muddy.

"That little thing?" Zadie sounded disbelieving.

"That little frog's skin contains enough poison to kill ten people," insisted Sicky. "Frog eats insects that have eaten very poisonous plants in jungle. Indians catch frogs and rub arrowheads and blowgun darts on frog's skin to make them act more quickly. Him plenty lethal."

Sicky lit a cigarette and held it near the little frog which, disliking the proximity of the hot end and the tobacco smoke, leaped away into the bushes.

"Flipping heck." Groanin looked anxiously at Mr. Vodyannoy. "Is he dead?"

"He's not dead," said Philippa. "Quite sick, I think, but not dead." She bent closer to Mr. Vodyannoy.

His eyes closed tightly, Mr. Vodyannoy whispered something.

"Don't touch him, miss," said Sicky. "Best you don't. Maybe some of frog's poison still on mister's skin. Wait for rain to wash off first." Gingerly, Sicky opened the old djinn's shirt, allowing the rain to cascade onto his bare chest.

Mr. Vodyannoy shuddered visibly.

"Him got plenty fever," observed Sicky. "If human, he be plenty dead. But since he djinn, then maybe he stay alive. Need medicine, though."

Carefully, Philippa leaned over the sick djinn. "Mr. Vodyannoy," she said. "You've been poisoned. By a poison dart frog. A yellow one."

"*Phyllobates terribilis*," he muttered deliriously. "Terrible frog. Batrachotoxin. Lethal to humans and almost lethal to djinn. I need . . . need to get back inside my lamp. Need time to recuperate. Get warm. Feel very cold. Very ill. Only chance to stay alive is to be inside lamp. Get warm again. Do you hear? Find my lamp, child, and bring it to me quickly. Put it in my hands. Or I'll be dead within the hour. Do you hear?"

Philippa looked at Sicky. "We have to find his lamp," she said.

Sicky was already emptying Mr. Vodyannoy's backpack onto the sodden ground. Moments later, a black Fabergé bottle decorated with solid-gold filigree appeared in his hands. Quickly, he handed it to Philippa, who removed the scepter-sized stopper and placed the bottle in Mr. Vodyannoy's trembling hands.

The sick djinn smiled thinly and sighed a great, long, almost mortal sigh that slowly turned into a djinn transubstantiation, which seemed to last forever. As they watched, the rasping breath leaving his body became visible while the body itself started to disappear in a cloud of thin smoke until only the hands holding the bottle were left, then they, too, disappeared inside the black glass. Instinctively, Philippa stoppered the bottle and wiped the rain from her face.

Then Zadie took the bottle from her and placed it carefully back in Mr. Vodyannoy's backpack, next to the map.

"And then there were five," said Zadie.

"I expect Nimrod and John will be back soon," said Philippa.

"I hope so," said Zadie. "Because I don't mind telling you, I think we're in trouble. I never thought I'd be wet and cold in the Amazon jungle. I tried uttering my focus word a minute ago and nothing happened."

Philippa shook her head. "I don't think you understand, Zadie. Mr. Vodyannoy said you can't use djinn power inside a propugnator."

"It's you who doesn't understand," said Zadie. "A propugnator doesn't continue after the djinn who laid it down has transubstantiated. So I should to be able to use my power. We both should. You try."

"FABULONGOSHOOMARVELISHLYWONDERPIPICAL," said Philippa, but nothing happened.

Zadie tossed her pet bat, Zotz, into the air and took Philippa's hands in her own. "Perhaps if we were to try together," she said, closing her eyes tightly.

"And let's think warm thoughts for dry clothes, water-proof tents, and a big blazing fire in the center of our camp," added Philippa. "Perhaps we can persuade ourselves that it's not as cold and wet as it is. Mind over matter."

"Good idea," said Zadie. "Mind over matter. Lots of lovely warm thoughts."

"Warm thoughts," repeated Philippa.

"Hot fires. Baking Polynesian beaches. Thick fur coats," said Zadie.

"Deserts," said Philippa. "Sand. The Sahara. The pyramids."

"Sauna baths and steam rooms," said Zadie.

"A New York subway in August," said Philippa.

"The Dead Sea in July."

"Magma, volcanoes, lava."

"A boiled egg."

"A steak on a barbecue."

"Scalding hot coffee."

"Chili powder, peppers, curry, hot toast."

Zadie squeezed Philippa's hand. "Let's go for it, Philippa."

"FABULONGOSHOO —" said Philippa.

"KAKORRHAPHIOPHOBIA," said Zadie.

"— MARVELISHLYWONDERPIPICAL," said Philippa, finishing her focus word.

Neither djinn needed to open her eyes to know that nothing had happened. At least nothing had happened that was the result of djinn power, anyway. Silently, Philippa and

Zadie released each other's hands and looked around in the gloom. Things were the same and yet they were not. Somehow the camp seemed to have become much smaller. Sicky was crouched down on the ground with his head completely enclosed by his huge hands. Groanin was standing quite still and looking more than a little worried. Muddy, too. Hector, the dog, had disappeared.

"Sorry," said Philippa. "But nothing seems to be working in the djinn department. Perhaps if it stops raining and we can get dry, we might warm up a bit, but until then . . ." She shook her head.

Groanin started speaking out of the side of his mouth. "I hope that's sooner than later, miss," he said. "Because in case you hadn't noticed, we've got company. And I don't think they want tea, neither."

Philippa blinked and rubbed her eyes as she understood how it was that the camp seemed to have become smaller. They were surrounded by Indians. Perhaps as many as a hundred warriors, all of them as silent as the trees and all of them painted like jaguars, so that they blended perfectly with the thick jungle that surrounded them.

"Do you think they're friendly?" asked Zadie.

One of the Indians, who appeared to be in charge of the others, had sharpened bones protruding from almost every part of his face. There was a small bell hanging in his nose. The jaguar camouflage covering his body wasn't paint but tattoos — hundreds of tattoos. Around his neck he wore a necklace made of claws and teeth and a large black stone about the size of a tennis ball. Except that the stone was a head. A shrunken human head.

"Not especially friendly, no," said Philippa.

"Close your eyes, Miss Philippa," whispered Sicky. "You, too, Miss Zadie. Mr. Groanin. Muddy. All of you. Close your eyes. I'll do my Medusa thing."

"Do as he says," hissed Philippa. "Quickly."

Suddenly, Sicky stood up and, with a loud shout, he pulled up the front of his wet T-shirt, exposing the deadly tattoo on his huge belly. The three Indians who were close enough and sufficiently unwise to look at this tattoo immediately turned to stone. The others let out a terrible ululating cry, and the next second, Sicky was struck on the head with a war club and bundled into a sack.

At the same time strong hands caught one of Philippa's wrists and then the other.

They were prisoners. Prisoners of the headhunting Xuanaci Indians.

CHAPTER 10

HOW LIKE A GOD

The giant anaconda is an aquatic member of the boa constrictor family of snakes. This means that it kills its prey by coiling its enormous elongated body around its victim and squeezing until the prey is suffocated or crushed to death. Then the snake dislocates its own jaw and swallows the unfortunate creature whole. The name "anaconda" comes from a Tamil word, *anaikondran*, which means "elephant killer." South Americans call this huge snake *el matatoro*, the "bull killer." Both names are good indicators of the snake's enormous power and fearsome reputation. Anacondas are slow-moving and rely on the element of surprise to catch their prey, which most often includes alligators, deer, and even jaguars, and it is seldom that a snake like an anaconda is itself the subject of a surprise attack.

The *giant* giant anaconda was caught quite unaware. The two jaguars were on the snake's suitcase-sized head in a matter of seconds. With sharp claws bared, each big cat raked itself a firm hold of the snake's huge body and held on tightly. But it was only now that they had the trunk in their grasp that they realized how big the snake really was. It was fifty or sixty feet long and, in the middle, perhaps two feet thick.

John sank his fangs into the creature's throat and fixed his jaws tight, like a dog hanging onto a blanket. But Nimrod struggled to get an equally firm bite on the head, such were its proportions. The snake hissed like a steam engine and twisted back on itself, trying to envelop the two jaguars in its massive and lethal coils, but each time Nimrod and John managed to scramble clear of the body, which threatened to squeeze them to death. Finally, Nimrod got a good grip behind the head and between the snake's yellow-button eyes and bit as hard as he could.

The anaconda's huge nostrils flared as it sensed the intelligence behind the two-pronged attack, but it was hardly finished yet. Suddenly, like a crane, the snake reared twenty or thirty feet up in the air carrying the bodies of the two jaguars with him. It shook itself vigorously so that the two cats found themselves waved around like twin flags on a huge flagpole and then dove toward the forest floor as if hoping that the fall would dislodge both its attackers. The impact with the wet ground winded John but still he held on. So long as there was a breath in the snake's huge body he had to hold on or die trying. His mouth was full of blood but he had no idea if it was his or the snake's.

Nimrod pressed his fangs against the creature's head and realized that if either one of these teeth gave way before the snake's skull was punctured, he and John would probably die. Closing his eyes he concentrated all of his strength in closing the aching muscles on either side of his lower jawbone.

Changing tactics now, the snake pushed quickly through the thick undergrowth hoping to brush off the two cats that were affixed to its head and throat. John almost let go as he was buffeted against a tree and then dragged through a bush backward. Nimrod growled with pain as the snake's fast-traveling weight scraped him across a sharp rock and an equally jagged log. But somehow he and John managed to hold on.

The rain forest had seldom seen or heard anything like it: the roaring of the two jaguars, the desperate hisses of the snake, the crashing undergrowth, and the birds and bats knocked out of their nighttime roosts — it was as if a mad bull elephant had gone on the rampage.

The minutes turned into an hour.

John's jaws were at breaking point. The pain went all through the top of his head, down his neck, and into his muscular shoulders. His claws felt like they were being wrenched out of their sockets. But then, detecting a change in the snake's breathing, John tightened his bite on the snake's throat and immediately he saw the black nostrils flare again as if the lack of air in the snake's oil-pipeline of a body was now becoming critical.

Nimrod saw it, too, and finding another two percent of strength somewhere in his chest muscles he made a last attempt to pierce the cranium. A second later he felt something crack in his mouth like one of Groanin's extra-strong mints and something hot and gelatinous filled his savage mouth. It was the snake's brain.

The anaconda twitched for several horrible minutes until finally it lay still.

"Is it dead?"

"I very much hope so," answered Nimrod.

John opened his mouth and rolled away. To his surprise the sun was rising. It would soon be light. But it was still raining. He tried to stand and found his legs trembling underneath him. Exhausted, he dropped down on his belly again and took a long deep breath. "Are you all right?" he wondered.

"Yes." Nimrod's thoughts weren't much more than a whisper. "I think so. How are you?"

"I feel very, very tired," admitted John.

"Me, too." Nimrod limped over to where John was now stretched out and began to lick one of the larger scratches on his nephew's side.

John looked at the anaconda's huge body and felt something close to shame. "What a magnificent creature," observed John. "I almost feel sorry for it."

"Don't blame yourself," Nimrod advised him. "Blame whoever put it here with the intent of killing one of us. And believe me, given the chance, it would have done."

"I wonder what it tastes like."

"That's the jaguar in you speaking, John." Nimrod let out a sigh. "Do you want to find out?"

"Not particularly. I'm too tired to open my mouth. I may never eat again. I just want to sleep."

"There's no time to eat and there's no time to sleep. We should be getting back. We've done what we set out to do."

"Do we have to?" John growled irritably. "Can't we just stay here for a while?"

"The others will be wondering where we got to. Before long they'll be worried. Do you want them to be worried, John?"

"I'm too tired to care. I just want to sleep."

"Come on. We'll take it slowly. A nice cool bath in the river on the way back should help to make you feel better."

"Sounds good." John stood up and put one paw in front of another.

They started to walk back, along the side of the trail. Neither was in a mood to communicate. Both were too preoccupied with their aching bodies to think very much. But after a while John felt he had to ask Nimrod if, when he left the jaguar's body and reclaimed his own, the pain he was feeling would disappear.

"Yes," answered Nimrod. "It will. That's why I'm keen to get back. I thought you knew that."

"I do now."

They walked on with Nimrod leading the way as before. But a tired animal is like a human in that it makes mistakes. No fully fit and well-rested jaguar would have walked into a man-made trap, even a trap made by local Indians. One minute John and Nimrod were moving in single file along the side of the trail, and the next a large net carrying Nimrod was flying up into the air above John's head.

John turned to flee and sprinted toward some undergrowth, straight into another net attached to a tree sapling that catapulted him off his feet. For a moment he hung there, swinging like a bag of coconuts. Then, a half-naked man wearing a white mask with a big red grin on it ran toward him, shouting loudly and gesticulating wildly. A second man appeared at his side. This one was dressed in the skin of a jaguar, wearing the jaguar's head like a kind of hat. This did not bode well. John growled at both men fiercely and lashed out with his claws. The man wearing the white mask waved a club in the air. The club was black and shaped like a piranha. The man held it by the tail. The head was fatter than the tail and full of small sharp teeth. The club disappeared behind the man's head and then reappeared suddenly again. John felt a sharp blow on his head that left him stunned. The white mask came closer now and the big red grin painted on it seemed to defy all John's earlier resistance. Behind the mask there was loud and mocking laughter. John closed his eyes and then all was black and silent.

When John recovered consciousness, he found himself upside down with all four of his paws tied to a length of wood and being carried through the jungle by two Indians. He was sensible enough to play dead. This wasn't so difficult since there was a pain in his head that made him think it might be better if they didn't hit him with that club again. So he let his long tail and his head hang loose and tried to make a plan about what to do. Did they think that they had killed him? And if so, did that mean they had killed Nimrod? It was hard to understand very much at all when his world view was upside down and the language around him was one he had never heard before. But at last it had stopped raining.

As they reached the Indian village, he arrived at some idea of what his next course of action might be. And letting his djinn spirit slip out of the jaguar's body he floated invisibly at one side of the trail and took stock of their situation. The other jaguar that was Nimrod was similarly trussed and insensible and being carried on the pole behind. John slid into the second jaguar's body and was relieved to find his uncle alive but still unconscious. He was enormously relieved because his first thought had been that Nimrod was dead.

Finding that there was nothing he could do for him, John lifted his disembodied form out of the other jaguar and, having made a careful note of where the village was located, he retraced his spiritual steps to the place in the forest where he had been captured. From there he quickly found his way back to the tree where Nimrod had left his travel lamp.

The moment John was possessed of his own atoms again he transubstantiated himself and, with Nimrod's lamp now safely in his hands, he returned to the camp where they had left the others, to get some help in mounting a rescue. He was sure Mr. Vodyannoy would know exactly what to do, and that Sicky would know who these Indians were.

Muddy's dog, Hector, stepped out of the bushes where he had been hiding and, whimpering piteously, came up to John and licked his hand. But of Philippa and the others there was no sign. The backpacks were still there but the fire was quite cold and the tents showed signs of having been attacked by some kind of wild animal. There was no blood, however, and no other signs of an attack.

"What happened here, boy?" John asked, folding the dog's ears affectionately.

Hector looked around and barked.

"What was it this time? A giant sloth? A giant alligator, perhaps?"

And then he saw them.

In a shallow grave, covered with tree branches and leaves, as if someone had tried to bury them in a hurry, lay three stone statues of Indians. John realized first that these were different, rather fiercer-looking Indians than the ones who had captured Nimrod and himself; then he realized that the most probable cause of how three stone statues came to be there at all was the tattoo on Sicky's stomach. John thought that Sicky must have tried to defend the others against an attack. The question was, had Sicky done enough to drive them off? And if so, where were the others now?

"Did they run away?" John asked Hector. "Did they get away in the boats? Let's go and look."

John walked down to the riverbank and found the boats remained beached and quite undamaged, and with all of the equipment and gear still in camp it was clear to John that the rest of the party must have been taken prisoner. He would have shouted out to them but for the fact that he didn't want to get captured again, and by a different tribe of Indians. Obviously, he was going to have to mount some kind of rescue. But who was he going to rescue first? Nimrod? Or his sister and the others?

"What am I going to do?" he asked Hector anxiously.

Hector whined and licked John's face encouragingly.

Sick with worry, John pushed Hector away and tried to concentrate his thoughts in case djinn power presented some obvious solution. It didn't. But the still-vivid memory of the fact that one of the Indians who had captured his uncle had been wearing the skin of a jaguar helped John to decide the matter. He would try to rescue Nimrod first. After all, John could hardly be sure that Nimrod might not be skinned himself. Perhaps his uncle would revive and slip out of the jaguar as John had done, but the boy djinn decided he could not afford to wait and take that chance.

And a plan presented itself in his mind. Looking at Hector, he saw how a dog — even a dog carrying a magic lamp in its mouth — might walk around the Indian village unnoticed, at least for as long as it took to work out exactly how to rescue Nimrod. Becoming a dog so soon after he had been a jaguar was not an attractive proposition. He was tired of being an animal. His mouth still tasted horribly of raw turtle and snake's blood. But he could see no alternative.

John was on the very point of transubstantiating and then slipping inside Hector when something flew through the air and landed on Zadie's backpack. It was Zotz, her adopted pet bat and, noticing something shiny around Zotz's leg, he went over to take a closer look at it. But when he tried to pick up the bat to see what this might be, the bat took to the air and circled the camp for a minute or two before landing once again. This happened several times before John hit on the idea of feeding it some banana and, in this way, he was at last able to take hold of the creature and remove the metallic object from its leg.

It was a tube, in diameter about as big as a nickel, and in length about as long as a paper clip. Inside was a piece of rolled-up paper. John slid the paper out.

"I've heard of homing pigeons," he told the bat as he placed it back onto Zadie's pack. "But never a homing bat."

The message, addressed to Zadie, left the boy djinn feeling utterly astonished.

John learned nothing about what had happened to his friends from being inside Hector — only that it was Muddy's dog himself who was responsible for chewing the tents, and that following a beating from his master when this had been discovered, he'd run off before the second tribe of Indians had turned up.

Carrying Nimrod's travel lamp partly hidden in his mouth, John followed the trail all the way back through the jungle to the Indian village where he had left Nimrod. There he walked almost invisibly among the local people. As he had suspected, no one paid much attention to yet another stray dog.

The village was — most of it — a series of longhouses built on stilts, and occupied a clearing in the forest on the edge of a fast-moving river. Some of the Indians lived here, but others lived in the wreck of an old steamship that was located halfway up a hillside, as if stranded there by some freak storm. Two stories tall and about sixty feet in length, it was the kind of vessel that belonged properly on the Mississippi River but, overgrown with creepers and overrun with children and chickens, it looked as if it had been there for a very long time.

Much more recent was the presence of the dead body of the giant anaconda. This had been carried into the village by other members of the tribe and was now laid out lengthwise alongside the steamship, which gave a better idea of its size.

Seeing the snake in daylight, John wondered just how he and Nimrod had ever contemplated fighting such an enormous creature. The snake was slightly longer than the ship and as thick as a tree trunk. The Indians also seemed properly impressed by the snake but even more so by the two *otorongos* that, they surmised, must somehow have killed it. It seemed these were being held in a small stockade in the center of the village and treated as something holy. Led by the man wearing the jaguar skin, who appeared to be some kind of witch doctor, a group of warriors were kneeling around the stockade and, as far as John could tell, they were now worshipping the two jaguars.

John went over to take a closer look and was horrified to discover that only one of the jaguars was standing up and walking around; the other one — the one that contained Nimrod — was already dead. Its pink tongue lolling out of its mouth, the jaguar lay on the ground with a rigidity that was all too eloquent. John swallowed a large lump of emotion. If the jaguar was dead, did that mean Nimrod was dead, too? John recognized that he was going to have to enter the stockade and find out for sure.

Almost as bad was the realization that their ceremony of worship now completed, the Indians seemed to be getting ready to kill the second jaguar. They were fitting arrows to their bowstrings as if preparing to sacrifice the big cat to whatever god it was they believed in.

Someone threw a stone at Hector to drive him off, but realizing that there was no time to lose, John ignored the pain and stood his ground. There wasn't going to be any time to be subtle about this manifestation of djinn power, he told himself. He was just going to have to do what he had to do regardless of the superstitions and beliefs of the Indians. The Indians, he felt, were about to get a probably well-deserved fright.

John dropped the travel lamp onto the ground and, lifting his spirit out of the dog, reentered the lamp to pick up the atoms he needed to effect transubstantiation. It was impossible to tell from the parts of himself that Nimrod had left behind if he was alive or not. He looked like a very lifelike statue. John stared at his uncle for a moment, as if reminding himself of how important he was to him, and then hurried out of the bottle in an extra-large cloud of smoke. It was extra-large because he wanted to make quite sure it drove away all of the Indians from the stockade. Even as he was still making himself flesh, he could tell that he had succeeded. Shouting loudly and gesticulating wildly, the Indians were already running away to what they considered to be a safe distance. Only Hector stayed put. Recognizing John, the dog licked his hand fondly before staring crossly at the Indians. Most of these were now hiding underneath the longhouses or on the upper tier of the steamboat, and pointing excitedly at John.

John picked up the travel lamp and was about to jump into the stockade when a voice said, "I wouldn't do that if I were you. That's a jaguar in there. And they're none too friendly when they're being held prisoner."

"Nimrod?" John grinned with relief and glanced around. Seeing nothing, he guessed that Nimrod was still in his spiritual form. "Is that really you?"

"Who do you think it is? A ghost? I saw your smoke and guessed you must be here with the lamp. And not a moment too soon."

"I was worried when I saw that dead jaguar."

"Yes. One of those chaps hit the poor beast a little too hard. Pity, really. He was a fine fellow. Anyway, I got inside the other jaguar and, finding you weren't there, reasoned you must have gone back for the lamp. I was just about to skedaddle out of him, too, when you turned up."

"And you're all right?"

"I'm fine. I have a sore head but that will feel better the moment I'm back in my own body. So, if you'll forgive me, I'll go and take care of that and be back in a moment."

"Yes. Sure. Go ahead. Be my guest."

John felt something move inside the lamp and put it down on the ground while Nimrod went about reentering the lamp to reclaim his human shape. At the sight of yet more smoke emanating from the lamp, the Indians started shouting again, and it was clear to John that they were terribly frightened.

"Serves you right," John shouted at them. "That'll teach you to go around hitting defenseless jaguars on the head, shooting arrows at them and throwing stones at little dogs."

Hector barked at the Indians in complete agreement. Now that he had his body back, he was feeling the pain of the stone that had hit him on the side.

"And as for headhunting," added John, "that really is totally unacceptable."

"They're not headhunters," said Nimrod, finally appearing in the flesh out of a cloud of smoke. "And, really not such a bad lot, either. These are Prozuanaci Indians. The same tribe as Sicky. Very different from the Xuanaci. It's not their fault. They're just a bit excited about what happened to that anaconda. You see, they worship a god who looks like a snake." Nimrod smiled awkwardly. "Or at least they did. Look."

A large crowd of Indians was now approaching on their hands and knees.

"I think we're about to be worshipped," he said.

"Cool," said John.

"No, it's not cool at all," said Nimrod, and tutted loudly. "This is so embarrassing. I do hate it when people mistake me for a god. Of course, it's inevitable when we're obliged to perform transubstantiation in the open. I mean, for them we're the nearest thing to a god they've probably ever seen."

"Sorry about that," said John. "But there didn't seem to be time to do anything more subtle."

"No need to apologize, dear boy. It can't be helped. These things happen. Still, we'd best get out of here before this gets really serious. Offerings and sacrifices and that kind of thing. Heaven forbid that they should start another religion. We've got quite enough of those already." Nimrod was already walking toward the jungle.

"Wait," said John. "What about the jaguar? We can hardly leave him there to get killed like his poor brother."

"No, you're right. Not after all he did for us." Nimrod urgently waved at John. "Well, do it, boy, do it. You have the power."

John nodded and, muttering his focus word, which was ABECEDARIAN, he made the stockade enclosing the big cat vanish in a purple puff of smoke. Hardly believing its luck, the jaguar galloped into the jungle without a backward glance at the now prostrate and loudly wailing Indians.

"Why the purple smoke?" Nimrod asked John.

"Because I still think they need to be taught a lesson," answered John.

Nimrod shook his head with disapproval. "I told you," he said. "They're not such a bad lot, the Prozuanaci." He turned on his heel and walked on.

John went running after him, followed closely by Hector the dog. "By the way," said John. "I've got something important and extremely worrying to tell you. Philippa and Groanin and Mr. Vodyannoy and the others. They've gone. Disappeared without a trace. If these are the Prozuanaci, then I think they've been captured by some other Indians. I found stone statues of three Indians near our camp; they were covered with leaves. My guess is that Sicky showed them the tattoo on his belly. The one that turns living things that look at it to stone? Like Medusa, the Gorgon? And that their friends tried to bury them where they were because they were too heavy to carry back home."

"Is that so?" said Nimrod, quickening his pace. "That's not good."

"And that's just the half of it," John said urgently. "I also need to tell you about Zadie. She's a traitor. She's the one who's been making all these giant-sized animals."

"Are you sure?" asked Nimrod.

John told him about the message he'd found on the leg of Zadie's bat.

"And you'll never guess who the message was from," added John. "Virgil McCreeby."

CHAPTER 11

THE PIRANHA POOL

"At least it's stopped raining," observed Groanin.

"I don't see how that helps our situation," said Zadie through chattering teeth. "We're still cold and wet. Too cold and wet to use our power to get out of here."

This was undeniable. With the exception of Sicky, they were all imprisoned in a wooden cage that was partly underwater in a large cave that overlooked the Xuanaci village. Fed by a mountain stream, the water in the cave pool was freezing.

"Do you think they know?" Philippa asked Zadie. "About djinn being made of fire? And that younger ones like us are powerless when we're cold?"

"I don't know," said Zadie, and told herself it hardly mattered since soon enough Virgil McCreeby would surely realize what had happened and come and rescue her. After all that she had done to help McCreeby's expedition — the gigantist binding on Sicky's centipede and the mosquitoes, and then the anaconda, to say nothing of the poison frog she had put in Mr. Vodyannoy's camp bed — they simply had to come.

"They'll come soon," she muttered through cold, clenched teeth. "They'll come. They have to."

"Yes, well, let's hope they do," said Groanin, who presumed wrongly that Zadie was talking about Nimrod and John. "Otherwise some of us will be shorter by a head. Like those poor blighters on the wall."

Groanin nodded up at a collection of shrunken human heads that was hanging on the cave wall immediately above Sicky and the box containing Pizarro's skull. Sicky himself had been tied up and placed inside a sack, which was a wise precaution given the terrible, medusan properties of the tattoo on his belly. It seemed that the Xuanaci had no wish to be turned into stone statues of themselves.

"I don't think that's what they've got planned for us, Mr. Groanin," said Muddy. "There's no honor in taking a bald head or a girl's head. Not for proud warriors like the Xuanaci. No, I'm thinking we've got only half of this pool to ourselves. There's a wooden barrier dividing it in two. See? Only it's more like a sliding door that can be opened."

"Yes, I was wondering about that," admitted Groanin, peering over the wooden barrier into the water. "The water on the other side appears to be quite warm. I can feel it on my face."

"If only we were in that half of the pool," said Philippa. "Then we could be warm and use djinn power to get ourselves out of here."

"If we were in that half of the pool, we'd be dead," said Muddy.

"How's that?" asked Philippa.

"The other half of the pool is filled with piranha," Muddy explained.

"You what?" exclaimed Groanin.

"A fish with an appetite for meat that's as big as its teeth," said Muddy. "Word *piranha* means 'fish with teeth.' A school of the biggest piranha can eat a living cow in minutes. Like shearing a sheep."

"I know what piranha are," moaned Groanin. He glanced over the barrier and then at Muddy. "Are you quite sure about that, pal? You're not just winding me up? I mean, the water looks peaceful enough. Doesn't it?"

"At first I wasn't sure," said Muddy. "Then a few minutes ago, I saw something come up and look at me, like it was me looking at fish in a restaurant."

But Groanin wasn't yet convinced. "You're joking," he said.

"No joking."

Muddy leaned over the barrier, spat copiously into the warmer water and, for a fleeting moment, Groanin was reminded horribly of the disgusting way that Muddy made *chichai* beer. But the very next second, several sets of extremely sharp teeth rose to the surface and began to chew the air expectantly. Hundreds of other fish quickly joined them so that the water almost seemed to be boiling with fish.

"See?" said Muddy.

"Flipping heck," yelled Groanin. "Here. You don't think they mean to — to slide open that door, and let them lunch on us, do you?"

"I reckon that's the idea," said Muddy. He thought for a moment and then sighed. "You know? Is a pity we are on the menu and not them. Piranha is pretty good eating fish. In my time I cooked and ate plenty." He laughed almost philo-sophically. "I guess it's their turn now."

Groanin gulped loudly. "If I ever get out of this, I swear I'll never eat fish and chips again."

While Muddy and Groanin had been discussing the prox-imity of the piranha, Philippa had been paying more attention to their surroundings. The unguarded cave was illuminated by a burning torch on the wall.

"If we could only get to that torch," she said. "We could make a fire and warm ourselves up." She looked at Groanin. "How's that superstrong arm of yours, Mr. Groanin? Do you think you could break open the door of this cage?"

"I already tried, miss," Groanin said ruefully. "But what-ever this enclosure is made of, it's too strong for me." As if to demonstrate the hopelessness of the task she was suggest-ing, he took hold of the cage and attempted, without success, to pull two of the bars apart.

"It's lignum vitae," said Muddy. "A local wood that's almost as strong as metal."

Philippa examined the material that lashed the wooden struts of the cage together. "And what is this cord made of?" she asked Muddy.

"Is made from plaited leaves of coconut palm," said Muddy.

She nodded.

"Now all we need is a saw," muttered Zadie.

"We already have a saw," said Philippa. "In fact, we have hundreds of them." She pointed at the other half of the pool where the piranha were at last beginning to calm down. "All we have to do is to persuade them to start work. And, like any other workers, all they need is an incentive."

"Is that a joke?" asked Zadie. "If so, it's not a very funny one."

"It's no joke," insisted Philippa. "I was thinking that a little blood dropped onto those cords lashing the wooden bars together just above the water line might persuade them to start biting."

Groanin inspected the bars and nodded. "By heck, you're right, miss," he said. "It might just work, at that. With their razor-sharp teeth they could gnaw through them bindings in no time. And then I might push these bars apart."

"Exactly," said Philippa.

"In the absence of another plan," said Muddy, "the ingenuity of using piranha teeth to get us out of this cage is terrific. Not to say, most ironic."

"I think it's a preposterous idea," scoffed Zadie.

"The only question," said Philippa, ignoring her fellow female djinn, "is where we are going to get a supply of blood. Does anyone have a pin? Or some other small sharp object?"

"You mean something other than Miss Zadie's tongue?" Groanin asked.

"Very funny," sneered Zadie, who was feeling too cold and guilty to have much of a sense of humor.

But no one had anything small and sharp.

"How are we going to get blood if we don't have a pin?" demanded Zadie.

"I've an idea," said Muddy. "Mr. Groanin. You must please to punch me on the nose, please."

Groanin winced. "I couldn't possibly, old chap," he said. "I say, I couldn't possibly punch you on the nose."

"Sure you can," said Muddy, and pushed his face toward Groanin. "Nothing to it. You just gotta punch me. You know how to punch me, don't ya? You just put your fingers together, make a fist, and land me a blow." He closed his eyes. "Come on, Mr. Groanin. Punch me on the nose."

Groanin made a fist and looked at Muddy uncertainly.

"I can't," he said. "I can't hit an unarmed man. It's just not British."

"Sure you can. Tell me. What soccer team do you like?"

"Manchester City, why?"

"Well, maybe if I insult you then maybe you'll find it easier to hit Muddy, yeah?" Muddy slapped Groanin lightly on the cheek. "Maybe then you can hit me, you stuck-up English slaphead. You pompous British donkey. You dumb ugly gringo, you." He slapped him again, a little harder this time. "And by the way, Manchester City is a really bad team. Next to Manchester United, they are a bunch of losers."

"Now steady on, Muddy," said Groanin, coloring a little. "You're talking about a great soccer team."

"Manchester City couldn't beat an old carpet," said Muddy. "Better hit me soon, old-timer, or I'm going to hit you."

Groanin shook his head. "Still not working," he said.

And then Zadie punched Groanin hard, on the nose.

"Yaroo!" Groanin pressed both fingers to his nose. "What did you do that for? You daft bat."

"Zadie," said Philippa. "Why did you hit Mr. Groanin?"

"Why? To save time, that's why. All that polite English 'I couldn't hit you, Muddy, old chap.'"

Groanin touched his nose with his fingers and then looked at the blood on them. "Flipping heck," he said. "I think she broke my nose." He stared bitterly at Zadie. "No one could accuse you of being polite. You've been a right nuisance since you came along."

"What's done is done, I suppose," said Philippa, and helped the hapless English butler to direct some of the blood from his nose onto the plaited palm leaves lashing the wooden beams of the cage together.

The effect was electric, which is to say it was as if someone had directed a strong electric current into the water containing the school of ferocious piranha. One moment there was barely a ripple on the surface, and the next, it was as if the water itself had come alive and was tearing at the bloody lashings.

"I think that's enough blood," Philippa told Groanin.

"Right, miss." Groanin pinched his nose. But there was still so much blood flowing from his nostrils that it was impossible to stop more of it from dropping off his fingers and onto the sliding barrier separating them from the piranha fish. Instinctively, Groanin turned away and made his way to the opposite end of the pool. Yet more blood dropped into the water.

"I said that's enough," said Philippa.

"I can't help it, miss," said Groanin. "Only it seems to me that if she hadn't hit me quite so hard, I wouldn't be bleeding quite so bleeding much."

Muddy looked at the lashings on the wooden cage. "But it's working," he said. "Them fish are chewing up the bindings like it's fresh meat."

Philippa cheered.

"I hate to rain on your parade," said Zadie. "But it's not just the cage they're chewing. Look." She pointed at the wooden barrier separating them from the hungry piranha.

Muddy looked and then groaned. "She's right," he said. "They are chewing the bindings on the barrier, too."

"You mean the barrier that's keeping them piranha away from us?" Groanin asked through his bloody fingers.

"That's right. There's too much blood in the water. The craziness of these fish is terrific."

Experimentally, Philippa pressed lightly at the barrier. "The question is," she said. "Which is going to give first? The bindings on the cage or the bindings on the barrier."

"That's just marvelous," moaned Groanin. "To be fish food, at my age. I might have known something like this was going to happen when I came to South America."

The barrier shifted ominously.

"They'll be through in a minute," said Muddy.

"Quick, Groanin," said Philippa. "Have another try at pulling these bars apart."

"Very well, miss." Groanin took hold of the wooden bars and pulled. "They're shifting. Quick, Miss Philippa. Squeeze through."

But Zadie was there ahead of her, climbing up onto Groanin's shoulders without apology, and pulling herself through the wooden bars. Philippa quickly followed. The two girl djinn picked themselves off the cave floor and stared into the seething water.

The barrier shifted again.

"It looks like it's going to give at any moment," said Zadie. "I'd say you've got about sixty seconds to get your butts out of there before you're history."

"Go on, Muddy," Groanin shouted bravely, and pulled the bars again. "On you go."

Muddy scrambled through the wooden bars and slid onto the stone floor. As soon as he was on his feet he turned and took hold of the bars, holding them apart so that Groanin might escape. But he wasn't nearly as strong as Groanin. Few human men were.

"If your limey stomach wasn't so fat," said Zadie, "you would probably be out by now."

"I'll give you fat in a minute," said Groanin. He grunted as he pushed his head and shoulders through the bars.

At last the barrier gave way.

"Push, Groanin, push," shouted Philippa.

With a loud grunt, Groanin lifted himself up and out of the water. For a moment the bars seemed to tighten around his waist, before, with a superhuman effort, he pushed them down and then lifted his legs clear of the water and the piranha. All except one, which had a tight grip of his trousers and, it seemed, a small part of Groanin's behind.

"Yaroo!" yelled the butler as he rolled onto the floor.

Zadie bent down to observe the piranha more closely as, flapping like a letterbox in a strong breeze, the metallic-looking fish kept its jaws tight on what it had hoped would be its next meal.

"Don't just look at me like it's in an aquarium," said Groanin. "Get the brute off me."

Zadie stood up and turned away as if she cared nothing for the English butler's obvious discomfort. She walked to the edge of the cave and looked out. "Get it off yourself," she said.

Meanwhile Muddy kicked at the fish, which, like a cartoon bulldog, remained stubbornly attached to Groanin's substantial behind.

"Yaroo!" he yelled again as the piranha's prognathous bite tightened desperately.

Philippa fetched the burning torch down from the wall and, for a second, held it under the piranha's tail. Immediately, the fish let go and dropped onto the floor.

Groanin let out a breath and rubbed his backside painfully. "Thank you, miss." He looked irritably at the piranha, which now lay on the ground biting at thin air and then booted it across the cave. "Ugly nasty thing."

"I daresay the fish had the same thought," said Zadie, which earned her a look of reproach from the butler.

"That's a relief, I must say," said Groanin.

"I wouldn't start ringing any bells," said Zadie. "Those Indians are on their way back here. They must have heard you bellowing."

"I'm only human, you know," answered Groanin.

"Don't remind me," said Zadie.

Muddy ran to the edge of the cave and looked down a hill at the Xuanaci village. A large party of Xuanaci warriors was already coming up the hillside path. They were carrying spears and longbows. "She's right," he said. "We gotta do something quick before them Indians come up the hill."

Philippa was untying the sack in which Sicky lay, bound hand and foot. "Sicky's tattoo," she said. "The one on his belly. It turns anyone who looks at it to stone. Like the

Gorgon. They won't dare come up here if there's a risk of seeing that." She loosened the gag on Sicky's small mouth.

"Thank you, miss," he said.

"How do you feel, Sicky?" asked Philippa.

"Sick," he said, sitting up and untying his feet.

"Ask a silly question," said Zadie.

"But I'll be all right."

"Just tell him to bring his belly over here," said Zadie, tap-dancing on the floor nervously. "And quick."

"No good," said Sicky, and showed Philippa his belly. "I'm not well at all. Before they put me in the sack, the Xuanaci blindfolded themselves and covered my tattoo with liquid latex. Rubber. From the *Hevea* tree. It'll take ages to peel off."

"That's unfortunate," remarked Philippa. "Because it will take at least an hour to build a fire and get warm enough to have djinn power again."

"I hate to sound like I'm stating the obvious, but we don't have an hour." Zadie screamed and then ducked as an arrow and then a spear flew through the air and into the cave.

"She's right," said Sicky. "We gotta get out of this place. If it's the last thing we ever do."

"How I wish Pizarro and his whole army were here now," yelled Zadie. "To teach these horrible people a lesson they'd never forget."

Philippa picked up the torch and then retreated into the back of the cave. "Here," she cried. "This way. There's a kind of curtain in the rock."

She peered inside the fissure and saw that the torch had illuminated a steep natural stairway that was enclosed between narrow walls of cold damp rock. Philippa stepped inside. The others followed quickly. There was no time to debate where the passage might lead them.

At the bottom of the narrow stairway, Philippa scorched the wall with the torch. "In case we need to find our way back again," she said.

"I hardly think we'll want to come back this way," observed Zadie. "Not unless we want to wind up on the Xuanaci menu."

"We don't actually know that they're cannibals," said Philippa. Remembering that she had been completely wrong about headhunters, she glanced at Sicky and said, "Are they?"

"Not cannibals as such," he said. "Xuanaci like to eat raw piranha that have just feasted on living human flesh. This is why you were in the rock pool. Piranha stuffed with fresh human meat is a great delicacy for Xuanaci."

This made everyone hasten their steps even more, although there was no indication that they were being pursued.

"Why don't they come after us?" asked Groanin, looking around nervously. In a small backpack, the butler was carrying the box containing Pizarro's skull, which he'd grabbed just before leaving the cave, to avoid Nimrod — if he ever saw Nimrod again — scolding him for losing it a second time.

"Because we have the only torch," said Philippa, heading farther down into the secret depths of the cave and making another scorch mark on the wall. "They'll probably follow as soon as they've brought more light."

They wound this way and that and eventually found themselves descending a precipitous path into a spacious cavern from whose dripping ceiling hung virtual chandeliers of stalactites. Leaving this cavern, they progressed down to another cavern that was full of stalagmites growing out of the ground like so many stone trees. And beyond this, at an even deeper level, was a vast cavern where stalactites and stalagmites had come together in fantastic glittering pillars and in which everything was a shadow or a pool of darkness. The light from the burning torch in Philippa's hand seemed quite unequal to the task of illuminating the tomblike gloom. And now, for the first time since the excitement of their escape, the silence of these deep, underground caves laid a chill hand upon their spirits. It hadn't escaped anyone's attention that the light from the torch was getting smaller and that all too soon they would be in cold darkness.

"I was kind of hoping that we might find something to burn down here," Philippa said as they climbed down a new passageway. She put her finger in a freezing rock pool and tasted it carefully.

"Duh," said Zadie. "Most plants and trees that you could burn don't grow underground. Any fool knows that. And with nothing to burn, there's zero prospect of getting warm."

"I was thinking more of mineral deposits," admitted Philippa. "Oil or sulfur or coal."

Groanin shot Zadie a sarcastic smile. "See? She knows what she's doing."

"Unless we find a mineral deposit we should go back, and take our chances with the Xuanaci," said Zadie. "One chance in a hundred with them is better than no chance stumbling around in the darkness."

Sicky took the torch from Philippa and wrapped the sack he'd been tied up inside earlier on around the flame. "We can burn some of our clothes for a while," he said. "We can do that."

"And get even colder than I am now?" demanded Zadie. "I don't think so. I'd give anything for a nice hot bath."

"Wait a minute," said Philippa. "A hot bath. Yes. That's it. Maybe there is something we can do. Back at Mr. Vodyannoy's house, when John was attacked by that big cat in the hall of shadows, he put his hand in the fire and pulled out a burning log."

When Zadie failed to respond with anything more than a shrug, Philippa shook her head and said, "Don't you get it? He wasn't burned. Perhaps if, together, we sort of washed our hands in the flame of this torch we might get a bit of djinn power back."

"Have you ever done anything like that before?" asked Zadie.

"No," admitted Philippa.

"Well, then. It sounds a bit far-fetched to me."

"Why? We djinn are made of fire. Everyone knows that."

Philippa shrugged. "And what's the worst that could happen? We get our fingers burned."

Somewhere in the distance they heard a shout echoing through the caves. The Xuanaci were on their trail again.

"Better hurry up," said Muddy. He peeled off his T-shirt and wound it around the burning torch.

"Look, why do you need me to do it with you?" asked Zadie. "Why don't you do it yourself?"

"All right, I will," said Philippa, and sitting down on the cold stone floor of the cave, she rolled up her sleeves and cracked her knuckles, like a conjurer preparing to perform a magic trick.

Sicky sat down in front of her and held the torch out. "You sure you know what you're doing, miss?" he asked. "This fire burns small but still plenty hot."

And seeing it close up, Philippa was bound to agree with Sicky in one respect, at least. The flame probably wasn't going to last long enough for what she had in mind.

A shirt lasted hardly any time at all. They were going to have to burn something else as well. Something longer-lasting that gave a more even flame. But what?

"Here," said Groanin, guessing the reason that lay behind Philippa's hesitation. "Why not burn this?" He laid the antique wooden box, which he had been carrying, on the ground between them before opening it and removing the skull of the infamous conquistador, Francisco Pizarro.

"Good idea," said Zadie.

Philippa considered the idea for a moment. Something about the ancient box gave her pause. "I don't know," she said.

"It's just an old box," added Zadie. "What harm could it do?"

"All right," Philippa told Sicky. "Go ahead and set fire to it."

Sicky lit his vest and then laid the box on top of the burning cloth.

For a moment the box smoked mysteriously and started to burn with a small clear green flame. Philippa was about to take a deep breath in order to concentrate but was put off from doing so by a strong sulfurous smell — like the vague stink of rotten eggs — that now filled the cavern's air. She waved her hand in front of her nostrils.

"That wooden box is inlaid with cinnabar," said Groanin. "I'll bet that's what we smell."

Philippa nodded and, extending one hand, held it over the growing green flame.

"Ouch," said Muddy.

"Give over talking," said Groanin. "She needs to concentrate. I say, she needs to concentrate."

Philippa nodded her thanks silently and continued to hold her small hand above the flame. To look at, it remained the same. Her hand did not change color and blacken as a human hand would have. Nor was it an unpleasant sensation that she experienced. Already she felt nothing more than the molecules in her hand starting to buzz, as if she were holding a wire attached to an electric current. But it was not enough and so she clasped both her hands together as if washing them in the pungent green flame, in the hope that heating both hands at the same time would achieve the desired result. Closing her eyes she pictured the heat now coursing through her body and the warmer blood moving more quickly in her veins, and prayed that the heat might stir something deep inside her supernatural being. And yet it was not enough. The return of djinn power still eluded her.

"It's not working," muttered Philippa. "Quick, Zadie, give me your hands for a djinncantation. I need to harness your power to mine. Immediately."

"Yes, but what shall we wish for?"

"To find a way out of here, of course."

For once Zadie did as she was asked without an argument. And holding hands tightly in the green flame the two young djinn waited for some sensation that the spark of djinn power had been reignited deep inside them.

But instead of Zadie harnessing her power to Philippa's, it was Philippa who found her own power harnessed to Zadie's. And almost immediately a wish was granted. Abruptly, Zadie let go of Philippa's hands and stood up with a yell, aware that power had been and gone, albeit in an instant. "No!" she said. "Not that. I didn't mean that."

At the same moment, Philippa felt an almost insignificant bat-squeak of power herself and quickly wished for a flashlight. Almost immediately a flashlight duly appeared. It was not much of a wish. It was not much of a flashlight. But it was all that Philippa was able to manage with just the thin sliver of djinn power that had been left to her by Zadie. Something else — another stronger, more powerful wish — had taken precedence and vacuumed up all the djinn power that she and Zadie had manufactured in the heat of the now spluttering green flame.

"What happened?" asked Philippa.

"The power went out of me before I could stop it," Zadie said forlornly.

"Yes, but what happened?"

Zadie shook her head. "It wasn't my fault," she insisted. "I must have wished for something a while ago. It was a simple case of earlier wish fulfillment."

"But what did you wish for?" demanded Philippa.

"I don't know," said Zadie. "I've forgotten."

"You great Sammy," said Groanin, and pointed at the box. The flame had gone out and it seemed unlikely that they would manage to kindle it again.

"Something happened," said Philippa. "I felt a surge of power. A wish got granted. Quite a big wish."

"Er, I think I know what she wished for," said Sicky, nervously pointing behind them.

Pizarro's skull was no longer just a skull. It had become something much more than just yellowing bone and ivory-colored teeth. It had become a tall, sinewy, yellowing man of about sixty years of age, with hollow cheeks and a thin gray beard. He wore an ancient steel helmet and a rather battered-looking breastplate, but the edge on his sword looked keen enough. This unexpected result would have been quite bad enough, but even while they watched yet more Spanish conquistadors and several dozen horses began to appear inside the underground cavern.

"It's almost as if an army is being assembled," observed Philippa.

"Blimey," said Groanin. "That's it. I remember what it was that daft bat wished for now. It was back in the cave when the Xuanaci were chucking spears at us. I heard Zadie wish that Pizarro and his whole army could be here now to teach them Indians a lesson they'd never forget. And now here they all are."

CHAPTER 12

GIVE A LITTLE WHISTLE

Back at the deserted camp, John handed Nimrod the message from Virgil McCreeby he had taken from Zadie's pet bat, Zotz, which was still clinging to her backpack.

Nimrod read the message and then read it again. Then he read it aloud:

ZADIE.

YOUR MONSTER CENTIPEDES, MOSQUITOES, AND SNAKES ARE MUCH APPRECIATED BY US AND WILL CERTAINLY HELP TO SLOW NIMROD UP A BIT.

OF COURSE, IT IS TO BE EXPECTED THAT HE OR MR. VODYANNOY WILL DEFEAT WHATEVER YOU CAN THROW AT THEM. AFTER ALL, THEY ARE POWERFUL DJINN.

BUT THE CONFUSION CREATED BY YOUR OWN POWERS SHOULD BE ENOUGH FOR YOU TO GET THE MAP AWAY FROM MR. VODYANNOY.

I AM VERY RELIEVED TO HEAR THAT YOU MANAGED
TO BRING THE TEARS OF THE SUN. YOU WILL REMEM-
BER THAT BOTH THESE AND THE MAP ARE ESSENTIAL
TO OUR [5]NAL PURPOSE.
VIRGIL MCCREEBY.

"You see?" said John. "What did I tell you?"

"Yes," agreed Nimrod. "It's disappointing."

"Disappointing?" John shrugged. "I'd call that an under-
statement. Still, I guess it explains why she wanted to come
along on this expedition. She's been working for Virgil
McCreeby all along."

"It looks that way," agreed Nimrod. "I suppose we'd better check to see if the map is still there."

Virgil McCreeby was an unscrupulous and unprincipled
English magus whom John and Nimrod had met before. He
was also the father of Finlay McCreeby, his estranged son,
who John regarded as one of his closest mundane friends.

John was already searching Mr. Vodyannoy's backpack.
"It's gone," he said.

"Let us hope that Frank has it on his person," said
Nimrod. "However, I do fear the worst."

He placed McCreeby's message in his pocket before
examining the three stone statues, especially their feet.

"I'm afraid that these are Xuanaci warriors, all right," he
pronounced finally. "Each of them has the scar of a letter X
on his heel. Sicky told me that this is a distinctive characteristic of the Xuanaci tribe. They make this mark so as not to

confuse the footprints of other men they might be tracking, with their own."

"Then we have to mount a rescue," said John.

Nimrod said nothing.

"They're headhunters. We have to go after them."

"All in good time," said Nimrod. "First we have to establish why three djinn were unable to protect themselves."

"That's easy," said John, and pointed at Hector. "Muddy's dog chewed up the tents, which then let in water during last night's heavy rain. They all got wet and were probably too cold to use djinn power when the Xuanaci turned up."

"While that might certainly be true of immature djinn like Philippa and Zadie," said Nimrod, "it doesn't explain why someone of Mr. Vodyannoy's age and experience failed to protect everyone from an attack. He would have to have been very cold indeed for his djinn power to have deserted him."

"That's right," said John. "What happened to Mr. V?"

"As I see it there are three possibilities," said Nimrod. "He abandoned his fellow travelers. He was murdered by someone. Or he was incapacitated by someone. Since I know Mr. Vodyannoy to be a djinn of some courage and resourcefulness, I must discount the first possibility. That leaves the second two possibilities. If he had died here, however, the Xuanaci would probably have taken his head as a trophy and, of course, we would have found his body. This leaves only the third possibility. That in some way Mr. Vodyannoy was incapacitated by Zadie. Perhaps, so that she might steal the map from him."

Nimrod and John glanced around Mr. Vodyannoy's tent.

"Maybe she put a djinn binding on him while he was asleep," offered John.

"I fear it was not a binding that she put on him, John," Nimrod said quietly. "QWERTYUIOP!" A thin latex glove appeared on the older djinn's hand even as he bent down to pick up a small yellow object he had spotted underneath Mr. Vodyannoy's camp bed. "I strongly suspect that she put this on him. A poisonous arrow frog. One of the most deadly creatures in all of South America. Any mundane man probably would have been killed by skin contact with this little creature. And while it wouldn't have killed him, even a powerful djinn like Mr. Vodyannoy would have been made very seriously ill if, as I think, it was placed on his head or chest." Nimrod put the frog on the ground and carefully peeled off his glove.

"It's true, I don't like Zadie all that much," admitted John. "Especially now in light of McCreeby's message. But I find it hard to believe she could have done something so wicked. I mean, she's from a respectable family. From a good tribe."

"What you say is quite true," said Nimrod. "But if Zadie does turn out to be responsible I'm sure it will be discovered that she has been acting under McCreeby's influence. McCreeby is without question a powerful magus and a hypnotist of some considerable skill. Let us ask Mr. Vodyannoy. I'm sure he'll be able to tell us what we want to know."

John glanced around. "You mean he's here? I thought he must have been captured, like the others."

"I think not." Nimrod delved inside Mr. Vodyannoy's backpack and took out the black Fabergé bottle decorated with solid-gold filigree. "I imagine he's inside this. Light my lamp, that's where I'd go if a poisonous frog had crawled all over me. You wouldn't see me for smoke. Indeed, it might be the only way he could survive such a terrible experience."

Nimrod disappeared inside the lamp to look for Mr. Vodyannoy, leaving John alone again. Hearing himself blamed once again for damaging the tents, Hector had skulked off into the bushes. And wondering what to do with himself, John started to search Zadie's backpack in the hope that he might find other messages from McCreeby and that these in turn might provide some further clue as to why she had betrayed her own kind and her friends. For John had not yet quite overcome his dislike of Zadie enough to accept the idea that she had indeed been hypnotized.

As he searched Zadie's things, the primordial quiet was pierced by the sound of someone expertly whistling a carefree, plangent tune, a hauntingly rapturous, inspired human sound that floated through the forest glade like a beautiful, summery, magic spell.

John stood up and listened. How he had always wanted to be able to whistle like that! It was hardly the kind of tune an Indian would have known, surely. And it certainly couldn't have been a bird. Not even a bird of paradise could have mastered a melody like that; there must have been at least nine notes in the tune, which was whistled perfectly, and with tremolos, too. So, who could it be? Sicky? Muddy? Zadie, perhaps?

He was reluctant to break the spell of the catchy tune but, eventually, John called out, "Hello? Who's there?"

The beautiful whistling stopped.

Picking up Sicky's machete, John slashed at some bushes and advanced into the forest. "Hello?" he repeated loudly. "Who's there? Come out and show yourselves."

Working his way around the perimeter of the camp, John came back to where he had started from, and cocking one ear he listened closely, hoping to hear the whistle again. All he could hear was the myriad sound of the birds twittering tunelessly, monkeys laughing like hyenas, frogs creaking like old ropes, and insects whirring like dozens of small clockwork toys. He might have used djinn power except he couldn't think what to wish for that could possibly have enabled him to determine the source of the whistling. As Mr. Rakshasas had been fond of saying: "Sure, knowing *what* to wish for is half of it."

Had he imagined it? He was beginning to realize just what a strange place the rain forest really was and how your mind could play tricks on you: sticks that turned out to be insects, leaves that turned out to be lizards, logs that turned out to be alligators. John had even heard of a fish called the corvina that came to the surface of the water to eat fruit and make a bizarre chirping sound. He listened again.

Maybe it had been a bird after all. Some of the birds looked extraordinary. Was it so hard to imagine that they might have sounded extraordinary, too? Even though it was broad daylight, John felt a little unnerved by what he had heard. And very alone. John shook his head and went back to searching Zadie's backpack.

He found no more messages from McCreeby, only a little notebook of canary-colored onionskin paper that she must have used for writing her own messages and, right at the bottom of the backpack, something that pricked John's curiosity. Sealed in a glass jelly jar, and just a little smaller in diameter than the lid, were three gold disks. John opened the jar and, kneeling down, emptied the disks onto the ground before picking one of them up. It was thicker than a quarter — about as thick as two or three quarters — and heavy. Very heavy. He stayed there looking at them for a while wondering what they were. They weren't coins or medals or plates. On each side were the faces of some Indian men — one of them very fierce-looking. He guessed they were possibly Incan but he wasn't even sure of that.

"Found something?" It was Nimrod, returned from his visit to the interior of Mr. Vodyannoy's lamp.

"These were in Zadie's backpack." John showed Nimrod the onionskin and the three gold disks.

"Interesting," said Nimrod, weighing one in his hand. "I've never come across gold that was quite as heavy as this." He turned one disk over in his fingers. "Supay the Incan god of death on one side, and Inti, the sun god on the other. That's unusual, too."

"What is?" asked John.

"To have the sun and death on the same artifact."

"Well," suggested John. "The sun gives life, doesn't it? So life and death. Aren't they just opposite sides of the same coin?"

"What you say makes sense," said Nimrod. "But look how one disk fits into another and how both fit into the third. It's almost as if they were meant to show that the sun and death were one and the same. That's what's unusual. I imagine that these must be the tears of the sun that McCreeby's message talks about. The Incas actually called gold the 'sweat of the sun.'"

"I guess we now know the true identity of the person who robbed the Peabody Museum in New Haven," said John.

"Of course," said Nimrod. "There were three golden disks stolen, weren't there? I'd quite forgotten about those."

"It wasn't Manco Capac who stole them at all."

"I think all he wanted was his mummy back," said Nimrod. "Yes, you're quite right, John, it must have been Zadie who stole them." He nodded back at Mr. Vodyannoy's black bottle. "Just as it was Zadie who tried to kill Mr. Vodyannoy. He told me just now that he woke up and found her in his tent. She said that she had been sleepwalking. Mr. Vodyannoy said she went back to her tent and that he didn't think any more about it at the time. But now, he's pretty sure she was wearing gloves. And that it must have been she who put the frog in his bed."

"How is he?" John asked anxiously.

"Really quite ill."

"Shouldn't we get him to a hospital?"

"And what could they do? Hospitals are for people, John. Not djinn. No, with warmth and rest, he'll recover. Eventually. When a djinn gets as sick as that, there's not much that can be done that he or she can't do for himself. He will have to stay there in his lamp for a good while longer, until he's rekindled his life force. Which might take several weeks. I'm afraid we've seen the last of him on this expedition."

"And does he have the map?"

"No. I'm afraid he doesn't."

"Then Zadie must have it."

"I fear so. But I am quite convinced she has been hypnotized. I cannot believe there is any other way she would ever have tried to murder Mr. Vodyannoy. For that matter, nor can he."

"So, what are we going to do?" asked John. "How will we find our way to the Eye of the Forest without the map?"

Nimrod tapped his forehead. "Fortunately, I have already memorized it."

"That's a relief."

"The message tube around the bat's leg," said Nimrod. "Did you keep it?"

"Of course." John retrieved it from his own pack and handed it to Nimrod.

"Excellent." Nimrod opened the little onionskin note-book and, taking out a pen, began to write. "We shall send our own message to McCreeby. As if it had been written by his young female accomplice. I think I can reproduce Zadie's hand accurately enough. She writes in capital letters, does she not?"

"That's right. With circles for dots and lots of fat curlicues."

"This sort of writing usually signifies a certain lack of confidence," said Nimrod. "Perhaps even a kind of moronic ignorance. It is almost as bad as forgetting to use capital letters altogether. Although of course there are some alphabets that have no capital letters. Hebrew, for example."

"Sometimes she draws hearts instead of circles. Like maybe she was in love with someone."

"Does she?" Nimrod said thoughtfully. "That is perhaps another indication that she has been hypnotized."

"What are you going to tell him? McCreeby."

"Only that we are all dead except her. Something that will serve to make him feel overconfident. And that he should now tell Zadie precisely where he is so that she can come and find them."

John grinned and, while Nimrod wrote the message, he tried not to think about the fact that his sister and Groanin and Sicky and Muddy — and quite possibly Zadie herself — were in the hands of the Xuanaci Indians. To keep up his spirits he started to whistle. The very same catchy tune he had heard just a few minutes before.

Nimrod carried on writing but spoke up with disapproval in his voice. "My dear young fellow. Didn't Sicky tell you? You must never, ever whistle in the rain forest. It is said that if you ever chime in by whistling the exact same tune as *el Tunchi*, then he will appear to you and play with you in a most horrible way."

John gulped. "Who or what is *el Tunchi*?"

"A spirit that protects the forest," said Nimrod. "A nasty mischievous spirit. Like a sort of poltergeist, I suppose. Only much, much worse. Or so I'm told. Just be careful, John. All right?" Nimrod looked up. "John?"

But John had disappeared.

CHAPTER 13

THE RETURN OF
THE CONQUERORS

Groanin had been right when he said that Francisco Pizarro had come back to life with his whole army. Because of Zadie's careless wish, the underground cavern where the party comprising Philippa, Groanin, Zadie, Sicky, and Muddy had taken refuge after their escape from the Xuanaci was now filled with one hundred and sixty-eight men at arms, sixty-two horses, and several Roman Catholic priests. This was the exact number of men and horses (and priests) with which Pizarro had conquered the Incas in September of 1532.

The Spaniards did not seem to need the light. They worked in darkness for it was from darkness they had come. And already they seemed intent on carrying out the second part of Zadie's wish, which was that they should teach the Xuanaci a lesson. And since there was only one kind of lesson that these hard-bitten soldiers had ever been capable of teaching anyone, they were sharpening their swords, and tightening the buckles on their armor with the obvious intent of reenacting the whole brutal business that had been the conquest of the Incas. Except that this time it would be the Xuanaci who would be put to the sword. Nobody had any doubt that this would be the result. Pizarro's small, ragtag army had easily defeated an army of one hundred thousand Incas, and it seemed unlikely that a few hundred Xuanaci would fare any better.

"We've got to stop them," Philippa told Zadie. "Those poor Xuanaci don't stand a chance against these murderers. They'll be massacred. Just like the Incas."

Zadie snorted with laughter. "Those poor Xuanaci?" She sounded incredulous. "Philippa. Hello? Those poor Xuanaci as you call them were going to feed us to the piranhas. The Xuanaci are the same guys who shrank poor Sicky's head, while it was still on his shoulders." Zadie looked at Sicky as if in search of some support. "Tell her, Sicky. Tell her how you feel about the Xuanaci."

Sicky scratched his shrunken head. Undeniably the Xuanaci had shrunk it. "Sick," he said. "I feel sick about what they did to poor Sicky, sure." But he was not a vengeful man. And now that he thought about it, he could see the contest between the heavily armored Spaniards and the half-naked Indians would be a grossly unequal one. "Xuanaci are fierce people, right enough. But then so were the Jivaro. And before them, the Prozuanaci. All Indians of the Oriente are pretty fierce, one way or the other. But Xuanaci are just ignorant folk. They don't deserve to get themselves beat up by a bunch of conquistadors like them Incas. You gotta speak to this Pizarro fellow, Miss Zadie, and persuade him to forget about the Xuanaci."

"Well, I won't," Zadie said firmly. "It would serve those Xuanaci right if they got their butts kicked by these Spaniards."

"From the look of them," observed Groanin, "I think this lot are planning a bit more than just a bit of butt-kicking. They mean business. Nasty business. Look."

"You're exaggerating," said Zadie. "As usual."

The entire army, including Pizarro, was on its knees, and receiving the blessing of the priests so that what they were about to do might meet with favor in the eyes of God.

"That's what always happens before one lot of people go and massacre another lot," added Groanin. "They persuade themselves that it's the will of God or some such malarkey. You ask me, God wants nothing to do with folk who go around killing other folk in his good name."

"Mr. Groanin's right, Zadie," said Philippa. "We have to do something."

"Like what?" demanded Zadie.

"This is your mess," said Philippa. "It ought to be you who cleans it up."

Zadie shook her head stubbornly. "Do what you like," she said. "But I think you're making too much out of this. I certainly didn't wish for any massacre. Just that someone should teach these headhunters a lesson, that's all."

Philippa shook her head, utterly exasperated with the other djinn and now very much regretting having asked her along on the expedition. John had been right. She could see that. The next time — assuming there was a next time — she would listen to her twin brother.

"Very well," she said. "I'll speak to him myself. As soon as they're finished praying."

Philippa didn't speak Spanish and she rather doubted that before he had died, Pizarro had spoken any English. Nevertheless, her recent acquaintance with a reincarnation of the Italian explorer Marco Polo persuaded her that this wouldn't be a problem. "Death is the most important passport you can obtain," Marco had told Philippa. "When you die, all the mysteries are solved. Including that mystery that is how the English language works."

The old conquistador bowed politely as Philippa presented herself in front of him. "*Señorita*," he said. "I am greatly honored." He spoke quietly but firmly, like one who was used to being obeyed, and with a slight lisp.

Philippa smiled and bowed back. "Don Francisco," she said, minding her manners, for a Don was a kind of Spanish knight. "Yours is a famous name. Perhaps the most famous name in all of Peru. And, of course, it is a very famous name in . . . er, history."

Pizarro bowed again.

"Look here," said Philippa. "I'm afraid there's been a mistake. Of course, it's entirely our fault and please be so kind as to accept our sincerest apologies, but you see, it's like this: You're not required to teach the Xuanaci a lesson, after all. In fact, we'd much prefer it if you went back to wherever it is that you came from. And left them alone."

"I don't understand," said Pizarro. "A wish was made, was it not? We certainly wouldn't have come back, *uninvited.*"

"Yes, that is true," admitted Philippa. "However, it was a wish made without any thought for the consequences. Even the djinn make mistakes."

"Forgive me, a wish is a wish: As I see it, making a wish is like pouring good wine onto the ground. When you have already done that, then it's hard to pour it back into the bottle. Truly, *señorita,* I would like to accommodate you, but I very much regret I cannot." He shrugged. "Unless of course, you *wish* it so. That would be a very different matter, you being a djinn."

"But I do wish it," insisted Philippa. "Very much indeed. We all do."

Pizarro looked around him for a moment and then shrugged again. "And yet I and my men are still here, are we not? Forgive me, O great djinn, but if you really wished it, I suggest that we would no longer be here. Your own power would make it so. No?"

"Ah," said Philippa. "Good point. Let me explain. You see, the djinn are made of fire and since it's a bit cold down here we've been unable to get warm enough to work ourselves up to full power. In fact we were obliged to set fire to the wooden box that had contained your skull in order to warm our hands long enough to make just one wish. Which came out badly, as I think I've explained. My friend spoke too quickly, you see. It's true, the Xuanaci are a tiresome and unpleasant bunch, but we don't mean them any real harm. All I ask is that you wait a little before doing anything, well, drastic."

"You mean like teaching them a lesson?" Pizarro was sounding reasonable.

"Yes, that's right," said Philippa. "I knew you'd understand. I promise you that as soon as we get our power back, we'll wish things back to normal and —"

"I'm sorry," said Pizarro, "but you of all people should know that a wish can only be rescinded in the normal way. By a second, third, or fourth wish."

"Yes, normally that's true," said Philippa. "But please, can't you make an exception? Just this once."

"My dear *señorita*." Pizarro sounded almost kind. "I didn't make the rules. You did. Or rather your kind did, many years ago. Is it not so?"

Philippa stamped her foot in exasperation. "Oh, look, you're not really going to hurt anyone, are you?"

"That's normal procedure in these situations," said Pizarro.

"What, all of them?" said Groanin.

"Yes."

"Isn't that a bit excessive?"

"Of course it is. Most certainly. Now, if you'll forgive me. I have to get back to my men. We have a job to do."

"Wait a minute," Philippa said in desperation. "If you teach them a lesson they won't forget, then you can hardly kill them all, can you? I mean they'll only be in a position not to forget if some of them are alive and able to remember. Don't you agree?"

"You have a point," agreed Pizarro. "Then we will certainly leave some alive."

"At least the women and children," said Philippa.

Pizarro looked shocked. "*Señorita*," he said. "We are not barbarians."

Philippa turned away. "That's not what I've heard," she muttered.

"Now what?" asked Groanin.

"We have to get back aboveground and into the warmth, as quickly as possible," said Philippa. "To avert a massacre."

But the horses were already moving back up the natural stairway in the cavern, blocking the way Philippa and the others had come. It was clear they would have to try to find another route out of the caverns. Philippa picked up the little flashlight.

"Come on," she said grimly. "There's absolutely no time to lose."

Zadie snatched up the still-burning torch. She had other, selfish ideas about what to do next.

Philippa seized Zadie's hand and pulled her along into the first corridor that offered another way out of the cavern.

Zadie hadn't gone very far before she snatched her hand away and stood as still as a stalagmite. "I'm not coming," she said. "You've no idea where you're going. This could lead absolutely anywhere."

Philippa pointed the beam of the flashlight ahead. The light disturbed a couple dozen squadrons of bats that came toward them flying in close formation. Everyone dropped onto their knees. Everyone except Philippa. Beyond the rank stink of the bats' droppings on the cave floor she realized that she could feel a cool fresh breath of air on her face.

"I don't think so," said Philippa. "That breeze you can feel on your face? That has to be another way out. I'm sure of it. Trust me, Zadie."

"You're so wrong about this, Philippa. Look, I'm going back up with them. With Pizarro and his men. Back the way we came. I'll be outside in the sun and have my power back while you're still groping around down here like a bunch of stupid moles."

"You can't go with them," said Philippa.

"Look, I'm getting claustrophobic being down here, and that's the plain truth. I'll go out of my mind if I don't see the outside again soon."

This was true. All djinn suffer from claustrophobia, which comes from some of them being imprisoned in old lamps and bottles for years on end. But of course there was another reason why Zadie wanted to get back to the surface with Pizarro and his Spaniards. Now that she had the map showing the way to the Eye of the Forest, she wanted to make contact with Virgil McCreeby's expedition as quickly as possible. It was true, she didn't have the tears of the sun with her, but she couldn't help that. The gold disks were still in her backpack back at camp. But she supposed McCreeby would know what to do about that. He was a magus after all. And magi are nothing if not resourceful.

"You have to stay with us. Leaving by yourself? That is not a good idea, Zadie."

"Watch me," said Zadie, and stepped back into the shadows. The last word she spoke was "Sorry."

"Let her go," said Groanin.

"Zadie, come back," begged Philippa.

But Zadie was gone.

Reluctantly, Philippa let herself be hurried on by Groanin who was too diplomatic to say what he really thought, which was that he was more than a little glad Zadie had left.

Presently, they arrived in another cavern at a tiny trickle of a spring whose basin was encrusted with a scrambled egg of glittering yellow crystals — the same yellow crystals that covered the walls and the floor. The water in the crystal basin was hot. As hot as a cup of coffee. But there was not enough of it to return Philippa's djinn power. So they merely drank some of it without any apparent ill effect and then traversed a narrow ledge that led to the only route out of the cavern, and squeezed along a murky corridor into the secret depths of the caves.

All the time the breeze on their faces grew stronger so that now their sense that they were on the right route was ever increasing. Finally, they arrived at a gaping circular pit about fifty feet in diameter and from which a violent current of hot, sulfurous air rose from the depths of the earth and up through a high chimney to a small point of dim light high above their heads. Intuitively, Philippa guessed that this might even be the very pit from which Manco Capac and his seven djinn brothers and sisters had emerged from a djinn-made world to rule the Incas many centuries before. But there was no way across the pit. And it seemed they would have little choice but to return the way they had come.

"There's the source of your breeze," said Groanin. "And there's no going on from here." He sighed. "I guess we'll have to go back." Then he smiled. "Not your fault, miss. I say, it's not your fault. We all thought this was the way out. Didn't we, Muddy?"

"For sure, we did," said Muddy.

"Zadie was right," said Philippa. "We've been descending these caves and passages for several hours." She looked up at the point of light above their heads that was the top of the chimney. "I guess that's ground level, up there."

"Reckon," said Sicky.

"How far up would you say that was?"

Sicky pursed his lips and, leaning his little head back on his enormous shoulders, said, "Could be five or six hundred feet. Could be more. Long way, at any rate. Long, long way." He looked around the walls, broke off a piece of the yellow rock in his hands. "No good to climb, either." He threw the rock violently across the pit. The rock had not traveled more than two or three feet before the current of hot air blasting up from the pit carried it high above their heads and out of the chimney top.

This gave Philippa an idea.

"I saw a movie on TV once," she said. "It was about this man who called himself a base jumper. He jumps off very tall buildings in places like New York, with a parachute. And skydives through the streets. Sometimes he dives into huge holes in the ground. So, I was thinking perhaps we could do the same. But instead of skydiving, it'd be more like sky flying. In other words, going up instead of down."

"You mean jump into that pit, without a parachute?" said Groanin.

"Yes. Except that we'd hardly be jumping into the pit. It would be more a case of jumping onto the current of hot air that's coming out of it and riding that current of air all the way up through the chimney."

"You're mad," said Groanin, and sat down on a large yellow rock.

"I don't think so. Heat rises. And so would we."

"You make it sound like we're no heavier than a handful of leaves, miss," said Groanin. "Myself I weigh more than two hundred pounds. I'd like to see the current of air that could blow me around like a bubble."

"I think you're looking at it, Mr. Groanin," argued Philippa. "But I bet that boulder you're sitting on must weigh quite a bit. Why don't we throw the boulder into the current of air and see what happens to it?"

"Good idea," said Muddy.

"You're mad," Groanin told Muddy. "Here, Sicky, how do you feel about this idea of hers?"

"Sick," said Sicky. "Sick to my stomach. Still, best we chuck the rock into the air current first and then figure if there's another way to get out of here. Experiment first, like she says. Then argue. Okay? That's scientific."

"I'm not doing it," said Groanin. All the same he stood up, and he and Sicky carried the yellow boulder along the path to the edge of the pit. "This rock is warm, you know."

"And plenty heavy," said Sicky.

"Aye, but how heavy?" Groanin grunted with the exertion of moving the boulder. "That's the sixty-four-thousand-dollar question."

"More expensive than that, I reckon," said Muddy. He would have helped but there was no room for three on the path. "Much more." He chuckled. "My life is, anyway."

"This rock is at least a hundred pounds, maybe," said Sicky. The guide's head may have been unusually small but there was nothing wrong with his ability to guess the weight of something heavy.

"At least," said Groanin. "Right, then. Here goes."

Groanin and Sicky stood cradling the boulder at the edge of the pit and began to swing their arms.

A second later, the two men tossed the yellow boulder into the pit and then watched in amazement as the hot current of air quickly carried it up the shaft like a pellet in the barrel of a BB gun.

"I think that answers your doubts, Groanin," observed Philippa.

"I'm still not doing it," he said. "I never liked jumping out of a plane when I was in the British Army. And that was with a flipping parachute on my back."

"You mean you've done this kind of thing before?" said Philippa.

"This kind of thing? No, miss." Groanin smiled thinly. "That was merely dangerous. This is foolhardy. I'm an English butler, not a flipping daredevil. Look here, suppose the air batters us against the walls of the chimney. We could be knocked senseless. And what happens to us when we shoot out of the top? How high up will we go before gravity takes over? We could land on anything. And anywhere. We could find ourselves lost in the Amazon jungle. Or senseless at the top of a very tall tree."

"You're forgetting," said Philippa. "I'm a djinn. The minute I'm in sunshine, I'll have my power back."

"I'm not doubting your word, miss," he said. "But what if it's still raining? Underneath the tree canopy there's not a lot of sunshine on the forest ground. It might be several hours before —"

"I'm going to try it," said Sicky.

"Me, too," said Muddy.

Philippa shrugged as if to say, "Me, too."

Groanin muttered darkly. "I'm certainly not staying down here by myself."

"If you've done a parachute jump before," said Philippa,

"then perhaps you can demonstrate the best way to do this. I mean the best way to make this jump."

Groanin nodded. "Very well, miss. I reckon the best thing to do would be to take a running jump at it. To launch yourself into the center of the current of air so that you aren't buffeted on the sides of the shaft as you shoot up the chimney." He wagged a forefinger at Sicky, and then Muddy. "As soon as you hit the air current, you should throw out your arms and legs in a star, so that the air can catch as much of you as possible."

"Who's going to be first?" asked Sicky.

"It ought to be me," Philippa said bravely, and put her glasses inside her pocket for safety. "After all, this was my idea. Plus, we might get lucky. I might shoot straight up and out of here into a beam of hot sunshine and find my power restored before I hit the ground."

"Stranger things have happened," said Groanin, and then told himself that they probably hadn't.

Philippa walked back along the path and prepared to make her run. She'd never been much of a long jumper. Thinking was her stronger suit, which was one of the reasons why her last thought before sprinting toward the gaping pit was to wonder what the yellow crystal that encrusted the walls of the cave was made of, and to put a piece in her pocket so that later on, if she survived, she might examine it more closely.

At the last second and just as she jumped, Philippa heard Sicky shouting and saw Groanin waving as if urging her on, and she was already airborne by the time she realized that they'd actually been shouting at her to stop. It was easy to understand why. The air current had stopped. For one sickening, heart-stopping moment Philippa hung in the air above the pit, instead of being blasted all the way up the shaft. Then she started to fall.

CHAPTER 14

EL TUNCHI

For several minutes, absolutely certain that it was not he who had disappeared into thin air but Nimrod, John walked around the deserted camp, shouting for his uncle and hacking at the thick undergrowth with the machete. He wondered if Nimrod's disappearance was self-inflicted or if there was some other force involved. Nimrod wasn't the type of uncle who disappeared without telling anyone. Almost immediately, John heard the whistling again and this time he was careful not to answer it with some whistling of his own, quite unaware that it was already too late, and that the wrath of *el Tunchi* had now fallen upon his young head.

This time it actually seemed possible to follow the source of the whistling, which grew stronger as John went deeper into the forest. He was not afraid. He was, after all, a djinn and, as he emerged into a sunlit clearing, the power felt strong in him. John was not even afraid when finally he laid eyes upon the fearsome-looking author of the melodious whistling.

The man wore a filthy fur rug around his large waist, and his black hair was long and shaggy. The upper half of his face was painted black and the lower half white. The upper half was remarkable on account of the fact that he had only one eye. The lower half was chiefly remarkable in that the man held the head of a living lizard in his mouth, with the rest of the black-and-white reptile's tail and body wrapped around his neck, like a necklace. It was through this lizard's head that the man seemed to do his whistling and, as John quickly discovered, most of his talking, too. Indeed, it almost seemed as if it was the lizard that was in charge of the man. Most odd of all, perhaps, was the jaunty little tune itself — quite at odds with the man's appearance — that continued to be whistled from the lizard's mouth.

"You whistle extremely well," said John. "For a lizard."

The lizard stopped whistling. "I whistle splendidly well for any sort of being," it said sibilantly.

"And that's a nice tune," said John.

"Didn't your mother ever tell you," demanded the lizard man, "never to whistle in a theater? Or on a ship? Or in a house, in case you invite the devil in? And above all, never to whistle in the rain forest?"

"No," said John, "she never did. But then my mother isn't like most mothers. In fact, she's not even particularly like my mother. At least not since she started to look like someone else."

"You make no sense, boy," hissed the lizard man.

"It's a long story," said John. "Some other time, perhaps."

"You don't seem to be afraid of me."

"I'm not." John shrugged. "What's the big idea making my uncle Nimrod disappear like that?"

"He didn't disappear. You did."

"Well, who are you to go around making people disappear? Are you a ghost?"

"No, not a ghost. I am *el Tunchi*. A shaman. The spiritual echo of a witch doctor who took his last breath in the rain forest, having been tortured to death by Spanish conquistadors about five hundred years ago. They were after gold, of course. And thinking that they were all going to be rich, they liked to whistle. They even whistled while they were torturing me. Nobody ever whistled in South America before they turned up. Nobody knew how. Ever since then, I have been here to punish all those, like them, who dare to whistle in the jungle. It is my revenge."

"But I'm not like them. And where I come from, people whistle when they're happy. And I think it's pretty sick of you to take revenge on people for doing something as ordinary as that."

"Who are you to tell me what I can and what I can't do?"

"My name is John Gaunt. And I'm on a quest to find the lost city of Paititi. And to save the world from the great destruction. The *Pachacuti*."

"I care nothing about that, John Gaunt. All I care about is my revenge." He grinned horribly. "First I'm going to drill a hole in your head. Then I'm going to suck out your brain. And then I'm going to use your empty skull for a note on my organ."

"You mean like a pipe organ? In a church?"

"Yes. Except that instead of pipes I use human skulls. My organ has sixty-one notes and five octaves. Would you like to see it?"

John shrugged coolly. "Sure."

He followed *el Tunchi* to a little hut in the forest, where John now gazed upon the strangest musical instrument he had ever seen.

"The five keyboards are made from locally sourced horn and bone," *el Tunchi* explained proudly. "Jaguar teeth and antelope horn. The stops are made from tapir vertebrae. The pedal board is made of human shinbones. The pipe casing is made of armor taken from the bodies of many dead conquistadors. Curses be upon them all. And of course, as you can see, the pipes themselves are human skulls arranged by timbre and pitch into ranks and mounted vertically onto a wind chest that's really just a wooden box over an ancient hole in the ground from which hot air comes forth. There are lots of holes like that in this part of the jungle. When the wind whistles through these pipes it makes a truly infernal noise."

El Tunchi sat down and started to play. And soon John was obliged to cover his ears. *El Tunchi* had spoken the truth: It was a truly infernal noise. Like something from the deepest, darkest pit.

"I think your playing really stinks," said John.

"I never learned to play," admitted *el Tunchi*. "Not that it matters here in the jungle. There's no one around to listen. Besides, I don't play for other people. I play for myself. But if ever I wanted an audience I'd just whistle one up."

John thought carefully. It was beyond his power and imagination to figure a way of restoring himself to the parallel world he had occupied with Nimrod just a few minutes before. For that he knew he needed *el Tunchi*. But he did not think it was beyond his power to goad the shaman into some kind of contest out of which he might make some kind of advantage for himself.

"Speaking of whistling," he said. "You're not much better at that, come to think of it. I bet I could beat you in a whistling contest."

El Tunchi grinned and the lizard head fell out of his mouth. Popping it back in again, he said, "Are you challenging me?"

"Sure." John grinned back at him. "But look here, if we are going to have a contest there had better be something worth competing for."

"Like what?"

"Like you get my skull if you win, and if you lose, you fix it for me to go back with my uncle Nimrod."

"All right," said *el Tunchi*. "It's a deal."

"Who goes first?" John asked.

"It ought to be you," said *el Tunchi*. "Since you're the challenger."

John shrugged. "Fine by me," he said, and muttering his focus word, "ABECEDARIAN!" wished that he was the best whistler the world had ever heard.

After warming up with a few bars of "Dixie" and "Yankee Doodle," which are commonly whistled tunes in most parts of the United States, John began in earnest with a tune called "Buffoon," followed it up with another called "Lovely Lady" and, by the time John finished "Moonlight," the whistling jungle shaman was looking worried.

"Truly, I never heard such magnificent tunes so wonderfully performed," admitted *el Tunchi* and set about whistling a much more complicated version of the same tune that John had heard earlier. But even he was forced to admit that his whistling hadn't the dexterity and melodic breadth of John's near symphonic whistling. "Perhaps you can, it's true, whistle a better tune," he said, angry with himself. "But I doubt there's anyone who can touch me for the sheer power of my whistling."

"All right," said John. "But this time you go first."

El Tunchi took a deep breath, pursed his lips, and let out a long, piercing whistle that sent several birds and quite a few insects heading nervously for the comparative quiet of the clouds.

John nodded. "Not bad," he admitted. "But I can do better." And wishing that he could whistle up a storm, as is the saying, he put his fingers in his mouth and started to blow.

At first the whistle was merely loud — indeed it was very

easily as loud as *el Tunchi*'s. But as the whistle continued, the wind generated by the considerable movement of air from John's mouth began to gather in power until the bushes and trees surrounding them began to move. Then *el Tunchi*'s head-dress blew off, revealing his bald head. Next the shaman's fur rug blew away, leaving him standing there in just a loincloth. Last of all, the lizard in his mouth was carried off. John might have laughed but for the fact that this would have required him to stop whistling.

"Please," yelled the shaman in his own squeaky billy-goat voice, which wasn't in the least bit frightening.

John reflected that when you heard a thin, reedy voice like that it was easy to understand why *el Tunchi* had used a liz-ard to do his talking for him.

"Stop, I beg of you," wailed the shaman, who looked much smaller now that he had lost his curious wig and his fur wrap. He put his fingers in his ears, closed his eyes, and cow-ered down on the ground as if he thought the very forest would blow away. "Please. Stop that whistling. It's driving me mad."

But John kept on whistling like the north wind, deter-mined to teach *el Tunchi* a good lesson. Never was whistling heard like it. Not ever at the South Pole nor at Cape Horn nor on the Russian steppes nor on the high seas, which are all places where great whistling winds carry all before them. And when he had blown away *el Tunchi*'s clothes, John blew away the shaman's morbid organ: the stops made from tapir vertebrae, the pedal board made of human shinbones, the pipe casing made of armor, and, of course, the pipes themselves that were made of human skulls; all of them were blasted over the treetops or shattered into dust and never to be seen again.

After his experience with the Prozuanaci Indians, John was in the mood for handing out lessons. And while he sympathized with anyone who had been a victim of the Spanish conquistadors, he did not think this was sufficient justification to go around drilling holes in people's heads and using their empty skulls as the pipes for some horrible organ. Only when he was quite satisfied that he had blown away every part of the organ did John finally take his fingers out of his mouth and stop whistling.

Gradually, the forest settled down again.

"Er, do you give in?" asked John, although it was quite clear that *el Tunchi* was beaten.

Looking very shaken, *el Tunchi* got up slowly, flexed his ears — for by now he was a little deaf — and bowed gravely to John. "Sir," he said. "Most esteemed sir. Never before have I heard the like. Not in all of the five hundred years I have haunted this forest. Such whistling. The mere word doesn't do it justice. My abject apologies, sir. I will restore you to your uncle, immediately."

"Wait a minute," said John. "All this whistling to catch people for their skulls has got to stop, do you hear? It's not civilized."

"Yes, sir. As you wish, sir. My organ is gone, so there's nothing to take their skulls for."

"Do you promise never to do it again?"

"Yes, sir. You have my most solemn promise. Never to do it again."

John felt sorry for the poor creature. Now that he had destroyed his terrible organ and forbidden him to torment people in the forest it was clear *el Tunchi* would have nothing with which to amuse himself throughout all eternity.

"You know, you could use a real organ," said John. "A proper organ with pipes and stuff, like the kind you get in a church." And muttering his focus word, John made a facsimile of an organ he'd once seen in a cathedral.

El Tunchi regarded it, openmouthed and awestruck, like a sort of spaceship.

"It's amazing," breathed the shaman. "Astonishing. What an instrument. I just wish I knew how to play it."

"You're right," said John. "It's not much good to you if you don't know how to play it. Your wish is my command." And using his djinn power again, he gave *el Tunchi* a new talent. He made him a very great organist.

John spent the next five minutes persuading *el Tunchi* that his wish had been granted before at last he sat down and played some great organ music by Bach and Handel, and when he finished he knelt before John and kissed his hand.

"Thank you, great sir, thank you," said *el Tunchi*. "You have given me my dearest wish in the world. I never liked making people disappear and then stealing their skulls. Only part of the reason for what I did was revenge. Mostly it was borne of frustration at not being able to play on a proper organ."

"I'm very glad to hear it." And he was. The huge organ sounded fantastic in the jungle. Indeed, to John's ears it was the sound of civilization.

"But before I restore you to your uncle," said *el Tunchi*, "there is something important I must give and tell you. Something that will help you on your quest to find Paititi."

"There you are," said Nimrod. "I was wondering where you'd wandered off to."

"I didn't wander off," said John. "I disappeared. On account of the fact that I answered *el Tunchi*'s whistle."

John told Nimrod about *el Tunchi* and the whistling contest.

"That explains it, then," said Nimrod. "A little while ago, there was a violent wind that swept through the forest for no apparent reason. So it was you."

"Where exactly was I? When I disappeared?"

"Difficult question." Nimrod shrugged. "The next world. The one before. The one beside it. None of these words really means anything when applied to where you were. Or, to be more accurate, where you weren't. You were here and there at almost the same point in time and space. Which is almost nowhere at all."

"You mean like two dimensions?"

"Yes. But not quite."

"So how is it possible that you felt the wind from my whistling?"

"Ah well, that's the thing about whistling. If the sound keeps on going long enough, then it can actually move between these two so-called dimensions. There are a lot of hurricanes that get started by the idle whistling of ghosts."

"I see," said John, although he didn't. Not quite.

"Anyway," said Nimrod, "you're back now. That's all that matters. We've got to get moving. While you were off having fun, Zadie's bat, Zotz, came back with a message for her from Virgil McCreeby. He says that he's lost in the jungle. He asks Zadie to take on the shape of the bat so that she might come to him and help him discover exactly where he is."

John nodded gloomily, still very worried about his sister and the others.

"Does that mean there's time to go and look for Philippa and the others?" he asked.

"I'm afraid not," said Nimrod. "Look, John, they'll have to take their chances. Need I remind you of what Faustina commanded us to do? To secure the Eye. And if we can't do that, then we can't prevent anyone from finding the lost city of Paititi. If that's where McCreeby is trying to get to, it won't be for anything good. You can bet on that much. We have to stop him. At all costs. Do you understand? At all costs."

John nodded. It wasn't often that Nimrod sounded so alarmed about something.

"Speaking of which," said John, "*el Tunchi* gave me this.

Said it might help us find the city. Although I have absolutely no idea how, or even what it is."

John handed Nimrod what looked like a necklace made of several hundred lengths — many of them knotted — of colored string.

"It's a *khipu*," said Nimrod, examining it carefully. "Unlike any other Bronze Age civilization, the Inca had no written language and so this was the way in which they encoded and recorded important information."

"Yeah? So what does it mean?"

"I have no idea," admitted Nimrod. "I don't think anyone does. *Khipu* are as much of a mystery today as Egyptian hieroglyphs were until Champollion deciphered their meaning. Let us hope that a solution to how these things work presents itself. But since hope is seldom enough by itself . . ."

Nimrod opened Mr. Vodyannoy's backpack and removed a book. "*Inca Khipu Made Simple*, by Terence Forelock. Frank Vodyannoy brought this from his library at New Haven because he thought it might come in handy. You'll remember that it wasn't just the tears of the sun that were stolen. Faustina reported several *khipu* and a golden staff stolen from that museum in Berlin. Perhaps this book will tell us something of what we need to know in order to understand the message contained in these pieces of string."

"So, where to now?" asked John.

"We must press on, to the Eye of the Forest," said Nimrod. "Along the route I memorized from Faustina's map."

CHAPTER 15

THE RISING

As Philippa plunged down the huge underground shaft she wished for — what else? — a parachute. But sufficient heat had not yet returned to her body for her djinn power to function and by the time she uttered her own focus word and a parachute did not appear, the last syllables of FABULONGOSHOOMARVELISHLYWONDERPIPICAL had turned into a scream. Of course, she could not help it and she screamed loudly, like someone falling from the window of a very tall Manhattan skyscraper.

Or out of an airplane without a parachute.

And then, just as she closed her eyes and thought she might actually die of fright — for her heart felt as if it was beating faster than the hooves of a galloping horse — the rate of her descent slowed suddenly until, for a moment, she seemed to remain almost stationary. Philippa heard herself gasp with relief and opened her eyes again. The current of air had returned and was already strengthening.

"I've stopped," she gasped. "Thank goodness. I've stopped. I've stopped."

Gradually, she began to ascend the shaft. And when she reached the ledge from where, just a few heart-stopping seconds before, she had jumped, she was moving up almost as quickly as she had been moving down. There was just time to wave and to shout at Groanin, Sicky, and Muddy that she would see them at the top or on the outside.

If she had been going only a little slower she might have heard Groanin's remark as he turned away from the edge of the shaft with a tear in his eye.

"I thought she was a goner for sure," he said. "I say, I thought that little lass was a goner, for sure." He shook his head, and took out a handkerchief. "I'd never have forgiven myself if something had happened to her. What we've been through together. I couldn't begin to tell you. The times she's saved my bacon." He blew his nose loudly. "Sorry."

His small head still observing Philippa's progress up the chimney shaft, Sicky whistled. "Even for a djinn girl, I reckon she's got plenty of guts," he said.

"That she has," said Groanin.

Intermittently poking a hand into the severe current of air now blasting up the shaft, Muddy said, "Ain't never seen anything like this. The way the current of air goes on and off like a gigantic hair dryer." He started to walk back along the rocky path. "I figure if I stopped to think about this, then maybe I wouldn't find the nerve to go after her. So I ain't gonna do it."

"That's the way I feel about it, too," said Groanin, quite mistaking the thrust of what Muddy was talking about. "I don't think I could ever jump now."

"Stop to think, I mean," added Muddy and, taking a long run at it, he jumped into the current of air and went sailing up the shaft after Philippa with a loud whoop of relief and exhilaration.

"Flipping heck," said Groanin. "I thought he meant he wasn't going to do it. Not that he was actually going to jump." He looked at Sicky uncomfortably. "How do you feel about doing this, Sicky, old mate?"

Thoughtfully, Sicky stroked the pieces of string that had been threaded through his lips by the Xuanaci Indians, and which looked like the whiskers of a Chinese Mandarin.

"Sick," he said, shaking his shrunken head. "Pretty sick. My stomach feels like I swallowed something nasty. But maybe Muddy is right. Maybe it's best not to think at all. Maybe it's best just to do, huh?"

Sicky was already walking back down the path that led to the edge of the shaft. Then he turned, clenched his fists, and readied himself like a sprinter.

Groanin gulped loudly. "Sicky," he said weakly. "Sicky, old mate. Let's talk about this. If you jump, it'll be just me down here on my own, and I'm not sure I can do this."

"You is the one who has done the parachute training," said Sicky. "Not me. I never jumped off anything before. Not even a bed, on account of the fact that I always slept in a hammock. I ain't got no head for heights. Truth be told, I hardly got a head at all. But Muddy's right. How's that old poem go? 'Theirs not to reason why, theirs but to do . . .'"

Sicky charged back up the path without bothering to finish his quotation. Indeed, he hardly knew that it was a famous poem by Alfred, Lord Tennyson. But Groanin did. Moreover, he knew the last two words of the line Sicky had spoken and uttered them quietly as the guide launched himself off the edge of the chimney shaft: "'Theirs but to do and die,'" he said, and grimaced uncomfortably.

But Sicky did not die. The guide's head may have been unusually small but there was nothing wrong with his ability to judge a long jump and, like a shuttlecock, he quickly sailed up the chimney.

"What the heck did you want to go and quote that poem for?" Groanin shouted after him. "'Charge of the Light Brigade.' Hardly inspiring of confidence, is it? 'Into the Valley of Death rode the six hundred.' It shows a want of consideration, that's what it does, a want of consideration." Groanin shook his head. "Still, what can you expect of a foreigner?"

Groanin hefted another yellow stone into the shaft and, as it followed Sicky up the shaft, he had an idea. Just before he started his run up he would throw another stone, and if the air carried the stone up he would run, and if it didn't, he would wait. That way he might avoid what had happened to Philippa. And this was what he did, although such was the strength with which he threw the rock that it almost went straight through the powerful current of air without stopping. Of course, thanks to the twins (and Dybbuk) Groanin was possessed of an extra-strong arm. But because of his largish stomach he was no athlete and certainly not much of a runner, and when he did jump, instead of jumping feetfirst, he jumped headfirst. This had the effect of turning him upside down and, yelling noisily, Groanin sailed up the chimney like a large and loudly deflating balloon.

Instead of exiting the chimney at ground level and in the open air, Philippa found herself flying up through a broken crystal ceiling and into a large stone chamber. Fortunately for her and the others who followed, the crystal ceiling had been smashed when, to test its strength, Groanin and Sicky had tossed the yellow boulder into the maelstrom of warm air. But for that they might have met the same sticky fate as a few bugs squished on a car windshield.

Being young and agile, Philippa landed on her feet, but her first thought was for her larger, heavier companions and how *they* might land. She glanced around at her surroundings. The chamber was circular, as large as a circus tent, and covered by a larger glasslike roof, which was mostly overgrown with jungle vegetation that allowed only a few shafts of greenish light to shine through. The air was thick, wet, steamy, and larded with a strong smell of decay. Philippa thought it was like being in a giant aquarium. But already she was warm enough to feel djinn power returning to her bones. And she had just enough time to mutter her focus word and conjure a large pile of thick mattresses on the floor all around the shaft's crystal ceiling before Muddy shot up into the air like a Ping-Pong ball in a carnival shooting gallery. He managed to twist his way through the air like a large cat, and to fall safely on the pile of mattresses Philippa had thoughtfully provided.

Guessing their origin, Muddy smiled at Philippa and nodded his gratitude. "Thank you, miss," he said, picking himself off the floor. "'Preciate it."

Sicky arrived less than a minute later. He seemed to go higher in the air than Muddy or Philippa and, but for the fact that his head was so small, he might have banged it on the roof. Picking himself up off the mattresses he said, "What is this place?"

"I don't know," said Philippa, who hardly dared to think about where they were until she knew Groanin was safe. "But it's kind of creepy."

"That's for sure."

"Where's Mr. Groanin?" she asked Sicky.

"Guess he'll be along in a minute. Soon as he's plucked up the nerve."

And then he was there, yelling loudly and flailing his arms and his legs as he attempted to right himself, and looking more than a little like a trapeze artist whose act had gone very wrong. As he reached the roof he reached for a creeper, clung on to it tightly and stayed there, swinging twenty or thirty feet above the heads of Philippa and the others.

"Let go," said Philippa. "This pile of mattresses will break your fall."

"Come on, Mr. Groanin," said Muddy. "Jump."

"I'm all right up here, thank you very much," Groanin said stiffly, for he was still unnerved after his unusual flight. "I'll come down when my stomach has caught up with my head."

Philippa shrugged. "He'll come down in a minute," she said, and followed Sicky around the strange chamber.

"Bit like an Incan greenhouse in here," said Sicky. "Sure is warm enough."

"Yes," agreed Philippa. "It feels great to be warm again." She smiled up at Sicky. "I'm sorry, but we're like lizards, we djinn. We only thrive in warmth."

Strange plants were growing out of the cracks between the huge stones in the floor. They had leaves as big as dinner plates and smelled unpleasant.

Around the circumference of the chamber were more than a dozen squarish alcoves. Each was about three or four feet tall and covered with an opaque, grayish material that was like a window you couldn't quite see through.

"What is it?" asked Sicky. "Glass? Plastic?"

Looking closely at the opaque material, Philippa saw that it was full of little strands and spirals. She tapped one experimentally with her fingernail.

"You know what I think this is?" she said. "I think it's fossilized gossamer. This is made of ancient spiderwebs."

"Spiderwebs?" Alarmed, Sicky took a step back. "Pretty big spider," he said.

"Or a lot of spiders working together," Philippa said hurriedly. "Don't worry. This stuff must be hundreds of years old. The spiders who wove these webs are long dead. Like the men who built this place."

"Maybe that's what I don't like about it." Sicky sniffed the air suspiciously. "The smell of death. This whole place stinks of it."

"I thought it was just me being fanciful." Philippa sniffed the air and made a face. "But you're right. And it is kind of overpowering, isn't it?" She took his big hand and squeezed it encouragingly. "All the same, I think it's just the cloying smell of tropical plants in the heat. That's what. Nothing to worry about."

She tapped the ancient gossamer glass again, only this time it felt sticky to the touch. Almost as if it was softening.

"That's odd," she said. "This gossamer glass. It seems to be melting." And then it dawned on her. "Of course. The heat from that shaft. For centuries it was probably blocked by the ceiling on the chimney shaft. Until we broke it. The heat is melting these gossamer glass coverings."

"Maybe it's best we're not here when they melt, eh, miss?" said Sicky.

"On the whole I tend to agree with you. Come on. Let's look for a way out of here."

Continuing their trip around the circular chamber they walked down some stone steps and out into the open air and found a very long rope bridge that stretched across an apparently bottomless chasm. The chasm was apparently endless, too, for the bridge led into a thick cloud of mist. The rope itself was made of a very finely stranded black material that shone like silk.

Philippa peered over the edge of the chasm. She realized she had little appetite for a journey upon an old rope bridge when you couldn't even see the bottom of the space you were crossing.

"A door," shouted Muddy. "I found a door."

They looked around and for a moment failed to see him.

"Over here," shouted Muddy.

Down a few steps at the opposite side of the chamber from the bridge, they found Muddy staring at an ancient door. Philippa stooped to inspect it. As well as the mold of several centuries, it was covered with the same creepers that continued up to the roof. She took hold of a creeper that was stuck fast to the door and pulled it. The door moved inside its frame, but only just. "It seems to be locked," she said. "From the outside."

"Reckon this is the way out, miss?" asked Muddy.

"If we can get it open, it might be," said Philippa. "But don't worry. I'm sure I can shift all these creepers with djinn power. And then we'll know for sure."

She muttered her focus word and a machete appeared in Muddy's hand. He grinned and then struck at one of the creepers with the razor-sharp blade as if it had been a dangerous snake.

"I say," shouted Groanin from the rooftop. "What about me? I say, what about me? Stuck up here, like a dusty old chandelier."

"I'd forgotten about poor old Groanin." Philippa laughed. She stood back from the door and shouted up to the butler, who continued to remain dangling at rooftop level. "All you have to do is let go," she told him. "The mattresses will easily break your fall."

"It's not breaking my fall that I'm worried about," said Groanin obstinately. "It's breaking my flipping leg. Or worse. I don't bounce as high as I used to. I say, I don't bounce as high as I used to."

"Hey, can you see anything out of that glass roof?"

"'Tisn't glass," said Groanin. "It's something else. Something like glass. As a matter of fact, I can see something. I'm not sure what, but it's on the same bearing as that there rope bridge you were looking at a moment ago. I daren't reach for me glasses to make sure. But there's a mountaintop. And there might just be a city sitting on top of it, like a cherry."

Meanwhile the gossamer glass coverings had all but melted in the heat. Sicky walked over to the one of the alcoves and was inspecting the now visible occupant closely. "Miss," he said. "I think you'd better take a look-see at this, quick."

Philippa stood beside him and felt her jaw slowly drop.

In the alcove were the mummified remains of what looked

like an Incan warrior. He was seated with his legs bent and his arms resting on his ample stomach and, but for the tightness and color of the skin on his face he looked to all the world like he was just sleeping. On his head was a golden helmet decorated with eagle feathers, a golden breastplate, and beside him on the ground were a rectangular shield, a spear, a bow and arrows, and a short, vicious-looking club.

"Fascinating," said Philippa. "He must have been a warrior or something. Look at all those weapons."

"Reckon he's more than just a warrior," said Sicky. "All that gold and feathers on him. Reckon he's a king, maybe." He pointed at some of the other alcoves where yet more Incas were now being slowly revealed. "Them Incas used to carry the mummies of all their dead kings around with them," said Sicky. "I wouldn't be surprised if these are them. And now we know what that smell was. This place. It's a crypt." Sicky shouted back across his shoulder. "Better hurry up with that machete, Muddy. I've got a feeling we're going to have company soon."

"Oh, Sicky," said Philippa. "They've been dead for at least five hundred years. Besides, even if they did come to life, which they won't, you've got a djinn here to protect you. Nothing's going to happen to you so long as you've got me around."

"Okay, miss. All the same, I'll feel better when I'm out of here. Don't like being around no dead people. In case it's infectious."

Philippa assumed he was making a joke. "It's not at all infectious," she said, scolding him.

"That's what you think," said Muddy. He swung the machete again and wrenched a huge length of creeper away from the door and the wall. And he kept on pulling, even as he found the creeper extended all the way up to the roof, to a spot only a few feet away from Groanin.

Groanin felt the creeper he was holding on to shift ominously. "I say," he said. "What's that you're chopping, Muddy, me old mate?"

Muddy hacked at another creeper. "Just the green stuff that's jamming this door," he said.

"Well, be careful," said Groanin, and felt the creeper he was holding shift again.

He was just about to shout a warning to Muddy when the creeper suddenly came away from the roof and, like Tarzan swinging through the jungle while holding on to a liana — a kind of creeper — Groanin started a rapid and pendulous descent.

"Look out, miss!" he yelled as he swung down from the roof, for it was clear that he would surely collide with Philippa. "Look out, I say!"

Too late Philippa turned to see what she was being warned about. Groanin's heavy swinging body struck her like a wrecking ball. The impact carried her clean off her feet and into one of the alcoves, where she collided with one of the mummified kings and then lay still.

Groanin, who was unaffected by the impact, picked himself up off the floor and ran to Philippa's side. Much to his
relief she was breathing, but unconscious. And gathering
her up in his arms, he kicked the Inca king's mummified
body aside, carried her out of the sinister alcove, and laid
her down by the door that Muddy had found earlier. There,
Groanin set about trying to revive her, patting her cheeks
and then her hands, and even fanning her with his jacket.

Sicky knelt down beside Philippa and took her pulse.
"That was quite a collision," he remarked. "Like a crunch
tackle in American football. This little djinn girl will be out
cold for a while, I reckon."

"She's alive at any rate," said Groanin.

"She's not the only one. Look."

Muddy pointed to the alcove recently vacated by Philippa
where the mummified Inca king was now on his feet. His
movements were slow and jerky as might have been expected
after five hundred years of immobility. But his intention was
clear enough. He was arming himself with the bow and arrow
that had been placed with him in the alcove. More of the Inca
kings were coming back to a kind of life, as well, and they,
too, were collecting their primitive weapons.

Primitive but effective. An arrow flew through the air,
narrowly missing Groanin's ear.

"I say, steady on," yelled the English butler. "You'll have
someone's eye out with that thing."

"I think that's the general idea," said Sicky. "Maybe you
shouldn't have kicked him."

"It's not my fault he's come back to life," said Groanin as another arrow flew through the air. "Do something."

Sicky, who had finally succeeded in removing the last piece of *Hevea* tree rubber the Xuanaci had used to cover the magical tattoo on his stomach, now thought to show this to the advancing Inca warrior kings in order that they might be turned to stone.

"Cover your eyes," he told the others, and then showed the marauding Inca kings his intimidating belly.

It didn't work. None of them were turned to stone. And it was plain to see why. Their dead-looking eyes didn't see things the way ordinary human eyes saw things. Either that or his stomach was still too dirty for the tattoo to work its Gorgonlike effect.

"Oh," said Sicky. "Now we're in for it."

Muddy brandished the machete in his hand. "I'll give them a taste of this if they shoot any more of them arrows at me. I'll fix them old kings. Kill a few. See how they like that."

"That might not be possible," objected Sicky. "If they be dead already."

"Good point." Muddy hacked the last creeper from the door and tried to haul it open.

Groanin made another vain attempt to revive Philippa. "Miss Philippa," he said urgently. "We need your help. Quick. Before these zombies make pincushions of us."

"It's no good," said Sicky. "Maybe you should apologize. After all, it was you who kicked that old king back there."

Groanin sprang up and bowed gravely toward the war-like Inca kings. "Esteemed sirs and princes," he said in an extremely servile fashion. He was British after all and no one can speak to a king or a queen quite like an English butler. "Your Highnesses. Your Majesties. Your Imperial Majesties. Please, forgive this intrusion. Begging your royal pardon, but I think there's been some kind of mistake. We are not your enemies. Just unwitting travelers. We had no intention of disturbing your privacy. But if we have offended you, then please accept our respects and abject apologies and our unworthy assurances that it will not happen again."

An Incan spear clattered onto the flagstones and skidded sharply toward Groanin's shoe. And recognizing the futility of further conversation, the butler turned and pulled hopelessly at the door.

"It's no good," said Muddy. "This door is still stuck fast."

"We'll all be stuck fast unless you can get that flipping door open, Muddy." Making a fist, Groanin hammered loudly on the door. "I say! Is there anyone there? Please, someone, could you open the door? I say, open the flipping door!"

CHAPTER 16

THE EYE OF THE FOREST

Shouldering their backpacks, John and Nimrod moved up the trail, hacking their way through the thick jungle for several hours until they came to the spot where, earlier on, as two fierce jaguars they had fought and killed the *giant* giant anaconda. The place was easy enough to recognize. There were broken bushes and trees and, in a hollow on a rock, a large pool of blood.

The two djinn did not linger, however, to savor their earlier triumph. At Nimrod's insistence, they pressed on so that they might reach the Eye of the Forest before nightfall. And, after another hour or two of walking and a series of jungle clearings, finally they found it. Or rather Nimrod did, for the stones of the doorway were so green and over-grown that they might easily have missed their square silhouettes in the encroaching Amazon darkness. And to John's tired eyes, only the neatness of the extremely large and old trees that surrounded these stones looked in any way remarkable. But, too tired to take much in, the two djinn quickly erected their tents and tumbled into them.

The next morning, John awoke feeling desperately hungry and with an intense sense of anticipation. Nimrod had already cooked a hearty breakfast of bacon, sausage, and eggs, and as soon as it was eaten they set about exploring the curious, decaying edifice, which was obviously Incan in its proportions and detail, and a foot or two smaller than any ordinary doorway in a normal sort of house. Most curious of all, on one side of the ancient door was a bolt secured with a giant knot that appeared to have been fashioned from braided human hair.

"They must have been quite small, the Incas," remarked John.

"Yes, I think they were, probably," said Nimrod.

"Are you sure that this is it?" asked John.

"Yes," Nimrod said flatly, "quite sure. There was a set of coordinates on the map that Faustina gave Frank Vodyannoy. An exact latitude and longitude. And this is the place. Look." He showed John his handheld satnav unit as it confirmed what he had just said.

"Only it doesn't look anything like the photograph that was in the newspaper," said John. "For one thing, the door's not really shaped like an eye at all."

"No, it's not," said Nimrod.

"And unlike the door in the picture, this one appears not to be made of wood but metal. To say nothing of the giant knot securing it. I mean, that wasn't even in the photograph."

"I must confess to never having actually seen the Eye of the Forest before, until, like you, I saw it in the newspaper," said Nimrod. "Or at least until I thought I'd seen it in the newspaper. But you're quite right, of course. This does look very different from what we saw in the *Herald Tribune*. As you say, that one was shaped like an eye, and this one clearly isn't. It's noticeably rectangular."

John hacked carelessly at the vegetation covering the stone doorway, which led nowhere but to the jungle on the other side. The noise and movement of his machete disturbed a flock of parakeets overhead that made a sound like the slashing violins in a Hitchcock movie. To his suspicious ears, the monkeys in the trees almost seemed to be laughing.

"It's also curious, wouldn't you say," John continued carefully because he could see that Nimrod was a little annoyed about something, "how there's no evidence of any expedition having been here at all? No one has even attempted to strip these ruins bare of creepers with their machetes. Which they would have done to take a picture, right?" John's keen eyes scanned the forest floor. "Either they did a very good job of hiding their tracks or they were never here at all. In fact, I'd say no one has been here for several hundred years."

"You tread heavily," said Nimrod, "but what you say is quite true, John. It would seem that the *Herald Tribune* and, more important, the djinn world, has been the subject of a hoax. It's clear to me now that the photograph in the newspaper was a fake, and very likely a fake that was made by Virgil McCreeby."

"Do you think he meant it to lure us here?" said John. "So that *we* could lead him to the Eye of the Forest?"

"I believe he did," agreed Nimrod. "As usual it would seem that McCreeby is in search of power and gold. Perhaps both. The door itself is not without considerable intrinsic value."

"What does *intrinsic* mean, when it's at home?" growled John. He was beginning to feel very slightly aggrieved that Nimrod had prevented him from mounting a rescue mission for Philippa and the others on the strength of the urgency of finding the secret door to a lost city that looked very likely to remain lost for some considerable time to come.

"It's valuable," said Nimrod. He hacked some of the creepers away and, using the tip of his machete, began to scrape some of the mildew and mold off a small area of the door. "Look."

To John's astonishment a small patch of something bright and shiny was already becoming visible to his eye.

"Holy Peru," said John. "It's gold."

"That's right," said Nimrod. "Solid gold. It was part of the trap Ti Cosi meant for the conquistadors who were, of course, obsessed with gold. That they might think that this was some kind of symbolic doorway to El Dorado, the fabled city of gold. Given the size and weight of this door I should say that the gold alone is worth several million dollars."

"But you don't think McCreeby's just after the door itself," said John, "do you?"

"No. It's what lies beyond this door that's probably more important to a villain like Virgil McCreeby. And it must have something to do with those three gold disks."

"You mean the tears of the sun?" asked John.

Nimrod nodded. "Perhaps he means to go through the door with those tears. It's just a thought but it may be that he has discovered the details of the forgotten *kutumunkichu* ritual once carried out by Manco Capac."

"So that he can learn the secret of making gold," added John.

"He does have an excellent library," said Nimrod. "Perhaps the best of its kind anywhere in the world. And of course making gold would be very much in keeping with his character."

John looked at one side of the door and then the other. "Maybe this'll sound dumb," he said, "but this is a door that looks like it leads not much farther than the other side of the door."

"If that were the case," said Nimrod, "Ti Cosi would hardly have gone to the trouble of creating such a large and elaborate knot with which to bind the bolt."

"Yes, but if the door was meant to be a trap," objected John, "then why bother to secure it at all? Also, I can't imagine that the knot would have presented much of a problem to conquistadors armed with Toledo steel. No more than the more famous Gordian knot presented much of a problem to Alexander the Great. Instead of untying the knot, he just hacked it in two with his sword, right?"

"This knot was for the protection of the local natives," explained Nimrod. "So that they wouldn't go through the door by accident. The natives would never have dared cut or undo a sacred knot that had been tied by an important priest like Ti Cosi. That would have been sacrilege. No, the idea was that if the conquistadors showed up they would probably cut the knot and their greed for gold would do the rest. I mean, obviously they would have tried to remove the door and to do that they would need to step through it."

"But what happens when you step through? Where does it go? And please don't say 'the other side' or I'll be forced to bang my head against one of those trees."

"I'm not entirely sure what is on the other side," confessed Nimrod. "To find out we would have to untie the knot, which I'm not going to do."

"What? We come all the way here and we're just going to leave it and go back home again? That doesn't make any sense at all."

"On the contrary," said Nimrod. "It makes perfect sense. It seems to me now that if McCreeby *has* lured us here, to the Eye of the Forest, very possibly with the intention of discovering its exact location, then the last thing I'm going to do now, John, is untie that knot. Even if I could."

"But suppose McCreeby just cuts the knot in two like Alexander?" John shrugged. "It's my impression of old Virgil that he might not be too bothered about committing a sacrilege or two."

Nimrod sighed again and glanced around. "Yes. Perhaps that's also true. It's beginning to look as though Faustina was right and that that this site needs some protection other than a sacred knot and a few lupuna trees."

John looked at the dozen or more trees surrounding the Eye. At least one hundred and fifty feet tall, each one of these trees was as big as a house at its base.

"I don't see how a few old trees were ever going to stop a guy like Virgil McCreeby," he said.

"These trees contain ancient spirits that are supposed to protect the rain forest," said Nimrod. "Spirits that will haunt you if you don't respect the trees or the *chacras* — the sacred forest clearings — they sometimes protect."

"If they can't stop a few loggers from chopping them down, what chance are they going to have against a bona fide magus like McCreeby? Surely what this particular area needs is a propugnator. A perimeter binding. Like the one you made for our camp after we were attacked by the giant centipede."

"Unfortunately, that's not nearly so simple as it sounds." Nimrod lifted his gaze to the treetops. "It turns out that there's a good reason no loggers have ever come to this place. Just look again at your surroundings. Don't they remind you of something?"

John followed Nimrod's gaze and saw how the highest boughs of the trees — he counted sixteen lupunas — seemed to join in arches, creating a sort of vaulted roof above their heads. He shrugged. "I dunno," he said. "I guess it's kind of weird the way these trees grow so neat and straight. Almost like pillars. And the way they all join up at the top. Sort of like they were designed that way." He shrugged again. "I guess it reminds me of a church."

"That's exactly what it's like," said Nimrod. "You see, this is more than a *chacra*. This is a holy place. This is an *abadía de árboles*, an abbey of trees. I would no more use djinn power to make a binding within an abbey of trees than I would use it in a church, a mosque, or a synagogue. I don't think God would like it."

"We have to do something," said John. "You said yourself this site needs some extra protection against Virgil McCreeby."

"Yes, but what?" muttered Nimrod. He shook his head. "Light my lamp, but this requires some careful cogitation. I shall retire to my tent for a short time while I suspend consciousness and consider the matter through introspection."

John nodded although he had no idea what Nimrod was talking about. But he was more used to that than he had been of old.

"Will you be all right on your own for a while?" asked Nimrod.

"Of course," said John. "Maybe I'll look at that book

about the *khipu*. Try to figure out what the one *el Tunchi* gave me means."

"Good idea," said Nimrod, and handed the book over to John, who then left him alone in his tent.

The boy sat down, leaned against a lupuna tree, and started to read.

Minutes passed and John felt his eyelids begin to droop. He'd never been much of a reader. The longest book he had ever read was a copy of the *Arabian Nights* given to him by Nimrod to which a djinn binding had been attached that caused him to stay awake long enough to finish it all in one sitting. But this book was different. It was all about mathematics, which had never been John's strong suit, and it was soon patently clear that the writer only had the vaguest idea of how *khipus* worked.

Much clearer to John were his own ideas, if things dreamed when you are asleep inside a tree can ever properly be called ideas. Not that these were his own ideas any more than they were his own dreams, for everything that swirled around his soundly sleeping mind informing him about the *khipu* in his hand came from an ancient spirit deep within the lupuna tree. For although the wood of these trees is very hard, lupunas can easily absorb unwary people who fall asleep leaning against them, sometimes for a short period of time and sometimes for much longer. People have been known to disappear inside a lupuna tree for several centuries. But, recognizing John as a djinn — and a good djinn at that — this particular lupuna tree absorbed him for only an hour or two. It was long enough for the tree spirit to pass on to John an understanding of what a *khipu* was and how it worked, as well as the true meaning and solution of the knot on the door of the Eye of the Forest. This was both complicated and simple at the same time.

John awoke again with a start, certain that he had heard something unusual. One glance at Nimrod's tent told him his uncle was still cogitating within, like Achilles (although not nearly as bad-tempered), and that he was not the source of the noise. For a moment, all thoughts of the true meaning of the *khipu* gained from his time inside the lupuna tree were forgotten. And tossing the very learned book he had been reading aside, John stood up and walked around the campsite before finally he realized what it was that had disturbed his wooden slumbers. The door in the Eye of the Forest was shaking very slightly, as if someone on the other side was trying to open it.

Walking around the free-standing Eye of the Forest in a wide circle, John wondered if he should call Nimrod. There could be no doubt about it. Someone, or something, was trying to open the door. It was like a scene in a horror movie when a poltergeist or a ghost moves something inanimate, like a toy on a bookshelf. For as far as he could determine, John knew there was nothing on the other side of the door.

Ignoring his own goose bumps, John picked up his machete, went a little nearer, and tapped the door with the razor-sharp blade. "Hello," he said. "Is anyone there?"

For a moment the door stopped moving, as if someone on the other side had heard him. That was, he thought, like a horror movie, too: the way an object became ordinary again when it ceased to move for no apparent reason.

He went closer still, finally bending his head and then his ear down toward the small shiny golden patch that Nimrod had cleaned with the point of his machete. "Is there anyone there?" he repeated. "Look, the door won't open because there's this big knot binding a bolt on the other side. So there's no point in trying to open it. See?"

Again the door moved within the stone frame, more noticeably this time and then there was someone banging loudly on it, which gave him such a fright that it made his heart leap in his chest like an excited puppy, and caused him to take a few steps back.

"Oooer," he said, holding his chest. But not before he heard another voice. A voice from very far away. As if from another lost, invisible world. It was a voice he was quite sure he recognized. The voice belonged to Mr. Groanin, and he sounded like he was in trouble.

CHAPTER 17

COMING THROUGH
THE DOOR

Upon hearing what he thought must be Groanin's cry for help, John's first instinct was to hack with his machete at the large and complicated knot securing the door in the Eye of the Forest, and it was fortunate that his sleeping head had been temporarily absorbed in the lupuna, for the tree had informed the young djinn's subconscious mind that somehow the knot contained an important and ineffable or secret word. Knotted within the cipher that was the knot, this secret word had been passed on through generations of Incan priests and revealed only to the Inca kings. This fact became more apparent to John only afterward, but now, with his blade less than a millimeter away, he checked himself from cutting the knot and instead set about the business of untying it.

"Hang on, Mr. Groanin," John shouted through the door. "I'm coming to get you."

Untying the knot did not take him very long. As with many apparently complex problems beloved of mathematicians, the solution was actually a simple one and began with John pouring the contents of his water bottle onto the knot itself. Because before it had been tied, the rope had been soaked in water, and after it had been tied, the knot had been exposed to direct sunlight which, of course, made it shrink. Thus, by wetting the coils of the knot, John helped to make them looser and, therefore, easier to manipulate.

Not that it would ever have been possible for an adult to have manipulated the knot — wet or dry. Not ever. Manipulation of the rope could only ever have been carried out by the small and more dexterous fingers of an Indian or a boy such as John. It was one of the reasons why the lupuna tree had told John the secret in the first place.

But the most important thing John had learned about the knot from the lupuna tree was that it was not really a true knot with two separate ends, but an ingenious loop that had been cleverly disguised only to look like a knot. The loop had been folded to make two ends and in this had been tied two multiple overhand knots; the two ends of the loops had then been pulled several times over the two knots and the rope then shrank until it was as tight as a miser's fist.

Knowing all of this made it a matter of less than a minute for John to unravel it.

"John. What on earth do you think you are doing?" It was Nimrod, who had been summoned from his tent by John's shouting through the door. Despite all of his "careful cogitation," Nimrod had devised neither a solution for the untying of the knot nor a solution of what to do about Virgil McCreeby. And he was astonished to see that the knot on the door had disappeared and that his young nephew was now holding in his two hands the loop of human-hair rope with which it had been tied. "How did you untie that knot? And, light my lamp, why?"

"It's all right," said John. "I didn't need djinn power. I just worked it out in my head."

"But why, John, why?" Nimrod looked at him fiercely for a moment. "I thought I made it perfectly clear that we should leave the knot tied. To prevent Virgil McCreeby from ever going through that door."

"Yes, but that was before," John said breathlessly.

"Before what?"

"Before I saw the door move," said John. "And before I heard Mr. Groanin. He's on the other side of the door and he sounds like he's in trouble."

"What?" Nimrod stepped quickly toward the Eye of the Forest and, pressing his ear to the door, listened carefully. Sure enough, albeit from a very long way away, he could hear his own butler shouting. "Light my lamp, but you're right, boy. Here. Help me draw this bolt."

Instinctively realizing the importance of the hair rope, John wound it around his waist, like a belt.

The spindle of the golden bolt, which had two large golden handles was, after several centuries, hard to turn in the hole and, in its fastening, even harder to draw back.

"You're not angry then?" said John, pulling on the bolt with all of his strength. "That I've untied the knot? And that we're going to open the door?"

"Given that Groanin is already on the other side, the question seems academic and no longer important." Nimrod grunted with the effort. "Let us hope that the others escaped the Xuanaci and are with him."

At last the bolt shifted and the door was free, although not yet open.

"Stand farther away," Nimrod ordered John. "We don't yet know what's on the other side. If Groanin is in danger, we may also be at some risk."

As Nimrod hauled at the creaking door, John took a step back. With all his exertions the rope had come loose around his waist, which John thought was just a little ironic given how tight it had been as a knot. He took it off for a moment to retie it, which was when he noticed the colored dots on the inside of the rope and realized he'd seen the same order of colored dots somewhere before. But there was no time now to think about that. The door was open. And on the other side he could see . . .

. . . nothing at all. Just a gaping black hole. It was, he thought, extremely weird. Even Nimrod looked surprised.

"Strange," remarked Nimrod.

"But where's Groanin?" asked John.

Nimrod took hold of his nephew's arm and stopped him from going through the open door. "Wait a minute," he said. "There's movement."

Inside the doorway that was the Eye of the Forest, a strange optical distortion of space was underway, as if light itself was bending. Then, on the other side of the doorway, like an old movie flickering into life, a large stone room appeared. This ancient-looking room was stacked high with hundreds, possibly thousands of gold objects, but of Groanin and the others there was no sign.

And yet there was also something unreal about the room and its fabulous, glittering treasure. As if it didn't quite exist at all.

"What are we looking at?" asked John.

"It's an illusion," said Nimrod. "Something those ancient Incan priests must have intended for the greedy eyes of the conquistadors. Only *they* would probably have called it a vision. Don't ask me how an Inca like Ti Cosi achieved such a thing. I don't know. But I think we're looking at an image of something that really happened. An image that was meant to lure the conquistadors on.

"You see, when Pizarro showed up in Cuzco, he managed, against all the odds, to capture King Atahualpa and promised him his life if he agreed to cooperate. And noticing the Spaniards' fascination with gold, Atahualpa made a proposition to Pizarro. The king drew a chalk line high on the wall of the room in the Temple of the Sun, where he was now held prisoner, and told Pizarro that if he spared his life, within twelve months he would fill the room with gold objects up to the height of the mark. Pizarro agreed, of course, and the king was as good as his word, even if Pizarro wasn't. It is said that more than forty thousand pounds in weight of twenty-four-karat gold was turned into ingots by the Spanish. The Incan priest who made the Eye of the Forest undoubtedly knew that seeing a vision of all that gold would, almost certainly, have been interpreted by the Spaniards as some kind of good omen."

Another moment passed and then the image of the gold disappeared like a mirage and, for a few seconds, it was replaced by a frozen image of Groanin and Sicky hammering at the door. At their feet lay Philippa, unconscious, and behind them stood Muddy in the act of brandishing a machete at some strange-looking Incan warriors. A second later, the four figures had changed their positions and were now stretching slowly through the door, like something escaping from a black hole.

"Philippa's hurt," said John, and bent forward to help Groanin, Muddy, and Sicky drag her through the doorway.

"Don't touch them," Nimrod told John. "They're moving between two dimensions. Which can be dangerous."

"Will they be all right?" asked John. "I mean, they look kind of weird. Sort of stretched out. Like spaghetti."

"It might take a few minutes for them to come through," said Nimrod. "I imagine this was designed to be an entrance, not an exit. But, yes. They should be all right. So long as we are patient."

"You mean it might be quicker going in than coming out?"

"Exactly. As soon as they are out, we must close the door. Otherwise the Incas, who seem to be chasing them, will also be chasing us."

"Zadie doesn't appear to be with them," observed John.

"I was wondering about her myself," admitted Nimrod.

Groanin, Muddy, and Sicky were still dragging Philippa through the doorway, but very slowly, as if they were walking through molasses. Then, an arrow appeared in the air above John's head. It was an unusual arrow because it wasn't moving more than about half a mile an hour. And, but for Nimrod's earlier warning, John might easily have reached up and grabbed it.

"That looks like one of Zeno's paradoxes," said Nimrod.

"Zeno's what?"

"Never mind," smiled Nimrod. "While we're waiting, you might like to tell me how you managed to untie the knot. I don't mind telling you, I'm impressed. I know I couldn't have done it."

John told him. But because he had no memory of his head having been inside the lupuna tree he left that part out, which made his achievement seem all the more impressive to Nimrod.

"Remarkable," said Nimrod.

"I noticed something else," said John. "When I was untying the rope."

"Oh?"

"There is a series of colored dots on the rope's inside," said John. "Interestingly, they correspond with the series of colored knots that appear on the *khipu* given to me by *el Tunchi*."

"That *is* interesting," agreed Nimrod.

"I'm pretty sure that the position and number of these dots mean something important," he said. "I'm not sure what yet. Only that it will come to me. In time."

Nimrod was pleased with his nephew. "You've already done more than I thought was possible," he said. "Perhaps your experience with *el Tunchi* has sharpened your wits."

"No," said John. "No, it wasn't that. But I do feel more intelligent, sort of, since I had that nap." He pointed at the doorway. "Look, they're nearly through."

Nimrod put his hand close to the door, ready to close it the second he was able to do so without hitting Philippa, who was the last to emerge from beyond the Eye of the Forest. A fierce-looking Inca king was close on their heels with a large war club in his raised hand, as if he was in the act of bringing it down on Groanin's head. Momentarily, Nimrod glanced at John. "When were you asleep?" he asked.

"When you were thinking in your tent," said John. "I sat down to read that book about *khipus* and must have dozed off. Books do have that effect on me, I'm afraid."

Nimrod tutted loudly. Then he said, "Where were you sitting, exactly?"

"Over there." John pointed at one of the huge lupuna trees.

"You mean you were resting against one of the trees?"

"S'right."

"That explains it, then," said Nimrod. "You must have learned something from the spirit of the lupuna."

"You mean I didn't come up with the solution to the knot all by myself?" John sounded a little disappointed.

"I'm afraid not," said Nimrod. "But there's no shame in that. After all, you do know what you know. And rest assured, I certainly won't tell anyone your secret." He glanced back at the doorway. "At last. I think we're about ready to close the Eye."

The very next second, he slammed the door in the face of the slowly advancing Inca king, and John suddenly understood what Nimrod had meant by closing the Eye. Nimrod picked up a piece of wood and used it as a temporary fastening on the bolt. "That should hold them for a little while," he said.

As soon as the door was closed, Groanin, Sicky, and Muddy suddenly came to life, as if somewhere a switch had been thrown that brought them up to normal speed.

"Thank goodness," bellowed Groanin. "That wasn't a second too soon. I say, that wasn't a second too soon." He rubbed the back of his neck and shivered. "That maniac's war club must have missed me by only a millimeter."

"If my head wasn't so small," said Sicky, "he'd have combed my hair with it for sure."

Groanin put a hand on his chest. "My heart," he said. "It feels like I've got the whole Nelson Riddle Orchestra in my chest. And they're playing 'I Get a Kick Out of You.'"

Nimrod and John knelt down by Philippa.

"We had a bit of a collision, she and I," Groanin explained. "It were an accident, so it were. Couldn't be helped. But I'm right sorry, that I am. I wouldn't have hurt the lass for all the world."

"I know, Groanin," Nimrod said kindly. "I know."

"We have to get her to a hospital," insisted Groanin.

John put his ear to Philippa's chest. "She'll be all right," he said. "I can tell. She's just a bit concussed."

"What are you, a flipping doctor?" demanded Groanin.

"No, but I am her twin," explained John. He tapped his head and then his heart. "I'd have known in here if she wasn't all right."

"Yes, of course," said Groanin. "Stupid of me."

John was right. A moment or two later, Philippa groaned and moved her head. And within just a few minutes she was sitting up and sharing explanations of what had happened since Nimrod and John had parted from her and the others.

"Zadie's a traitor," John told his friends. "That's probably why she managed to persuade you to invite her along in the first place, Phil. All along she's been in cahoots with Virgil McCreeby, trying to slow us down so that he could catch up with us and she could give him the map. She stole it from Mr. Vodyannoy's pack."

"That would explain why she went off with Pizarro and his men," said Philippa. "She obviously intends to go and find McCreeby while the Spaniards are busy dealing with the Xuanaci Indians." Then she gasped. "Oh, for goodness' sake. We have to do something to help them. The Xuanaci. Pizarro and his men will massacre them for sure."

But John was almost as offended by this idea as Zadie had been. "What? Are you kidding? They were going to feed you to the piranhas. And then eat the fish."

"Philippa's right, John," said Nimrod. "It was an unequal struggle back in November 1532 when the Spaniards first turned up on the Incas' doorstep. And it's an especially unequal struggle now. After all, even the Xuanaci can hardly defeat an enemy that's already dead."

"I guess you have a point," agreed John.

Philippa rubbed her head and stood up. She felt a little like she'd been hit by a truck. But nothing was broken. "So, what are we going to do?" she asked Nimrod.

"I think there's only one thing we can do," said Nimrod. "And that's to give the Xuanaci a powerful ally."

"Who?" asked Philippa.

Nimrod looked at Sicky. "Can you remember the way back to the Xuanaci camp?" he asked.

Sicky pointed at the Eye of the Forest. "You mean, down there? Through that door?"

"No, through the jungle."

Sicky shrugged. "Sure, no problem," he said. "My head might be small but there's nothing wrong with my sense of direction. Or my memory, boss. Twice I've been a guest of the Xuanaci and twice I've gotten away with my life. I'm not exactly anxious to be visiting with them Xuanaci a third time."

"Not visit, exactly," said Nimrod. "All you have to do is lead some warriors near to the Xuanaci camp." He laid a hand kindly on the jungle guide's broad shoulder. "How do you feel about doing something like that, Sicky?"

"Sick," said Sicky. "Pretty sick. But I'll do it. Only, what warriors are you talking about, boss? There ain't no warriors hereabouts who're crazy enough to take on no headhunters like the Xuanaci."

"Yes, there are," said Nimrod, and looked at the door in the Eye of the Forest. "Who better than some dead Incan warrior kings to go and fight with some dead conquistadors? Who is harmed, if everyone is already dead?"

"Your logic is unanswerable," said Philippa.

"I think maybe you is the crazy one, boss," said Sicky.

"Sicky's right, sir," agreed Groanin. "We only just got away from those nutters. And you're proposing to open that door and let them out. How do we know that they won't bash our heads in first?"

"We can protect ourselves with djinn power, of course," said Philippa.

"I'm afraid we can't, no," said Nimrod. "Not here. This is a holy place." And he told Philippa what he had already told John: that under *The Baghdad Rules*, which govern the use of djinn power, it is strictly forbidden to use djinn power in a church, a mosque, a synagogue, or any holy place where worship had been conducted within the last thousand years.

"It doesn't look much like a church," observed Groanin. "At least not the ones I've been to."

"Nevertheless it is, and that's the rule," said Nimrod.

"So what are you proposing to do?" Groanin said acidly. "Persuade them with quiet diplomacy not to bash our heads in. Is that it?"

"Yes," said Nimrod.

"The man's mad." Groanin looked at Philippa and shook his head. "I say, the man's mad."

Nimrod smiled. "Well, not just diplomacy," he said. "Eh, John?"

"What's that?"

"It was John who solved the secret of the Gordian-like knot that was used to bind the bolt on the door," said Nimrod.

"Er, yes, it was," John said a little uncomfortably.

"And it's John who knows now how to speak diplomatically to these Inca kings, not me. It's he who will know exactly what to say."

"I do?"

"Yes. I think you do. I think when the moment comes, you'll know exactly what has to be said."

"I will?"

Groanin rolled his eyes. "Doesn't sound like it," he remarked caustically. "The lad doesn't sound like he even knows what day it is."

Nimrod was already walking back to the door in the Eye of the Forest.

"Hang on a minute," said John. "You're not going to open it again right this minute, are you?"

"That's the general idea," said Nimrod.

"But, look, I'm not ready yet. Really I'm not."

"Listen to him, will you, sir?" said Groanin. "Don't bully the lad so. If he doesn't know, he doesn't know. For Pete's sake, you always think you know better than anyone else."

"Think about it, John," said Nimrod, ignoring his butler. "You just knew how to solve the problem of the knot, didn't you?"

"Yes."

"Then you'll just know what to say to the Inca kings in the same way," insisted Nimrod.

"But suppose I don't understand," said John, "what it is I'm supposed to say. What if it makes no sense?"

"Then I suggest you say it anyway," said Nimrod, and removing the piece of wood from the bolt fastening, he opened the door once again.

CHAPTER 18

SPEAKING IN TONGUES

With the door in the Eye of the Forest now wide open, the heavily armed, mummified Inca kings — like Philippa and the other humans before them — slowly started trooping out into the Peruvian jungle clearing. Given their speed, or more accurately, their lack of speed, it seemed, after all, that John would have a few more minutes to remember what he was supposed to remember. Not that he could have ever really remembered what he had never learned in the first place. What was happening inside his mind had nothing to do with memory and everything to do with the lupuna tree, as Nimrod had wisely guessed. But none of this made it any easier for John to know what he was supposed to say that would persuade the kings not to attack them.

Instinctively, John glanced at the *khipu* from *el Tunchi* and the hair rope with which the knot in the door had been tied. The colored marks on both these strange artifacts were starting to mean something. Something important, yes. But what? Some words began to crowd into his mind. Only none of them made any sense to him. It was gibberish, he thought. Could he really speak something without understanding any of it?

It was a word of power, like SESAME in *Arabian Nights*, or an incantation such as ABRACADABRA in the Hebrew kabbalah. A word of power, he was sure of that much. Like a focus word it was a long word, too, only it was much longer than any focus word ever spoken by a djinn. How could he ever hope to pronounce such a long word? It was a much longer word than the longest two words he had ever read — but never pronounced — which were, of course, "FLOCCINAUCINHILIPILIFICATION" and "HONORIFICABILITUDINITATIBUS."

"Hurry up, lad," said Groanin as one of the mummified Inca kings turned slowly to face him. To the butler's horror, he realized it was the same king whose mummified body he'd kicked out of the way when he had picked up Philippa's unconscious body. Groanin felt certain the king would hit him as soon as he was able. Moving rapidly away, he added, "They're speeding up. They'll be hopping around like us in a minute."

"Shhh, Groanin," said Philippa, and took her twin brother's hand, telepathically offering him her own djinn and intellectual power to help enhance John's strength of mind.

"Let me help you, brother. Use my brain as well as your own to help you concentrate. Take my mind and make it yours."

And then . . .

"It's not one word, I don't think, but many words together. Quechua words. That's the ancient language of the Incas. And it's the order of the words that is important. Like a cipher or a code. The order of the words. Speak them as they appear on the *khipu*. As if these were a series of code words you were telephoning to the CIA. That's all you have to do. It's as simple as that."

"Flipping heck," said Groanin, and ducked as an Incan war club swung quickly through the air. "They're up to speed. Say something quick, John lad, or my head is going to look like a bowl of gazpacho soup."

Suddenly, John felt the words in his mouth and blurted them out in a language that he had never heard before. It was a most peculiar sensation. He spoke fluently but — to himself at least — quite unintelligibly.

"Yana chunka," said John. *"Yuraj pusaj. Puka tawa."*

Immediately all of the mummified Incan kings turned to face and then advance upon the one who had spoken.

"It's working," said Groanin. "I've no idea what he's saying but it's working, by Jove."

"Sounds a bit like Quechua to me," said Sicky.

"What's he saying?" asked Muddy.

"Glossolalia," said Nimrod.

"Glosso what? I say, glosso what?"

"Willapi qanchis," said John, continuing. *"Kellu kinsa. Komer phisqa. Sutijankas iskay. Kulli sojta. Chixchi jison. Chunpi uj."*

All of the mummified kings stopped what they were doing and stood still.

"It means 'speaking in tongues,'" said Nimrod. "I've heard of it being done, but never seen it before."

"Does it matter?" said Groanin. "It's had the desired result, hasn't it? The main thing is they no longer seem intent on bashing our heads in."

Surrounded by the Inca kings, who now seemed to be awaiting his next command, John said, "I think it means black ten, white eight, red four, yellow seven, lemon three, green five, blue two, violet six, gray nine, and brown one. The colors are also the names of birds of the same colors."

"Excellent," said Nimrod. "A color and numeric code. What could be simpler?"

"What shall I tell them?" asked John. "I don't know any more words of Quechua."

"Tell them in English," said Nimrod. "I'm sure they'll understand. All languages sound much the same after you're dead. Besides, when they're abroad and speaking to a foreigner, most English people — Groanin for example — just speak English as if they were speaking to a dead person. Which is to say slowly and loudly. And that often works."

"That's a bit unfair," grumbled Groanin.

"All right," said John. "I'll give it a try." He cleared his throat and, reasoning that he was about to address several Inca kings, attempted to sound commanding. "Listen to me. We are your friends, not your enemies. Your true enemies are Pizarro and the conquistadors who, even now, are planning to fight your young brothers, the Xuanaci."

John looked at Nimrod, who nodded his approval.

"Good, John, this is good."

"You must help the Xuanaci to fight and defeat the Spanish conquistadors. Now then, this man." John pointed at Sicky and, almost to his surprise, the Inca kings also looked at him.

"This man. Sicky. He will show you where the Xuanaci village is to be found. And where you can fight the ancient enemies of the Incas. Now go. And do not fail."

"Well done, John," said Nimrod. "As stirring war speeches go, it wasn't exactly Winston Churchill and 'we shall fight them on the beaches,' but still, not bad at all." He looked at Sicky. "All right, Sicky?"

Sicky smiled thinly.

"I never had to guide ancient mummies through the jungle before," he said uncomfortably.

"Just think of them as a bunch of stupid English football hooligans," said Nimrod. "Should be easy enough. They're armed. None of them is wearing much in the way of clothes. And they're covered with tattoos."

"All right, I'll give it a try."

"We'll make camp here," said Nimrod. "And wait for you to come back."

"Okay, Your Majesties," said Sicky. "This way."

And then he and the mummified Inca kings set off into

the jungle. Sicky thought it was about the strangest tour group the jungle had ever seen.

"What now?" asked Philippa.

"I'll tell you what now," said Groanin. "I'm going to put the kettle on and make us a brew. If I don't get a cup of tea soon, I'm going to perish of thirst."

"An excellent idea, Groanin," agreed Nimrod. "I could use a cup of tea myself. And while you're busy doing that, John, Philippa, and I will see if we can't find room to plant some more lupuna trees in the ground around here."

Groanin muttered darkly and then, with Muddy's help, he set to work building a fire.

"Talking about the ground around here," said Philippa, and handed Nimrod the piece of yellow rock she had in her pocket. "A lot of it seems to be made of this. I took this sample when we were underground."

Nimrod weighed the rock in the palm of his hand.

"Heavy, isn't it?" remarked Philippa.

"It seems to be uranium," said Nimrod.

Both twins took a step back from Nimrod.

"Isn't uranium radioactive?" said John.

"Yes," said Nimrod. "But this is quite safe. The alpha radioactive particles released by raw uranium don't absorb through the skin. Microscopic amounts can even be eaten, harmlessly. We all of us manage to consume about one microgram of uranium a day in nearly everything we eat and drink."

"Speak for yourself," muttered John.

"Interesting," Nimrod said, and tossed it playfully to John, who caught it nervously and then put it in his backpack.

From his own backpack, next to the lamp containing Frank Vodyannoy's transubstantiated djinn body, Nimrod produced a small plastic bag. It was full of tiny trees.

"These are bonsai lupuna trees," he told the twins as they walked into a jungle clearing nearby. "Miniaturized using djinn power. And genetically modified by Faustina herself so that they can grow more quickly. I've been planting them ever since we arrived in the upper Amazon. The idea is that they start growing immediately at about ten times the normal speed so that in just twenty years you have a tree that's as big as one that's two hundred years old. It goes without saying that the whole rain forest is important to planet Earth. But there are no trees that put out as much oxygen as the lupunas. To say nothing of the spirits that live within them. It's the lupunas that are the most important ones, especially for us."

"So why do the loggers cut them down?" asked Philippa. "If they're so important."

"Not all loggers do," said Nimrod. "As I told John, some loggers are afraid of them. But most of the loggers have to do what they're told by the logging companies or they'll lose their jobs. And for the companies these lupuna trees are one of the most important saw-logs in Peru. The timber is used for furniture, plywood, and pulp. Even the fiber surrounding the seed gets used as filling for pillows."

"But why do spirits go and hide in these trees and not others?" asked John.

"Spirits like anything that's been in existence for a long time," said Nimrod. "In developed countries that usually means old houses and castles. But here in the jungle, the lupuna trees are the oldest things around." Nimrod looked around the clearing and nodded. "This looks like a good spot to plant some trees." He handed each of the twins a pointed wooden tool.

"What is it?" asked Philippa, looking at the simple implement.

"A hole dibber. You make the holes and I'll put the little trees in them."

It was hard work but after about an hour they had planted the clearing with as many as a hundred new lupuna trees.

"Now all we have to do is protect them from being cut down when they become mature trees," said Nimrod. "John? Philippa? Any ideas on how to do that?"

"How about one of those giant centipedes?" suggested Philippa. "I can't see anyone arguing with one of those horrible things."

"True, but not very subtle. I was thinking of something a little less lethal. After all, these are decent men who are only trying to make a living."

"I don't see what's so decent about it," said Philippa. "Everyone knows it's important to preserve the trees in the rain forest."

"And what about Christmas trees? Did you have one of those last year?"

"Er, yes," said Philippa. "But those are different, aren't they? I mean, Christmas wouldn't be Christmas without a nice tree."

"Rank hypocrisy," Nimrod snorted. "You want some poor Peruvian loggers to desist from making their living by cutting down trees in the rain forest. But you don't want to give up your own Christmas tree."

Philippa pursed her lips and nodded thoughtfully. She had to admit he had a point.

"But let's get back to the problem at hand," said Nimrod. "How are we going to protect these new trees?"

"Why not make them invisible?" said John. "After all, you can hardly cut down what you can't see, now can you? I can't think of anything more subtle than that."

"No, nor can I," said Nimrod. "Good thinking, John. Actually, I've been doing the same thing myself with the trees I already planted. I just wanted to see if your ideas coincided with my own in this matter. Do you know any good invisibility bindings?"

"No," said John. "I'm not very good with those. Whenever I try to make something invisible, it disintegrates."

"Me, too," confessed Philippa.

"Then it's fortunate I know a good one," said Nimrod, and, muttering his focus word, the small tree plantation disappeared.

*　　*　　*

When they got back to camp, they found tea waiting for them, which Nimrod decided to complement with cucumber sandwiches and a large chocolate cake, and scones with lots of cream and jam.

"Beats me why you didn't make the tea as well," complained Groanin. "I say, it beats me why you didn't make the tea as well, sir."

"Because, my dear Groanin, it is an established fact that tea always tastes better when someone else makes it. And what's more, when someone makes it properly, as only an English butler can. In a teapot, with boiling water. And then serves it with milk. Never with lemon. You have many good qualities, Groanin, and you have many faults, as well. But no one makes tea quite like you."

"Thank you, sir."

"I don't know about the tea," said John, "but this cake is fantastic."

"Cucumber sarnies aren't bad, either," agreed Groanin.

"After all that we have been through," said Nimrod, "I thought we could do with a treat. There's nothing boosts morale quite as well as an English high tea."

"I couldn't agree more, Nimrod," said a polite English voice. "Milk and two sugars for me, Groanin. Oh, and I say, doesn't that chocolate cake look nice? It is fresh cream, isn't it? Silly me. Of course it is. You wouldn't have any other kind of cake, would you, Nimrod? Not a man of your taste and sophistication. But I wonder if that cake tastes as good as my wife's famous lemon drizzle cake."

CHILDREN OF THE LAMP

Everyone looked around to see a man walking toward them, grinning affably and waving Faustina's map. He wore a safari jacket, puttees, and a solar topi, which is a kind of hat. On his chin was a beard that looked like a shoe brush, and he had a smooth, well-spoken voice that always reminded John of an actor in a play by William Shakespeare. And but for the gun in his hand, the man might even have seemed quite friendly.

"I was wondering when you'd show up," said Nimrod.

Of course, it was Virgil McCreeby and he was accompanied by Zadie Eloko and a tall, moody-looking boy of about thirteen who wore a rock band T-shirt, jeans, a leather jacket, and a pair of motorcycle boots that looked like they'd been around the Daytona International Speedway by themselves.

"Dybbuk," exclaimed Philippa. "Dybbuk, what are you doing here?"

Dybbuk made a noise like a bassoon and rolled his eyes up to the top of his long-haired head. "Buck," he said. "Just Buck, okay?"

CHAPTER 19

THE HOSTAGE

"Give me one good reason why I shouldn't turn you into an ulcerous toad, McCreeby," said Nimrod.

"Because he already is an ulcerous toad?" offered John.

"I say, that's not very hospitable, Nimrod," said McCreeby. He swallowed a mouthful of Nimrod's cake and washed it down with some hot sweet tea. "Considering that I'm a fellow Englishman out here in the Amazon jungle and all that rot. But since you ask, I'll give you a number of jolly good reasons why you ought to restrain yourself. And this goes for all of you." He pointed first at the twins and then at Groanin and Muddy before stuffing some more chocolate cake into his mouth. Clearly he was enjoying it. He even managed to smear some of the chocolate icing on the handle of the gun he was still carrying.

"I'm listening," said Nimrod. "You were about to list the reasons why I should restrain myself from turning you into a toad. And I suggest you do it very quickly."

"Well then, let's see." McCreeby licked chocolate off his fingers' ends as he started counting off the reasons. "One is that this is a holy place and I know that out of a stupid sort of respect for other belief systems, you people won't use djinn power in a holy place." McCreeby glanced up at the cathedral of lupuna trees. "What do they call this kind of thing? An *abadía de árboles*, isn't it? So. As long as we're here, I figure I'm perfectly safe. Especially with this gun in my hand. Which is, of course, another reason why you should restrain yourselves. And I will use the gun if I have to, so I advise you all not to try anything. That's two reasons." He slurped some tea noisily.

"But you djinn do like things in threes, don't you? Such as wishes. Oh, yes. So I'll give you a third reason. And perhaps you'll think, as I do, that it's the most important reason of all. You see, I have a hostage. My followers — druids, they call themselves, although to be honest, the little cult I have going in England these days has nothing at all to do with true pagan druidry — are holding John and Philippa's father, Mr. Gaunt, at a secret location. Which is to say, he's been kidnapped. But don't worry. He'll remain quite unharmed as long as you keep out of my way."

"I don't believe you," said John.

"No? Well, naturally I didn't expect you just to take my word for it, boy. I've brought some proof, of course. And you can thank your lucky stars that I'm a civilized sort of man and that I'm not about to hand over your father's ear or little finger."

Virgil McCreeby nodded at Dybbuk, who dropped his backpack on the ground and silently began to search inside for something. Apart from insisting that people should call him Buck, Dybbuk still hadn't spoken. The sense of shame he was feeling in front of his former friends had, so far, prevented it.

"Mr. Gaunt was kidnapped," explained McCreeby, "on his way to work one morning in Manhattan while you were all in New Haven."

"Mr. Senna would never have allowed anyone to kidnap my father," insisted John. "He's Dad's bodyguard as well as his driver. And he's pretty good at it. He's ex–Special Forces."

"Oh, is he?" McCreeby made a face. "Well, Special Forces or not, your Mr. Senna has a stomach like anyone else. Which means it can be upset. Especially when my people managed to give him something nasty to put inside it. Such as a potion of my own devising that makes it impossible to leave the bathroom for three whole days. I mean, that's what I really call 'Special Forces.'" McCreeby chuckled unpleasantly. "As a result, on the particular morning in question, he just wasn't there to drive your dad to work. One of my followers was. Mr. Haddo. Anyway, your dear old dad didn't even notice that old Sennapod wasn't in the driving seat. Until it was too late. Show him, Buck."

Dybbuk took a small laptop out of his backpack. He folded open the computer, attached it to a satellite phone, switched it on, logged on to a popular Web site featuring lots of videos, and then turned it toward John.

John tried to meet the eye of his old friend but Dybbuk avoided it.

"And here I was thinking it was Finlay who was helping McCreeby," said John, "when it was you all along. I might have known. Why are you doing this, Buck? I thought we were friends."

But Dybbuk did not answer. This — the moment when he faced John and Philippa — was the moment he had most dreaded. Now that he was here with his former friends, enduring their sense of disappointment in him, he felt even worse than he had expected to feel. After all the adventures they had come through together, he knew exactly what they must be thinking about him. Dybbuk winced as if someone had burned him with a hot iron when Groanin said loudly, "I never liked that lad. I always thought he were trouble. I say, I always thought he were trouble."

Meanwhile, Groanin, Nimrod, Philippa, and Muddy had grouped around the laptop and were waiting to view what had been recorded.

In the video, Mr. Gaunt was seated on a chair inside a cage. He was wearing an orange jumpsuit and holding up a copy of the *New York Daily Post* with manacled hands. The video zoomed in on the front page and then the date of the newspaper so that the fact of his imprisonment might easily be proved to anyone's satisfaction. He looked a little tired and unshaven but otherwise seemed quite unharmed.

"Hi, kids," said Mr. Gaunt. "Hi, Nimrod. I guess you know by now that I've been kidnapped and that I'm being held hostage by three English hippie weirdos. I have no idea who they are or what they want, but they're treating me well enough. I'm getting plenty to eat and to read and I'm watching a lot of TV. I've been told to tell you that if you do exactly what they say, they'll let me go unharmed. But that if you don't cooperate, then things might get a bit rough for me. Their words, not mine. That's pretty much all that I'm going to be allowed to say, except that John? Philippa? I miss you both and love you very much and hope to see you again soon. And not to worry about me. We've come through bad times before and we'll do so again."

When the video ended abruptly, they watched it once more.

"Most heartwarming," said McCreeby.

"Is it for real?" John asked Nimrod.

"Of course, it's for real," McCreeby said irritably. "Whatever makes you think otherwise?"

"You faked the photograph in the newspaper," said John. "The one of the exploration party supposedly discovering the Eye of the Forest."

"Yes I did," admitted McCreeby. "Rather a good fake, though, don't you think? Amazing what you can do on a computer these days."

"So, maybe you faked the video, too," suggested John.

"If I did, then I'd have nothing to bargain with," said McCreeby. "Which is hardly likely. I'd be taking a terrible risk, wouldn't I? Risking the wrath of three powerful djinn? Four if we include your mother. It was a lucky break her not being on the scene right now, wasn't it?" McCreeby shook his head. "No, I'm not brave enough to fake it, lad. Or sufficiently foolhardy. Besides, now that you've guided me here to the real Eye of the Forest, it's not like I'm asking anything from you people except to stay out of my way. If you do that, then your father will be returned to you unharmed. You have the word of Virgil McCreeby."

"Whatever that's worth," Nimrod laughed. "What exactly are you after, McCreeby?"

"I should have thought it was obvious. I intend to find the lost city of Paititi."

"Now I'm beginning to understand," said Nimrod. "There's something in this for both of you. You're planning to carry out the *kutumunkichu* ritual, aren't you?"

"I've never heard of it," McCreeby said innocently. "You're mistaken. *Kutumunkichu?* What's that?"

"Using the *kutumunkichu* ritual, you, McCreeby, hope to gain the power of turning base metal into gold." He looked squarely at Dybbuk. "While you, Buck, you think you can restore your power. Like Manco Capac himself. Isn't that right?"

"Why not? The *kutumunkichu* ritual worked for him," said Buck. "Why not me?"

McCreeby winced. "It might have been better not to have mentioned that," he told Dybbuk.

But Dybbuk ignored him. "It will work for me," he told Nimrod. "It has to work."

Philippa almost felt sorry for him.

"Is that what you've told him, McCreeby?" asked Nimrod.

"I haven't told him anything." McCreeby sounded indignant. "Buck read the ancient Incan texts for himself. In the library back at my castle in England. You remember my library, Nimrod, don't you?"

"What ancient text might that be?" Nimrod asked. "After all, the Incas wrote nothing down."

"The Incan priest Ti Cosi, nephew of King Titu Cusi, who was himself nephew of Atahualpa, described a number of Incan myths and legends to a Spanish chronicler in about 1550. Including the *kutumunkichu* ritual. I have the only extant copy of that chronicle. What I didn't have was the map of how to get here. Thanks to you that's no longer a problem. And before you suggest otherwise, it was Dybbuk who sought me out, looking for a solution to his problem. In return for my help, I'm getting not three wishes but six. That's three from Zadie, and three from Buck. At least he will give me three wishes as soon as he gets his djinn power back. The only reason I'm not insisting that any of you give me three wishes, as well, is because even with your father under my control, I still don't trust you not to do something unpleasant to me."

At this mention of her father, Philippa wiped a tear from her eye.

"Ah, yes," said McCreeby. "That reminds me. The tears of the sun that were in Zadie's backpack? We need them for the ritual. So please, hand them over."

When no one moved, McCreeby added, "I only have to use the satellite phone to tell Mr. Haddo that you're being obstructive. And he'll just post another video of your father for you to watch that won't be as easy on the eye as the first one. Come on. Hand them over. Best save your father the heartache, eh? Oh, yes, and you'd best hand over your satellite phone, as well. Zadie told me you've got one."

John went into his backpack and found the three gold disks that had been stolen from the Peabody Museum. To his surprise they were quite warm. Almost hot, even. He handed them to Dybbuk. And then the phone.

"Listen to me carefully, Buck," said Nimrod. "It's possible that this Incan ritual you've read about has something to do with the *Pachacuti*. The great earth shaking that presages the end of the world. It might very well be dangerous. Very dangerous."

"You don't really believe that prophecy, do you?" scoffed McCreeby. "If that kind of force had been available to the Incas, don't you think they'd have used it against Pizarro and his conquistadors? Of course they would."

"Manco Capac died," Nimrod told Dybbuk, ignoring McCreeby. "Have you thought about that, boy?"

"Manco was old and sick already," said Dybbuk. "Anyway, without djinn power, I might as well be dead. To live without djinn power is no life at all."

"You're still alive," said John. "That's something, isn't it?"

"Easy for you to say, John," said Dybbuk. "You still have your power. I don't."

"And whose fault is that?" said John.

"John is right. You were warned not to waste your power," said Nimrod. "By everyone. Me. Your poor mother. Everyone. But you chose not to listen. You abused your gift by performing cheap magic tricks for the entertainment of mundanes."

"That's a little unfair, Nimrod," said McCreeby. "They were hardly cheap tricks. Some of them were rather good, I thought."

"On television." Nimrod spoke the word as if it had been something disgraceful.

"I did what I did," Dybbuk said angrily. "But it sure doesn't make it feel any better that everyone told me not to do it. And what would you do? If you were in my position? John? Philippa? What would you do if you lost all of your power? Wouldn't you try anything to get it back? Of course you would."

"We all of us have to live with the consequences of our actions," said John. "That's what life is all about."

"Easy to say," said Dybbuk. "But not so easy to do."

It was Philippa's turn to be angry now. But not with Dybbuk. She was angry with Zadie.

"I can understand why he's doing this," she told Zadie. "He was always headstrong. It's you I don't understand. How could you be in cahoots with them? How could you betray my confidence like that?"

Dybbuk took Zadie's hand. "Leave her alone," he told Philippa. "She did it for me."

"I love him," said Zadie. "That's why I've been helping them since we got here. Delaying you with those monsters to help Buck and McCreeby catch up with us when we fell behind. Putting clues on the ground so that you would think an expedition party had gone ahead of us. I want to help Buck get his power back." She looked at Dybbuk and smiled warmly. "I'd do anything for him. I don't expect someone like you, Philippa, to understand something like that. After all, who could fall in love with someone like you?"

McCreeby smiled and waved his hands mysteriously in front of Zadie's face. *"L'amour, toujours l'amour,"* he said. "Love conquers all."

"Speaking of conquest," said Philippa, trying to ignore Zadie's hurtful insult. "What happened to your friend Pizarro and his conquistadors? Where are they now?"

Zadie gave Philippa her most sarcastic smile and then shrugged.

"The last time I saw them they were in a pitched battle with your friends, the Xuanaci," she said. "And serves them right, too."

"That's right," said McCreeby. "That's right, Zadie. I agree with you. Listen to my voice and only my voice. Forget everything else. Only my voice matters." He waved his hands in front of her face again.

"You've hypnotized her, haven't you?" said Nimrod. "That's why she's helping you. She only thinks she's in love with Dybbuk. Because you've told her she is. To help persuade her."

"What rubbish," said McCreeby. He glanced nervously at Dybbuk. "Of course she's in love with my young friend."

But Dybbuk now gave him a strange look.

"Aren't you, Zadie?"

"Yes," said Zadie. But there was something in her voice that sounded mechanical and automatic. "I'm in love with him. Always have been. Always will be. Love. *L'amour, toujours l'amour.*"

"You see?" McCreeby smiled and pointed at the door in the Eye of the Forest. "Well," he said. "I'm sorry to break up this very touching reunion, but we have to go in there. Clever of you to work out how to untie the knot on the door lock, Nimrod. Myself, I should just have cut it with a machete and been done with it. Like that other famous chap from Greece."

"It wasn't me who solved the secret," said Nimrod. "It was John."

McCreeby smiled at John.

"Then it was clever of you, boy. Perhaps you will now go ahead and conquer the known world. Oh, yes. One more thing. My information is that there's a rope bridge made of human hair that leads all the way to Paititi. Would that be correct?"

"Correct," said Philippa.

"And the guardians? The Inca king mummies."

"They've gone somewhere else," said Philippa. She shot a sarcastic smile back at Zadie. "To help the Xuanaci."

If she and John were being honest with McCreeby it was because they were anxious about their father.

"As usual, McCreeby, you are very well-informed," said Nimrod.

"I like to read," he said. "It gives one such an unfair advantage over those other humans who look only to television and radio for their information."

"In which case," said Nimrod, "hasn't it occurred to you that, perhaps, Ti Cosi sought to mislead his Spanish chronicler? That the *kutumunkichu* ritual will actually bring about the *Pachacuti*? The great destruction?"

"I come back to my previous question, Nimrod. If that kind of destructive force had been available to the Incas, don't you think they'd have used it against Pizarro? No, I don't think the *kutumunkichu* ritual will actually bring about the *Pachacuti*." McCreeby shook his head and lifted up his backpack. "But nice try all the same."

He looked at Dybbuk and Zadie. "Come on, you two. Let's get moving."

"What about my dad?" asked John.

"He'll be all right," said McCreeby. "Provided no one tries to follow us or to interfere. As soon as I'm safely out of Peru, I'll call Mr. Haddo and tell them to let him go. Simple as that. Believe me, I have no interest in incurring the wrath of your mother, Layla."

"To say nothing of my own wrath," said Nimrod.

"Which is why I shall have need of six wishes, I expect. You see, Nimrod? I've thought of everything."

McCreeby opened the door in the Eye of the Forest and, closely followed by Dybbuk and Zadie, he walked on through. At which point all three disappeared.

"I dislike that man intensely," said Groanin.

"So do I," said Nimrod, closing the door behind them.

"Now what? I say, now what?"

"You heard what McCreeby said. Our hands are tied, Groanin."

"Normally," said John, "when someone is kidnapped, you try to find them before the ransom is paid."

"That's not so easy when you're up the Amazon," said Groanin.

"If only your mother were in New York," said Nimrod, "instead of Brazil."

"We need to get a message to her," said Philippa. "We need to tell her to go home and look for Dad."

"Does anyone have the telephone number of Dr. Kowalski?" asked Nimrod. "Her plastic surgeon."

"No," said Philippa. "She didn't give it to us. Besides, McCreeby took our satellite phone."

"So we'll make another," said John.

"Not here," said Nimrod. "Not in this place. Remember?"

"All right," said John. "We leave this place. Make a phone somewhere else."

"Why not use djinnternal mail?" said Philippa. "It's probably quicker."

She was referring to the facility that exists between mature djinn who are also brother and sister, whereby it is possible for one to swallow something and it then to appear in the other's mouth. No matter how far apart they might be.

"It's normal to telephone first and warn the other person," said Nimrod. "The last time Layla sent me something by djinnternal mail, I was in the dentist's chair. It was very embarrassing." He shrugged. "On the other hand, it might take a while to find Kowalski's number. And time is of the essence in this case. I mean, the sooner she finds your father, the sooner we can go after Virgil McCreeby and stop him."

CHAPTER 20

IN SEARCH OF MR. GAUNT

Dr. Stanley Kowalski pushed himself away from the wall on which he'd been leaning and handed Layla Gaunt a hand mirror and a photograph taken more than a year before the terrible accident that had destroyed her original face and body.

Layla looked from one to the other and then back again, for several minutes until, recognizing herself for the first time in months, she smiled broadly.

"I can't believe what a great job you've done," she said. "I look exactly like my old self. And I mean exactly. I absolutely couldn't tell that this face didn't start out as my own. That's how good a job you've done. Among plastic surgeons you're a genius, do you know that? A genius."

Dr. Kowalski took the match he'd been coolly chewing out of his mouth and smiled modestly. "Cut it out." He hardly dressed or behaved like a surgeon at all. Underneath his white coat he wore a plain gray T-shirt, a pair of jeans, and heavy work boots.

"No, it's true," insisted Mrs. Gaunt. "If I didn't know better, I'd say it was magic."

"You know something?" said Kowalski. "That's what all my patients say. If only they knew, huh?"

"That you're a djinn? If they knew that, Stanley, they'd probably expect the impossible. Instead of the mere miracles you actually perform."

"If it was anyone else but me doing it, plastic surgery like the surgery you've had would be impossible, of course." The doctor shrugged modestly. "But most people who come in here just want to look like a better version of themselves. Not someone completely different, like you did, Layla."

"Look who's talking. You're hardly the guy I remember from school."

Dr. Kowalski scratched himself and put the match back in his mouth. He was an unusual man in that he looked exactly like a famous movie actor — now dead — named Marlon Brando. Not the old Marlon Brando who had appeared in movies like *The Godfather*, but the young Marlon Brando who had appeared in movies like *A Streetcar Named Desire*. Years before, Kowalski's djinn father, Victor, who was a plastic surgeon in Beverly Hills, California, had, at his son's request, made Stanley the spitting image of an actor many people once thought the handsomest man in the world. Doctor Stanley Kowalski even spoke like Marlon Brando.

"Sure, I've changed." Kowalski shrugged again. "For the better. And you know why? Because I wanted to be comfortable. That's always been my motto in this business. Be comfortable with yourself. And if you can't be that, then you change yourself until you *are* comfortable. Simple."

"Thanks to you, I feel more comfortable with myself than I have in ages." Layla looked at both profiles, one after the other, and then kissed Kowalski on the cheek.

Kowalski looked embarrassed.

"No, really, I am very grateful. Now then. You've known me for years, Stanley. We were at school together. So tell me honestly. Surgery is one thing. I look like myself again. But am I still glamorous?"

"I never met a dame yet that didn't know if she was glamorous or not without being told. Sure, you're glamorous, Layla. Like you always were. Beautiful with a cherry on top."

Layla smiled happily. The next second, however, she started to cough in a horrible choking way and put her hand onto to her chest.

"What's the matter?" Kowalski asked anxiously. "Are you all right?"

"Bottle me," said Layla, and uttered some more gurgling choking noises that sounded like steam emerging under pressure from an espresso coffee machine. "There's something coming up in my throat."

By now she had guessed what was happening and how an object — whatever it was — came to be traveling up from her stomach and into her windpipe. "It's my brother, Nimrod."

For a brief moment she cursed Nimrod for using djinnternal mail without telling her, but then another moment passed and she put her hand up to her mouth and spat the object onto the palm of her hand. "Djinnternal mail," she said.

"That's a relief," said Kowalski. "For a moment I thought it might be some kind of reaction to the plastic surgery. That can happen sometimes. Just the idea of looking like someone else can stick in people's throats."

Layla Gaunt unfolded a message written on greaseproof paper and read it quickly.

"I have to get back to New York immediately," she said. "Possibly even quicker than that. My husband, Edward, has been kidnapped."

"That's too bad. Do you know who's behind it? The Ifrit? The Ghul?"

"Nimrod thinks they're mundanes."

"Asking for trouble, aren't they? Messing with a djinn like you?"

"Yes," Layla said grimly. "They are."

Since it seemed unwise for Layla to risk creating another whirlwind — she hadn't forgotten the one she'd released on New York from the roof of the Guggenheim Museum — Kowalski drove her to an airport. But not just any airport. He drove her to an airport belonging to the Brazilian FAB, the aerial warfare branch of the Brazilian armed forces. Layla had decided to hitch a ride aboard the fastest airplane she could find which, as Kowalski had informed her, was — in

Brazil at any rate — the new Mirage 2000 jet fighter, with a top speed of more than fifteen hundred miles per hour.

The pilot, a captain named Alberto Santos, had little choice in the matter of course since Layla put a powerful djinn binding on him. So that when Santos took off he was quite convinced the person sitting in the seat behind him was none other than a major brigadier in the Brazilian Air Force.

Before she took off, Layla thanked Kowalski for all his help and kissed him again.

"Oh, stop, please, you're embarrassing me," he said. "Besides, I haven't finished helping you yet." And he proceeded to point out that since New York was almost five thousand miles from Rio de Janeiro and the jet had an operating range of about nine hundred miles he was going to have to get on the phone and impersonate the real major brigadier — who just happened to be a client of Kowalski's, and who'd had an operation to make him look more obviously heroic — to divert a series of refueling jets into their flight path.

The flight was a smooth one, at least until Captain Santos decided to demonstrate what a proficient pilot he was, and performed a series of aerobatic maneuvers that would have had anyone but a djinn like Layla reaching for the sick bag. Otherwise things went well until, less than four hours after taking off from Rio, the Brazilian jet entered American air space near New York and a squadron of USAF F-15 fighter eagles was scrambled to intercept it.

Seconds later they were under fire. Captain Santos took evasive action but it was an unequal combat. There is only so much a Mirage can do against four F-15s and when a warning signal in the cockpit told them that a missile had locked onto their tail, they had little choice but to eject.

They parachuted down into the sea where a naval vessel was already steaming into the area to pick them up. But Layla had already decided she couldn't afford to be arrested. Not when she was in possession of her old face. So as soon as she hit the water, she let herself sink beneath the surface, conjured herself a self-contained underwater breathing apparatus, a wet suit, and some fins, and, under the noses and binoculars of the sailors searching for her, swam all the way to the Long Island shoreline.

Meanwhile, the poor Brazilian air force captain was arrested. Mrs. Gaunt resolved to go to his assistance, but only later, when the more pressing business that had brought her back from South America was concluded.

She came ashore at Westhampton, which was a lucky break for her. From Westhampton Beach it was but a short distance to the Gaunt family's summer house in Quogue. And under cover of the encroaching darkness, she walked quickly home. Once there, she changed her clothes, made a light supper and, using the computer in her husband's study and the code word Nimrod had given to her through the djinn-ternal mail message, she logged onto the Web site to search for the kidnappers' video.

As soon as Layla had viewed the film she enlarged one frame onto a computer, analyzing the smallest details of what she could see for some clue as to where the video had been made. Finally she found what she was looking for: Behind her husband's cage, in the very corner of the frame, was a tall arched window and after magnifying what was visible through this window several times she ended up with a tantalizing picture of the edge of an old suspension bridge.

"Where is that?" she murmured thoughtfully.

She stared at this picture for a long, long time before she realized that she recognized this bridge. It was the Brooklyn Bridge across New York's East River. And from the angle of the concrete piers and the Manhattan skyline beyond, she was able to deduce that her husband was on the Brooklyn side of the bridge in a building somewhere immediately underneath the bridge itself.

Back on the computer, Layla searched for images of Brooklyn and its famous bridge and in a matter of minutes found a likely location. Right under the bridge was a promenade and a semi-derelict waterfront building called Molloy's Warehouse. The warehouse had tall arched windows just like the one in the video.

Molloy's Warehouse was where her husband was being held by Virgil McCreeby's followers.

Her eyes narrowed angrily as she looked at a picture of the warehouse and imagined what her husband must have been going through.

"I will have such revenges on these creeps," she muttered darkly. "I know not yet what they may be. But they will be the terrors of the earth."

It was dark by the time she got to Brooklyn in her car. The bridge was noisy with traffic and a strong cold wind was blowing off the East River. With powerful binoculars, she scanned Molloy's Warehouse, especially the arched windows. It was a curious, eerie-looking place, like something from a bad dream someone was having in a nightmare. Made of limestone with a steep red tile roof and two polygonal towers, there was only an ancient sign with the name MOLLOY'S WAREHOUSE across the L-shaped stoop to say that it was a warehouse and not a miniature, Romanesque castle. From the outside, the place looked quite deserted. But that was no reason to assume that she had been wrong or that Virgil McCreeby wouldn't have taken a few anti-djinn precautions, just in case. Even a djinn went carefully where Virgil McCreeby was involved.

She went up to the splendid entranceway with its twin arches, noting the ornamental letters on the stones over the front doors. Like runic letters, she thought, as used by the ancient druids. These were common enough in England and Germany, she knew, but rarely ever seen in New York. Layla was about to put her hand on the door handle when her keen nostrils collected the scent of something strange on it. Something that smelled like flowers but was much stronger.

Taking her hand away, she bent closer and sniffed fastidiously at the door handle like a suspicious leopard sensing a hunter's trap. And in the moonlight she saw a tiny frozen wave of something greasy thickly smeared on the handle. It was an unguent of some kind!

Something scuttled through her memory as she remembered what the smell was that was in her nostrils. The unguent. It was a skin-absorbed enzyme made from the venom of a deathstalker scorpion which, if she'd put her hand on the handle, would have left her paralyzed for several hours, perhaps longer, depending on how concentrated it was. Realizing she'd had a lucky escape, Layla muttered her focus word, and a few seconds later, her hands were safely inside thick leather gloves.

She reached for the handle again, and turned it quietly. The door was not locked. But she did not open it yet, either. Layla knew that with a powerful magus like McCreeby, even a door squeak or a creaking floorboard could be put to some sinister use. There were some door squeaks that didn't just raise the hairs on the back of someone's neck but the whole neck and head with it until a person was strangled in midair. And creaking floorboards could turn into a kind of invisible bear trap with powerful jaws that could crush a man's leg. There were even gusts of wind whistling through broken windowpanes that could be turned from the sound of a wolf howling in the distance to an actual timber wolf stalking you hungrily through the darkness.

Layla wasn't afraid of stranglers or bear traps or even wolves, but she was extremely wary of the unexpected. Even so, she still managed to brush away the cobwebs that covered the door to oil the hinges without thinking more than that these were home to just a few common house spiders. That was her first thought. Fortunately, it was not also her second thought: that was to remind herself that Virgil McCreeby was a keen collector of spiders and had made himself almost immune to even the most venomous arachnid. Very likely this was because he knew that whereas poisonous snakes were harmless to djinn, poisonous spiders and scorpions were quite lethal. Quickly, she closed the door again. Just in time, as she caught a glimpse of something large and hairy move in the room behind it. *Much too large for a spider,* she thought. And yet the movement had been triggered by the web, she was sure of that.

Layla went back to the car to leave her body somewhere safe, thinking to make herself invisible before entering the warehouse. Reasoning that she might be gone for a while, she sat in the back where there was a bit more leg room, and locked the doors from the inside. Then she muttered her focus word and, for a moment, it was like growing taller, much taller, except that when she looked down, she found herself looking at the rooftop of the car.

She floated back to the warehouse and through the front door. Immediately, she felt glad she had observed this small precaution because behind the warehouse door was what she took at first glance for a very large spider. Invisible eyes can take longer than physical ones to adjust to darkness, and it was at least a couple of minutes before she realized that what she was really looking at wasn't a spider at all, but rather an unusual large antique engraving of what seemed to be a man on all fours, albeit one who had more than a little of the spider about him, for he was depicted crawling up or possibly down a wall.

Invisibly, she moved forward to take a closer look at the engraving. Dressed all in black, with a white hourglass on his back, the strange man had long, horribly thin arms and legs, tiny hands and feet, and a head bent down so that only a white domelike forehead and a few straggling hairs could be seen. Not so much a spider man as a sort of human-spider. Layla thought it quite the most revolting picture she had ever seen — even outside the Museum of Modern Art — and reflected that an abandoned warehouse was perhaps the best place for it. But it was not something that seemed likely to cause her any harm.

Backing away from the picture, she glanced around the cold and deserted entrance hall. From both sides of the hall a rickety old stairway led upstairs into deeper darkness. Several bentwood chairs were piled one on top of the other against one bare, damp wall and, in an empty fireplace, lay a large sleeping dog. Now dogs famously have a sixth sense and while they can't see into the invisible world, they can sometimes feel when it has been disturbed, and Layla chose to ascend the stairway farthest away from the dog to find only that this led to a brick wall.

Returning to the entrance hall once more she paused by the dog and, thinking that she might use its body for a while, she slipped under its mangy fur and even managed to take several stiff steps before she realized that the dog was dead. And that the only reason it had even looked alive was that it had been stuffed by an expert taxidermist. Doubtless, it had once been someone's favorite pet.

Leaving the dog's stuffed body beside the fireplace, she started to mount the second set of stairs and hadn't gone up more than a few steps when she heard something behind her. Looking around, she saw several dozen footprints in the thick layer of dust that covered the bare floorboards. For just a second, Layla thought that the footprints were her own. Then she looked behind the door and saw that the strange man crawling on all fours in the creepy engraving was no longer there. He was gone. But where? And was it possible that those were his footprints? She glanced around nervously.

Layla's answers were not slow in coming. A cold current of air slipped down the chimney and into the fireplace, turning the entrance hall as cold as a meat locker. This sudden change in temperature served to make her a little more visible than before and therefore more vulnerable to attack. It was all that the strange human-spider from the engraving needed. The hideous thing dropped from the ceiling right into the middle of Layla's ectoplasmic being and with its loathsome mouth parts — the creature had no nose, just a mass of solid tissue around a mouth opening that served as a straw through which it began to suck at her spirit — made a hideous slavering noise like a wet vacuum cleaner.

Suddenly, Layla realized just how well McCreeby had guarded this place against a djinn like her: The creature from the engraving was an exorbere, a special kind of elemental, which was once used by ancient druids conducting exorcisms to suck spirits and other invisible things into its gut. Something similarly horrible had happened to poor Mr. Rakshasas, who had not been seen since a terra-cotta warrior had absorbed him at the Temple of Dendur in the Metropolitan Museum of Art in New York.

She felt some small part of her detach from her invisible being and disappear inside the exorbere. And then something else. She was being slowly sucked into oblivion.

CHAPTER 21

THE TEARS OF THE SUN

What do you think will happen?" Philippa asked Nimrod. "If they complete that ritual you were talking about? The Kutu-mun-something."

It was now almost an hour since Dybbuk, Zadie, and Virgil McCreeby had gone through the door in the Eye of the Forest. And Nimrod's party was still pondering its next course of action. Groanin had made some more tea, which was what he always did when no one could think of anything else to do. This is the English way: If in doubt of anything, sit down and drink a cup of tea while you have a jolly good think about what you're planning to do. It's one of the principal reasons why Britain once had the largest empire the world has ever seen. John and Philippa didn't much like tea, and neither of them wanted to rule the world — they just wanted to see their father safely returned home and their South American expedition successfully concluded. So they drank some lemonade instead.

"The *kutumunkichu*? I honestly don't know," said Nimrod. "But nothing good, I fear. Dybbuk is playing with fire."

"I'll say," said John, and laughed. "Almost literally."

Nimrod frowned a puzzled sort of frown. "Meaning?"

"Meaning that you should have seen the look on his face when I put the tears of the sun in his hand. It was the weirdest thing, but those golden disks were quite hot. Well, one of them was, anyway."

There was a longish silence while Nimrod finished his tea. And then, almost as if John's words had only just caught up with him, Nimrod said, "John, what did you say? About the tears of the sun?"

"One of them was hot."

"Hot? How hot?"

John shrugged. "I dunno. Hot. Not burning hot like it was on fire so that you'd drop it. But too hot to have against your skin for very long. Not hot like it'd been in a fire. But hot like it'd been lying in the midday sun. Or on a radiator. That kind of hot."

Nimrod looked up at the thick tree canopy from which very little really hot sun ever penetrated, and then across at John's backpack. "How could one disk be hot?" he wondered aloud. "All three were inside your backpack."

"That's right," said John. "I mean, I thought that was kind of weird, myself. But at the time, I guess I had other things on my mind. I only just remembered it, actually. What with McCreeby and Buck and what's happened to Dad and that witch Zadie and everything else, it sort of slipped my mind."

"But why should the tears of the sun get hot inside your backpack?" Nimrod got up and went to look inside John's backpack. "Why? It's not like they were in sunlight. Or near the fire for Groanin's kettle."

Groanin lifted his kettle off the fire and poured some more boiling water into the pot. "More tea, sir?"

"No, not at the moment. Thanks, Groanin."

Nimrod lifted the flap of the backpack and began to toss John's possessions onto the forest floor as if he was urgently searching for an answer.

"Hey, be my guest," said John. "That's just my personal stuff, you know? Nothing important. Help yourself, okay?"

Nimrod ignored him. And by now everyone was grouped around John's backpack, wondering what Nimrod might find that could explain why the tears of the sun had been hot.

"I could have something private in there," said John.

"Like what?" said Philippa.

"If I told you it wouldn't exactly be private, now would it?" John told her, with unerring logic.

"Zadie's the one with the secret life, John, not you," said Philippa. "Can you get over that double-crossing little witch?"

"I think I'll get over it a lot quicker than you will," admitted John. "What I can't get over is Buck being in love with her." Her shrugged. "Or her with him. I mean Buck was always a pretty prickly guy."

"He was that," muttered Groanin. "And no mistake."

"I didn't even know he and Zadie were friends," said Philippa.

"I don't even understand that much. I'd have said that Zadie was way too annoying for him."

"Isn't that always the way?" said Groanin. "Nothing perplexes us quite like our best pal's choice in a partner. Eh, sir?"

"Do I have to remind you all that Zadie has been hypnotized?" said Nimrod.

"It seems you did," said Philippa. "Sorry."

"Hmm," said Nimrod, and tossed something in the palm of his hand. It was the piece of yellow rock Philippa had brought up from the underground tunnels. "I thought as much. This is the culprit. The uranium sample. It is still quite warm. Here. Feel it."

He tossed the rock to Philippa who let it fall to the ground, without even attempting to catch it. "Thanks, but no thanks," she said. "If it's hot, it's hot for a reason that doesn't sound safe."

But Muddy picked it up and looked at it more closely. He was used to handling hazardous things. Like guns and cigarettes. And the odd crocodile.

John shook his head. "I knew that rock was dangerous." He started to refill his backpack with all the things Nimrod had thrown onto the ground. "Hey, you don't suppose it's contaminated my underwear, do you?"

"I wouldn't worry about it, bro," advised Philippa. "There's nothing on this planet that's more hazardous than your underwear."

"Funny," said John. "Real funny."

"The rock shouldn't be dangerous," said Nimrod. "Not unless —"

"Not unless," said Philippa, "those three gold disks weren't made of gold at all, but something else? Something that reacts badly to being near uranium."

"Yes, indeed," said Nimrod. "Go on."

"Well, might it be that the tears of the sun only looked like gold? That the tears were only disguised with a thin layer of gold so as to conceal what they really were? I mean, suppose those Incas just dipped them in gold."

"Exactly," said Nimrod. "Clever girl. Now then. What could they be made of? If my memory serves there was only one disk out of three that seemed much heavier than normal gold."

"How about lead," suggested Groanin. "I say, what about lead? There were lots of folk who used to gild a bit of lead and pass it off. Counterfeiters and coiners. It's why folk still bite gold coins. To check that they're the real McCoy."

"Not lead," said Nimrod. "Lead doesn't react with uranium."

And then he swore loudly.

It was the first time the children had ever heard their uncle curse and for a moment, they were a little shocked.

"Wash that man's mouth out," said Groanin. "Swearing in front of young'uns like that. You should be ashamed of yourself, sir."

"Forgive me, everyone," Nimrod added quickly. "But I suddenly had a very, very bad thought." And then he was silent for longer than a minute and walked nervously around the camp, shaking his head and wringing his hands.

"Are you going to tell us what it is or are we going to have to club it out of you?" demanded Groanin. "Sir."

"It might be best not to know," Nimrod said darkly. "I mean, there's a lot I know that sometimes I wish I didn't. What was it Mr. Rakshasas used to say? It is better not to remember what is best forgotten and better never to forget what is worth remembering."

"What rot," said Groanin. "I say, what rot. Tell us and be done with it, man, or I'll never make tea for you again."

"That's quite a threat, Groanin." Nimrod smiled wryly. "Very well. I was thinking this: that the heaviest of the three disks might have been made of pure polonium."

"Never heard of it," said Groanin. "I've heard of the Palladium. I saw Judy Garland live at the London Palladium once. When I were a lad. Marvelous stuff. Now that lass could sing."

"There is a rare earth metal element called palladium," said Nimrod. "But I'm not talking about that. I'm talking about another metal called polonium."

"Well, I've never heard of it," said Groanin. "I say, I've never heard of your polonium."

"Well, you wouldn't have, probably," said Nimrod. "It's not the kind of metal you find in some loose change in a butler's trouser pocket. In fact, it's extremely rare. It was discovered only as recently as 1898. By Pierre and Marie Curie."

"Wait a minute," said Philippa. "If it was only discovered in 1898, how come a disk made from polonium has been passing as an Incan artifact in the Peabody Museum for the better part of a century? Either Hiram Bingham was lying about where he found those tears of the sun, or —"

"Or the Incas discovered the secrets of pitchblende five hundred years before the Curies," murmured Nimrod. "Yes, exactly."

"Pitchblende?" said John. "What's that?"

"German miners used to come across a rock they called pitchblende, which was full of metals that were considered too difficult to extract."

"I might have known them Germans would be involved, somehow," said Groanin.

"In fact," continued Nimrod, "one of the metals in pitchblende was lead, another was uraninite, which is a major ore of uranium, and another was a new element that the Curies managed to separate from the pitchblende. They named this new element polonium after Marie Curie's native land of Poland."

"Happen they did the right thing," said Groanin. "Them Poles have always been good at causing trouble. 1939 for one thing."

"Groanin, you're a racist," said Nimrod.

"Yes, sir," said Groanin.

"But how would the Incas have managed something like that?" asked John. "They were just a bunch of savages, weren't they? Not scientists."

"Now you sound like Francisco Pizarro, John," said Nimrod. "He was also a racist."

"Sorry," said John. "You're right, of course. In their own way I guess they were pretty civilized."

"You're also forgetting that Manco Capac was a djinn," said Nimrod. "He knew secret things about all of the atomic elements that were not then known to man. Do you remember your Tammuz? In Egypt? And what I told you about how a djinn makes things from the fire that burns within? And how an understanding of all the atomic elements is essential to understanding how djinn power works?"

"Sure," said Philippa. "The inner fire? It's called the Neshamah."

"Then perhaps you remember how I also told you how we djinn use that energy source to affect the protons in the molecules possessed by objects."

"Of course," said Philippa. "You told us how making something appear or disappear requires us to add or remove protons and thereby change one element into another."

"Or how subtracting neutrons from the various atoms of a rock will make it disappear," added John.

"Exactly," said Nimrod. "Well, don't you see? Djinn power is just simple physics. Or to be more accurate, simple nuclear physics. The Spanish belief in the existence of a city of gold may not have been fantasy. One of the reasons the Incas possessed so much gold in the first place was that Manco Capac was very good at turning lead into gold. And here's another thing: It's impossible to understand how lead works without also understanding how its isotopes work."

"An iso what?" said Groanin. "What's an isotope? And speak English for Pete's sake."

"Isotopes are different forms of the same element. The same element with a different number of neutrons. Lead has four stable isotopes and one common radioactive isotope."

"Radioactive," said John. "I was kind of hoping you wouldn't use a scary word like that."

"I'm afraid I had to," said Nimrod. "You see, it's my belief that Manco Capac managed not only to isolate polonium five hundred years before the Curies, but that he also understood the fundamentals of radioactive physics. And that one of the tears of the sun we just handed over to Virgil McCreeby might actually be the detonator for a crude nuclear bomb."

"What?" Groanin threw the rest of his tea into a bush. "Flipping heck." He bit his lip. "I told you not to tell me about all this. I said I told you not to tell me. I am a much happier man when I am ignorant. And that's a fact."

"My guess is that one of those other tears of the sun was made of lithium," said Nimrod, ignoring him. "And that

McCreeby already possesses whatever else he needs to complete the device. Possibly some kind of rod also made of pure uranium."

"Wait a minute," said Philippa. "Didn't Faustina say that some rare Incan artifacts, including a golden staff, were stolen from the Ethnological Museum in Berlin?"

"Yes, she did," said Nimrod. "A golden staff might be just such a rod."

"If that was made of uranium instead of gold, too," she said.

"Yes, that's right." Nimrod rubbed his chin thoughtfully.

"But how does it all work?" asked John. "These three disks and perhaps a rod."

"The idea is that you blast the rod and your lithium disk down some sort of tube, like a bullet. At the bottom of the tube are the polonium disk and a piece of uranium about as big as a baseball."

"Never liked the game," said Groanin. "It's a simpleton's version of cricket, if you ask me."

"That's all there is to it," added Nimrod. "To an atomic bomb. Smashed together, your polonium and your two pieces of uranium start a chain reaction and a small nuclear explosion. About the same size of atomic bomb that destroyed Hiroshima."

"A baseball?" said Philippa. "Is that all?"

"I'm afraid so," said Nimrod. "Perhaps less."

"Gee, that's one baseball I don't want to catch," said John. "Could that be an Incan artifact, too?"

"Easily," said Nimrod. "Just as long as it hadn't already started to get hot. That would make it too unstable to handle."

"Do you think McCreeby was carrying that, as well?" John asked Nimrod.

"He must have been," said Nimrod.

"Wait," said Philippa. "Don't you see? Maybe he didn't need to. This whole area is just one huge deposit of uranium. And it's warm, too. That's why there was hot air being blasted up that underground chimney shaft."

"Light my lamp, you're quite correct, Philippa." Nimrod shook his head. "The uranium is right here. Underneath our feet. There's so much uranium in this area that there must be a natural chain reaction that's constantly in progress. The whole area's just fizzing with it. That must be how Manco thought he had managed to revive his own djinn power. Using the country's own deposits of uranium."

"So let me get this straight," said Groanin. "In order to revive the lad's djinn powers and because McCreeby thinks it's going to give him the power to make gold, he and Dybbuk are planning to carry out some daft Incan ritual unaware that in so doing they will actually set off a nuclear explosion."

Nimrod nodded. "As usual, you reduce things to their absolute common denominator. But that's about the size of it, Groanin, yes. In a nutshell."

"But that's just the point," said Groanin. "The size of it. There's tons of uranium down there. I mean if one flipping baseball can destroy a city the size of Hiroshima, then —"

"The *Pachacuti*," said Philippa. "The Incan prophecy. Talk about global warming. Wow!"

"Exactly," said Nimrod. "They could destroy the whole world."

Everyone stayed silent for a long while as they tried to contemplate the terrible consequences of what McCreeby and Dybbuk were planning to do. It was John who spoke first.

"I'm no good at making speeches," he said. "But it seems to me that with something as important to the future of the planet as this, Dad is going to have to take his chances with his kidnappers." He picked up his backpack. "Don't get me wrong. I love my dad. But we've simply got to go through the door in the Eye of the Forest and go after those loonies. We've got to stop them before they manage to blow up the planet."

"John's right," said Nimrod, hoisting up his own back-pack. Catching Philippa's anxious eye, he added, "We can't afford to wait to hear from your mother, Philippa. We've got to go after them. Now."

She nodded silently.

"Groanin? Muddy? You two had better stay here and wait for Sicky to return."

Groanin gave Nimrod a look. "Leave me behind? I should

say not, sir. I'm a butler, not an umbrella. Besides, you might have need of me. Not to mention my arm. Since it was kindly replaced by your niece and nephew, I can do a lot more than make a good cup of tea, you know. Just as long as you don't ask me to chuck a baseball at someone."

CHAPTER 22

HANNIBAL AND THE CANNIBALS

Sicky's head may have been unusually small, but there was nothing wrong with his social skills. He may have had long red laces strung from his lips, but he still liked to talk to his clients. He liked people. Even when they were mummified people. And it was only natural that in the time it took for him to lead the mummified Inca kings through the jungle to the camp of the Xuanaci Indians, he should have tried to offer them some interesting conversation. Sicky tried to talk about the weather, tourists, the local fauna, Fidel Castro, carbon trading, the Xuanaci, the Shining Path guerrillas, deforestation, the Incas, the conquistadors — he even tried to talk about the dreadful state of Peruvian soccer.

"You're all Peruvian," he said gamely. "Doesn't it bother you that we're the third-largest country in South America and yet we can't field a decent national team? It sure bothers me. I mean, we haven't qualified for the World Cup since 1982. Argentina is only a bit bigger than us, and they're one of the best soccer countries in the world."

If any of the Inca kings cared about soccer and the fortunes of the Peruvian national team, they didn't show it. Their eyes remained nearly closed while their squashed-up, ash-gray faces stayed as impassive as Easter Island statues. Very occasionally, Sicky thought he saw one of them smiling but that was always just the teeth in the skull showing rather horribly through the mummy's parchment-thin skin. As they walked silently through the steamy jungle, Sicky doubted that the kings were even capable of speech, and the discovery that they could indeed talk was just one of many surprises that lay ahead of him.

The first of these surprises was the existence of an animal Sicky had never seen before. In a forest clearing, they came upon a herd of what looked like a variety of tapir — a large piglike mammal with a short prehensile proboscis or trunk that is indigenous to South America. Except that these were about twice as big as any tapir Sicky had seen in all his many years as a jungle guide. Not only that, but these creatures had tusks and resembled small mastodons, or prehistoric elephants, as much as they resembled large tapirs.

Just as surprising to Sicky was the discovery that these animals were quite tame, for they permitted the mummified kings to mount them like horses and, hardly wishing to walk when his taciturn companions seemed more inclined to ride, Sicky took hold of one beast by the thick hair at the base of its neck and hoisted himself onto its back. After this, they made swift and easy progress through the forest, and before long, Sicky was quite certain that the sudden discovery of these strange and ancient-looking beasts was connected with the appearance of the mummified Inca kings.

"So what is this animal we're mounted on?" he asked the nearest Inca king as his mount bulldozed a small tree out of the way. "It looks kind of rare. Maybe even extinct. Like them dinosaurs in that movie."

No reply. But Sicky wasn't taking no reply for an answer.

"Some kind of prehistoric tapir, is it? An elephant perhaps? It sure is comfortable. I'll give you that. Up here I feel like that old Carthaginian general, Hannibal. The one who rode across the Alps on the elephants to conquer the Romans. I suppose that's the idea, is it? To use these beasts to give you a bit of an edge in a fight?"

Nearing the Xuanaci village, Sicky heard the unmistakable sounds of a bitter conflict that was in progress and, standing upon the sturdy back of his mount, Sicky caught sight of three Spanish horsemen armed with twelve-foot lances, riding through the jungle in pursuit of several fleeing Indians and endeavoring to spear them. In the village itself a pitched battle was in progress with Pizarro's armor-plated Spaniards and a host of near-naked Xuanaci warriors engaged in hand-to-hand fighting, while close to the center a group of Spaniards emerged from the largest hut clutching golden vessels and plates and shouting triumphantly to their colleagues. That was also a big surprise to Sicky.

"I never figured the Xuanaci had so much gold," he said quietly. "Who'd have thought it possible? No wonder they were always so fierce. Probably scared that someone was going to steal all their treasures."

"Which ones are the Xuanaci?"

The Inca king nearest Sicky had spoken and was now looking at him directly for the first time. There was a curious glow in his eyes, like a dimly burning electric lightbulb, while his voice sounded similarly incandescent, as if it had been smoked over a slowly burning fire.

"You spoke," said Sicky. "I do believe you spoke."

"Certainly I spoke," said the mummified Inca king. His fellow kings were all looking at Sicky now, as if waiting for his answer. "We were ordered to help the Xuanaci. By the young master."

"You mean that kid, John?"

"Yes. John. We came back from the *hana-paca*, the upper world, where food and warmth were plentiful. We came back to send our enemies to the *okho-paca*, the place of unending cold. The young lord and son of the sun commands and we obey. Tell us now, llama dung, which of these are the Xuanaci?"

Sicky didn't much like being described as llama dung, especially after all the trouble he'd taken to guide the kings to the Xuanaci village, and he was half inclined to tell the mummified Inca king to go and boil his head. But at the same time he was anxious to finish the job of guiding this strange party and to get back to Nimrod and the children.

"Er, Your Majesty, the Xuanaci are the ones painted like jaguars," he said. "That's the big cat, not the car, of course. Ain't no call to look like a luxury sedan in the jungle. Nor any call to own one, neither."

As more Spanish horses galloped about, several Xuanaci women and children screamed as they tried to flee the pandemonium. Many of the more sensible ones started to climb trees and creepers in order to escape. Some managed it and some didn't.

"Usually the Xuanaci are pretty good fighters, but as you can see — I think — them Spaniards are armed to the teeth, and mounted on horseback, which makes them pretty hard to kill. Not to mention the fact that they are already dead, of course. It's not so easy to kill a fellow who's been dead for nigh on five hundred years, even for people as mean as the Xuanaci."

As if to demonstrate the truth of what Sicky was saying a Xuanaci war hatchet flew through the air and neatly beheaded one of the mounted conquistadors, who carried on riding and waving his lance as if the loss of his head was a matter of small inconvenience.

The decapitated head bounced in the undergrowth and, still wearing its distinctive Cabasset helmet, rolled all the way to Sicky's feet. The guide stared down at the Spaniard's bearded face. The blue eyes continued to blink, and

the face to move as if it was still attached to the Spaniard's body. Then, fixing him with a lively, sarcastic smile, it
said in a lisping Castilian accent, "What are you looking at, pinhead? Haven't you ever seen a severed head
before?"

"No, nor never seen one that talked back to me, neither,"
said Sicky, and booted the head away into the undergrowth.
"See what I mean?" he told the Inca king. "The Xuanaci have
got their work cut out to beat these dead Spaniards. But I
guess you understand how that is, sir, on account of the fact
that I guess you are dead yourself." Sicky shrugged. "If you'll
pardon my saying so, Your Majesty."

The mummified Inca king did not answer. Instead, he
blinked his eyes slowly and raised his spear, which appeared
to be a signal to all of the other mummified Inca kings,
who tightened their grip on their mounts and their weapons and prepared to charge the greater force of cowardly
conquistadors.

"Uh-oh," said Sicky as the beast he was sitting on snorted
excitely. And hardly trusting it not to follow the rest, Sicky
swung his leg over its neck and, not a moment too soon,
slipped down its big furry flanks and onto the ground. This
was not his fight.

The next second, the Inca kings, urging their mounts
forward with fierce and ululating war cries, attacked the conquistadors, who hardly knew what hit them; such was the
ferocity of the first attack that the heads of several dead
Spaniards were soon bouncing like soccer balls along the

jungle floor, although with no more lethal result than the conquistador whom Sicky had seen beheaded earlier on.

"This looks like it's going to be a long battle," said Sicky and, in the absence of his paleomastodon — for that was the name of the beast he had been mounted upon — Sicky was obliged to climb to the top of a tree to get a clearer view of the action. Which was where he encountered several howler monkeys, a three-toed sloth, and those members of the Xuanaci who, very sensibly, had run away when the Spaniards showed up "to teach them a lesson."

Much to Sicky's relief, the many Xuanaci who were hiding in the tree recognized that it was he who had brought the mummified Inca kings to help them and, as a result, greeted him like a liberator.

"At first we tried to fight them," said one of the Xuanaci people. "But when we realized that they couldn't actually be killed, we ran away."

"You can't kill them because they're already dead," explained Sicky.

"Ah, that explains it," said the Xuanaci. "And then you turned up with these other warriors. And I must say they fight very well. With no heed for their own safety."

"They're dead, too," said Sicky.

"Ah, that explains it."

The Xuanaci speaking to Sicky, a man named Nicnax, recognized Sicky, on account of the small size of his head, and now apologized for what the Xuanaci had done to Sicky and said it was all the fault of their chief Pertinax.

"He was a very bad chief," said Nicnax. "He was always telling us that your tribe, the Prozuanaci, wanted to go to war with us and made us very afraid of you. It was he who wanted us to go around collecting human heads and to eat people. Myself, I have never liked eating people all that much." Nicnax shook his head and sighed. "No doubt about it. Pertinax was a very bad man."

"Was?" repeated Sicky. "You said 'was.'"

"Pertinax and his two witch doctors, Chenax and Condonax, are dead," said Nicnax. "The conquistadors killed them first. They might have killed all of us perhaps but for the very timely help of your Incan warriors, Sicky."

Sicky and Nicnax watched as, immediately under the tree they were hiding in, one of the conquistadors cut off the head of an Inca king and, in turn, had his own head cut off. The two then proceeded to hack at each other with swords, although most of the time they missed because they couldn't see anything at all. Just occasionally they hit each other and managed to sever an arm or a leg. But there was no blood. As battles went, it was one of the most bloodless bloodthirsty battles Sicky had ever seen.

"How long do you think this battle will last?" said Nicnax.

"Difficult question," said Sicky, "given that the two armies are made up of dead people. But you know something, Nicnax? It occurs to me that the world would best be served if all wars were fought by dead soldiers. And then nobody could get killed."

"You're a very wise man, Sicky," said Nicnax.

Sicky yawned and scratched his grapefruit-sized head. "Not really. It's just that when you people shrunk my head, my thoughts got more, well, concentrated. I used to wonder why that was. And now I know it's because most people have more brains than ever they need. You see, when God made man, he made him with a brain that'll be big enough to cope with all the stuff he's going to need to know in about a million years' time. Which'll be a lot, of course. But right now, people don't need ninety percent of the brain they've got. Not for watching TV and basketball and rap music and things that don't require any thinking at all. Me, I've got exactly as much brain as I need and no more. Which means I never have a surplus thought. And I never have to think about a lot of stuff that ain't ever going to happen." Sicky smiled. "You don't know it, but you people actually did me a favor."

Nicnax nodded thoughtfully, impressed by Sicky's great wisdom. "Look here," he said. "Now that Pertinax is dead, we Xuanaci need a new chief. And you sound like you might be the very man for the top job. Everyone is very tired of being warlike and fierce. All we want is to live in peace with our neighbors. So how would you feel about that?"

Before answering, Sicky thought about the idea very carefully. He rather enjoyed being a jungle guide. At the same time he felt a greater responsibility to his tribe, and to all the peoples of the upper Amazon. For years, the Prozuanaci had lived in fear of the Xuanaci. Maybe he could bring them together. Sicky's head may have been unusually small, but there was nothing wrong with his sense of civic responsibility.

"Well, there's a thing," he said. "Old Sicky the chief of the Xuanaci. I wouldn't have to wear a crown or nothing like that, would I?" He grinned. "'Cause my head is too small for most kinds of hats."

Nicnax grinned back at him. "Pertinax was a real big head. I mean, he really thought he could change the world, you know? I think someone with a much smaller head would be good for us."

"I can see how that might work," admitted Sicky.

"And there are some big pluses that come with the job," added Nicnax.

"Like what?"

"There's a nice house with a chef and a couple of maids to clean up and stuff. Widescreen TV. Sunken bath. And plenty of gold."

"Yeah, I saw some of that just now. Hey, I never knew you Xuanaci were so rich."

"We could never sell it, of course. Most of the gold is early Incan stuff that the Spaniards couldn't find. Including El Dorado, the famous city of gold that the Spaniards were always looking for."

"You know where that is?"

"Sure. It's right here."

Nicnax turned around and picked up a heavy object wrapped in sackcloth. He unwrapped it to reveal a large model made of gold and enamel with an ebony base. It was a beautifully made, intricately wrought solid-gold sculpture of Machu Picchu, perfect in every detail.

"El Dorado," said Nicnax. "Our most precious artifact."

"This is really it?"

"This is really it." Nicnax grinned. "I mean it wasn't called El Dorado when it was made. But, over the years, and for obvious reasons, that's what people started calling it.

"The Incas made it out of solid gold when they were still planning Machu Picchu. I guess you could say that it's an architect's model for how the finished thing was supposed to turn out. Nice, isn't it?"

"Yeah," said Sicky. "I like all sculpture and stuff like that."

"The Spaniards got to hear about the so-called city of gold, El Dorado. Only this was it. They never did figure out that the city of gold was just a model. A very valuable model, but a model nonetheless."

"No wonder they could never find it."

Nicnax grinned happily. "It's our biggest secret."

Sicky thought for a moment.

"You sure you don't want the job yourself, Nicnax?"

"I'm no leader," said Nicnax.

"Me, I'm just a jungle guide," said Sicky.

"That's a kind of leader, isn't it?"

"I never thought of it like that. But you're right. Okay, I'll do it. But only after I finish guiding the *yanqui* children and the Englishmen. I must get back to them as soon as this battle is over."

Sicky looked down at the raging battle. Pizarro's men had fallen back and regrouped while the mummified Inca kings were already beginning to pursue the harried Spaniards. But it was clear from the number of heads and arms and legs on the ground that this particular battle was only going to be over when both sides had completely annihilated each other.

"Whenever that might be."

CHAPTER 23

THE WRATH OF LAYLA

When the great escapologist Harry Houdini died in 1926, it was said that his secrets would only be revealed to the world in 1976, after the passage of fifty years. In fact, all of his papers went to the Library of Congress, in Washington, D.C., where they remain to this day.

As a young student at Georgetown University (also in Washington, D.C.), Edward Gaunt was fascinated with the life of Houdini and, before becoming an investment banker, had even contemplated a career as a cabaret magician. To this end Mr. Gaunt had read all of Houdini's papers and learned quite a few of his escape secrets.

There had been a time when Mr. Gaunt had helped pay for his studies by performing cabaret escape tricks. But this was many years ago, and he guessed he was now a little out of practice. But his opportunities for even attempting an escape were limited by the fact that the three peculiar Englishmen guarding him took shifts to watch the cage in which he had been locked. And many nights had passed before the routine they had established of watching their wealthy prisoner turned to mind-numbing tedium and Mr. Gaunt finally found the right opportunity to put his old skills to the test. Mr. Haddo, who appeared to be in charge of his three kidnappers, was asleep. And quite unaware that his own wife was downstairs in Molloy's Warehouse, Mr. Gaunt lassoed the end of the screw in the old-style cuffs with his shoelace, and yanked the bolt back. Almost miraculously the cuffs sprang open, which only left Mr. Gaunt with the task of now unlocking the cage itself.

That was more difficult. It was fortunate that like his hero, Harry Houdini, Mr. Gaunt was small, and agile, too. And he was almost able to squeeze through the bars. Almost, but not quite. He was not as small as he used to be. He might have reached the keys to the cage if these had been on Mr. Haddo's belt, which was where he sometimes kept them. But this time they were on a hook on the back of the door.

Now in many ways Mr. Gaunt was an eccentric man for whom old habits died hard. And, during his long fascination with Houdini, it had been his peculiar habit to copy his boyhood hero and always to travel with an unfolded paper clip concealed in the thick layer of skin that grew upon the soles of his feet — so that he might pick the lock to his own front door if ever he managed to lock himself out of his own house. Which, indeed, had happened, for Mr. Gaunt usually had so much business going on inside his head that apparently trivial details like house keys and cash and credit cards often slipped his mind. Denizens of East 77th Street were not unused to the sight of the multimillionaire banker sitting on his stoop and pulling off his socks and shoes so that he might extract his emergency paper clip. As far as local residents were concerned it was just one of many strange things that happened in or out of number 7.

It had been several years since Mr. Gaunt had seen a chiropodist and the skin on his feet was as thick and hard and yellow as a piece of smoked haddock and while this is unpleasant, it is also important to remember that this did not make him a bad person. With skin on his feet that was this thick and hard, it took poor Mr. Gaunt almost two whole minutes to extract the long thin paper clip that had lain concealed in there, untouched, like a neglected mousetrap, for several months. But it was the work of only a few seconds for him to pick the small padlock on the door of his cage.

Now all he had to do was open the door without it squeaking. The tray containing the remains of Mr. Gaunt's dinner lay on the floor of his cage. He had to admit that they had fed him quite well. But he'd never much cared for salad, and the ingredients of its dressing — olive oil and balsamic vinegar — were quickly put to good use lubricating the hinges of the cage door.

Mr. Haddo let out a snore and shifted in his chair, as silently the door swung open. It was then that Mr. Gaunt dropped his paper clip. In the silence of that room it sounded like an iron bar falling onto the bare wooden floor. Haddo shifted again, rolled his head on his shoulders, yawned, stretched his arms above his head, and then opened his eyes. The now-empty cage was the last thing he saw for several minutes because Mr. Gaunt picked up the large skillet in which his supper had been cooked earlier on, and fairly clobbered Mr. Haddo on the back of the head with a sound like a dinner gong. Haddo returned to his unconscious state with a half-witted, crinkle-cut smile on his ugly face.

Mr. Gaunt put down the skillet and, collecting his shoes and socks off the floor of his cage, as well as the olive oil, he tiptoed toward the door. Having lubricated the door hinges — for these were no less squeaky than the ones on the cage — he paused several seconds to allow the oil to take effect and then, turning the door handle, he stepped outside.

He found himself standing on a landing at the top of a dilapidated flight of stairs, which he started running down immediately, pausing only to collect an old brass poker that stood by an empty fireplace. He wasn't about to be recaptured without a fight.

"Help me, Edward. Help me."

At the bottom of the stairs, he stopped and listened again for the tiny, quavering bat-squeak voice he thought he had heard. A terrified voice that raised the hairs on the back of his neck and sent a long shiver down his spine. Had he imagined it?

Meanwhile, an odd scene presented itself to Mr. Gaunt's tired eyes. In another empty fireplace stood a stuffed dog, and on the heavily cobwebbed wall behind the door was a large antique engraving of what looked like a bare church wall. But this was not what made the scene odd. It was the atmosphere. The room at the foot of the stairs was charged with a powerful sense of conflict, as if something had disturbed the very air that surrounded him. As if the voice had been real.

For a moment he held his breath and put all of his effort into listening.

"Is there anyone there?" he whispered fearfully.

After a while, he shook his head. All he could hear was his own heartbeat. "I must be hearing things," he said. But something invisible kept him rooted to the spot.

"Help me, Edward."

There. He *had* heard it. Not only that but he was certain he recognized the voice.

"Layla? Is that you? Where are you?"

The next second something terrible happened.

For a split second it was as if his human spirit had been cut in two with a very sharp and invisible knife and made him yell with fright. And being cut into two wasn't so very far from the truth.

As she desperately tried to pull away from the horrible thing that threatened to suck her into oblivion, Layla and the exorbere had actually passed right through Edward Gaunt's physical body. It was, he reflected later, a most peculiar sensation. In that same instant Edward Gaunt saw a fleeting image of his wife's horrible predicament. Felt it, too. She was wrestling for her life with a repellent creature that seemed to be half man and half spider. With a horrible slurping noise, like someone drinking hot soup from a large spoon, the exorbere was trying to draw Layla's disembodied djinn spirit into its hideous, trunklike mouth part. If he didn't do something to help her she was going to die. He knew that as a matter of fact. Simultaneously, Edward heard his wife's desperate voice cry out inside him.

"Help me, Edward," she cried. "Help me, please, or I shall die." And then, "You must destroy the picture. Destroy the picture, Edward, before it's too late."

Mr. Gaunt hardly needed to be told twice, and advancing rapidly on the antique engraving that hung on the wall behind the door, he dealt it a savage blow with the poker, and then another. Even as he hit the picture again and again, the crawling creature reappeared on the surface, as if summoned to defend itself. But it was too late. Mr. Gaunt struck the exorbere on the head and on the back, poking holes through the thick antique paper until a deep, black, and unendingly hellish void lay visible beyond. There was a terrible shriek and then the paper started to burn. Instinctively Mr. Gaunt knew that whatever it was had been destroyed.

At least he thought this particular knowledge had been instinctive. But when he looked around to find his wife, he found that Layla was already inside his body, and that what little he now knew about the exorbere had originated in his wife's powerful mind.

"Thank goodness, Edward."

Her thoughts were in his head and, for several moments he struggled to make his own thoughts the dominant ones.

Which felt strange because, after all, it was Mr. Gaunt's head. But quite soon he gave up trying to make himself heard. That was quite common where his own wife was concerned.

"Here I am come to rescue you, Edward dear, and I find it's me who needs to be rescued. That horrible thing was about to absorb me. Like Mr. Rakshasas. You remember him, dear? He got absorbed by one of those terra-cotta warriors in the Metropolitan Museum. The children were terribly upset about it. Anyway, I'm sorry to invade your body like this, Edward, but I left my own body outside in the car. I thought to take the precaution of coming in here invisibly, but, as you can see, it looks like Virgil McCreeby was prepared for something like that. I don't think you've met him. You'd remember if you had. He's English. Bit of a creep. Only more of a magician — a real magician, not the stuff you used to do when you were in college — than I'd given him credit for. Still, that was clever of you to get out of that cage. With a shoelace and a paper clip. Just like Houdini, yes. And there are three of them upstairs, yes? And they're English, too? I see. Well, I don't care where they came from. They're about to find out what it's like to cross a djinn like me."

Mr. Gaunt tried and failed once more to gain the mastery of his head and thought processes. To that extent it was just like being back home in East 77th Street, with his wife very much in charge. The only difference was that he couldn't flee to the sanctuary of his own den and read quietly or just watch television. In fact, he couldn't even sit down to put on his own socks and shoes, which was what he'd have liked to have done. That and get the heck out of that place. Layla was already marching his own body back up the stairs he'd just come down.

"It's all right, Edward." Her thoughts came at him in a stream of consciousness that was as fast and powerful as a white-water rafting trip down the Colorado River. He felt overwhelmed. Swamped by the strength of her presence. "You're perfectly safe now I'm in here with you. We'll deal with them and then we'll be on our way home back to East 77th Street. I'm sure you're anxious to get home and have a nice hot bath. It's not that far. We're in Brooklyn. Right under the bridge."

Mr. Gaunt found himself at the top of the stairs, where he threw open the door, and stepped, more than a little reluctantly into the room he had just vacated, where Mr. Haddo was rubbing his head and picking himself up off the floor.

With his sharp teeth and elongated nose he reminded Layla of a species of rat or shrew.

"I certainly didn't expect to see you again," Mr. Haddo told Mr. Gaunt. "But now that you are here, I can tell you this. You're going to regret it. No one hits me on the head and gets away with it. And don't tell me you're married to a genie with a temper, mate. I just don't care." Mr. Haddo opened a drawer and took out a small blackjack. Evidently, he intended on hitting Mr. Gaunt with it.

"Well, you ought to care." Mr. Gaunt heard his own voice but hardly recognized the words as his own. "Because they're the last words you'll ever hear with human ears." The next word was certainly not his own and though he'd heard it before, the word was not a word he'd ever been able to — or for that matter had ever dared to — pronounce. He did know the meaning of the word, however. The word had been coined by a Greek playwright named Aristophanes and meant "Cloud-Cuckoo Land," which is to say, a place where everything was perfect: in other words, somewhere that doesn't exist. It was Layla's focus word: "NEPHELOCKOKKYGIA!"

And there was anger in it, too. The strong smell of sulfur in the air that accompanied the utterance of Layla's focus word told him that much. Cloud-Cuckoo Land had probably never sounded so real and powerful as it did in Layla's mouth.

With a loud bang Mr. Haddo vanished in a puff of smoke, and in his place now stood a rather bemused-looking creature that Mr. Gaunt momentarily took for a somewhat loathsome-looking species of giant brown rat with an extremely elongated snout.

"It's not a rat." Layla was already explaining what it was. "It's a Cuban solenodon, also known as the almiqui, and it's almost extinct, even in Cuba. You can see why, I think. It's incredibly ugly. This is why I chose it, of course. And because he reminded of me of one. Incidentally, the solenodon is not just unusually ugly. It's unusually dangerous. Its saliva is venomous."

The loud noise summoned the other two kidnappers from a back room. One of them had unusually hairy ears while the other had an unusually hairy nose.

"How did you get out?" asked the one with the hairy nose.

"Where's Haddo?" asked the one with the hairy ears.

"What's that smell?" asked Hairy Nose.

"And what's that hideous-looking animal?" asked Hairy Ears.

"It's your friend Haddo." Mr. Gaunt's voice sounded menacing. "Or at least it used to be. Now it's a rare Cuban shrew or soricomorph."

"A sorry what?"

"No, it's not sorry," said Mr. Gaunt's voice. "But you will be. NEPHELOCKOKKYGIA!"

This time Layla chose a different animal, although one no less rare or ugly than the Cuban solenodon: a northern hairy-nosed wombat. The second kidnapper — whose hairy nose had put her in mind of a hairy-nosed wombat — disappeared with a loud bang and in a large puff of smoke. This made the third scream with fright and run for the door. He didn't get very far.

"NEPHELOCKOKKYGIA!"

She might even have turned both of the two remaining kidnappers into wombats except that by now there was a method in Layla's — and by extension, her husband's — mind. The third kidnapper disappeared like the second and the first before him, and in his place the hairy-eared dwarf lemur he had reminded her of now sat on the floor chattering like a monkey. A second or two later, the hairy-nosed wombat chased it up onto the mantelpiece above the fireplace.

"I'm fed up with turning people into dogs and cats." Layla was answering the question Mr. Gaunt had been about to ask. "What the world doesn't need are more dogs and cats. So I picked the animals they reminded me of. It so happened I also picked three of the world's rarest animals. We can give the Central Park Zoo a call when we get home and they can come and collect them. It'll be good for the reputation of the zoo and good for the breeding future of these animals. Don't you think?"

Mr. Gaunt was on the verge of answering when his wife said, "Let's get out of here. Before someone else shows up. I know there's just the three of them you've seen, but you never know with a man like Virgil McCreeby."

She turned him around and started them down the stairs. In the street outside, a man was standing next to Layla's car and fiddling with the lock. Unfortunately for him, there was something lupine about his face, which is to say he reminded Layla of a wolf.

"Can you beat that?" Layla was outraged. "I'm actually sitting in the backseat, and he's still trying to steal the car."

At last, Mr. Gaunt managed to get a word in edgeways. "It's dark. Perhaps he hasn't seen you." He was about to suggest that being turned into an animal — albeit a rare animal — was quite a severe punishment for auto theft, but Layla's thoughts were already there ahead of him. "I think what the world needs are a few less car thieves and a few more red wolves."

She paused but before Mr. Gaunt could think to stop her, Layla's focus word was already out of his mouth.

"NEPHELOCKOKKYGIA!"

The rare red wolf, once common in the river forests and swamps of the southeastern United States, barked loudly and then loped off into the streets of Brooklyn.

Layla slipped out of her husband's body and into the car, where, once she was herself again, she unlocked the door to let him in. Silently, he got into the passenger seat, put on his seat belt and — since he didn't actually hold a license himself — waited patiently for her to drive them home.

"It's good to see you again," he said quietly. "I mean the real you, not Mrs. Trump. You look . . . er . . . you look, great. Wonderful. Quite like your old self."

"You really think so?"

But after a moment he let out a long sigh.

"What?" she asked, although the fact was she already knew the answer.

"I didn't say anything."

"That's what I mean," she said, already regretting her anger and how she had dealt with those four miscreants — not because she thought they deserved some lesser punishment but because having been inside Mr. Gaunt's mind, Layla now knew exactly what her husband thought of what she had done and, as a consequence, what he thought of her. In short he was afraid of her. Terrified. Because it's no small thing for a man to be married to a wife who can turn him into a rabbit or a sheep with just one word.

Mr. Gaunt tried to contain his fear, but it was no good. His hands were trembling and there was a film of sweat on his forehead. He was only human, after all.

"I'd never do something like that to you," she said. "Surely you know that, Edward."

"But the fact remains, you could," he said. "In a moment of anger, you could transform me into anything you liked. Like my two brothers, Alan and Neil."

"In case you'd forgotten, they were plotting to murder you, Edward," said Layla.

"Yes, I know, and I was very grateful to you for saving my life."

"Plus, they're back in human shape now, aren't they?"

"Yes. And they certainly learned their lesson. They'll never do anything like that again. They're the most loyal brothers anyone could have. But they do what they do out of fear of you. Not out of love for me. And I'm a little worried that the same thing might be happening to me."

"I don't understand."

"Suppose I disagreed with you about something."

"We never disagree."

"But suppose we did. Like who to vote for in an election. I mean, you vote one way and I vote the other."

"Don't remind me."

"I'm just a little worried that I may begin to feel I have to watch what I say and do. Just in case."

"Just in case I turn you into an animal?"

"Something like that, yes."

"Over something as trivial as who we're going to vote for?" She shook her head. "It wouldn't ever happen."

"Something else then. Suppose I smacked one of the children."

"We don't believe in smacking."

"All right, suppose I ever hit you," said Mr. Gaunt. "If I was married to anyone else the worst that could happen is that they'd hit me back and maybe report me to the police. And deservedly so. A man should never hit a woman. But with you, the worst that could happen to me can't even be guessed at. Since I've met you, Layla, you've turned people into dogs, cats. Our own cat, Monty, for example, used to be human. You've turned people into fleas, fish, parking meters, a cactus, cat litter, wombats, venomous shrews, wolves. You've even turned them into bottles of wine."

"Which you drank."

"Only to steady my nerves." Mr. Gaunt paused. "But that's not the only thing."

"You mean there's more?"

"One of the things we mundanes take for granted is the privacy of our own minds. It's about all we mundanes have left that we can truly call our own. But my own inner domain of thought has been violated by you, Layla. Just as if you had read my private diary."

"I'd never do something like that," protested Layla.

"Maybe not. But a few minutes ago you were inside my mind. Albeit for a good reason. And now you know all my darkest secrets."

"Oh, I don't care about those," said Layla. "Everyone has things like that."

"Yes, but everyone usually manages to keep them private."

Layla shrugged. "Sorry. But I didn't think you'd mind."

"The point is it happened once and it might easily happen again," said Mr. Gaunt. "I simply can't live with the thought that at any moment, you might come bursting into my mind, like someone gate-crashing a party, because you'd left your physical body somewhere else."

"So, what are you saying?"

"I don't know," said Mr. Gaunt. "I surely don't. But your magic is too rough for me."

"It's not magic," insisted Layla.

"But that's what it seems like to one such as me. And believe me, it's pretty rough when a man ends his life as a dog or a cat."

Layla was struck to the quick by what Mr. Gaunt had said, but being no less intelligent than him, understood exactly what he was talking about. And thinking herself no less kind than her softhearted husband, whom she loved deeply, Layla Gaunt promised to renounce her djinn power. Only this time it would be forever.

Solemnly, she held up her hand as if giving an oath in a court of law and spoke with great gravity.

"No more will I dim the sun at noon," she said, "nor turn the grass the color red, nor call forth the mutinous wind, nor put the sea and sky against each other, nor make thunder, nor split an oak with fire, nor shake the trees, nor put men out of their senses, nor make music from thin air, nor make windows in men's souls. This rough magic, as you call it, I here abjure. From now on, what strength I have's my own. And let your indulgence, Edward, set me free. Hear me, God."

She kissed her husband's hand but there were tears in her eyes.

"Let's go home," whispered Mr. Gaunt.

Layla started the car.

"What happens now?" he asked.

"Now?" Layla sighed. "I'm just going to concentrate on being a wife and a mother. That's what happens now."

CHAPTER 24

THROUGH THE EYE

Entering the Eye of the Forest proved to be a lot quicker than leaving it. Or, put another way, coming out of the eye was many times slower than going into it. Nimrod and John, who had not yet been on the other side of the golden door, spent several moments looking around their surroundings with interest. Philippa spent those same moments looking puzzled. And so did Groanin. For instead of the large pile of mattresses Philippa's djinn power had created to ensure that she, Groanin, Sicky, and Muddy had enjoyed a safe landing at the end of their rapid ascent up the chimney shaft, there were now several beds of very sharp nails, of the kind that are sometimes employed by ascetic Indian holy men, or fakirs, for lying on — much to the astonishment of the credulous.

"I wouldn't have fancied landing on those very much, Miss Philippa," observed Groanin. "Not without a suit of armor, anyway."

"No, indeed," agreed Philippa. "Odd, isn't it?"

"What is?" inquired Nimrod, tearing his attention away from the shaft and the column of warm air that continued to blast out of it.

Philippa explained how the mattresses had been replaced by the beds of nails.

"Hmm," said Nimrod. "Are you quite sure about that?"

"Of course, I'm sure," said Philippa.

"No doubt about it," confirmed Groanin. "You could ask Sicky and Muddy if they were here. They landed on them."

Making a fist, Nimrod thought for a moment and then, uttering his focus word, opened the palm of his hand to reveal a black chess piece.

"What is it?" asked Groanin.

"It's a chess piece," said Nimrod. "From an English Staunton set, which is the best type, of course. A black queen, to be precise."

"I can see that," said Groanin.

"Then I wonder why you asked."

"I meant, what are you doing with it?"

"Conducting an experiment, old fellow."

Nimrod laid the chess piece on the ground and, with a piece of chalk from his pocket, drew a neat circle around it. No sooner was the circle complete than the black queen had turned into a white king.

"I thought as much," he said. "It seems that when Manco Capac created this place he attached an Enantodromian wish or binding to it. To protect it from the power of any other djinn."

"What the heck is an Enantodromian wish?" said John who, despite once having read the *Shorter Baghdad Rules* from cover to cover, had never heard of such a thing. Although he did think he might have heard the word "Enantodromia." Possibly it was some other djinn's focus word.

"It's quite simple really," Nimrod said airily. "It means that whatever it is you wish for, you end up with the exact opposite. You wish for black, you get white, and so on. Manco Capac must have been quite a fellow. Quite a clever sort of wish really."

"But the mattresses I wished for remained mattresses for much longer than that black queen remained a black queen," objected Philippa. "Several minutes. Perhaps as long as half an hour."

"Of course. The Enantodromian wish made by Manco is five hundred years old, which means it's rather slower to take effect. Probably, when the binding was made, the effect was much quicker. Which was lucky for you. Otherwise you would all have had a very sticky landing."

"And the chalk circle?" asked John.

"Completing a circle around something always speeds up a wish," said Nimrod. "Especially an old wish. Didn't you know that?"

"No," said Philippa.

"At least it does just so long as it is a perfect circle," explained Nimrod. "And only a djinn can draw a perfect circle with a free hand — which is to say without using a set of compasses. Did you know that?"

"Yes," said Philippa. "I believe you did tell us that before."

"When we were in Venice," added John.

"It's the perfection of the numbers in a perfectly drawn circle that helps an ancient wish to achieve its original result. Like giving an old man a stick to help him walk."

"We get the point," Groanin said sharply. "Sir."

"Do you?" Nimrod smiled. "I wonder if that's correct. You see the point, my dear Groanin, is this: There can be no more wishing from here on in. In case it turns out the wrong way."

"You mean no djinn power?" said Groanin.

"That's exactly what I mean," said Nimrod. "John? Philippa? Is that quite understood by you both? Positively no unauthorized wishing."

"Yes, Uncle," they said meekly.

"But surely," said Philippa, "all you have to do is think of what you want to come true and then wish for the exact opposite."

"You might think that, yes," said Nimrod. "But it's not so easy to do in practice. Believe me, I've tried."

"But what if something goes wrong?" asked Groanin. "What if we need to protect ourselves? What if there's some horrible great beastie lying in wait for us? Another zombie? Or a giant thingummy?"

"Then we shall just have to rely on our wits," said

344

Nimrod. "And that remarkable arm of yours. You were right. It seems we will have need of you after all, Groanin." He smiled kindly at Philippa. "Now, why don't you show us this rope bridge you were talking about?"

Philippa led the way outside to the human-hair rope bridge where, to their surprise, on the edge of the yawning chasm that it spanned, they found a midget submarine. The hatches were open, and there was a large dent in the bow end, as if it had run into the ground at speed. But there was no sign of any water.

"This certainly wasn't here before," said Philippa, running her hand across the sub's smooth metallic hull, which was completely dry.

"What the heck's a midget submarine doing on dry land, anyway?" said Groanin. "It's about as much use round here as a bicycle to a fish."

"Precisely, Groanin," said Nimrod. "You put it very well."

"Do I?" Groanin looked pleased and confused at the same time. "Still doesn't explain what it's doing here."

"My guess?" said John. "Buck, McCreeby, and Zadie were worried about crossing the chasm on this bridge."

"Can't say as I blame them," said Groanin, staring uncertainly over the edge. Not only did the chasm drop hundreds of feet away into a cloud of mist, but the other end of the bridge itself could not be seen. "But I can't for the life of me understand as how a submarine would have helped."

"So they tried to get across the chasm using a small plane that Zadie created using her djinn power," continued John. "But just as they got airborne, the Enantodromia took effect, and the plane turned into its exact opposite. A submarine. Luckily for them, they weren't over the chasm when it happened. Which accounts for the dent in the bow."

"That's so crazy it makes perfect sense," said Groanin. "Almost."

"I think you're right, John," agreed Nimrod. "That must be exactly what happened."

"Must have been quite a hard landing," said Groanin.

"I'll say," said Philippa, and showed them some blood on her fingertips from when she'd touched the submarine's hull. "Looks like someone got hurt."

Nimrod tasted the blood on the submarine. "McCreeby," he said.

"How can you tell?" asked John.

"Human blood is cooler than a djinn's," said Nimrod. "Saltier, too. Djinn blood tastes more sulfuric. Like a mixture of asparagus, pumpkin seeds, cabbage, garlic, beans, and broccoli."

"Ugh," said John, who hated vegetables and wondered how he could be a djinn at all if that was what his blood tasted like.

The four advanced to the stone anchor that marked the beginning of the bridge. There were two cables acting as guardrails and another two at a lower level, which supported a footpath made of trimmed matting, also made of human hair.

"The Incas were fond of this sort of bridge," said Nimrod. "Not least because they did not use wheeled transport. But more usually these bridges were made of woven ichu grass than human hair."

"I've been wondering about that," said Groanin.

"I imagine human hair makes it much stronger than a simple grass bridge," said Nimrod.

"Well, let's hope so, at any rate," said Groanin. "I'm none too happy about going for a stroll along that thing."

"I certainly can't think of any other reason why anyone would want to make a bridge using human hair," admitted Nimrod.

Groanin wiped his bare pate clear of sweat with his hand-kerchief. "Speaking as someone who's a bit thin on top, neither can I."

"So," said Nimrod. "Who's going to be first?"

No one spoke.

"I suppose it had better be me," said Nimrod. "And try to look on the bright side, everyone. If there was anything wrong with the bridge, McCreeby and the others would hardly have chosen to use it, now would they?" He pointed along the sagging length of the bridge into the mist ahead of them. "After all, since they are not here on this side, we must presume they are already on the other side."

"Yes," said Groanin. "But the other side of what exactly?"

"Exactly?" said Nimrod. "I believe we are inside a djinn-made world. Manco Capac's djinn world."

"You mean this is like the inside of a djinn lamp?" asked Philippa.

"Exactly so. Only much, much bigger. And it's now clear to me that, in the beginning, anyway, Manco Capac must have been a much more powerful djinn than anyone has ever suspected."

"Then how's Groanin still alive?" asked John. "Humans can't exist inside a djinn lamp."

"They can't," said Nimrod. "But perhaps the sheer scale of this djinn-made world is what allows him to breathe. On the other hand this may be the actual cave system through which Manco Capac and his brothers and sisters moved from the djinn world into a human world. Which in itself is highly unstable. Not to say, dangerous. These two worlds should never be connected."

"The underground chimney," said Philippa.

"Yes, it must be," agreed Nimrod.

"Well, that's all right then," said Groanin. "For a moment there I was worried I was in trouble."

Nimrod put his foot on the bridge and, turning to look at the others, said, "Leave a space of about ten feet between each of us, so as to spread the load. Groanin? You bring up the rear. And try not to look down."

"Yes, sir."

As they started to walk on the bridge it began to wobble. At first the wobble was no more than a sideways oscillation, but gradually it began to sway like a pendulum.

Groanin stopped walking. "It's a bit wobbly," he observed.

"It's nothing more than a positive biofeedback phenomenon," declared Nimrod. "Also known as synchronous lateral excitation."

"It's still wobbly," grumbled Groanin as he started walking again. "I say, it's still wobbly."

"Groanin's right," said John, "the sway is increasing." He looked over the edge and felt his stomach sink inside his body, almost, he thought, as if gravity had an increased effect while he was so high above the ground. Not that he could even see the ground below. It was like walking down the aisle of a flying plane in which the rest of the plane had been removed.

"Those Incas must've had nerves of steel," said Groanin. "Either that or the designers were having a laugh at our expense."

"Try not to walk in step," said Nimrod. "That should help to break up the amplitude of the bridge oscillations."

"He means it'll stop wobbling if we stop marching," said Philippa, who always understood what Nimrod was saying better than any of the others.

Nimrod's suggestion seemed to fix the problem of the wobble and they made slow but steady progress along the rope bridge.

Each time Philippa put her hand on the silky smooth black handrail, she wondered about the many Incas whose hair had gone into its making. Had they been dead when their hair was taken, or alive? She'd read about the human sacrifices of the Aztecs. Hearts cut out of living victims at the tops of pyramids and horrible things like that. Had the Incas also practiced human sacrifice, like the Aztecs? She thought about asking Nimrod and then decided against it in case the explanation was more than she could cope with.

After a while, she became aware that she was out of breath and that the route along the bridge was getting more diffi-cult. The bridge was going up. The air was getting colder, too. She turned around, nodded at Groanin, and saw that the stone anchor that marked the beginning of the bridge and the midget submarine next to it had disappeared into the mist. With only mist ahead of them, it was almost as if the bridge was suspended by nothing. This she found more than a little disconcerting.

"Keep up, Groanin," she said. "I can hardly see you."

"Doing my best, miss," he said, panting audibly. "I don't know whether it's exertion or fear that's making me breathe so hard. I can't say I like this place very much. If it is a place. Being neither here nor there, it's like being in limbo."

"That's a happy thought," said Philippa, and winced as she felt the vibration of something heavy strike one of the rope bridge's handrails. And then again.

"Everyone take a tight grip of a handrail," shouted Nimrod.

"Why? What's happening?" yelled Philippa.

"I could be wrong," said Nimrod, "but it feels as if someone — probably McCreeby — is trying to cut the bridge, with a machete."

"Did you have to say that?" moaned Groanin. "I say, did you have to tell me? I'm a much happier man when I'm an ignorant one."

As all four of them took a firm grip of the handrail, they felt another powerful vibration of something striking it hard. And then, just as suddenly, the vibrations stopped. For a moment, everyone remained braced for a fall. But the bridge remained suspended in the air.

"It's stopped," said John.

"Thank goodness," said Philippa.

"Talk about white knuckles," said John, inspecting his two fists, which were still clenched on to the handrail. "My heart feels like it's in my mouth."

"Mine feels like it's trying to climb out of my ear holes," said Groanin. "If I do catch sight of my heart, I'm going to strangle the thing just to put it out of its misery."

"I wonder what it really was," said Nimrod. "That vibration."

"Please don't," pleaded Groanin. "I don't think I could bear it. If you say McCreeby's gone to fetch a sharper machete, I think I shall just jump and have done with it."

"It's a thought, you know," said Nimrod. "When human hair is bound and braided like this, it's extremely strong. You'd probably need a very sharp machete to cut through it."

"Oh, well, that's all right then," said Groanin.

Experimentally, Nimrod bounced the blunt edge of his own machete on the handrail.

"What the heck do you think you are doing, you blithering idiot, sir?" demanded Groanin.

"The tensile strength of this hair is indeed remarkable," said Nimrod. "Maybe as strong as steel cable."

"I wish the same could be said of my nerves," said Groanin, mopping his brow again. "They feel like they've been put through a shredding machine."

"Relax, Groanin," said John. "The bridge is still aloft. And we're still here."

"I wish I wasn't, young Master John. I really do wish I wasn't here at all."

"No wishing in here," Nimrod said sternly. "I thought I made that clear."

"Yes, sir. Sorry, sir. It's just that I didn't think that applied to me, sir. For obvious reasons."

They walked along the bridge for another two hours before they began to see an end in sight. And near the stone anchor at the far side was a vaguely human figure. At first it looked like something vaguely monstrous and hairy, like a human-sized fly. It was only when they neared the thing that they realized it was a human being enveloped in millions of strands of the same hair from which the bridge was constructed. Nimrod put his ear to what appeared to be the head and listened carefully. But it was Philippa who first recognized who it was.

"It's Zadie," she said. "Look at the boots."

Sure enough, the hair-wrapped being was wearing Zadie's distinctive purple boots.

"And there's something sticking out of the mouth," said John.

"Her toothbrush," said Philippa.

"It is Zadie," said Groanin. "At last, someone or something managed to stop her from dancing. She looks like a caterpillar before it becomes an insect. You know. A thingy."

"A pupa," said Philippa.

"Aye, a pupa," said Groanin.

"Talk about a bad hair day," said John.

Groanin chuckled. "That's good. Very good."

"Is she dead?" asked John.

"No," said Nimrod. "Not dead. I can just about detect some signs of life. But she's been completely immobilized, obviously. And I've an idea why. Look at this." He ran his hand down from the head to what were only just recognizable as a shoulder, an arm, and then a hand. In the hand was the vague shape of something metallic.

"A machete," said John.

"Exactly," said Nimrod. "It would seem that this bridge is designed to protect itself against destruction. From the look of her I'd say that when she started to cut the handrail, the hair fibers she'd severed managed to reconnect themselves. And along the way, made her a part of the bridge."

"How are we going to get her out?" asked Philippa.

"How?" Groanin sounded outraged. "Why on earth should we bother? She was cutting the bridge. Need I remind you that we were standing on it at the time?"

"Zadie didn't know that," said Philippa.

"She didn't know we weren't, either," said John. "I agree with Groanin. She wouldn't bother trying to get you out."

"We can't just leave her here," said Philippa.

Nimrod smiled and handed her his machete. "Would you care to try and cut her out?"

"Er, no," admitted Philippa.

"A wise choice, Philippa," said Nimrod. "I fear you'd only end up like her. Wrapped up like — what was it again, Groanin? A pupa. Except that this is one butterfly that's not going to fly anywhere."

Groanin pushed his way off the bridge to stand on the rocky outcrop on which the stone anchor had been built. "If you don't mind," he said, "I'll only feel more comfortable discussing this on terra firma."

"Me, too," said John, joining him.

Nimrod shrugged and followed them. A set of steps led steeply up the side of a mountain and around a corner.

"Uncle Nimrod?" There was a note of strong protest in Philippa's young voice.

"What?" said Nimrod. "Look, there's nothing to discuss. It's entirely up to John what happens to her now."

"Me?" said John. "I don't see why. I don't even like her."

"Hear, hear," said Groanin. "Look what she did to Mr. Vodyannoy. Tried to kill him with one of them frogs. Not to mention that giant centipede that nearly ate me for supper. I can be quite a forgiving man, it's true. But I draw the line in front of anyone who's set a giant Peruvian centipede on my trail. The image of that thing underneath my hammock will live with me forever."

"Which is about the length of time Zadie will be here, unless John releases her," said Nimrod.

John looked at the machete in his hand uncertainly. "I don't see why I should be the one who has to risk going the same way as her. Mr. Groanin wasn't the only one who nearly got eaten. You're forgetting that giant anaconda." He shook his head.

"Need I remind you again that, whatever wrong she's done, she has done because she was hypnotized by that scoundrel McCreeby?" asked Nimrod.

"Exactly," said Philippa.

"I don't care," said John. "I'm not going to do it. She can stay there forever as far as I'm concerned. I'm not chopping this bridge. Not for her. Not for you. Not for anyone."

"Nobody said anything about chopping the bridge with a machete, John," said Nimrod.

"What then?" demanded Groanin. "I wish you'd make yourself clear to the lad. We're facing nuclear annihilation, after all. Blimey, I don't half wish old Rakshasas was here. He certainly couldn't make less sense than you, sir."

"No wishing, Groanin," said Philippa. "Try to remember."

"Sorry, miss."

Nimrod touched the handrail opposite the one that had enveloped Zadie in a web of human hair. "Haven't you noticed these colored spots? They're in the same order as the ones near the other side of the bridge."

"So?" asked John. "What about them?"

"Well, it's just a thought," said Nimrod, "but it strikes me that if you were to pronounce those Quechuan words again in the same order that you learned them when you untied the knot on the Eye of the Forest, you might very well facilitate the release of Zadie."

John thought for a moment.

"What if I can't remember them?" said John.

"Then I suppose poor Zadie will be hair for the rest of her life," said Nimrod.

Groanin chuckled. "That's good, too," he said.

"I don't think it's funny," said Philippa.

But John and Groanin were laughing.

"John," said Philippa. "This is me talking. I know you're lying. I know you can remember the words. And you know I know."

"Yes," sighed John. "All right. I'll do it. But she'd better be grateful. Not to mention a lot easier to get along with than she was before."

"Amen to that," said Groanin.

"If she gets out of line, I'll zap her myself," said Philippa.

Nimrod winced. "I do so hate that expression. Zap. It makes you sound like a pest controller."

"Zadie is a pest," said Groanin. "And she does need to be controlled."

John frowned as he tried to remember the words. "*Yana chunka,*" he said. "*Yuraj pusaj. Puka tawa. Willapi qanchis.* What was it now? *Kellu kinsa. Komer phisqa. Sutijankas iskay. Kulli sojta. Chixchi jison.* Wait a minute." He tapped his forehead impatiently. "Yes, I've got it. *Chunpi uj.*"

Immediately when John had uttered the last Quechuan syllable, the hair binding Zadie to the bridge started to unravel. It was like watching a time lapse film of a plant growing, only in reverse. Several minutes passed before Zadie was able to speak. And when she was finally free she spent several more minutes weeping and apologizing for all her bad deeds.

"I couldn't even speak my focus word," she said through gulps of tearful air. "As soon as I had cut some of the hair, it bound my jaws tight together. If I hadn't had my toothbrush in my mouth, the bridge would have smothered me."

Zadie was still holding the machete and the realization that she might have been killed was enough provocation for her to take another swing at the handrail of the bridge, cutting more of the hairs so that once again she was quickly enveloped in another massive beehive of human hair.

Groanin groaned loudly. "Flipping heck," he complained. "Is the girl daft or what? I mean, you'd think she'd
have learned her lesson, wouldn't you?"

"Actually," said Nimrod. "It's my fault. I completely forgot to bring her out of the hypnotic state that McCreeby put
her in."

Once again, John was obliged to repeat the Incan words
of command. Only this time, Nimrod relieved Zadie of the
machete as soon as she had been released by the hair.

"I think I'll take that," said Nimrod. "Just in case."

And his voice had altered. To the others he sounded
exactly like Virgil McCreeby. It was the first time they realized that among his many other talents, Nimrod was also a
brilliant mimic.

"Listen to me, Zadie," he said. "Listen to my voice. And
only my voice. Forget everything else. Only my voice matters.
When I snap my fingers, you will no longer be hypnotized.
You will come out of the trance I put you in and behave quite
normally. You will remember everything. But you will behave
quite normally."

Nimrod snapped his fingers in front of Zadie's eyes.

She blinked and looked around with a look of bewilderment. "Oh," she said, and bit her lip as a tear welled up in
her eye. "Oh."

Nimrod put an arm around Zadie's shoulders to comfort
her. For a moment, Zadie could not speak. Then she said,
"I'm sorry. I'm sorry for all the terrible things I've done. I
owe all of you an apology. I don't have an excuse, only an

explanation. I did all that I did because I thought I was in love with Buck. But I realize now I wasn't in love with him at all. Dybbuk and Virgil McCreeby were using me. I know that now."

"It's all right," said Philippa, taking Zadie's hand and squeezing it affectionately. "You were hypnotized. You couldn't help yourself."

"Yes," said Zadie, realizing this for the first time. "I was, wasn't I?" Then she shuddered. "When the bridge wrapped me up with hair, Dybbuk didn't even stop to try and rescue me. He said he'd come back and rescue me when his power was restored. But I just knew he was lying. And that he would never come back for me. Just as he didn't try to find me when the Xuanaci were holding us prisoner."

"I'm afraid we've no time for explanations now," said Nimrod. "But one thing I must tell you, Zadie, and it's extremely important. On no account must you use your djinn power while we're on this side of the Eye of the Forest. There's an Enantodromian wish at work here. That's a wish that —"

"I know what an Enantodromian wish is," said Zadie. "Whatever you wish for with djinn power you get the exact opposite." She nodded. "It would certainly explain the midget submarine. I can't tell you how mad they were when that happened. McCreeby bashed his head and is making no sense at all. I think he has a concussion. And Buck called me the most useless djinn he'd ever met and said I was of no use to him if I couldn't fly them across a chasm. I tried to explain about the whirlwind situation, and how nobody can make one right now, but he simply didn't believe me. After that, I think he was just looking for an excuse to leave me behind. Sometimes —" She shook her head, exasperated. "You know, sometimes it seems like there are two Bucks. Good Buck and Bad Buck."

"You say more than you know," said Nimrod. "Come on. We'd better move."

CHAPTER 25

SLIPPED DISK

In the beginning, when first they had met and Dybbuk had been feeling quite sorry for himself about losing all his djinn power, he had quite liked Zadie — enough to allow himself to believe that he was as fond of her as she appeared to be of him. But that had been before he guessed that Virgil McCreeby had hypnotized her into believing she was in love with Dybbuk, as a way of making her obey him. Dybbuk was satisfied he himself had not been hypnotized. But at the same time, he half wondered if McCreeby hadn't been using Zadie as a way of controlling him, too, by way of ensuring that it was McCreeby who remained in charge of things and not Dybbuk.

Since this discovery, Zadie had become something of a nuisance to Dybbuk. Clingy and overattentive, she was always looking at him, smiling in a cloying, saccharine-sweet sort of way, reciting the love poetry of Elizabeth Barrett Browning, humming happily, and trying to stroke his hair or move it back from his brow so that she could look him tenderly in the eye. Dybbuk loathed people trying to touch his hair. Especially when they were humming or reciting poetry. Even if they had been hypnotized into behaving in that way.

And then, of course, there was the tap dancing and the toothbrush that was forever in her mouth like a lollipop. Those things really drove Dybbuk mad. So, all in all, he was quite pleased when at last they were able to leave Zadie behind. Besides, they had little choice but to do so. It was clear that any attempt by himself or Virgil McCreeby to cut the hairs of the rope bridge that now held her fast would only have resulted in their getting tied up like Zadie. He felt sorry for her, sure. It was a tough break, her ending up looking like a set of New Jersey hair extensions, but what was he to do? It wasn't like he had any djinn power to help her.

Dybbuk leaned as close as he dared to Zadie's nearly mummified head and told her that after his power had been restored he would come back and try to help her out. At the same time, however, somewhere inside himself he knew the truth was different and that in all likelihood he probably wouldn't bother. As soon as he had his power again, he was planning to make a whirlwind and fly off to the Bahamas for a few weeks. On his own.

Virgil McCreeby ought to have been more upset about leaving Zadie behind than he was, reflected Dybbuk. After all, he stood to lose the three wishes she had promised him for helping them. Then again, he was hardly himself since the blow on the head he had received when the plane/submarine

Zadie had made for their journey across the chasm crash-landed. McCreeby had hit his head hard on the periscope, and Dybbuk had been obliged to drag him out. Ever since then, McCreeby had been repeating himself and looked puzzled whenever Dybbuk told him something. Dybbuk guessed he had a concussion. He himself was still puzzled how a small plane ended up turning into a midget submarine. Was it just Zadie's incompetence as a djinn, or something else? Some other manifestation of djinn power interfering with hers, perhaps? Nimrod's, or the twins'. Or even Manco Capac's.

So, leaving the bridge and Zadie behind, Dybbuk and McCreeby proceeded up a winding yellow stone path above the chasm. It was a bracing walk and the clear mountain air tasted pure and sweet. Even McCreeby seemed invigorated. He kept inhaling noisily through his nostrils like a personal trainer trying to enthuse a client. And, after an hour or two, McCreeby had sufficiently recovered his senses to notice Zadie was no longer with them. But when he asked where she was, Dybbuk felt obliged to provide him with an answer that would not delay their steady progress up the mountain for long. Indeed, he felt quite justified in filling McCreeby's head with what he wanted him to believe because that was, he strongly suspected, what McCreeby had been doing to him with Zadie.

"She's dead," he said, affecting some sadness.

"Dead?" repeated McCreeby. "How? What on earth happened?"

"You really don't remember it?"

"I think it's not that I don't remember," said McCreeby. "It's just that I've not been thinking straight since we were in a midget submarine. Can that be right?"

Dybbuk nodded. "You had a blow on the head, that's all."

"I'm better now. So tell me about Zadie."

"Well," said Dybbuk, "do you remember when you told her to cut the bridge? With a machete? To stop anyone like Nimrod from coming after us?"

"Did I?"

"Yes," lied Dybbuk, "you did." In fact, it was Dybbuk himself who had suggested that Zadie do this. "And you remember how it was made of human hair?"

"Yes," said McCreeby, "I do remember that much. Who'd have thought there were so many Incas willing to have a haircut?"

"So, when Zadie cut the bridge, some of the hair fibers, well, they sort of came alive, like a boa constrictor, and strangled her as they repaired the bridge. Before she could utter her focus word, the hair had wrapped itself around her neck. There was nothing she or I could do."

"Good grief," said McCreeby. "Poor Zadie."

"Could have happened to any of us," said Dybbuk, and shrugged nonchalantly.

"To any of us who had cut the bridge with a machete, you mean," said McCreeby.

Dybbuk nodded gravely. "You were very brave," he said.

"Was I?"

"Yes. Don't you remember? You tried to cut some of the hair that was strangling her with your own machete and narrowly escaped being strangled yourself."

"Good grief," said McCreeby. "It sounds as if I had a lucky escape."

"You're very lucky, yes. I'd say so."

"Then again. Poor Zadie. Dead, you say?"

"Dead."

"That's a pity," said McCreeby. He made a tutting sound and then kicked a stone out of his path. "She was going to give old Virgil McCreeby three wishes. I was rather counting on those. Just to protect myself from Nimrod."

"I'll give you an extra three myself," said Dybbuk. "When my own power is restored. To make up for the three you've lost from her."

Of course, McCreeby ought to have contradicted him. Told him that a fourth wish always undid the first three. But he didn't. And Dybbuk concluded that maybe McCreeby hadn't yet completely recovered from the bump on his head. Either that or he was too diplomatic to contradict him. After all, without Dybbuk, Virgil McCreeby had no chance of getting even three wishes.

They walked on, and after another hour or so they came around a corner to see where the yellow stone path led through an avenue of tall, sinuous plants. These were about the height of a man, brown, with a bright pink flower like a drainpipe, and looked vaguely fungal. At first, Dybbuk thought it was the wind. And it was only after watching them for almost a whole minute that he noticed the plants were moving very slightly, like a strange species of undersea animal. It was then he realized the plants were probably carnivorous.

"What are we waiting for?" asked McCreeby and, pushing past Dybbuk, stepped onto the path. "Paititi is just up ahead of us."

Dybbuk grabbed McCreeby's pack and hauled him back.

"What is it? What's the problem?"

"Watch," said Dybbuk as a small tapir came blundering onto the path.

The pink flowers turned in the direction of the animal as if they possessed eyes. The next second, Dybbuk and McCreeby heard a series of spitting sounds, and then gasped as they saw several sharp tubular filaments fired from each flower, like a dart from a blowpipe, that hit the tapir's leathery gray flesh. A split second later, the animal hit the ground, dead. Another few seconds passed and these tubular filaments filled with red. It was like watching a transfusion in a hospital. The plants were drinking the tapir's blood.

"Good grief," said McCreeby. "Those plants are carnivorous."

"That's putting it mildly," observed Dybbuk.

"Sort of like Venus flytraps, but on a larger scale."

"Much larger. I'd say they could kill a man, wouldn't you?"

One of the plants stopped gulping for a moment and let out a noise that sounded very much like a burp.

"Since we have to get past them without getting hit with a poison dart ourselves, I suggest we take advantage of the fact that they're feeding and move past them as quickly as possible," Dybbuk suggested.

And before McCreeby could say anything, Dybbuk sprinted along the path and past the vampire plants.

"Good idea," said McCreeby, and ran after him. Which Dybbuk thought was unusually courageous for a man he considered a craven coward, and he concluded that McCreeby was indeed still suffering the effects of his concussion.

But not every plant had fired a filamented dart at the tapir and, as McCreeby hurried up the path, two of the plants spat their lethal feeding apparatus at him. One missed him altogether. The other hit McCreeby's backpack. It was lucky for him the pack was so large. The magician did not notice, however, and kept on running. At least he did until the filament reached its full length and brought him and his pack up short; such was the strength in the dart and the filament that it jerked McCreeby off his feet.

As he hit the ground hard, his mess tin, knife, fork, and mug slipped out of the top of the poorly fastened backpack. McCreeby lay there for a moment, waving his arms and legs, trying to right himself, like a great black beetle.

"I say, help," yelled McCreeby. "Those horrible things have got their hooks into me."

Dybbuk made a noise like a bassoon and rolled his eyes up to the top of his long-haired head. Yet he had little choice but to turn back and help McCreeby. In his backpack,

McCreeby was carrying Manco Capac's golden staff and some of the other Incan artifacts needed for the *kutumunkichu* ritual. Without those, the journey to Paititi would have been a complete waste of time.

Reaching McCreeby, he flipped him over onto his stomach and sliced the vampire plant's filament off the dart with his machete. Oozing a surprising quantity of malodorous red liquid onto the yellow stone path, the filament snaked back to its owner like the tentacle of an injured octopus. But Dybbuk was even more surprised to hear the plant emit a loud hissing noise, like a threatened cockroach.

McCreeby picked himself up and shuddered with disgust. "Ugh," he said. "Horrible, horrible, horrible. Did you see it? That big ugly potted plant almost got me."

Virgil McCreeby looked at his backpack, wrinkled his nose with horror, and pulled the slimy dart out of his pack. It was about six inches long, barbed, and as sharp as the spine on a cactus. He threw it away before picking up the several objects that had bounced out of his backpack.

"Thanks a lot, Dybbuk," said McCreeby, forgetting just for a moment the boy djinn's enormous sensitivity regarding his oddish name.

"Buck," said Dybbuk. "Just Buck, okay?"

Not more than an hour away from the vampire plants, the lost city of Paititi lay on a ridge that rose like a tall crown in the middle of the cloud-filled valley. A more magical place could hardly have been imagined, thought Dybbuk. Even by a djinn. A narrow landing strip of rock led out on to the summit and the main buildings which, although obviously Incan in their origin, were in a much better state of repair than Machu Picchu, or for that matter, the Eye of the Forest. Although worn and smoothed by time, none of the large, ingeniously placed, perfectly fitting stones were overgrown like other Incan ruins. The squarish buildings themselves were little more than shells, however, without windows or doors and no obvious purpose except that one of them was filled with Incan weapons and armor. The main central building was different, however. This was shaped like a small dome and was chiefly remarkable for its heavy golden door.

"A palace?" said McCreeby.

"Could be," said Dybbuk.

"Just look at this door, Buck," said McCreeby breath-lessly. "It's even bigger than the one in the Eye. And it's solid gold. This must be priceless."

Dybbuk shrugged. He wasn't much interested in gold. There had been a time when he'd been able to make the stuff appear with just a word and he'd never really understood why mundanes were so fascinated with it. Gold was just a metal, after all. More brightly colored than iron and copper but a metal nonetheless. Power was what interested him. Djinn power. Especially now that he didn't have any.

More curious than the fact that the door was made of solid gold was the design engraved upon it, which appeared to be that of a large mushroom.

"Mushroom worshippers?" said Dybbuk, and laughed.

"Very likely," agreed McCreeby.

"I was joking," said Dybbuk.

"I'm not. Certain kinds of mushrooms were sacred to the Incas. And more especially to their holy men. They called them *teonanactl*, or the 'flesh of the gods.' The Aztecs actually considered these mushrooms divine."

"I hate mushrooms," Dybbuk sneered. "I can never imagine why anyone would want to eat a fungus."

"When the Incan priests ate these mushrooms, they thought they saw visions. But quite what mushrooms have to do with the *kutumunkichu* ritual, I have no idea."

"Maybe we'll find out inside," said Dybbuk, and pushed open the heavy gold door.

"Look how heavy the door is," said McCreeby. "And how snugly it fits the doorway. Those Incas were amazing engineers, when you think about it."

Even Dybbuk had to admit that McCreeby was right. The dome itself was perfectly spherical like a bubble and about thirty or forty feet tall. Each of its giant, smooth stones had been fitted together perfectly. Inside, the atmosphere was cool, almost clinical. A series of stone steps led up to a circular white rock, in the center of which was a tall rod made of gold.

"It's almost as if the dome had been built to contain something," observed McCreeby as he mounted the steps. "Hey, come and look at this."

Dybbuk came up the steps, and standing beside him, saw

that the gold rod descended for several hundred feet below them into the darkness. "What is it?"

"I don't know," said McCreeby.

"So what do we do now?"

McCreeby shrugged. "According to the ancient chronicle that was dictated by the Incan priest Ti Cosi, the final part of the *kutumunkichu* ritual would be found in here."

"Could that be it?" said Dybbuk, and pointed to an inscription on the back of the door through which they had entered the dome over the rock.

"Yes. That must be it."

They went to look at the inscription.

"That's curious," said McCreeby.

"What is?"

"The words of this inscription," said McCreeby. "They're in Spanish."

"What's curious about that?" said Dybbuk. "Everyone speaks Spanish in this country."

"But not back in the mid-sixteenth century," said McCreeby. "This is an Incan temple, after all. They spoke Quechuan. What's more, the Incas never wrote anything down. Least of all in Spanish. They hated the Spaniards. The Spaniards had stolen their gold and killed their kings."

"You're forgetting Ti Cosi's own chronicle," said Dybbuk. "That's in Spanish."

"That was dictated to a Spanish priest," said McCreeby. "For all we know it might even have been dictated in Quechuan. And translated by the priest."

Dybbuk shrugged. "Then what's the problem? You can read Spanish. So go ahead and read it."

"Doesn't anything of what I've told you strike you as being just a little strange?"

"Maybe if you read the inscription, I could decide for myself." Dybbuk shot McCreeby a sarcastic sort of smile.

"Be patient, boy," said McCreeby. "I'll get to it."

Dybbuk bit his lip. He disliked being called "boy," as if he worked in the lobby of some expensive hotel, and he disliked being told to be patient by a mundane. *Him. Dybbuk, the djinn. AKA Jonathan Tarot, the television star. The son of Iblis, the Ifrit.* It was another reason for him to dislike Virgil McCreeby. Because by now, Dybbuk disliked McCreeby almost as much as he disliked the venomous pet spider the English magus kept in his shirt pocket. He disliked his fingernails, which were long and sharpened to points, like tiny swords, and he disliked the way McCreeby was forever filing them with an emery board. He disliked the way McCreeby reminded him of his son, Finlay, who Dybbuk had never really liked even when they'd been friends. He disliked McCreeby's beard and his fat belly and tweed suits and his singsong, hoity-toity stage actor's English accent. But he especially disliked McCreeby's strange smell, which was referable to the ointment he rubbed on himself. McCreeby called it his flying ointment and it was made of moonlight, honey, and myrrh. It was nonsense, of course. McCreeby couldn't fly. It was just something he said to make people think he was powerful. All part of the great magician's pose. Back in Lima, when first they'd arrived in the country, a hotel manager speaking to Dybbuk had mistaken McCreeby for his father and Dybbuk had felt like strangling him.

As McCreeby's greedy eyes ran across the inscription, his lips muttered the words in Spanish. "Oh, I say, this is fascinating." With fingers rippling excitedly, McCreeby took a notebook out of his pocket and began to write with the stub of a pencil. "It's a set of instructions about what to do next to perform the ritual."

Dybbuk sighed impatiently. "Well, what *do* we do? Are you going to tell me, or do I have to kick it out of you?"

McCreeby looked taken aback. "I say, there's no need for that kind of talk," he said. "Not after coming all this way together. I thought you and I were friends."

"We are," said Dybbuk. "I'm sorry. Tired, I suppose. Maybe it's the altitude. I'll feel better when I get my power back." He smiled encouragingly at the older man. "I suspect we both will."

McCreeby grinned back. "Quite. Well, let's get to it. Where's that backpack of mine?"

"Outside," said Dybbuk. "I'll go and get it."

"Thanks. Decent of you."

While Dybbuk went outside again, McCreeby mounted the steps, peered down the length of the gold tube, and shook his head in wonder. He looked at it for a moment and then, taking hold of the rod, shifted the top as per the instructions on the back of the dome door. "Extraordinary," he muttered.

Dybbuk came back with the backpack.

"Now then," said McCreeby. "If you would be kind enough to pass the pieces to me as I ask for them."

Dybbuk opened the backpack and began to lay the pieces on the floor of the containment dome.

"The tears of the sun," said McCreeby.

Dybbuk handed him two gold disks and McCreeby looked at them carefully. "As you can see, this is not a rod at all, but a tube. And, according to the instructions, we drop the first disk into the tube," he said.

McCreeby held the disk above the tube, lining up the edges of the matching perimeters. Then he let it go. For a moment the disk stayed where it was before settling a little and then sliding perfectly down the length of the tube with an audible and metallic sigh.

"Look at that," he said with admiration. "The extraordinary precision of those Incan craftsmen. Quite takes your breath away, doesn't it?"

Dybbuk made a noise like a bassoon and rolled his eyes up to the top of his long-haired head. "If you say so," he said.

"I do say so," said McCreeby. "Now then. The second disk goes in after the first." He took the next disk and dropped it down the tube. Once again it looked like a perfect fit. "Marvelous. It won't be long now. Your djinn power, and me with the power of making gold." McCreeby chuckled and rubbed his hands. "Now then. If you could hand me that rather wonderful-looking gold staff."

Dybbuk picked up the staff. It was heavy, about fifteen inches long and two inches in diameter. At the top was a squat little Incan god wearing a semicircular sort of crown, like a risen sun. The god was quite ugly and bowlegged and, under his crown, had earlobes as big as turkey wattles, which contained studs of jade and lapis lazuli. The rod itself was perfectly cylindrical, as if milled on a machine and, as he handed it over, Dybbuk noticed that the diameter of the rod was about the same as that of the disks. Small though it was, it weighed more than five pounds.

"We'll just check the mechanism, shall we?"

"Mechanism? What mechanism?"

McCreeby took the staff and, having consulted his note-book, turned the body of the god through ninety degrees. There was an audible click and the rod fell away in his hand. "This mechanism," said McCreeby.

"Neat," admitted Dybbuk. "But why does it do that?"

"Well," said McCreeby, "the idea is that we insert the gold rod into the gold tube. I imagine it will fit perfectly, like the two gold disks. When we decide that we're ready, we twist the body of the god, which releases the rod, and it falls down the length of the golden tube. It's my guess that the tube is as tall as this mountain, which means that by the time the rod reaches the bottom of the tube, and collides with those two disks, it will be traveling as fast as a bullet in a gun barrel. Well, almost."

"That's it?"

"Yes, all we have to do now is attach the third disk to the bottom of the rod."

"How are we going to do that?"

"Again, I'm just guessing here, but I imagine the disk is magnetic."

"But pure gold's not magnetic," said Dybbuk.

"No, well, obviously the rod is not made of pure gold," said McCreeby. "Gold is not a metal that's of much use in magic. Except as an end result, of course. We like to make gold. Not use it for something else. If this were real gold, we'd hardly be dropping it down a tube into the bowels of the earth. No, I imagine the rod is made of lead. Lead is much more useful for an alchemist. There's so much more you can do with it."

Dybbuk nodded. It all sounded quite convincing to him.

"Now then," said McCreeby. "Please hand me the third disk. The heaviest of the three."

"*Three* disks?" Dybbuk frowned. "But there were only two."

"No, no. There are three." He paused as Dybbuk began to search his backpack for the third disk. "There were always three disks. Surely you remember." He paused. "Look, don't muck around. A joke's a joke, but we're supposed to be performing an important and sacred ritual here. I distinctly remember Nimrod's nephew giving you three disks." He snapped his fingers at Dybbuk impatiently.

"I'm not mucking around," said Dybbuk.

He started throwing things out of the backpack all over the dome in his desperation to find the missing disk. By the time the backpack was empty, he was furious. "It's not in here."

"It must be," said McCreeby, coming back down the steps.

"See for yourself." Dybbuk turned the empty backpack upside down over McCreeby's head.

Irritated, McCreeby snatched it from Dybbuk's hand and searched all of the pockets. "It's not there," said McCreeby.

"I told you," said Dybbuk.

"What are we going to do? We can't complete the ritual without the third disk."

Dybbuk thought for a moment.

"Do we really need the third disk?" he asked. "I mean, we've got two down there already. What's a third one going to achieve? Perhaps it's just a spare."

"Rituals involve observing a prescribed procedure for conducting a ceremony," McCreeby said stiffly. "You can't mix and match those parts that suit you and those parts that don't. That third disk might well be the most important of all our Incan artifacts."

Dybbuk turned and faced the inscription on the door as if hoping for some kind of clue about what to do next. "What does this say, anyway?"

"Mostly, it's a description of what to do," said McCreeby. "Disk two follows disk one, the way to release the rod from the restraining little god at the top. The last part I really don't understand. *'Si el fulgor de mil soles fue a reventar a la vez en el cielo, que seria como el esplendor del podero. . . .'* Roughly translated it means something like 'If the radiance of a thousand suns were to burst at once into the sky, that would be like the splendor of the mighty one.'"

"Whatever that means," said Dybbuk. "A nice tan, I guess."

"I rather think the mighty one was Manco Capac," McCreeby said. "But it might well be you, too, if we manage to pull this off. You, my dear Buck, might be the mighty one. But we simply have to find that third disk or we can't be sure of anything."

Dybbuk smacked his own forehead. "Of course," he said. "The third disk. I bet I know where it is. In the avenue of vampire plants. It must have slipped out of your backpack when you fell. It's probably still lying on that path. One of us will have to go back and get it."

"It won't be me," said McCreeby. "I haven't forgotten what happened to that pig thing."

"It's called a tapir," Dybbuk said wearily.

"Well, whatever you call the thing, it was a supersize Coke for those creepy plants." McCreeby shook his head. "Look, I'm older than you. And tired. It's an hour's walk back down to that path. And an hour back. That's nothing to a young chap like you, Buck. Besides, you're quicker than me. More agile. That gives you a much better chance of dodging those poison darts."

Dybbuk thought for a moment and then yawned. "I think

you should go and get the disk. You see, now that you've told me what to do, you're more expendable than I am." He smiled a crafty sort of smile. "Look here. Suppose something were to happen to me. You do want three wishes, don't you?"

"You cowardly little swine," said McCreeby.

"Or maybe six wishes, like I said before." He shrugged. "As many as you like."

"You must think I'm an idiot," said McCreeby. "We both know that a fourth wish given by the same djinn will undo all the previous three."

"All right, all right. I tell you what. You go, and as soon as I get my power I'll go and sort Zadie out. She'll give you three wishes, just like we figured at the beginning of this expedition."

"I thought you said Zadie was dead."

Dybbuk grinned awkwardly. "I just said that so we wouldn't waste any time trying to release her."

"Poor Zadie," said McCreeby.

"Poor Zadie nothing. She was driving us crazy, and you know it." He shook his head. "Besides, it was obvious there was no way to cut her loose from that bridge without ending up the same way ourselves."

McCreeby smiled wryly. "You're really quite ruthless, aren't you?" he said. "I can see you are your father's son. Yes, indeed, I shall have to be careful of you, Buck."

Dybbuk's grin dried on his face and then disappeared. "What do you know about my father?"

"I know who he is," said McCreeby. "And what you are, son of Iblis. Two djinns, not one. Half Marid, and half Ifrit. Jekyll and Hyde. Like twins. Good and bad. In fact, I rather think that the twins the prophecy speaks of are both you, dear boy."

"If you know all that, then I wonder why you don't just do what you're told," said Dybbuk. "Look here, you'll be fine. You can wear some of that Incan armor we found in one of the other buildings. There's even a shield you can carry."

"All right, I'll go," said McCreeby. "But just remember this: You swore an oath on your mother's life to give me three wishes if I helped you. Well, I'm helping you. I expect you to keep your word." Ominously, he added, "And, if she knew, your mother would expect the same of you. While I'm gone, I suggest you think about that promise. And what it might mean. To her and to you."

CHAPTER 26

STRAWBERRY SLIPPERS

My feet hurt," said Philippa, and sat down heavily at the side of the yellow stone path.

"Everyone's feet hurt," said John.

"I'm not at all surprised," said Zadie. "We've been walking for hours."

"What did you expect on an expedition into the Amazon jungle?" demanded John. "A chauffeur-driven limo?" He was still adjusting himself to the idea that Zadie was not the same person she had seemed to be before.

Zadie shook her head and shrugged. "Sorry," she said. "I was just saying."

"No, I'm sorry," said John. "There was no need to bite your head off like that."

Nimrod anxiously inspected the way ahead. He was eager to keep on going but recognized that his companions needed a rest. "All right," he said. "We'll have a fifteen-minute break. But that's all. We can't afford to waste any more time."

Groanin sat down beside Philippa and mopped his brow with a handkerchief the size of a pillowcase. "I can't decide which feels worse," he said. "My feet or my stomach. I say, boss, I'm not half hungry."

"I'm afraid you'll have to wait a while before the next meal," said Nimrod. "If Dybbuk and McCreeby manage to set that bomb off you won't notice you're hungry."

"Haven't you heard? An army marches on its stomach." Groanin's stomach proceeded to rumble very loudly. "And in case you hadn't noticed, this one is becoming mutinous."

Meanwhile, Philippa had pulled off her walking boots and socks and was inspecting her feet, prompting John to hold his nose.

"My feet do not smell," protested Philippa.

"Everyone's feet smell," said Groanin. "Of cheese, mostly." He unlaced his own boot and stared unhappily at a sock that looked greasier than a fish-and-chips wrapper. "I say, everyone's feet smell. T'ain't natural to have feet that don't pong a bit after a bit of a route march. I know mine do. Like a strong English cheddar. Or a nice bit of Stilton. Or maybe a slab of Yorkshire blue. There are times — this being one of them — when I get a whiff of my own feet and I think to myself, if only I had some bread and pickles, some rad-ishes and spring onions, and a pint of bitter beer." Groanin grinned at the thought of eating his own feet. "Yes, indeed, there are times when I think that my feet'd make a mighty good lunch."

"Ugh, Groanin," said John. "That's disgusting."

"To you, maybe. But no one's asking you to eat with me, are they? I say, you're not invited to the handsome spread me and my feet are putting on."

Zadie picked up Philippa's boot and looked at it critically. "Your boots don't look as comfortable as mine," she remarked. "But we're exactly the same size. Would you care to wear mine?"

Philippa smiled and delved into her own backpack. "That's kind of you, Zadie," she said. "But I thought I'd wear these for a while." She took out a pair of gold-colored shoes. "They're fantastically comfortable. And what's more, they don't smell of cheese. They smell of wild strawberries."

"It'll make a pleasant change from cheese, I suppose," said John.

"Strawberries is all very well," said Groanin. "But they're not what I'd call a square meal. Strawberries is not very substantial."

"May I?" asked Zadie.

"Sure." Philippa handed Zadie the shoes, and the other djinn pressed them to her nostrils.

"Oh, my goodness, these smell wonderful," said Zadie. "I don't think I ever saw a pair of shoes that were as fragrant as these."

"Strawberries come from the genus *Fragaria*," Nimrod said absently. "Which comes from *fragans*, meaning odorous. Everyone eats strawberries today, of course, and yet, in parts of South America, they were considered poisonous until the mid-nineteenth century."

"There's not many people what know that," said Groanin, and pulled a face. "But I don't know why."

"These shoes are like a breath of summer." Zadie took another deep breath from the inside of the shoes. "The curious thing is that you can even taste the strawberries." Zadie handed them back to Philippa. "Where did you get them? New York? Fifth Avenue? Somewhere expensive, I'll bet."

"Actually, they were a present from someone," said Philippa, slipping on the shoes. "When we were in China. A great djinn called Kublai Khan gave them to me."

"What, *the* Kublai Khan?"

"Yes." Philippa stood up. "You know, it's odd, but now that I've got these on I feel I could walk forever."

"Got a spare pair there, have you?" asked Groanin. "Because my poor dogs are barking like the Oakley Hunt hounds. I swear, they feel like they walked to Tipperary and back. I wish . . ."

"Don't," said Nimrod. "Remember what I said. Nobody wishes for anything. No matter what the provocation."

"In case you'd forgotten," said Groanin. "I'm the one person in this team who doesn't happen to be a flipping djinn. And therefore what I wish for me and my feet is of absolutely no consequence to anyone."

Nimrod frowned. "Break is over," he said, and picked up his backpack.

"Slave driver," muttered Groanin.

On they trudged. Although in Philippa's case, she felt more as if she were walking on air.

After another hour or so they came around a corner to see where the yellow stone path led through an avenue of tall, sinuous plants. It wasn't the pink flowers of the plants they noticed first, or even their uncanny, sinister movement so much as the man dressed in full Incan armor who was crawling on the ground among them. Cowering behind a large rectangular shield, he appeared to be looking for something.

"That's Virgil McCreeby," said John.

"Yes," said Nimrod.

"He seems to be afraid of something," said Groanin.

"It's those flowers," said Philippa. "They're like blowpipes."

"Thus the armor and the shield," said Nimrod. "Those plants must be firing poisonous darts."

As if to confirm Nimrod's theory, several darts hit McCreeby's Incan shield and bounced off it with a metallic sound, like raindrops hitting a corrugated iron roof. McCreeby yelped cravenly. And then whooped as his fat fingers chanced onto what he was obviously looking for. A gold disk.

"That's one of the tears of the sun," said Zadie, recognizing it immediately. "I stole them from the Peabody Museum, in New Haven."

"They must have dropped one of them the first time they came past here," said Philippa.

"Most likely they were running away from those plants," agreed Nimrod.

"And now he's come back for it," added Philippa.

"Then we're not too late," said Nimrod. "They have yet to complete the ritual."

Still whooping, and now clutching the gold disk, McCreeby picked himself up off the path and retreated to a position of safety on the far side of the vampire plants and about thirty yards away from his pursuers. He was just about to run away when Nimrod shouted at him.

"McCreeby, wait a minute, please."

McCreeby turned and, seeing Nimrod, waved him forward. "Come over here and have a chat, why don't you?" he said.

"I think not," said Nimrod. "We'll just stay here for now. Until we figure out a way past these poisonous plants."

McCreeby laughed. "Not just poisonous, I'm afraid. They drink blood. But I should still like to collect one. It would be interesting to see their effect at the Chelsea Flower Show. And I think I'd need more than green fingers to cultivate one. Don't you?"

One of the vampire plants nearest to McCreeby spat a dart that fell just short of his shield.

"See what I mean?" said McCreeby. "Well, maybe you'll find some armor. Then again, maybe not. You know, I wonder why you don't make a wish to get rid of them or me and have done with it." McCreeby searched the sky above him as if looking out for some form of djinn attack from the air.

"I wanted to give you a chance first," said Nimrod, bluffing. "To make amends."

"Decent of you, old boy, I'm sure. By the way, it's a relief and a pleasure to see you're okay, Zadie. No hard feelings, I hope. It certainly wasn't my idea to leave you behind."

"No hard feelings, Virgil," said Zadie.

"This is your last chance, McCreeby," said Nimrod. "Put the disk down and give up. Or I'll turn you into that toad I mentioned the last time we spoke."

But McCreeby shook his head. "I'm afraid I don't buy it, Nimrod. If you haven't put the hex on me or these vampire plants yet it's because there's a jolly good reason. Quite possibly you can't. Wait a minute — yes. Now I understand everything. Zadie wished for a plane and we ended up trying to fly in a midget submarine. Not very successfully. That's it, isn't it? There's something about coming through the Eye of the Forest. Something about it that means you don't dare use your power." McCreeby chuckled. "Oh, my goodness, how very unfortunate for you all."

"Listen to me, McCreeby," said Nimrod. "Just for a moment, please."

"A matter of life and death, is it?" McCreeby's tone was mocking.

"No, it's more important than that. Please listen."

"What, no more threats to turn me into a toad? That wasn't very polite, you know, Nimrod. Not very polite at all."

"Listen to me, McCreeby. You're probably not aware but this entire area is one huge chunk of uranium. Those yellow stones you're standing on? They're uranium, too. That's the power you're planning to call on with the *kutumunkichu* ritual. Atomic power. This whole mountain is a natural nuclear reactor that's been undergoing one continuous chain reaction over several centuries. I think the three tears of the sun are made of polonium, lithium, and steel. The Incan rod you've got is also made of uranium. Probably even purer than the stuff we're both standing on."

McCreeby continued chuckling. "Don't stop. I'm enjoying this. It's very entertaining."

"It's my guess that there's some kind of barrel or pipe into which you have to put two of those disks. The third you probably attach to the Incan staff, which you then fire along the pipe and straight into the heart of this uranium mountain."

"This is really ingenious," said McCreeby. "I'm impressed. You're not just a pretty powerful djinn; you're a pretty powerful djinn with a good imagination."

"Listen to him, please, Virgil," said Zadie. "It's true."

"When the rod hits the mass of uranium rock, the whole mountain goes critical," said Nimrod. "The uranium molecules will become so excited they start to boil."

"And so they blow up. Is that right?"

"Not quite. That's where the tears of the sun come in. By itself the whole mountain would become massively radioactive, but without an atomic explosion. To make that happen you need those disks. Look, McCreeby, I'm not a nuclear engineer. Left apart, all the various pieces are harmless, but when you bring them together you have a very big bang, indeed. I think it's the tears of the sun that will start a chain reaction and cause the mass of uranium — namely the mountain — to blow itself to pieces. And not just the mountain. The whole country. The whole hemisphere. You're talking about an explosion that would be a million times bigger than the first atomic bomb."

"Oh, stuff and nonsense. Are you really telling me that the Incas knew the secret of atomic energy, Nimrod? You must take me for an idiot, old boy."

"Manco Capac was a very powerful djinn. Even you should know that's true, McCreeby. Throughout history there have been several djinn who knew the secret of nuclear fission hundreds of years before humans learned it. And the idea of you carrying out the *kutumunkichu* ritual, like Manco? This was all Ti Cosi's idea for getting revenge on the Spanish conquistadors. To bring about the *Pachacuti*. The great destruction. This is what it's all about. You're not completing a ritual to give yourself the power to make gold, McCreeby, or to help Dybbuk to recover his djinn power. You're building an atomic weapon that is going to destroy the world."

"I can't see how it's got anything to do with the real world. We're in a different dimension, aren't we?"

"There's another way in here that doesn't require one to enter through the Eye of the Forest," said Nimrod. "This world and our world are connected. And that means they're both at risk of destruction."

McCreeby made a show of looking at his watch. "Nimrod? What can I say? It's been fascinating. Really. And I'd love to stay here chatting with you. However, I must be getting along. Dybbuk is expecting me, with the third disk."

And he turned around and walked away.

"We simply have to stop him from completing the ritual," said Nimrod, as they watched McCreeby start laboriously back up the hill toward the lost city of Paititi.

"But how?" said Groanin. "We can't get past those horrible aspidistras. And you said, none of you can afford to use your power for fear of it turning out wrong." He shook his head. "That's the thing about you djinn that annoys me the most. It always seems that when you need your power the most, it's never there. I can't remember the number of times this sort of thing has happened."

"Shut up, Groanin," said Nimrod.

"Yes, sir."

"I'll have to risk it," said Nimrod. "Let's see now. If I wanted to wish for a cup of coffee, I'd wish for — what?"

"A cup of tea?" suggested Groanin.

"QWERTYUIOP!" said Nimrod, and a bucket of mud appeared on the path in front of them.

Groanin dipped a finger into the mud and licked it. "Well," he said. "It does have two sugars, the way you like it, sir."

"I don't see how that helps," said John.

"It was an experiment," Nimrod said irritably. "In opposite wishing. I was wishing for a cup of tea in order that I might end up with a cup of coffee."

"Well, it didn't work," observed John.

"So, if you wanted a cat," said Philippa, "would you wish for a dog or for a mouse?"

"You see the problem exactly," said Nimrod.

Philippa shot John a sarcastic smile as if to underline the fact that she understood something that her twin brother didn't.

"The difficulty lies in how to properly fix the front of your mind on the thing you don't want, if the thing you do want is somewhere at the back of it."

"Sort that one out," muttered Groanin. "If you can."

"You managed it all right with the chess piece," said Philippa.

"That was an easy bit of opposite wishing," said Nimrod. "In a sense the word black is already built into the word white. Especially in the game of chess. Indeed, a chess piece becomes whiter if it exists in relation to another piece that's black."

Groanin threw his hands up and brought them down on top of his bald head with a loud and exasperated slap. "Virgil McCreeby will be gone by the time you work out all the linguistics on this," he said. "And so will we if he gets a chance to use that third disk."

Philippa stamped her golden heels on the yellow stone path and a strong fragrance of strawberries filled the mountain air.

"Oh, it makes me so mad," she said, and experienced a strong but pleasant taste of strawberries in her mouth, which she thought was very curious. She stamped her heels again, only this time things tasted and felt very curious indeed, especially underfoot, for when she looked down at her golden shoes she saw that these were no longer standing on top of the yellow brick path, but on the flattened body of Virgil McCreeby who lay prostrate, groaning underneath her on the ground like a quarterback who has been tackled in a game of football.

Meanwhile the golden disk that had been in McCreeby's fat fingers was now rolling back down the path toward the spot where Nimrod and the others were still standing; the spot where, not five seconds before, she had been standing herself.

"Curiouser and curiouser," said Philippa, who was now so much surprised that for the moment she quite forgot how to speak good English.

Nimrod picked up the disk and put it in his pocket.

Philippa looked at her uncle and, catching his eye at last, lifted her arms in bewilderment, as if to say, "I really have absolutely no explanation for why I'm over here when, just a few seconds ago, I was over there with you."

Anxiously, Nimrod started to walk toward his niece until one of the vampire plants turned its pink flower his way and, wisely, he seemed to think better of it just as a poison dart came flying through the air. It fell a long way short of Nimrod, but the thing's intent was clear enough. There was still no way past the vampire plants. At least, no way that either he or Philippa was able to explain.

"How I hate those beastly flowers." Philippa stamped her heels on Virgil McCreeby's back and once again, a delicious fragrance of strawberries filled the air and her mouth.

"Ouch," yelped McCreeby. "Oooof."

This time she remained exactly where she was. It was the vampire flowers that moved. Or, to be more accurate, disappeared. All of them. One second they were there, and the next, they were not. It was as simple and immediate as that.

Looking rather bemused by this fortunate turn of events, Nimrod and the others came slowly up the path.

"Er, what happened?" John asked Philippa.

"I don't know," said Philippa. "All I know is that I didn't make a wish. I never said my focus word. And yet, somehow, each time, what I was thinking is exactly what ended up happening."

"Gerroff," moaned McCreeby. "I can't breathe."

Philippa glanced under her feet and realized she was still standing on the Englishman. And a strong scent of strawberries remained in the air.

"What's that smell?" asked Zadie.

"Strawberries," said Philippa, and stepped off McCreeby's armor-plated back. "Somehow, stamping my feet seems to make the smell of strawberries coming off my golden shoes grow stronger."

"I don't think that's all it does," said Nimrod, kneeling down beside her feet, and scrutinizing her shoes. "I think these shoes given to you by Kublai Khan are gestalt slippers."

"Guest what?" asked Groanin.

"Gestalt," said Nimrod. "I've heard of them, but I never thought they actually existed. I'm sure the Chinese called them something different, but that's what we call them today. It's said that when a djinn wears them, the whole becomes greater than the sum of its parts. A djinn's true desires emerge spontaneously, without reference to the wish-making process. You just have to have a strong thought about something, and that thought emerges as complete reality immediately. It's your idea of order on matter. Those slippers must be immensely powerful."

"And here I was thinking that they were just a nice pair of shoes," said Philippa.

"If they're so powerful," said John, "it might be best if you were to take them off immediately. At least until you know how to control them better."

"Maybe you're right," said Philippa. "But what about Dybbuk? Shouldn't we — shouldn't I go and stop him, right away?"

"It's all right," said Nimrod. "Without the third disk, he can't cause an atomic explosion."

"You mean all that stuff about atomic bombs was true?" said McCreeby, sitting up and rubbing his shoulders painfully.

"Most certainly it was true," said Nimrod. "Ti Cosi really did intend to bring about the complete destruction of the conquistadors. Just as Manco Capac had promised."

"Odd, how we never saw Manco again," remarked John.

"Well, I never," said McCreeby, and let out a chuckle. "Oh, I say. That explains the mushroom. On the door of the ritual chamber in Paititi, there's an engraving of a mushroom. Well, obviously I thought it was the sacred mushroom. The *teonanactl*, or the 'flesh of the gods.' I say, you don't really think that I've been assembling a nuclear bomb, do you?"

"I do think," said Nimrod. "It's not a mushroom engraved on the door of the ritual chamber, but a mushroom cloud. Of the kind you might get over a nuclear explosion."

McCreeby whistled. "And there I was, blithely putting together the means of my own destruction."

"If it was just your own destruction, McCreeby," said Nimrod, "there would be no great cause for concern. But since it involves the destruction of a good part of this hemisphere, then we're obliged to do something about it."

Groanin cuffed the magician on the back of the head. "Your trouble, Virgil McCreeby, is that you judge everyone by your own despicably low standards," he said. "You wretched man. If anything happens to their father, I'll give you such a hiding."

"Oh. Yes. Look here. Let me call my followers right away," said McCreeby. "All I need is a satellite phone. I left my own in Paititi."

Philippa stamped her feet and handed him a phone. Fearfully, because he was beginning to realize just how awesome Philippa's power was, McCreeby took the phone and keyed in a number. "Er, what time is it in New York?" he asked.

"That's odd," said John. "My watch has stopped."

"Mine, too," said Groanin.

"Erm, this phone doesn't work," said McCreeby.

Nimrod looked at the phone and shook his head.

"Perhaps it's the effect of these gestalt slippers," said Philippa.

"Perhaps," said Nimrod.

"Look," said McCreeby. "It's just a thought, but young Dybbuk isn't what one would call a patient person, is he? In fact, I would say that Dybbuk's rather an impulsive, willful sort of chap. Not to say headstrong."

"That's him, all right," muttered Groanin.

"The reason I mention it is this: Before I left Paititi, to come back down here to look for the third disk, Buck was asking me if we could complete the *kutumunkichu* ritual without the third disk. Naturally, I said it was impossible. Thank goodness I stopped him, eh? Of course, it wasn't the answer he wanted to hear. In fact, he got quite cross about it, really."

"You showed him what to do?" said Nimrod.

"The details of the completion of the ritual are on an inscription in the main building," said McCreeby. "I just read them out. I didn't actually show him anything that he couldn't have read for himself. But it sort of occurs to me now to inquire what might happen if the boy just sort of went ahead and dropped the uranium rod down the tube and into the uranium rock, after the first two tears of the sun."

"The uranium in the rock would start to fizz," said Nimrod. "There would be no explosion, just a great deal of radioactivity."

McCreeby pulled a face. "Well, might that not explain why this phone isn't working? And why your watches have stopped?"

"Light my lamp, you're right," said Nimrod. "Electromagnetic radiation. If only we had a Geiger counter."

"You mean a machine that measures radiation?" said John.

"You mean one of these?" Philippa stamped her feet and handed Nimrod a strawberry-colored electrical box with a dial and a pinkish tube that was about the size of a duck call.

"That's it," said Nimrod. "That's a Geiger counter."

Taking the machine from Philippa, he switched it on and held the tube up to the air. The needle on the dial moved from one side of the machine to the other as the tube in Nimrod's hand registered the background radiation. Nimrod shook his head and almost bit his lip off.

"The fool," he said. "The little idiot."

"You mean, he's gone and done it?" said McCreeby. The magician stood up abruptly and, wrapping himself in his arms, looked around with mounting anxiety. "Oh, Lord, what have I done?"

"He must have gone ahead without the polonium disk," said Nimrod. "This whole area is a blizzard of radioactivity. We've got to get away from this place right now. Sooner if possible."

"Oo-er," said McCreeby.

Groanin cleared his throat. "Let me get this straight," he said. "Are you telling me that after coming thousands of miles to find it — not mention surviving headhunters and giant centipedes and whatnot — that we're not going to see the lost city of Paititi, after all?"

"I'm afraid not, old fellow," said Nimrod. "Radiation is awkward stuff. You can't see it. But it's quite deadly. It may already be too late for us."

"But what about Buck?" said John. "We can't just leave him up there in Paititi. We have to go and rescue him. We have to bring him home."

"I'm afraid there's absolutely no possibility of that," said Nimrod. "We have to go now or we won't be able to go at all. I'm sorry, but chances are he's already beyond our help. It may even be too late for us."

Philippa stamped her golden strawberry-slippered foot. "No, she said. "No, no, no."

Her voice sounded strange inside the concrete, lead-lined nuclear bunker that her will and the gestalt slippers had created within a split second. There had been a project about the Cold War at school and she had seen pictures of nuclear bunkers built during that time, and Philippa figured this one was pretty accurate in every detail, except for the color, of course. She was certain they weren't ever the color of strawberries, but for some reason she had strawberries on her mind. At least it matched the semitransparent, strawberry-mottled, anti-radiation suits that everyone, including herself, was now wearing. Not to mention the several bowls of strawberries that she had thoughtfully provided in case anyone got hungry. And the strawberry drapes on the lead-filled glass window.

"John's right," she said. "We can't leave him. Please wait and try to be patient. I'll only be gone for a second. All of you will be safe in here, I think. There's a decontamination chamber, working air filters and, through that door, a very comfortable living room with a TV and a library. And a refrigerator. I'm afraid it's mostly full of strawberries, Groanin."

"But why does it always have to be pink?" complained John, shouting through his strawberry-hued plastic hood. "Everything she makes. It's always pink. You know how I feel about pink, Philippa. Couldn't I have had a yellow suit? Or a blue one?"

"It's not pink," insisted Philippa. "It's strawberry-colored." She shook her head impatiently. "And I don't have any time for this. I need to go and find Dybbuk."

Philippa looked at her uncle, who nodded and then embraced her as fondly as their fully ventilated, gas-tight suits allowed.

"Please be careful," said Nimrod.

CHAPTER 27

SPLIT PERSONALITY

While he was waiting for McCreeby to come back with the disk, Dybbuk amused himself by dressing up in some of the Incan clothes they had found in Paititi and by fighting an imaginary enemy with a battle ax. The ax wasn't, he thought, particularly sharp. None of the Incan axes or lances were very sharp, and it seemed obvious to Dybbuk why the Spanish had easily conquered South America. The Incan weapons were junk.

The one weapon he did like was a sort of mace with a long wooden handle that had a ball of copper at the end with eight protruding points. It looked jokingly crude but effective enough to batter heads to a pulp. But he doubted that even these could have penetrated Spanish armor. No wonder Ti Cosi had looked for some other kind of weapon that would destroy the Spaniards.

When Dybbuk got tired of wielding the mace, he tried using a sling and spent a happy fifteen minutes throwing egg-sized stones at the head of what looked like a god or a king that was carved on a wall. He got quite good at it, too, and before long, his wanton boyish vandalism had quite obliterated the face on the ancient carving.

Looking around for something else to destroy, Dybbuk happened upon a bow and achieved a certain amount of pleasure in shooting arrows at a bronze shield and breast-plate of the kind McCreeby had taken to protect himself against the vampire plants. And it was quickly clear that nei-ther afforded much protection against an arrow.

So how would it fare, he wondered, against a poi-son dart?

To answer this question, Dybbuk went back to the containment dome to take another look at McCreeby's backpack — the one that had been hit by a dart from the vam-pire plant. And he was surprised to discover that the poisonous dart had apparently penetrated the tough nylon Cordura material and the contents of the backpack — including McCreeby's tobacco tin — to a depth of several inches. It was this last discovery — the hole in the tobacco tin — that persuaded Dybbuk that there was no point in awaiting McCreeby's return.

"Poor old McCreeby," he said out loud, because the profound silence and solitude of Paititi was beginning to weigh on him a little. "Gee, those darts must be sharper and tougher than we thought."

In this assumption Dybbuk was mistaken, however. The hole in Virgil McCreeby's tobacco tin had not been caused by the dart from the vampire plant but by the Englishman's Swiss Army knife, when he had fallen on the path.

Dybbuk glanced impatiently at his expensive gold watch — it was about the only thing he hadn't sold after the Jonathan Tarot affair — and told himself that McCreeby's return was well overdue.

"The lazy fat idiot, he should have been back by now."

Dybbuk was mistaken about this, too. It was an hour's walk to the place where the vampire plants grew, and an hour's walk back again. McCreeby had been gone for less than ninety minutes.

He smiled wryly. "For sure, the guy's a goner. Poor old McCreeby. Hey, wait a minute. Poor old me. I guess I'm on my own now."

Dybbuk went and sat cross-legged in front of the carving that a little earlier he had been using for target practice. There he spent several minutes considering the possibility of going to get the disk himself, and then telling himself the various reasons why he thought that this was not a good idea.

"First, there's the obvious danger," he said. "If McCreeby is dead, then I might get killed, too. Those plants are not to be messed with. The darts are lethal. Second, there's the fact that if McCreeby isn't dead, just injured, I might actually have to help him, which would be difficult on account of the fact that he's too fat to carry, and I don't know how to use any of that medical stuff in his backpack. Those are two pretty good reasons."

Clouds moved across the high peak on which Paititi was

positioned, casting strange shadows that undulated over the ancient ground. A condor wheeled in the sky near the sun. Except that Dybbuk thought it was a vulture and that it could be waiting to eat his dead body. He shivered.

"Third is the fact that this place is kind of cold and spooky and I don't much like being up here on my own, so the sooner I can complete the ritual and get out of here the better. I think the silence is beginning to get to me. I'd sure hate to be here at night." He tossed another stone at the carving. "I don't know how you stand it, pal.

"Fourth is the fact that fundamentally, McCreeby was a very picky sort of guy and was always one for doing things exactly by the book and the proper way, even though a lot of times, in most situations, you can always cut a few corners. That's certainly been my own experience. Frankly, he was a bit of a bore like that and just because he thought we couldn't do without the third gold disk, doesn't mean that it's really the case. If this ritual is half as powerful as it is supposed to be, then I can't believe that one little stupid disk is going to make all that much difference."

Another shadow moved across the ground, only this time it seemed human in shape. Dybbuk thought it must be McCreeby with the disk and felt a mixture of emotions. He was pleased to see McCreeby back, because he was lonely, but at the same time he was already looking forward to being rid of him again.

"Well, you certainly took your time," said Dybbuk. "Did you get it? Did you find the disk?"

Glancing up, he found himself staring at a figure silhouetted by the bright sunshine. A figure that did not answer him. A figure that seemed to be wearing a cloak of feathers.

Dybbuk sprang up. It wasn't McCreeby at all but someone else. Someone or some unspeakable thing. An Inca not unlike the little figure carved in stone. This Inca's face was also defaced, not by the stones hurled from some careless boy's catapult, but by that greatest vandal of all — time itself. The baboonlike visage was that of a near-naked mummified man, part skull and part flesh, hardened by centuries, with some sort of material thrust by its long-deceased embalmers into the ancient nostrils and question-mark ears to prevent the escape of something decayed and liquid. Several teeth were visible on the upper jaw of the stiffened mouth. But in the large recessed eye sockets, behind half-closed eyelids, some kind of sinister life still moved like goldfish in two bowls of very dirty water.

Instinctively, Dybbuk backed away from a figure he half recognized, half guessed must be Manco Capac. The same Manco Capac whose mummified figure had remained in the Peabody Museum, a gift from the explorer and desecrator of graves, Hiram Bingham, for a whole century.

"Was it you I was talking to?" Dybbuk asked nervously. "If so, I meant no disrespect to you or your people. I'm a djinn, too. Like you. Only I've lost all my power. Which is why I'm here. To complete the *kutumunkichu* ritual and get it back. The same way you did, right?"

"I see the twins have arrived," hissed the figure.

"Twins?" Dybbuk looked around. "They're not here, are they?"

"You, boy," hissed Manco Capac. "You're the twins. Two boys in one body. As if you didn't know."

"You're mistaken." He started backing away from Manco Capac's mummy. "So, look . . . nice to meet you, but I'll finish up and be on my way, okay?"

Anxious to be gone from Paititi as soon as possible, Dybbuk ran back into the dome and picked up the staff with a mixture of urgency and reverence. Swallowing his fright, he carried the heavy staff up the steps. He checked the release mechanism as he had seen McCreeby do, and then slid the rod precisely into the golden tube, appreciating for the first time the accurate workmanship of the ancient Incas who had fashioned these pieces of precious and semiprecious metal. Fear of Manco Capac and anticipation about what he was about to do — about what he was about to become — now dominated his thoughts. Would it work? Would the energy and heat released return his djinn power or would it destroy him? He was willing to take the risk. What else could he do? Dybbuk wiped the sweat from his hand and reached to twist the top of the staff.

Then a voice he recognized stopped him.

"Sure, before you do that, young Dybbuk, consider this: A trout in the pot is better than a salmon in the sea."

Dybbuk turned around in the direction of the familiar voice. He had to look hard to see who or what had spoken, although in his bones he knew exactly whose voice it was he had heard.

It was Mr. Rakshasas.

Or rather it was a thin, almost invisible, ghostly version of what had once been Mr. Rakshasas. Not so much a ghost as the ghost of an idea Mr. Rakshasas had once had, a long time before: the idea that one day Dybbuk would have need of some wise and fatherly advice of the kind he was unlikely to get from his real father, Iblis.

"Mr. Rakshasas," said Dybbuk. "First Manco Capac. And now you. It's becoming like a convention of freaks up here."

"I heard you talking to that old prune face. He started out a decent sort of djinn. But I'm afraid that too much time has curdled his soul."

"I rather admire him," said Dybbuk.

"There never was a scabby sheep in a flock that didn't like to have a comrade."

"What are you doing here?" Dybbuk asked Mr. Rakshasas. "I thought you were dead."

"I'm not so very dead that I can't spare a little time to come here and stop you from throwing away your life, you young eedjit," said Mr. Rakshasas. "It's not easy being a child of the lamp when the light gets taken away. Ages ago, when first we met, I decided to attach a pale ersatz version of myself to you and the twins, John and Philippa. Like a sort of personal recording, if you like. Or a conscience, if you prefer. So that in a moment of great personal crisis, I might turn up and give you some necessary guidance. Private-like. Sure, a whisper in Nora's ear is louder than a shout from the highest hill. Anyway, my advice to you is this, boyo: You might not have your power anymore, but at least you still have your life. You twist the head of that Incan staff to release yon rod, and you'll regret it to your dying day, if you live that long."

Dybbuk sighed. "There's no other way to get my power back. And I really can't live like a mundane. I know, I've tried. I don't know how anyone could live an ordinary life like that. So, please Mr. Rakshasas, do me a favor and go away."

"A silent mouth is sweet to hear, right enough. And if you really believe that, then you're a bigger eedjit than I take you for. Listen to me, Buck, lad. When the old cock crows, the young cock learns. You want your power back? This is not the way. There never was an old slipper but there was an old stocking to match it. In time, a better solution than this will present itself. I promise you."

Dybbuk shook his head. "What good are your promises?" he asked. "You're not even real."

"It's a stubborn one you are, Dybbuk Sachertorte," said Mr. Rakshasas. "You've a tongue like an adder, and no mistake. Just like your father. But sure, it's no more I'm telling you now than you know yourself in your heart of hearts. That this is a big mistake you're making."

"Then it will be my mistake," Dybbuk said sullenly. "Not anyone else's mistake."

"Another mistake in a long line of big mistakes."

"It's my right to make my own mistakes," insisted Dybbuk.

"Sure, the fox never found a better counselor than him-self." Mr. Rakshasas sighed and shook his head. "Listen to me, young fellow, me lad. There are no shoes on your feet. So what's the use of carrying an umbrella? Forget this idea. It will turn out badly for you and your other half."

"My other half?" Dybbuk shrugged. "What do you mean?"

"Sure, it's not just atoms that can get split, Dybbuk."

Dybbuk made a noise like a bassoon and rolled his eyes. "Buck," he said. "Just Buck, okay?" It was the last time he would ever say it.

"It's people, too," continued Mr. Rakshasas. "A man can lose more than just his hat in a fairy wind."

"Look, I don't know why you're bothering with me," said Dybbuk. "I'm not the person you think I am."

"If I didn't think there was some good in you, Buck, I wouldn't be here, and that's the truth. There's good and bad in everyone. In you, most of all."

"What do I care about being good?" said Dybbuk. "It's the good part that made me weak. Except for that, I might still have my djinn power. It was being nice to people, trying to entertain them, that got me where I am now."

"That's nonsense and you know it."

"I'm going to count to three, and then I'm going to turn this staff head," said Dybbuk.

"If you count three, Buck, you'll never hear the count of five, do you hear?"

"One."

"It's a different kind of energy you'll release, Dybbuk. And you won't like what it looks or feels like."

"Two."

"Even the light-bearer himself, the son of dawn, the morning star — he fell and lost his glory and hated himself for all eternity."

"Three."

"You will become hateful unto yourself."

"I am hateful to myself already," said Dybbuk, and turned the staff head. He felt the mechanism inside the little Incan god give a little click, and the heavy gold-covered uranium rod of the staff dropped away into the depths of the yellow rock mountain. He smiled a sarcastic sort of smile at Mr. Rakshasas. "It's done."

The old djinn's shade nodded quietly. "Well, I tried," he said. "But sure 'tis as much of a mistake to give cherries to a pig as good advice to a fool. I'll not be troubling you again."

And with that he disappeared.

"I thought you'd never leave," said Dybbuk.

He kept his hand on the little staff head but it was loose on the golden tube now so there seemed little point in holding it there. A few seconds passed and, wondering if anything had actually happened, he took a flashlight out of his backpack and peered down the tube into the depths of the atomic rock.

A split second later, he felt a wave of energy and a strong glow of courage. Something had happened. It was quite unmistakable.

For a moment, a great sickness took hold of him. This quickly subsided to leave a sense of something new and sweet. And for the first time he saw himself for what he no longer was. As something weak and disordered and fettered by the bonds of friendship and obligation and decency.

That person now stood apart from him.

While he himself was stronger and entirely careless of innocence and good. And Dybbuk knew himself, in the first moment of this new life, to be more wicked, a million times more wicked than he had ever dreamed was possible.

While that other Dybbuk, the good Dybbuk, the one who now stood apart from him with a face full of horror at what he had become, was now an object of contempt and derision.

And as the good Dybbuk collapsed onto the ground, the evil Dybbuk stretched out his powerful-looking hands, and the very thought of his own utter wickedness braced and delighted him like a hot shower.

Appearing inside the dome of Paititi a split second later, Philippa, wearing her anti-radiation suit, registered the radiation levels in the lost Incan city with horror. They were completely off the scale. What was most horrible, however, was the realization that there were now two Dybbuks. It was as if he himself had split like one of the atoms whose huge and lethal power he had sought to control.

One of these two figures — the Dybbuk she recognized more easily as her old friend — lay on the ground, huddled up against the blizzard of uranium neutrons that now raged inside the containment dome. He looked utterly exhausted. His skin was a deathly shade of gray and in his hands were large clumps of his own dark hair. Instinctively, Philippa knew that this Dybbuk was near death. And she might have gone to comfort him but for the presence of the other, the second Dybbuk.

This second Dybbuk was a livelier, obviously healthier version of the boy who lay on the ground. He was taller, stronger, and older than the other Dybbuk. More ruthless, too. All the good that had once appeared in Buck's eyes was now gone. Evil was written on his face so clearly that, for the first time, Philippa saw a strong similarity to his father, Iblis. And a powerful sense of misgiving that he would not permit her to come near the other Dybbuk kept her at a distance.

"Buck," she said, "what have you done to yourself?"

"Realized who and what I truly am," said the second Dybbuk. He uttered a little chuckle. "Discovered the real me. Taken charge from my better half. Better late than never, I suppose."

"I'm not talking to you," said Philippa. "I'm talking to the other Dybbuk. The good Dybbuk. I'm talking to you, Buck. It's me, Philippa. Can you hear me? Let me help you, if I can."

"It's too late for him," said the second Dybbuk, the evil Dybbuk. "I should have thought that was obvious. Even to you, Philippa."

"Buck," said Philippa, "listen to me. Come to me. I can help you, if you'll let me."

"You're wasting your time," said Dybbuk.

Philippa paused, searching for something else that might give the boy on the ground some strength. "Think of your sister, Faustina. And your mother. Buck, let me help you for their sakes. Think of their love for you."

"Love." Dybbuk made a noise of derision. But the boy on the ground raised his head weakly and stared ahead of him, as if seeing nothing. "Phil?" he croaked. "Is that you? Help me. Please."

"You're finished," said Dybbuk. "Dybbuk is my name and what I am. Malicious. Turned away. Dislocated. Like a split atom. What I was always meant to be. There's no mileage in being good. No recognition for it. People just think you are weak. It's strength that matters. Being pitiless."

"Don't listen to him, Buck," said Philippa. "You can still prevail against him. Against his evil." She held out her hands. "Come back with me. I can help you. My power is greater than his. Dybbuk knows it, which is why he doesn't dare come near me."

"Your power is greater than mine, true," said Dybbuk, and planted a foot squarely on Buck's shoulders. "But mine is much greater than his." And with that he crushed what remained of the part of himself that was still good.

"There," said Dybbuk finally. "Happy now? You've made

me kill him, I think. Whoops. Boo-hoo. Aw, look. Poor little me."

This seemed to make Dybbuk stronger.

Now that his good half was finally out of the way, Dybbuk felt a sudden exhilarating boost in his own newly recovered djinn power. Indeed, he felt much stronger than he had ever felt before; as if the good part of him had somehow always been holding back the extremely wicked part. Like that most pathetic of human things, a mundane's conscience.

At the same time Dybbuk guessed that Buck must have always known who and what Dybbuk really was. Poor Buck. How he had struggled against it. He must have been acutely aware that Dybbuk was every bit as nasty as his true father, Iblis. Possibly even nastier. And aware that Iblis had previously tried to destroy Philippa, Dybbuk did not hesitate. He resolved to try to do the same.

Up until now he had been cautious of Philippa, sensing that her own djinn power was somehow enhanced by some ancient force present in the strange golden slippers she was wearing. But that earlier caution no longer existed. Every decent feeling he had once had for Philippa was now gone. He had quite forgotten the many good turns she had done him in the past. And silently uttering his focus word, he tried to concentrate all of his new malignance upon his former friend. Wasn't it Philippa and her stupid brother, John, who had helped imprison his father inside a jade suit of armor, somewhere in China? She would pay for that. Dybbuk pointed at the sky over Paititi.

"I wish for a great black cloud," he said.

Immediately the sky darkened ominously and a storm cloud as big as a city materialized over Philippa's head.

"And out of that great black cloud I wish for a huge fork of lightning to blast you into oblivion," he yelled.

A split second later the mountaintop was hit by a bolt of lightning that was the size of the Amazon River itself. It split the rock to a depth of several feet and left a smoking scorch mark as wide as a bus. But it did not harm Philippa. As long as she wore the slippers she was protected by the ancient djinn power of the great Kublai Khan. A few seconds before the bolt of lightning struck the rock with a noise like a train wreck, she was transported a short distance away to a place of greater safety.

"Stop it," Philippa yelled. "Stop it, or I'll hurt you, Dybbuk. You're not the only one who can pull that kind of a stunt. My power is as great as yours. Greater."

But she did not finish her sentence. Dybbuk's next wish brought a huge boulder sailing through the air, which narrowly missed crushing Philippa to a pulp.

The sense that he truly meant to harm her was enough to make Philippa stamp her feet with anger and frustration. She was wasting her time. He was lost to the world of good. She could see that now. And this realization was enough to return her, in the blink of an eye, to the nuclear bunker where she had left her uncle, her brother, and her true friends. Not to mention Virgil McCreeby.

"There's no time to explain," she said and, stamping her

strawberry-slippered feet again, transported them all, in the wink of an eye, to their encampment on the other side of the Eye of the Forest even as Muddy was welcoming Sicky back from his journey to the Xuanaci village, and Hector the dog after being lost in the rain forest.

Philippa took another radiation reading with the strawberry-colored Geiger counter, and finding the levels quite normal, started to relax a little. "We can take off these stupid suits now," she said.

"You were only gone for a split second," said John. "What on earth happened?"

"More than I think I can say," said Philippa. "For the moment at least." Her eyes filled up with tears.

Nimrod placed a kind hand on her shoulder. "Tell us later," he said. "When you feel more equal to the task."

For an hour or two she sat quietly on her own, and gradually recovered her composure. And when no one was looking, she dug a very deep hole and buried the gestalt slippers.

A little later on John said to her, "Just tell me one thing. Is Dybbuk dead?"

"No," she said. "Yes."

"Well, which is it?" he demanded.

Philippa thought hard for a moment and felt her eyes fill with tears again. The memory of what she had seen in the lost city of Paititi would, she knew, stay with her forever.

"He chose," she said. "Unwisely."

"What does that mean?" said John.

"What I mean is that I think the Buck we knew is dead. There is another Dybbuk now. A different Dybbuk. A bad Dybbuk. Full of evil, like his father."

"I was afraid of that," said Nimrod.

"Me, too," said John, and walked sadly away.

"We should call home," said Philippa.

"I already did," said Nimrod. "Your father is rescued. Your mother is with him now, at home."

"Thank goodness."

"Thank goodness, indeed," said Nimrod.

CHAPTER 28

DOING THE RIGHT THING

After Pizarro's conquistadors and the mummified Inca kings had finished cutting each other to pieces, and peace reigned once more in the rain forest, Sicky was made chief of the Xuanaci in an impressive and lengthy ceremony that was attended by Nimrod, John, Philippa, Groanin, Zadie, Muddy, Hector the dog, and Virgil McCreeby, as well as many members of Sicky's own tribe, the Prozuanaci. Even poor Mr. Vodyannoy felt sufficiently recovered from his contact with the poison dart frog to come out of his lamp and attend, albeit briefly.

After the ceremony, Zadie decided not to come back to New York with the others but to remain in the rain forest and work with the Xuanaci.

"I know I was hypnotized and all that," she said. "But I really feel I ought to do something for them. With a little bit of djinn power, I was thinking I might set up a school."

"Good idea," agreed Nimrod. "But you'll need a good teacher to help you." He looked at Virgil McCreeby.

"No," said McCreeby. "Nimrod. You can't be serious."

"I think it's a very good idea," said Nimrod.

"Me, too," said Zadie.

"Have a heart, Nimrod," protested McCreeby. "Me a school teacher? Can you imagine it?"

"As a matter of fact, McCreeby," said Nimrod, "I happen to know that you were once the headmaster of a boys' school in Switzerland."

"Yes, but that was a long time ago. And the boys were Swiss. You can teach the Swiss anything, except perhaps how to be late."

"I'm sure you will do a very good job here," said Nimrod. "You shall stay here with Zadie and help her set up the school. Consider it your punishment. A punishment that Zadie will strictly enforce."

"Count yourself lucky that we don't let the Xuanaci put your head on a necklace," said Groanin. "Or feed you to them piranha. Or put a giant Peruvian centipede down the back of your shirt collar. Do the right thing for once, man."

"Just be careful he doesn't try to hypnotize you again," Nimrod told Zadie.

"It's all right. I'm wise to him now. I know all his little tricks."

When Philippa and John had finished saying good-bye to Zadie, they hugged Sicky and wished him luck in his new job. Sicky choked back the tears of emotion he felt at being parted from all his new friends.

"Come back anytime," said Sicky. "We'll give you a real jungle welcome." His head may have been unusually small, but there was nothing wrong with his heart.

"Muddy," said Groanin, shaking the boatman's hand. "It's been a pleasure. I say, it's been a pleasure."

"I heard you the first time," said Muddy.

"What will you do now?" asked Nimrod.

"Now that Sicky is an important chief, I'm going to give up being a chef."

Groanin nodded his approval. "Believe me, you're doing the right thing. In my opinion, you were a terrible cook. What will you do now?"

"Me?" said Muddy. "I'll take over Sicky's business as a tour guide."

And it was Muddy who took them back to Manu, where they awaited a plane to fly them to Lima.

"It will be a while before those lupuna trees we planted have grown and any of us djinn can safely fly by whirlwind again," said Nimrod. "Of course, I suppose Philippa could take us home just by stamping her feet if she wanted to."

"No, I couldn't," explained Philippa. "The gestalt shoes. I buried them somewhere in the jungle."

"You did what!" exclaimed John.

"It was too much power," said Philippa. "It's hard enough just being a djinn without having to cope with those slippers as well. I just had to think a thing and it happened instantaneously. I simply couldn't stand the responsibility. I'm sorry, but we'll have to take a plane home like anyone else."

Nimrod nodded gravely.

"Did I do the right thing?" she asked, and found herself being hugged tightly by her uncle.

"It takes great wisdom to know when one has too much power," said Nimrod. "Great wisdom and a great soul. So, yes, Philippa, you did do the right thing."

"But what about Paititi?" John asked. "What about the radiation levels on the mountain? What about the Eye of the Forest? Suppose someone goes through the Eye? Won't they be in danger?"

"Yes, they will," agreed Nimrod. "Which is why Sicky and the Xuanaci have agreed to stand guard over the door. To prevent anyone from accidentally entering the Eye. He's also going to lock the door. This should do the job until we can figure out something more secure." Nimrod held up two sturdy-looking brass combination locks.

"Did you make those with djinn power?" asked John.

"No," said Nimrod. "As a matter of fact these belong to Groanin. They were on his suitcase."

Groanin pulled a face. "Them baggage handlers at Heathrow Airport," he said. "You can't trust them."

"I'm sure that can't be true," objected Philippa.

"It is. I know. I used to be a baggage handler at Heathrow myself."

*   *   *

Several days later, Uncle Nimrod, Mr. Groanin, Mr. Vodyannoy, and the twins arrived back in New York.

Mr. Vodyannoy went immediately to his apartment in the Dakota building, where Nimrod had arranged for Marion Morrison, a djinn nurse, to come and look after him. (And within three months he was quite well again. Well enough to host another Djinnverso tournament at his house in New Haven.)

The others went straight to the Gaunt family house on East 77th Street, where the twins found both their parents waiting for them. Mr. Gaunt looked none the worse for his experience at the hands of his kidnappers. Mrs. Gaunt just looked fabulous, which is to say, very glamorous and exactly the way the twins remembered her. Even Mr. Groanin said how good she looked.

There was, however, one minor difference. For once it seemed to be their diminutive father who was in charge. Mrs. Gaunt seemed more deferential to her husband than before, although only her brother's keen eye spotted this and suspected what it denoted.

When the twins had finished hugging their parents and telling them all of their adventures, Nimrod made his excuses and the two Englishmen checked into the Carlyle Hotel around the corner, which was Nimrod's favorite hotel in the world.

"I don't know about you, Groanin, but I'm hungry," said Nimrod.

"I could eat a horse," admitted Groanin.

"Would a nice juicy steak, smothered in onions, do instead?" asked Nimrod.

"A steak would certainly hit the spot," said Groanin. "As long as they do it the right way, mind. Knowing how to do the right thing in a kitchen, well, how else is civilization to measure itself?"

But after they had eaten the steaks, which were excellent, Groanin found something else about which to complain.

"I just wish I'd taken a little more time to say good-bye to those kiddies," he said. "I miss them already. I say, I miss them already. Why did you hurry us out of there so quickly?"

"Because," said Nimrod, "I decided that the right thing to do would be to leave the reunited Gaunt family to itself. You see, my dear Groanin, that is all that any happy family — no matter how peculiar — really needs. To be left to itself."

"Sounds like the start of a novel," said Groanin. "Or perhaps the end of one."

ABOUT THE AUTHOR

P. B. Kerr was born in Edinburgh, Scotland, where he developed a lifelong love of reading. Although the Children of the Lamp books are P. B. Kerr's first for children, he is well known as the thriller writer Philip Kerr, author of the Berlin Noir series, including most recently, *The One from the Other*, *A Philosophical Investigation*, *Gridiron*, *The Shot*, and many other acclaimed novels. Mr. Kerr lives in London with his family. You can visit him on his Web site at www.pbkerr.com.